Edge of Forever

Ed Adams

a firstelement production

Ed Adams

First published in Great Britain in 2021 by firstelement
Copyright © 2021 Ed Adams
Directed by thesixtwenty

10 9 8 7 6 5 4 3 2

A CIP catalogue record for this book is available from the British Library.

ISBN 13 : 978-1-913818-12-8

Ebook ISBN : 978-1-913818-13-5

Printed and bound in Great Britain by Ingram Spark

rashbre
an imprint of firstelement.co.uk
rashbre@mac.com

ed-adams.net

To John Owens,
who knows his Trigax from his Tropus

Thanks

A big thank you for the tolerance and bemused support from all of those around me. To those who know when it is time to say, "step away from the keyboard!" and to those who don't.

To thesixtwenty.co.uk for direction.

To Topsham, for being lovely.

To the NaNoWriMo gang for the continued inspiration and encouragement.

To the edge-walkers. They know who they are.

To Donna J. Manifestly Haraway for the cyborg manifesto.

And, of course, thanks to the extensive support via the random scribbles of rashbre via http://rashbre2.blogspot.com and its cast of amazing and varied readers whether human, twittery, smoky, cool kats, photographic, dramatic, musical, anagrammed, globalized or simply maxed-out.

Not forgetting the cast of characters involved in producing this; they all have virtual lives of their own.

And of course, to you, dear reader, for at least 'giving it a go'.

Books by Ed Adams include

Triangle Trilogy		About
1	The Triangle	Dirty money? Here's how to clean it
2	The Square	Weapons of Mass Destruction – don't let them get on your nerves
3	The Circle	The desert is no place to get lost
4	The Ox Stunner	The Triangle Trilogy – thick enough to stun an ox
		(all feature Jake, Bigsy, Clare, Chuck Manners)
Archangel Collection		
1	Archangel	Sometimes I am necessary
2	Raven	An eye that sees all between darkness and light
3	Card Game	Throwing oil on a troubled market
4	Magazine Clip	the above three in one heavy book.
5	Play On, Christina Nott	Christina Nott, on Tour for the FSB
6	Corrupt	Corridors of power
		(all feature Jake, Bigsy, Clare, Chuck Manners)
Stand-Alone Novels		
1	Coin	Get rich quick with Cybercash – just don't tell GCHQ
2	Pulse	Want more? Just stay away from the edge
3	Edge	Power can't be left to trust
4	Now the Science	the above three in one heavy book.
Blade's Edge Trilogy		
1	Edge	World end climate collapse and sham discovered during magnetite mining from Jupiter's moon Ganymede.
2	Edge Blue	A human outcome, after a doomsday reckoning, unless…
3	Edge Red	An artificially intelligent outcome, unless…
4	Edge of Forever	Edge Trilogy

About Ed Adams Novels:

Triangle Trilogy		About
1	Triangle	Money laundering within an international setting.
2	Square	A viral nerve agent being shipped by terrorists and WMDs
3	Circle	In the Arizona deserts, with the Navajo; about missiles stolen from storage.
4	Ox Stunner	the above three in one heavy book.
		(all feature Jake, Bigsy, Clare, Chuck Manners)
Archangel Collection		
1	Archangel	Biographical adventures of Russian trained Archangel, who, as Christina Nott, threads her way through other Triangle novels.
2	Raven	Big business gone bad and being a freemason won't absolve you
3	Card Game	Raven Pt 2 – Russian oligarchs attempt to take control
4	Magazine Clip	the above three in one heavy book.
5	Play On, Christina Nott	Christina Nott, on Tour for the FSB
6	Corrupt	What goes on in Parliament
		(all feature Jake, Bigsy, Clare, Chuck Manners)
Now the Science Collection		
1	Coin	cyber cash manipulation by the Russian state.
2	Pulse	Sci-Fi dystopian blood management with nano-bots
3	Edge	World end climate collapse and sham discovered during magnetite mining from Jupiter's moon Ganymede
4	Now the Science	the above three in one heavy book.
Blade's Edge Trilogy		
1	Edge	World end climate collapse and sham discovered during magnetite mining from Jupiter's moon Ganymede.
2	Edge Blue	Endgame, for Earth – unless?
3	Edge Red	Museum Earth – unless?
4	Edge of Forever	Edge Trilogy

Ed Adams Novels: Links

Triangle Trilogy		Link:	Read?
1	Triangle	https://amzn.to/3c6zRMu	
2	Square	https://amzn.to/3sEiKYx	
3	Circle	https://amzn.to/3qLavYZ	
4	Ox Stunner	https://amzn.to/3sHxlgh	
		(all feature Jake, Bigsy, Clare, Chuck Manners)	
Archangel Collection			
1	Archangel	https://amzn.to/2Y9nB5K	
2	Raven	https://amzn.to/2MiGVe6	
3	Raven's Card	https://amzn.to/2Y8HLgs	
4	Magazine Clip	https://amzn.to/3pbBJYn	
5	Play On, Christina Nott	https://amzn.to/2MbkuHl	
6	Corrupt	https://amzn.to/2M0HnOw	
		(all feature Jake, Bigsy, Clare, Chuck Manners)	
Now the Science Collection			
1	Coin	https://amzn.to/3o82wmS	
2	Pulse	https://amzn.to/3qQlBvL	
3	Edge	https://amzn.to/2KDmYOW	
4	Now the Science	https://amzn.to/3iG5Nc2	
Edge of forever Trilogy			
1	Edge	https://amzn.to/2KDmYOW	
2	Edge Blue	https://amzn.to/2Kyq9au	
3	Edge Red	https://amzn.to/2KzJwjz	
4	Edge of Forever	https://amzn.to/3c57Ghj	

Author's Note

The series of novels Edge; Edge, Blue and Edge, Red discuss Earth after a major series of dystopian catastrophes. Fortunately, Earth has found an additional source of energy and transport by bringing magnetite back from Ganymede, a moon of Jupiter.

Edge, Blue and Edge, Red which deal with the end situation of Edge in two different ways. Some building blocks of the solution are similar, but the result creates two very different stories. Both Edge, Blue and Edge, Red start at the same moment but diverge in their outlook. Events from 300 years previously and described in the novel Pulse also surface in Edge, Red.

I hope you enjoy!

Ed Adams

TABLE OF CONTENTS

EDGE

EDGE, BLUE

EDGE, RED

Edge

Ed Adams

a firstelement production

Edge

First published in Great Britain in 2020 by firstelement

Directed by thesixtwenty

10 9 8 7 6 5 4 3

Every effort has been made to acknowledge the appropriate copyright holders. The publisher regrets any oversight and will be pleased to rectify any omission in future editions.

Similarities with real people or events is unintended and coincidental.

A CIP catalogue record for this book is available from the British Library.

ISBN 13 : 978-1-8380146-2-9

Ebook ISBN : 978-1-8380146-3-6

Printed and bound in Great Britain by Ingram Spark

rashbre
an imprint of firstelement.co.uk
rashbre@mac.com

ed-adams.net

21

PART ONE

Mastery

The economic transmission of power without wires is of all-surpassing importance to man.

By its means he will gain complete mastery of the air, the sea and the desert.

It will enable him to dispense with the necessity of mining, pumping, transporting and burning fuel, and so do away with innumerable causes of sinful waste.

Nikola Tesla

Monday evening

He heard the apartment judder from the impact. A mournful sigh. This one had been close, but not that close. He knew the building was meant to take it.

He looked towards the window. Grey night skies, something resembling clouds, thin trails, raked towards the horizon.

Now he looked at the clock. Ten minutes to midnight. This would go on until the morning. He expected there to be more crashes and thumps as the battering continued.

He was better indoors. Going out just added to the tension. If he could stay inside, he could watch some transmissions to take his mind off the situation.

He moved from his bedroom into the main living area. He flipped the switch and could suddenly hear the weather. A gentle rain and a rustling of leaves. The occasional spatter of water dripping from branches. He kept the weather set to April for several months now. Outside it was the end of summer but somehow it did not matter what the official calendar said, he had decided to run it at his own speed.

He flipped the main screen. Not the full screen but the one designed to show just entertainment transmissions and data. It opened on a standard news transmission and he gestured for it to move across to his messages. He expected they would ask for him, but so far there were only a few spams that had missed his filtering.

The main room had noise cancellation and so he was now no longer aware of the crashes from outside. Just a slight feeling underfoot as the building absorbed more impacts.

"Peter give me status," he asked.

A small pop-up window appeared on the top right of the screen. Everything was green. At this rate, he did not need to do anything at all.

He walked across to the kitchen area, flipped a tap and drank some water. The tap illuminated the water as it poured. The blue colour signifying that the source was both pure and cold. They had built his block in the 40s and it was still good at the management and monitoring functions. He knew it had originally been built for the military as an offshoot of the nearby base.

When he had arrived in the city, they had given him a choice of either staying on the base or moving out as long as the commute was less than 30 minutes. He had opted for off-base because it was already like living in a bubble and on the base was like living in a bubble inside another bubble.

A little information light on the screen briefly flickered to amber. The moment later it had returned to green. He realised another advantage of being away from the base was that smaller incidents were handled autonomously by the base management systems.

"Hi Peter," he said, "please provide an update on base status."

"Full base status is green. There was a short incident with a meteorite, but they cleared it with a grid gun. Incident duration 1.2 seconds. There are zero requests for your attendance at the base."

He walked to the kitchen cupboard and flipped open a compartment.

"Peter dispense modafinil. Two units."

To small capsules appeared in the compartment. He placed them in his mouth and took a small drink from the water glass. He could feel the rush at once. His senses heightened as if he had been over-clocked like a computer.

The modafinil was for mission use. He had someone fix Peter's system so that there was always a modest threat level running such that Peter would dispense the drugs. The same fix meant that Peter also lost track of how many drugs were dispensed.

He just needed to remember not to get the automatic updates for the health-care system in the apartment. That was another advantage of being off base. Living quarters on the base would always run with the latest and greatest versions of everything.

A chime sounded from the streamcom. "Peter accept," he said.

A small repeater screen in the kitchen showed the face of one of his colleagues.

"Hi Roelof, it's Jasmijn. There's something very unusual happening here. The incoming shower seems to be concentrated on our control centre. We've already lost the above-ground units and now the incoming are creating a crater where the underground centre is located. At this rate we'll have lost everything within another 15 minutes."

"What about the HSDA?" asked Roelof.

"I know. This is one of the times where our fast reflex friends should be able to solve this without us even noticing. I've seen the high-speed defence array running today almost non-stop. There's no question it's been working but it just doesn't seem to be enough to stop this. It's almost as if the meteors have their own avoidance telemetry."

"Do I need to come in?" asked Roelof.

"I don't think you would be in time to make any difference," said Jasmijn, "We are all being backed into a corner here. They've already given the order to flip command to another centre."

Peter interrupted the transmission, "I am stabilising the display, it exceeds my tolerance levels."

"Hi Peter, remove video stabilisation," requested Roelof.

Roelof watched Jasmijn on the display as the stabilisation was removed. He had never seen such a level of erratic framing. Most of the base was designed to withstand just about anything that could be thrown at it. Quakes, powerful winds, floods, fire. The original designers had borrowed the triple X symbol from the Earthside town of Amsterdam. Fire flood and pestilence. Three Xs. Three times "No".

Triple X Protection.

Jasmijn looked back towards the camera. "I'm gonna bail," she said. "I'm guessing this place is only going to be around for a few more minutes."

He heard the noise of a siren. Then a bleep and the screen terminated.

"Transmission terminated," said Peter.

"Peter please give me externals," requested Roelof, "Put it on the main wall."

He stepped back in the living space. All across the wall was a scene showing distant clouds, a red sky, and white streaks of light focused towards a smoking central area.

Roelof walked towards a console in the living space. He sat in a swivel chair and grabbed the controls. He looked around the sky and locked on to two monitor drones.

Requesting access to their video channels, he zoomed the drones towards the distant control centre. The external centre disappeared and that an ominous hole in the ground suggested the Secondary bunker was also compromised.

"Jasmijn, Jasmijn, do you copy?"

He repeated the request a couple more times.

Then a voice. "Copy that, Jasmijn here - I can hear you."

" What is your status?"

" The pod is secure, and I am outside the main ring of damage. Another 20 seconds and it would be very different. It looks as if some of the others have made it too."

"Okay, follow the protocol and join me here," said Roelof.

"Copy that"

Roelof knew that the profile had been designed to protect as many people as possible on the base. Everyone had been paired, and he had been selected to pair with Jasmijn. He was officially English, and she was officially Belgian, although neither of them had spent much time in their designated home countries.

Roelof flicked through some of the observation systems to check the wider impacts what had been happening. This was one of the worst storms he had seen since he had been active on Ganymede. There was also something very unusual about the focus of this storm. Usually anything that appeared in the weather systems was quite predictable in the way that it travelled across the winds of the surface. Although violent, the normal storms dissipated across large geographical tracts. This protected the mines and other constructions from acute damage.

A paradox was that the very substances wanted from Ganymede and the adjacent Europa for use on Earth were also capable of being harnessed within Ganymede's own biosphere.

For around two hundred years the magnetosphere of Jupiter's largest moon had been observable from Earth. It had only been for the last 40 years that dependable space transit had been possible. The discovery of two complimentary passive minerals that when combined created a magnetic field like that within an electricity generator had been a breakthrough discovery.

Small amounts of the minerals could be used to make powerful generators which could be used for domestic and commercial purposes back on Earth. The same technology could be used in-situ on Ganymede to create the required defence shields to protect the mining and other operations from danger. For planet Earth this had been a life-saving discovery such that as fossil fuels declined, the new availability of magnetite had become a complete game changer.

The original predictions of a six-year flight from Earth had been dramatically reduced to three years in each direction augmented with the creation of SkyTrains to provide a near continuous round-trip service. For a two year stay on Ganymede base there was the prospect of considerable wealth for those that pioneered the creation and exploration of the bases.

The sovereign structure of Ganymede had originally been incorporated into Earth's United Nations although a series of different and sometimes very unconventional procedures had been allowed. The Earth Council had superseded the United Nations although the exact sequence of events and their timing was hazy.

The jurisdiction was not so much 'out of sight, out of mind' as a series of procedures to support the necessities of developing a base to support the future of humankind so far from Earth.

Pioneers to Ganymede had taken the longer and slower six-year outbound trip, then 2+ years working and then the faster three-year return cycle using newer technology driven by Ganymede's own propulsion devices. In practical terms this was an 11-year absence and during that time the first settlers used a range of techniques to create the necessary labour capabilities for the mining to be successful. The roundtrip with work time was now reduced to eight years. Three outbound, two moonside and then three return.

Most people on earth were unaware of change taking place on Ganymede. It was much further than a distant small country and as long as the requisite technologies arrived in time to be useful than the main debates were about the rise in fortunes of those that had made the return trip.

Roelof and Jasmijn did not know much about the situation on earth. Their memories of it were very dim, as were the memories of many of the people they worked with. There were some individuals, sometimes referred to as the Sharps, who seemed to have a much better knowledge of life on Earth. Curiously, the Sharps were perceived by people like Roelof and Jasmijn as dim-witted and slow thinking.

The buzzer to Roelof's landing deck signalled the arrival of Jasmijn.

"Peter, please guide her in."

"Acknowledged," responded Peter.

A few minutes later, Jasmijn buzzed again, and Peter opened the main door to the apartment.

"Are you okay?" asked Roelof.

"Everything is fine," said Jasmijn, "That was a close thing, but I think most of us had evacuated each area before it was destroyed."

"It's still a very worrying change of situation," said Roelof, "It's the worst I remember, after nearly two years and despite the hostile environment, there has been nothing like this."

At that moment Peter interrupted, "I have an incoming transmission for both of you."

"Okay Peter, put it on the wall."

A newsflash appeared on the whole of the living space wall. It was accompanied by newscaster soundtrack music. There was a flash and both Roelof and Jasmijn momentarily tipped their heads sideways. Four seconds later, the news broadcast resumed with a good news story from Perth about a pet dog that had been found after it had run away from home.

"Okay then," said Roelof to Jasmijn. "I'll meet you at the alternate control centre tomorrow."

"That's fine," said Jasmijn, as she left the apartment.

Tuesday morning

Roelof awoke. It was 6:30 AM. He would be heading across to the base by around seven. He hurried through the bathroom noting his vital signs which were displayed automatically on the mirror when he stood on a certain tile in the bathroom.

Then to his travel pod, he took off for the control centre. He knew he would need to go to control centre seven today. His travel pod was already programmed with the flight path. During the flight he had screens down and used the time to look at the morning's telecasts. Another quiet day on Ganymede and another quiet day on earth with a few amusing stories.

At precisely 07:02 he arrived at the control centre. Jasmijn was already there, just leaving her travel pod. They walked in together.

"What is on our agenda for today?" Asked Roelof.

"I'll need to check with control. Last night was uneventful."

They busied themselves with starting their consoles and checking the relevant levels of supply of magnetite were available.

"There seems to be some shortages," observed Roelof, "Some of yesterday afternoon's shift is lower than expected."

"No, no," said Jasmijn, "There was a request to hold extraction for three hours yesterday. Taking that into account everything is as it should be."

They watched as handler automats loaded the sliced core elements into special holders ready for transport.

"You seem to be on top of this," came a voice behind them.

"Hi Mr Sadler," said Jasmijn.

"Good, good morning to you both. All our shipments are on schedule and we seem to be running at optimum efficiency. This is great news for me. It is my last week before I return to Earth. Another three years and one day and I will be back home."

"Do you know who will replace you yet?" asked Roelof.

"I think I will meet my replacement tomorrow. I keep hearing that there are changes, but I'm not sure yet who is taking my place," said Sadler.

Roelof and Jasmijn looked at one another. They knew that Sadler was one of the Sharps and so they were unsurprised at his lack of knowledge.

Ganymede

Ganymede had started small. After the first ships landed there was a general wonder at how far into deep space it was possible to see from this un-light-polluted landscape. There were lazy swirls of stars and distant galaxies, the blue-white smoke from further outside of the solar system.

But then like a kind of fast forward fuelled by the incoming train of ships. First small colonies and then an intricate web of transportation tubing had snaked across the surface of this moon of the mighty Jupiter.

Right from the start, the colony had been militarised. They didn't call it that. It was referred to as security, but the stakes were high, and no one wanted to see the vast investments in the mining get drained away by some kind of civil war or military coup.

Instead, every second ship in the continuous train was a fully armed gunship. Alongside the mining work, the deployment of security had prevented this new land from becoming like the wild west of the 19th century on earth.

That is not to say it was a full equilibrium. Instead there were zones run by different closed communities. The Eurussian zone, the Amerikan Mafia zone, a whole area operated by a mix of Chinese and Japanese called Sino-Nihon and run by the Japanese Yakuza.

The mining meant that there were plenty of hard materials around and these were used to create the new buildings, generate the power, and provide the resource to go back to earth.

Until the ships with hydroponics arrived, there was no local vegetation. The planet's raw surface was heavily ice-ridged, but the combination of the power generation technology and the ice created a natural and beneficial trade-off that more of the ice could be heated back to water and in limited areas could kickstart a microclimate.

The Yakuza were the first to bring in addictives. The Eurussians had thought as far as alcohol, but the Sino-Nihon soon brought first marijuana seedlings and then created synthesised methamphetamines, which soon became widespread throughout the mining community.

Miners initially saw it as a relief from the tedium of two years Moon-side, but it quickly created the first series of major accidents which culminated in the destruction of an entire Amerikan mine through misuse of the drug. The rumour was that the crime lords were drawing their boundaries between the areas on Ganymede.

That era had been short lived because once the big boundaries were drawn between the different mining nations each one ran its own turf and contained and policed its own operations.

Nowadays the whole of the inhabited non-mining part of Ganymede had been purified and there were sweet smelling perfumes in the corridors, quiet flooring, and tasteful entertainment complexes. For those involved with the administration it was like being permanently inside of a vast shopping mall filled with pleasant, though hardly overwhelming, experiences.

Inside it was possible to walk around in regular clothes but most people were only a few steps away from the hostile environment outside and chose to wear heavy clothing which could provide protection from any sudden incursions of the elements.

Torus Industries

Earthside, the entire New Delaware facility was run by Torus industries. They were established approximately 50 years earlier and had seen through the acceleration of the space program to support Ganymede. They had been a consolidation of several other companies, including Biotree, which had developed much of the nanotechnology prevalent on Ganymede and Earthside. There were two other equivalent huge corporations operating in other parts of the world. *AlfaCorporatsiya* (AlfaCorp) for Eurussia and *Kǎxīmǔ gōngyè* (Cassim Gongje) for Sino-Nihon.

These three separate divisions were mirrored on Ganymede with three individual areas each being mined by one of the large industry conglomerates.

For those that worked at Torus, it was considered a privilege. Since the Scourge and then the Klima War had wiped out large parts of the planet Earth there had been a small number of higher profile roles within which to operate.

The work involved with the space shuttles to Ganymede

was still a high-level engineering task suited to scientists although much of the Earth's work was now geared toward food production.

The smaller global population meant that there were sustainable foodstuffs left in the remaining habitable parts of Earth however the food tech had also moved to greater synthesis implying fewer proper foodstuffs to eat in many parts of the world.

The three global bands of Earthside had seen this occur. Most of the scientists lived in the middle band which is where New Delaware was situated.

Considerably south of the facilities was the start of the desert plains which led in turn to the desolation areas that were considered uninhabitable.

A similar effect had occurred within the sea and it now contained potentially dangerous chemicals and was unsuitable for use as a means of transport. Wherever water was needed there were new large-scale desalination units of the type used previously in desert areas to take the saltwater and purify it so that it could be used for supporting life.

The New Delaware facility like many other major population areas was largely enclosed. Although people would go outdoors in this zone, they would attempt to limit their exposure to sunlight and to the unscrubbed atmosphere.

It was the same with the rains which still fell but nowadays held a cocktail of chemicals which were generally non-harmful in small quantities although no one really wanted to stay outside for too long.

Most people would wear ruggedized suiting when outside in the natural elements.

Torus was one of the major conglomerates and also provided the clothing and other climate management facilities on earth. After the full perils of climate change had become clear, the pre-existing industries needed to pool their resources to develop the relevant remedies quickly enough.

There was still competition, but the scale of the endeavours was such that in each of the major continental zones a single company emerged as the leader to provide the coverage necessary.

 A few leaders had arisen in each of these companies and acted as sovereign rulers of the relevant areas. Earth Council had established a forum structure to provide regulation and many of the pre-war countries were represented through a kind of Senate.

However, there was a great need for speed to develop the required changes and Torus had used strong leadership to drive through its approach to the space program, to robotics, to climate management and to the feeding and wellbeing of the remaining population.

 The economic model had changed. There was still currency and exchange rates between nations, but most people would exist using tokens which were charged at the beginning of a month and which included pre-allocated deductions for food, transport and other necessary aspects of living.

In return for this, most people living within New Delaware could expect a stable lifestyle in exchange for their contribution through work. It was a very different role from the capitalist approach used prior to the start of the climate decline.

There were few people left now who remembered the world before the change to the new regime.

Communications, education, discussions about freedoms were all contained within this limited framework. Astride it all was Torus Corporation and the other similar sized behemoths.

Back in the 21st-century there had still been 200 countries and 20 major nation states that dictated how politics and major economics operated on earth.

The shifts in population and wealth and the redistribution of natural resources because of the climactic changes meant that this number now reduced to a smaller number of nation states with transnational corporations gaining the upper hand.

There had always been corporations joining and splitting themselves to optimise their global footprint to gain the greatest economic and political advantages whilst often paying the lowest taxation.

The situation with global corporations was not new and had origins right back to the Second World War when companies such as Cola manufacturers would retain both an Amerikan *"It's the real thing"* and a German *"Mach doch mal Pause"* presence. In effect, playing on both sides of the equation.

The three largest corporations together ran via subsidiaries and covered approximately 70% of the Earth's major businesses.

Because the Earth Council had found it necessary to bring everyone together during the times of deep concern, it would therefore become beneficial to be able to deal via these three large corporations.

It had also simplified global currency which was now three major currency types stably pegged to one another for exchange-rate purposes.

The major stakeholders in the corporations were now nation-states who contributed towards the shareholding of the companies and in return received the income streams necessary to sustain their populations.

The decline in the habitability of the southern hemisphere also meant that the three corporations operated from above the equator. Closest to the Equator were the reception areas for the return of the miners from Ganymede. The base in the Americas was the one in New Delaware and there were equivalent control locations in Europe's Barcelona and China's Shenhua.

Routine

Jasmijn and Roelof wore the standard uniform common to office-side workers in the complexes on Ganymede. These uniforms all included a large number sewn onto the front and back like a kind of reference code for each of them.

It was so commonplace that they did not notice it as unusual. It did mean that they could usually detect other members of their team from long distances and where security was involved it was easy to tell who was present.

They also had idents embedded in their suits and their work layers that could be used for close to surface work when they were in the complexes.

The uniforms were a light grey colour and featured colour coding on the shoulders which also helped identify the zone to which people belonged. The light grey stood out from the Ganymede surface colours as well as standing out when they were within the complex itself. It was both a matter of safety and of security and ingrained into the way that everyone operated on this moon of Jupiter.

Jasmijn and Roelof watched the arrival of a new mining ship. Even in the time that they had been active on the moon, the profile of the ships had been changing. Incoming ships were becoming more infrequent and when they did arrive, they would have dramatically changed profiles from the ships that arrived within the last 10 years or so.

This one landed smoothly with a minimum of noise and fuss. Because the new ships used the technology of the magnetite, their whole power systems had been dramatically scaled down, the power to weight ratio had completely changed from the days of the ships requiring huge booster rockets to leave Earth's atmosphere.

Watching the new ship arrive through the observation deck meant that the experience was viewed in silence. The originally thin atmosphere of Ganymede also meant that most of the original landings had been perceived as quiet, but as the ice had melted the microclimate became established and then the expansion of the individual colonies. It had created an increasing industrial soundscape.

There was an irony that most of this could be solved using industrial processes to create noise suppressors. Building small devices from the magnetite technology had allowed much of Ganymede's rapid progress to be possible.

This same technology had only been dreamt of on earth until the first ships were able to get back. Once the technology was seeded back on Earth it became a virtuous circle with improvements to the incoming technology from Earth and from the outgoing technology back from Ganymede.

Roelof likened it to Earth's industrial revolution and the steam age when steam locomotive designers had built standard metallic chassis onto which increasingly powerful steam engines could be constructed.

These spaceships used similar ideas. They had a loading gauge for width and height, they incorporated standard couplings for their hatch accesses and many of the control systems ran on a standardised electronic bus and with similar controls. It meant the ships could be interconnected and that operation of the ships was straightforward, once the core controls had been learned. Consistency between designs meant that there was little threat of system redundancy.

All of this had improved general efficiency and had a knock-on effect towards the way that Ganymede was being operated.

The size of inbound crews to Ganymede had been reduced as the efficiency of the moon-side workers improved. This incoming ship seemed to have only included primary crews for piloting and navigation. It held inbound supplies but even these were reduced now because Ganymede had become increasingly self-sufficient.

By contrast the outbound ships from Ganymede had become much larger because of the net export of raw materials and the increasing inventory of completed machinery back to earth. The increasing use of robotics and AI to create and finish product meant that Ganymede was a dramatic exporter back to Earthside. Roelof wondered how the Earth Port was handling such dramatic increases in quantity of goods. The main effect was to improve the conditions for Earth through these transfers.

Intergalactic, planetary, planetary, intergalactic

You're on earth. There's no cure for that.

Samuel Beckett

Earth

"These system updates are taking longer and longer," said Sam Walker, "This time we had to wait for nearly four hours to get the new command centre online."

"I know," replied Cindy Shaw, "They told us this time it was the new extraction modules that were being introduced."

"Anyway," said Sam, "We seem to have everything back now. Just about every system is already green and a couple of the minor ones are still restarting."

"There are still some discrepancies, though," said Cindy, "If I add together the time for a reload plus the transmission times, even with those new modules, we should see the return to ready state within maybe a couple of hours.   There is no hint that the systems were ready - it looks like a complete restore. "

They both studied the console for moment. Sure, the transmission time for the command up to Ganymede were about 34 minutes. That made a round trip of just over an hour. All the new software had already been transmitted so it should have just been a case of firing it up.

"Let's take a look at the log," said Sam.

"Yes," said Cindy, "I see this was an update that created a new release level. We are on release seven now. It still seems strange that when we go through minor release levels, they take about two hours but the major levels are adding increasing amounts each time.

"See here," said Sam "There's this whole extra section for transfer..."

He looked at what was an extra section which had inserted itself into the update.

"Yes, that only seems to happen when we do one of these big levels," said Cindy.

Sam reached across to a mug which contained a kind of vegetable soup. As he lifted it from the work surface, it made a resonant chink sound which cut across the sounds from the faintly whirring technology.

"What is it?" Asked Cindy. She peered towards the brownish liquid with little white green and orange pieces floating in it.

"It's Italian," said Sam, "They call it minestrone. It's not bad for a sub."

Cindy grinned, "Happy Nutrition."

Cindy and Sam looked like a dream team. Cindy was slimly built, athletically bodied with dark hair and a friendly disposition. One of the people that if you saw, you'd think you already knew, and that she was a good friend. Sam was a similarly slim build, a shock of blond hair and a tanned face suggesting outdoor adventures. They both had that scaled-down look that somehow would look right for movies.

Cindy peered towards the observation windows.

"One day these subs will have proper vegetables in them again."

Outside she could see the land. An orange-brown colour. It was only just daybreak. She could still make out the outline for the moon and across the sky from it the second much smaller moon which had been created by man. Small pinpricks of light twinkled between the two moons indicative of transiting space hardware.

She looked across to the Meteo display. 40C degrees already.

"It is going to be a hot one today."

Sam nodded.

Their base was in New Delaware on the east coast of the United States. The whole island area of what had once been called Delaware and what had been the eastern half of Maryland had been re-designated as New Delaware when the efforts to bolster the space program had redoubled.

Global warming had affected the original sites further

south in the deserts and across on the eastern seaboard of Florida. The move further north still had the advantages of nearby sea as well as a convenience for any military reinforcement that may have be required.

New Delaware had then aggressively become a TEZ - total exclusion zone - permitting the wholesale development of first lunar and then interplanetary transport vehicles.

Secondary developments had sprung up around the bases providing supplies and other technologies for the agency. In the early 22nd Century it had been a race to find power sources to keep those functional and to avoid major global instabilities.

The very necessary race to space had itself created huge new industrial footprints across many parts of the globe.

Cindy and Sam had met at IPX school. Interplanetary Exploration was a career choice for the very brightest. They were selected early and then encouraged to form friendship groups and ultimately to pair off. The process was part of the selection for further duties, where couples were always selected together for space mission work.

Earlier attempts with longer flights and separated spouses had failed for all manner of reason and there was usually salacious reporting of the unfortunate outcomes. It had culminated when an early high-profile mission to the intermediate planet of Mars had been destroyed by an unhappy astronaut who had realised his wife was cheating on him back on earth.

Sam and Cindy had been deselected from space travel part way through the programme. The official story was that they were too precious to be gambled in space travel and that there were others more suited to the roles required.

It was a blow to them both after what had been training since their childhood. They'd been through the full process not disclosed to many normal earth dwellers and knew the concluding fate of the planet.

Most of the situation had been drilled into them through schooling, although the official story for the general populace stopped short of the more dramatic conclusions to which they were subjected.

Earth Class at IPX

Almost ten years earlier, Sam and Cindy met for the first time. They had attended the Earth Class at IPX.

Sam was aware of Cindy being on the programme, but Cindy didn't seem to have noticed Sam. Sitting together for a lecture, they soon struck up a conversation.

"I'm not sure about the Prof," said Sam, looking towards Cindy.

"No, he looks more like a stoner than part of the establishment," agreed Cindy.

"I'm thinking he must know something about the faculty that means he has one over them?" added Sam.

"Yes, maybe knows where the bodies are buried," quipped Cindy.

"That's almost eerie." Said Sam, "Here have an energy bar," He offered her a small packet.

"Energy bar?" queried Cindy, smiling.

"It's all I got," said Sam, "Consider it a love token."

Professor Marcus Garvey entered the auditorium. He was wearing a long overcoat, a scarf, and a headscarf. Around his wrists were a selection of beads and what looked like festival admission charms.

He looked up briefly and then started the talk. Sam and Cindy and the others present were indeed about to find out where the bodies had been buried.

"I'm gonna go fast," he said, "You'll need a good head today and a strong constitution for what I'm about to tell you." He tugged at one sleeve of his coat pulling out a remote.

He flipped towards a sensewall and some pictures appeared. It looked like the End of Days.

"See this, it looks like the lower half of a Bosch painting of Hell," he said, "Except Bosch underplayed it. These real scenes are worse. Worse than a World War I battlefield, worse than Genghis Khan on the Silk Road."

"Awesomely awful," he continued.

"So, let's get to it. Earth had a finite lifespan to support humanity, but it was been dramatically shortened because of post-industrial consumption. Mark Lynas predicted a hotter planet and set the outer edge around six degrees. Much of what he predicted has come true.

"Lynas said it was all about the temperature rises. Just a matter of a few degrees. Hardly enough to excite average thinkers, but enough to create special forces to be established in many governments.

"It was all politicised, and stupid politicians crashed past structural safeguards to bring about the end of the world.

Garvey swiped through the air and the sensewall showed a series of pictures of politicians. Sam thought he recognised one, a plump man with a grinning orange face and blonde hair.

"It had all begun back in the early 21st Century. It started as a barely noticeable single degree Centigrade shift, which was enough to ripple across climatic extremes.

"It started with more extreme hurricane seasons, there had been floods and loss of life, generally in small pinpointable areas. It made mainstream news and various aid agencies were dispatched but it did not really interfere with much of the western world's ways of working.

"The relief agencies were corrupted by local country bribes and big business just lobbied to carry on as before. A few large firms bid for the reconstruction work, just as they had done after the middle eastern wars. Fat politicians helped industrialists line their pockets.

"Then the North American dustbowls started to expand. Farming areas in Nebraska, Montana and Wyoming became bleached and prairies land started to revert to desert.

He flicked again and some Dorothea Lange pictures from the 1930s were projected.

"There, you see, this wasn't even when the main trouble occurred, but the black blizzards of the 1930s were like a forerunner of what was to happen. Even the Farm Securities Association couldn't stop what happened. Farmers ploughed the prairie grass as part of their Manifest Destiny to live on the land. The replacement wheat didn't have deep roots and then with a drought the entire topsoil blew away - some of it as far as New York.

He showed a photograph of dust approaching Manhattan.

"The old United States provided new technologies, ironically borrowed from the oil industry, to send water around in major pipelines to re-irrigate some of the areas affected. They couldn't stem things completely, but they did enough to maintain food crops where they were important to national wellbeing.

By now Garvey had fired up a second sensewall. Now, one showed monochrome portraits of the people from the dustbowl, the other showed colour images of the desolate effect. There we are, 1930 monochrome and around a century later, digital colour."

"Shit. It's awful," said Sam.

"No, this isn't awful, this is a precursor," said Garvey.

"It wasn't just America that suffered. The countries closest to the equator had it the worst. The one-degree rise created new droughts and freshwater shortages on top of what was already a dangerously disease-ridden part of the world.

"Over in well-developed northern Europe they were aware of what was happening, certainly in terms of changing economic fortunes, but in the early years the milder winters and more dependable summers were seen as a bonus. The sentiment of 'If this is global warming, then I'm all for it' was frequently expressed.

"Of course, the so-called Spanish flu appeared around this time. A little-known aspect is that it started in Kansas, in an army barracks. It was soldier migration to Europe, through Spain, that carried the virus across the Atlantic.

"Now we have the blend of climate change and virus attacks, simultaneously destroying the earth. The 1918 pandemic accounts for some 50 million deaths. Then, minor waves of epidemic and a further pandemic in the early 21st Century. The history of that one seems to be based upon a bat-shit dystopia movie from the earlier century. No-one really wanted to get to the real cause, in case it was engineered."

"Add to that internal combustion powered cars and goods vehicles and their side-effects. General economic wealth meant the increase in the use of dirty cars as well as of air conditioning. It managed the heat for living but merely dumped it back into the atmosphere, along with the extra power consumed and carbon dioxide created in the process.

"Scientists started to notice important changes. The Amazon dropped to a precipitously low level on part of its route. The Mississippi delta became alternately arid and then a major flood plain.

"In the same period, scientists quietly scrutinised the Arctic. The permafrost which had been frozen for thousands of years was thawing. Both poles saw temperature increases faster than the global average.

"This permafrost dissolved into mud and lakes, consequently destabilising whole areas as the ground collapsed beneath buildings, roads and pipelines.

"Earlier seasonal snowmelt meant more summer heat went into the air and ground rather than into the act of melting snow, raising temperatures in a feedback loop effect. More dark shrubs and forest on formerly bleak tundra meant still more heat was absorbed by vegetation.

"At sea, the pace was even faster. While snow-covered ice reflects more than 80% of the sun's heat, the darker ocean absorbs up to 95% of solar radiation.

"Once sea ice begins to melt the process becomes self-reinforcing. More ocean surface is revealed, absorbing solar heat, raising temperatures, and making it unlikelier that ice will re-form next winter."

Garvey paused and let the sensewalls catch up. They were showing glacial thaws and wildlife trapped on breakaway floes.

"There was a year when 720,000 square kilometres of supposedly permanent ice disappeared, and this illustrated the rapidity of planetary change.

"That was Earth crossing a tipping point."

Garvey moved the sensewalls along and it now looked more like a disaster movie on the walls.

Cindy looked at Sam, "He's surrounding us."

Garvey pressed another button. Sub-woofers kicked in. A dull roar.

"Yes, the mountains, too, were starting to come apart. In the Alps, most ground above 3,000 metres is stabilised by permafrost. In the summer of 2003, however, the melt zone climbed right up to 4,600 metres, higher than the summit of the Matterhorn and nearly as high as Mont Blanc. With the permafrost glue of millennia melting away, rocks showered down, and 50 climbers died. These were still early warning signs, yet the summits held by politicians and businessmen in nearby Davos were oblivious to all of this.

"Ah yes, a Swedish girl spoke out but was ignored by big business," remembered Cindy.

Garvey continued, "As temperatures edged upwards, it wasn't just mountaineers who fled. Whole towns and villages were at risk.

"Then, at the opposite end of the scale, low-lying atoll countries such as the Maldives prepared for extinction as sea levels rose, and mainland coasts – in particular the eastern US and Gulf of Mexico, the Caribbean and Pacific islands and the Bay of Bengal – were hit by stronger and stronger hurricanes as the water warms.

"Another bell-weather was Hurricane Katrina which, in 2005, hit New Orleans with the combined impacts of earthquake and floods and was a nightmare precursor of what the future held.

"Most striking was seeing how people behaved once the veneer of civilisation had been torn away. From Katrina, most victims were poor and black, left to fend for themselves as the police either joined in the looting or deserted the area.

"Four days into the crisis, survivors were packed into the

city's Superdome, living next to overflowing toilets and rotting bodies as gangs of young men with guns seized the only food and water available. The USA learnt, after Katrina, to put up tents and use refrigerated trucks to store bodies."

"Why was that?" someone behind Cindy asked.

"Stigma, purely stigma, so that an august building isn't associated with being a morgue," answered Garvey, "But it was still cosmetics for the politicians,"

"Perhaps the most memorable scene was a single military helicopter landing for just a few minutes, its crew flinging food parcels and water bottles out onto the ground before hurriedly taking off again as if from a war zone. This was Americans supporting other Americans."

"In scenes more like a Third World refugee camp than an Amerikan urban centre, young men fought for the water as pregnant women and the elderly looked on with nothing."

"It's what happens when people are desperate," Garvey paused and looked around. The auditorium was silent.

"I should add," said Garvey, "That there were some pandemics mixed in with all of this. New flu strains that adapted from earth mammals to be able to be hosted on humans. And what happened?"

Garvey paused to look around the auditorium.

He pressed a button and a new scene appeared on both sensewalls.

"Take a look," he said, "Long lines of people in lines. Like in the Great Depression. But you know something?" he flipped the screen forward.

A small gasp from the auditorium.

"You may well gasp. These people are not queuing for food, nor for medical supplies. No. These people are queuing for guns," he announced.

"So, are you going to tell us about the Warming?" asked Cindy.

"Yes," Garvey continued, "Let's go through the stages. Starting with between one and two degrees of warming.

"At this level, the hot European summer became the annual norm. Anything that could be called a heatwave was of Saharan intensity. Even in average years, people died of heat stress.

"The first symptoms were minor. A person will feel slightly nauseous, dizzy and irritable. It needn't be an emergency: an hour or so lying down in a cooler area, sipping water, will cure it. But what if there were no cooler areas, especially for elderly people?"

Garvey continued, "Once body temperature reaches 41C (104F) its thermoregulatory system begins to break down. Sweating ceases and breathing becomes shallow and rapid. The pulse quickens, and the victim may lapse into a coma.

"Unless drastic measures are taken to reduce the body's core temperature, the brain is starved of oxygen and vital organs begin to fail. Death will be only minutes away unless the emergency services can quickly get the victim into intensive care.

"As early as summer 2003, in France, the emergency services failed to save more than 10,000 French people. Mortuaries ran out of space as hundreds of dead bodies were brought in each night.

"Across Europe as a whole, that precursor heatwave is believed to have cost between 22,000 and 35,000 lives.

"Agriculture, too, was devastated. Farmers lost $12 billions worth of crops, and Portugal alone suffered $12 billions of forest-fire damage. The flows of the River Po in Italy, Rhine in Germany and Loire in France all shrank to historic lows.

"Barges ran aground, and there was not enough water for irrigation and hydroelectricity. Melt rates in the Alps, where some glaciers lost 10% of their mass, were not just a record – they doubled the previous record of 1998.

"Extreme summers take a much heavier toll of human life. Crops will bake in the fields, and forests will die off and burn. Even so, the short-term effects may not be the worst:

"From the beech forests of northern Europe to the evergreen oaks of the Mediterranean, plant growth across the whole landmass in 2003 slowed and then stopped. Instead of absorbing carbon dioxide, the stressed plants began to emit it. Around half a billion tonnes of carbon was added to the atmosphere from European plants, equivalent to a twelfth of global emissions from fossil fuels.

"This was feedback of critical importance, because it suggested that, as temperatures rose, carbon emissions from forests and soils also rose. As many were saying, if these land-based emissions were sustained over long periods, global warming could spiral out of control.

"Was that when they stated to name it a climate emergency?" asked Sam.

"Yes, global warming was just a bit too friendly sounding," answered Professor Garvey, "By the time we get to the two-degree world, nobody would take Mediterranean holidays. The movement of people from northern Europe to the Mediterranean reversed, switching eventually into a mass scramble as Saharan heatwaves swept across the sea area known as the Mediterranean. People everywhere thought twice about moving to the coast.

"When temperatures were last between 1 and 2C higher than they were in the 20th Century some 125,000 years ago, sea levels were five or six metres higher too.

"All this 'lost' water was in the polar ice.

"The 'tipping point' for Greenland wasn't until average temperatures had risen by 2.7C. Greenland was also warming much faster than the rest of the world at 2.2 times the global average.

"Didn't the politicians rail against this?" asked Cindy.

"Not really," answered Garvey, "There were some protests, but many significant world leaders played the whole thing down. The Amerikan leadership didn't believe in climate emergency at all. They said it was 'Fake News'."

"What even with predictions and modelling?" asked

Sam.

"Yes, it became fashionable for some of the really weak politicians to say they'd had enough from so-called experts, implying rather pompously that they were better than the scientists."

Garvey shook his head, "The ensuing sea-level rise was far more than the half-metre predicted for the end of the 20th Century. Some scientists pointed out that sea levels at the end of the last ice age shot up by a metre every 20 years for four centuries."

"It took the situation when Miami was set to flood and disappear, as was most of Manhattan. Central London, despite its river defences, flooded. That's when some of the political class started to pay attention. It was too late, of course."

"Like thermal runaway?" asked Sam.

"Kind of, like an exothermic reaction, where the heat from one stage accelerates the next stage, that's what happened, " answered Garvey, "Bangkok, Bombay and Shanghai lost most of their area. In all, half of humanity had to move to higher ground.

"Not only coastal communities suffered. As mountains lost their glaciers, so people lost their water supplies. The entire Indian subcontinent was fighting for survival. As the glaciers disappear from all but the highest peaks, their runoff ceased to power the massive rivers that delivered vital freshwater to hundreds of millions.

"Everywhere, ecosystems unravelled as species either migrated or fell out of sync with each other. You can see how the divisions on Earth were starting to form."

Garvey continued, "Of course, as we all know, it didn't stop there. Now let's look at what happened between two and three degrees of temperature increase."

"Assuming that governments had planned carefully, and farmers converted to more appropriate crops, not too many people outside subtropical Africa need have starved.

"But beyond two degrees, mass starvation became a huge problem. Millions, then billions, of people faced an increasingly tough battle to survive.

"To find anything comparable we have to go back to the Pliocene Epoch – The last epoch of the Tertiary period, 3 million years ago."

"Wow, that is a long way back," said Sam.

"Not really, in geological terms, the Pliocene Epoch follows the Miocene Epoch and is followed by the Pleistocene Epoch - It is one of the more recent Epochs, actually." Answered Professor Garvey.

"There were no continental glaciers in the northern hemisphere and trees grew in the Arctic. Sea levels were 25 metres higher than today. In this kind of heat, the death of the Amazon was as inevitable as the melting of Greenland.

"The warmer seas absorbed less carbon dioxide, leaving more to accumulate in the atmosphere and intensify global warming. On land, matters were even worse. Huge amounts of carbon are stored in the soil, as the half-rotted remains of dead vegetation.

The soil carbon reservoir contains some 1600 gigatonnes, more than double the entire carbon content of the atmosphere. But then as the soil warmed, bacteria accelerated the breakdown of this stored carbon, releasing it into the atmosphere.

"We are into 'end of the world' territory here," emphasised Garvey.

"The three-degree increase in global temperature threw the carbon cycle into reverse. Instead of absorbing carbon dioxide, vegetation and soils start to release it.

"So much carbon pours into the atmosphere that it pumped up atmospheric concentrations by 250 parts per million boosting global warming by another 1.5C.

"All soils were affected by the rising heat, but none as badly as the Amazon's.

"'Catastrophe' is almost too small a word for the loss of the rainforest. Its 7m square kilometres produced 10% of the world's entire photosynthetic output from plants. Drought and heat crippled it and then fire finished it off.

"Farming and food production tipped into decline. Salt water crept up the stricken rivers, poisoning ground water.

"Higher temperatures meant greater evaporation, further drying out vegetation and soils, and causing huge losses from reservoirs. The TV news shows featuring droughts became increasingly common.

"Grain yields declined by 10% for every degree of heat above 30C, and at 40C there was no more grain. The

Indian subcontinent was choking on dust.

"All of human history shows that, given the choice between starving in-situ and moving, people move. Pakistan was one of the early failed states as civil administration collapsed and armed gangs seize what little food was left.

"To summarise, it was bleak, but this wasn't even the end of it."

Sam nodded towards Cindy, "I've seen a screendoc about some of those nation states like Pakistan and India, which were the seat of much unrest."

"Yes," and there was that movie 'The Flatlands' about the flooding Netherlands," replied Cindy.

"Something for all of us?" asked Garvey, looking towards Sam.

"We were talking about that movie, "The Flatlands", he answered.

"Ah yes," continued Garvey, "They got some things right in that screenplay.   As the land burned, so the sea will go on rising. They didn't depict the situation in other countries though, just lowland Europe.

"At the time it was happening, they could have featured New York, or even London. New York flooded and the eastern part of England also. There was also mass migration away from the stricken areas. It made the earlier populist debates about migrants seem ridiculous, although it allowed resurgent fascist parties to still win votes by promising to keep foreigners out."

"It didn't even stop there, did it?" asked someone behind Cindy.

The sense wall briefly cleared, then on one side a giant 3 appeared and on the other side a giant 4.

"Yes, you are now entering the era of between 3 and 4 degrees of warming," said Garvey.

"The stream of refugees which started when the lowlands flooded will now include those fleeing from coasts to safer interiors – millions when storms hit.

"Where they survived, coastal cities became fortified islands. This wasn't pretty though. The world economy was in tatters. A few fat cats had bet on the decline of businesses and made huge sums from shorting the markets. They picked high land to develop into prestigious dwellings, with a castle-like fortifications and walls around them.

"Direct losses, social instability and insurance pay-outs cascaded through the whole system, with funds to support displaced people increasingly scarce. Certain of the politicians were also dipping into the money to be made from the catastrophe. Building works, Infrastructure, Military and Medical Aid, not to mention shorting the equities in weakened companies. It was cynical, amoral feeding from the trough."

"The earth couldn't deal with the rate of change. The poles were melting, which projected a 50-metre rise in sea level. It didn't happen, and would take millennia to complete, but even the metre every 20 years that did occur was way too much for civilisation to handle.

"China was also on a collision course with the planet. As

its people became richer and could consume at a rate similar to Amerikans, they were eating two-thirds of the entire global harvest and could burn through 100m barrels of oil a day, or 125% of the world's output.

"It was still worse because China's agricultural production also crashed, and it was left with the task of feeding 1.5bn much richer people on two thirds of current supplies. That's around when Sino-Nihon was first mooted. The joining of China, Japan and several other smaller countries – frankly to avoid expensive conflict in the region.

"Air-conditioning was mandatory for anyone wanting to stay cool. This in turn put ever more stress on energy systems, which could pour more greenhouse gases into the air as coal and gas-fired power stations ramped up their output, hydroelectric sources dwindled, and renewables failed to take up the slack.

"I'm originally from England, which had problems of its own. As flood plains became more regularly inundated, there was a general retreat out of high-risk areas. Millions of people lost their lifetime investments in houses that become uninsurable and therefore unsaleable.

These last moves also saw the start of the thawing of permafrost. This was another capsule of doom. The permafrost contained much carbon dioxide, which could then accelerate the warming further.

Garvey waved the remote again. The sensewall graphics of 3 and 4 gave way to 4 and 5.

"We can understand the Earth Council being formed to try to make sense of what was happening. A problem was that right from the start it contained many vested interests. These were people from major corporations who saw the angle to try to gain control of a larger slice of the planet.

"They were presiding over the Earth as we now know it. An entirely different planet. Ice sheets have vanished from both poles; rainforests have burnt up and turned to desert; the dry and lifeless Alps resemble the High Atlas; rising seas are scouring deep into continental interiors.

"One temptation may be to shift populations from dry areas to the newly thawed regions of the far north, in Canada and Siberia. Even there, though, summers may be too hot for crops to be grown away from the coasts; and there is no guarantee that northern governments will admit southern refugees.

"Right now, Siberia is only one stop from war, with Sino-Nihon ready to invade Siberia and let's not forget that Amerika has already incorporated Canada.

"Summer heatwaves scorched the vegetation out of continental Spain, leaving a desert terrain heavily eroded by winter rainstorms. Palm mangroves grew as far north as England and Belgium, and the Arctic Ocean was so warm that Mediterranean algae thrived.

"The total amount of carbon in the atmosphere during the Palaeocene-Eocene thermal maximum, or PETM, as scientists call it, was more than today's, but the rate of increase in we are seeing may be 30 times faster. It may well be the fastest increase the world has ever seen – faster even than the episodes that caused catastrophic mass extinctions.

"And we see globalism in the five-degree world breaking

down into something more like parochialism. Customers will have nothing to buy because producers will have nothing to sell.

"Where no refuge is available, civil war and a collapse into racial or communal conflict seemed the likely outcome. Isolated survivalism was as impracticable as dialling for room service. How many of us could really trap or kill enough game to feed a family?

"Even if large numbers of people did successfully manage to fan out into the countryside, wildlife populations would quickly dwindle under the pressure. Supporting a hunter-gatherer lifestyle takes 10 to 100 times the land per person that a settled agricultural community needs.

"A large-scale resort to survivalism would turn into a further disaster for biodiversity as hungry humans killed and ate anything that moved. Including, perhaps, each other.

"That's when the Zonal Laws were first proposed, and the power of the Earth Council extended. It should have been by country voting, but instead was declared a global emergency, so that everywhere could be incorporated.

"Of course, it met with huge resistance from some areas. Countries that had previously been power brokers, or countries that were doing okay, despite everything. It tipped into the Klima Wars, which started diplomatically a phony war, but then toppled into an actual war.

"To see the most recent climatic lookalike, we have to turn the geological clock back between 144m and 65m years, to the Cretaceous Period, which ended with the extinction of the dinosaurs.

"There was an even closer fit at the end of the Permian Age, 251m years ago, when global temperatures rose by six degrees, and 95% of species were wiped out.

"That episode was the worst ever endured by life on Earth, the closest the planet has come to ending up a dead and desolate rock in space.

Garvey looked around the auditorium," On land, the only winners were fungi that flourished on dying trees and shrubs. At sea there were only losers. Warm water is a killer. Less oxygen can dissolve, so conditions become stagnant and anoxic. Oxygen-breathing water-dwellers – all the higher forms of life from plankton to sharks – face suffocation. Warm water also expands, and sea levels rose by 20 metres." The resulting "super-hurricanes" hitting the coasts would have triggered flash floods that no living thing could have survived.

"That is small comfort, however, for beneath the oceans, another monster stirred – the same that would bring a devastating end to the Palaeocene nearly 200m years later, and that still lies in wait today. Methane hydrate.

"What happens when warming water releases pent-up gas from the seabed? First, a small disturbance drives a gas-saturated parcel of water upwards. As it rises, bubbles begin to appear, as dissolved gas fizzles out with reducing pressure – just as a bottle of lemonade overflows if the top is taken off too quickly. These bubbles make the parcel of water still more buoyant, accelerating its rise through the water. As it surges upwards, reaching explosive force, it drags surrounding water up with it. At the surface, water is shot hundreds of metres into the air as the released gas blasts into the atmosphere. Shockwaves propagate outwards in all directions, triggering more eruptions nearby.

Garvey pressed the remote again, the sensewalls changed. One showed a diagram of the gas-explosion. The second wall showed a real-world example, like a terrifically powerful geyser spouting water, but from within the sea.

"The eruption is more than just another positive feedback in the quickening process of global warming. Unlike CO2, methane is flammable. Even in air-methane concentrations as low as 5%, the mixture could ignite from lightning or some other spark and send fireballs tearing across the sky.

"The effect would be much like that of the fuel-air explosives used by the US and Russian armies – so-called "vacuum bombs" that ignite fuel droplets above a target.

According to the CIA, those near the ignition point are obliterated. Those at the fringes are likely to suffer many internal injuries, including burst eardrums, severe concussion, ruptured lungs and internal organs, and possibly blindness."

"But these last effects have not happened. Instead, we were able to reverse the trends through off-world discoveries. That's where all of you come in. To help us bring back the materials and the technologies that help us once again make the Earth self-sustaining."

"But what about the law of unintended consequences?" asked Sam.

"I get asked this every time I run this session," answered Garvey, "It would take a pretty bleak unintended consequence to be worse than a burnt, dead world filled with methane gas."

He looked around the auditorium. He was used to the ashen faces and exhausted looks of the attendees at this point.

"You'll need to go away and process all of this," he suggested,

" Try to find some up-sides. You are all going to help the recovery programme. The six-degree change can be reversed. We've found new technology that removes the need for carbon fossil fuels. There's a new form of lightweight, yet formidable material."

"You are all going to help find it, mine it and make new tech from it which can reverse what has been happening. We might be on an edge, but you are among the ones who can stop us from toppling over it."

Streamcom chimed

Both Cindy and Sam had been thinking back to their time at IPX. One thing, they agreed; it didn't prepare them for the command-based nature of life afterwards.

Interplanetary Expedition school had taught them about many things that the general public didn't know but hidden within it was the passive-aggressive command structure to which they were both linked.

The streamcom panel chimed.

Cindy pressed the accept button.

"Hi Cindy, Hi Sam, and how are you today?" asked Matson.

Matson was higher up the chain than Cindy and Sam and routinely they had little direct contact with him.

"Good morning," said Cindy.

"There's been something of a situation," said Matson.

"Since we changed to Version 6 of the control, we noticed some new anomalies. I'd like to talk it over with you both. I know we just added Version 7, but I'm expecting similar challenges. I'm thinking of forming a small team to investigate. Can you come over to the Block this morning? There'll be some other people for you to meet as well."

"Once the rest of the system is stable, we can come straight over," said Sam.

"Excellent, replied Matson, "I guess I'll see you in a couple of hours then?"

The streamcom screen went blank.

"I guess that's it," said Cindy.

Sam smiled, "Yeah- Command and Control; I think I was probably a little too eager," he chuckled.

He flipped a couple of switches and checked a status light.

"This is all fine," he said, "Come on; we might as well make a move."

They knew that when Matson referred to the Block, he wasn't talking causally about one of the housing blocks. No, he was referring to The Block, which was the central administration and command centre for New Delaware.

In the corner of their office was a glass lift shaft. It didn't go directly to the transit system and so they had to change at the mezzanine floor. Two other groups of couples were also waiting for transit to the Block.

"I guess these will be our company," suggested Sam. He looked at Cindy, then he looked at the two couples, although he did not recognise them from the complex.

A transit arrived. A soft wash as the doors opened, and they were soon on course for the Block. The other two couples had also taken seats in different areas and appeared to be making similar judgements about Sam and Cindy.

As the transit arrived at the Block's dock, all six of them prepared to exit.

"Hi guys," said Sam to the others, "Are you all here to see Matson too?"

"That's right," said one of the women, "We had a call about half an hour ago."

"Yes, he seems to be rounding us up for something," said Cindy. She looked towards first woman. A shock of pink hair cut straight across her forehead, with a chink around her left eye. A sharp chiselled chin, blue eyes and a small nose and mouth. She was wearing something that could be a sailor costume, powder blue dress with a vee-shaped collar and a white tie pulled loosely underneath the collar. Cindy thought she could be a teen-boy's image of a sexy avatar.

"I'm Cat, by the way," Cat looked towards her partner. He nodded. He looked older than Cat with shaggy dark hair, a bleached red tee-shirt with Reibu written across it and some Japanese writing underneath, canvas jacket and maroon trousers.

"Did you see anything unusual, based upon the reset?" asked Cat looking towards Cindy, "It would be good to know before we get in with Matson"

"Only that it seemed to take a very long time," said Sam, "Much longer than the calculated reset time."

"Yes, we noticed that with release six as well," said Cat, "But there is something else. Each time the reset occurs the location seems to drift sometimes as much as 5 km. In fact, each time the drift has increased."

"Are you sure it's not just the static based upon the large distances?" asked Sam.

"No, we've seen it too," said the man from the third couple, wearing a smart suit jacket over a dark hoodie, "My name is Lorenzo, and this is Francesca. We've also seen the drift and the timing changes. It's as if each reset is occurring from a different location. I can't work out why the delays increase, however," he looked towards his dark-haired partner, who was wearing tight fitting jeans and a loose-fitting top. Francesca nodded in agreement.

They were now approaching the entrance to the Block and prepared for the first level of security.

They would each have to go through biometric testing and identity comparisons with their individual implanted security tags.

There had been several situations where the tags had been removed from individuals and used illegally. At the Block the tests were very thorough to avoid any mistakes.

"Okay, we will scan you for terrestrial biology, then for no circuit implants, and compare you with the bio ident.

It should only take a moment," said the security guard, smiling.

The Block had multiple entry lanes and each of them selected a separate lane and began the process.

It was very fast. The security guards themselves had circuit implants tailored to their work and could operate certain processes much faster than a full human.

Sam and Cindy knew these security people were often referred to with a negative nickname of Sleds; they were fully functional humans with a special adaptation for their role. It was usually people who had been selected after an accident or other injury which had left them impaired. The adaptation for this role usually included modifications to offset their injury. It was a type of insurance scheme that had become more commonplace since the earth terrain had become more hostile because of the climatic changes.

For Cindy and Sam, the idea of these security guards was part of their routine existence. At their own complex, there was a similar type of system for visitor access but because they were regulars the security guards could make the tests largely based upon the physical access cards and physical glance at each person as they entered the building.

Cindy and Sam also knew that these people could bring a very tough level of security blockage into play if there were any transgressors. That was where their nickname had emerged, from the Brits on the campus. They could sledge anyone who tried to break in or defeat the security systems.

In this case all six of the visitors to the block needed to

go through the full protocol. Cindy hoped that if this worked the first time that they would then be given a speedier route in future. It certainly looked as if they would be making multiple visits to see Matson.

Around 10 minutes later they had all passed through the gates and were now in the main reception lobby of the block. They knew they would need to be escorted to see Matson and took seats in a small lounge area whilst they waited,

"It's a good chance for us to compare notes about what we all do," said Sam, "It looks as if we are all in a similar line of work."

"That's right," said Cat, "I've not seen you two before, but I've seen Lorenzo and Francesca around the complex. And yes, we monitor and revise the command packages being delivered to Ganymede."

"So, were any of you candidates for flights?" asked Sam, "We nearly made it but were dropped. We've visited Moon Two, however, which was still quite a blast."

"It's the same with us," said Francesca, "We've also been to Moon Two."

"And us," said Cat, "but no further. I was very ill during the orbits and we returned to Earth early, actually."

Sam noticed the small lapel pin that Lorenzo was wearing. It was like a small coloured disc with three small lines in colours on it. He quickly decoded its value. They were all supposed to wear them in the complex, if they were part of the elite teams. Most people didn't because it created a strange one-upmanship which could be counterproductive. The small disc provided an indication of intelligence based upon the complex metrics. Like the once revered intelligence quota but updated for the 22nd Century. It used coding from ancient Electronics to denote the values. Anyone aware would be able to decode this quickly but for most other people it was just a small badge.

"I see you are wearing a circle-badge," said Sam to Lorenzo.

Lorenzo smiled, "It's a bit of a first," he said, "I put it on because we were coming here. I don't usually wear it. I guess you guys got them too?"

"Yes," said Cindy, "but honestly, if they need that kind of information, they'll have it from our idents."

A well-groomed man approached them.

"Hello," he said, "You are the group to visit Matson?"

"That's right," said Cat.

"Please follow me, "he said, "we are going to the 107th floor.

He led them to an elevator.

"This will take us to the 80th," he said, "Then we change to another system."

The door closed and they each felt their ears pop as the elevator rapidly accelerated and then came to a cushioned halt at the 80th floor.

"I will be handing you to my colleague here," said the

man, "He will take you to the 107th floor.

"Yes, I'm afraid there are a few more formalities before we make the second part of the journey. Please could I ask you to step across into this room?"

He gestured politely, "Nothing to be worried about. It's all part of the security process for this building. Matson is one of the controllers and this whole area is rated as restricted."

Cindy

Cindy had been sponsored through college by Torus Industries. They had recognised from a very early age that she was extremely intelligent and well suited to the complex world of space engineering.

The whole concept of university studies had changed dramatically since the Klima War. Firstly, there were now far fewer people on the planet and secondly the nature of required skills had changed. For most people the choices were simply related to food production, energy production, climate management, infrastructure engineering, mining management associated with magnetite or space travel.

A major shift had been the reduction in the amount of leisure time compared with the 21st century.

Added to this were health scares because of new viruses appearing.

Cindy had originally studied to become a crew member on one of the space shuttles, without at the time knowing that it would be targeted towards Ganymede. It was a highly sought-after role and during the assessments it had become clear that she had a natural aptitude for complex pattern recognition, particularly when handling vast quantities of pre-analysed data.

Although this was useful in a space-jockey role, it was even more useful to have a role in the main control which would be centred on earth. It was during this time that she met Sam who had a similarly fast thought process associated with analytics.

There's had started as a purely working relationship, but they had gradually fallen in love over a period of their second year in the IPX.

When they had started, they had been given the usual introductory speeches and presentations and one of the Principals had even said that often people would find their life partners during their studies at the base. Neither Cindy nor Sam had believed this, but they seemed to have a natural affinity for one another.

During their third year of study, they had moved in together and became a well-recognised couple around the base.

Never Underestimate Technology Drift

"Humanity is acquiring all the right technology for all the wrong reasons."

-R. Buckminster Fuller

Matson

Matson had risen through the ranks in the control centre. He was known as a bureaucrat and administrator rather than as a bright scientist. That is not to say he was in any way stupid; he had a fantastic eye for problem-solving within projects.

He could keep the operation of the continuously returning ships from Ganymede optimised so they would spend as little time as possible offloading their precious content.

There was also a need to have a very high-quality communication back to the moon orbiting Jupiter although this needed to compensate for the 34 minutes delay in transmission times in each direction. In effect, Matson had become good at pre-empting situations which may not be capable of being answered directly.

The return flights of each spacecraft took three years to

reach Earth and the more recent ships included some manufacturing capabilities necessary as well as the magnetite materials. This meant that whereas the earlier return ships provided raw materials only, by now the ships were providing finished components ready to be assembled into new uses.

There was a curious technology drift; improved designs were being created on Ganymede but because they were being sent to new ships for fabrication it could be 3 to 4 years before the resultant products were available on Earth. Sometimes the raw materials were brought back to allow faster development of newer technologies.

Matson had also noticed that sometimes the new designs from the spacecraft were already anticipating changes that were being suggested from Earth. It was as if the manufacturing facilities were pre-empting some Earth designs.

Cindy was used to the protracted communications with Jasmijn and Roelof. They were the counterparts of Cindy and Sam on Ganymede.

She was impressed at how well they operated, always professional, always available. She sometimes suspected they didn't really sleep.

Now they had received the telemetry from the recent abnormal events on Ganymede, Cindy was anxious to re-establish contact with Jasmijn and Roelof. As usual, they appeared quite unflappable.

"Hi Jasmijn," Cindy had sent a message, "Please update status from recent on Ganymede event. We detected irregularities following Release 7 introduction."

They had waited an hour for the response, Normally, if something minor occurred Jasmijn and Roelof would pre-empt a request from Earth by transmitting a status update, They would usually cross in mid space. It kept the message exchange times to around 35 minutes for routine matters.

On this occasion Cindy had to wait the full hour and then some. Eventually the message came.

"Hi - thank you for message. We have resumed normal operation following a disturbance on Ganymede. All systems now resuming normal operation. No ongoing abnormal conditions to report."

Cindy looked at the message feed. It was voice only. Most routine transmissions were also with video, so this one implied that there had been some gaps in getting all systems back to full operation.

Cindy decided to send a second request, "Please supply status before and after disruption."

She had never requested this before and knew it would be more complex for Jasmijn to prepare this response.

Sam and Cindy were surprised to be once more separated from the others. Although they had only just met them, they had expected that whatever came next would be done as one group.

Instead, Sam and Cindy had to face a further range of tests, this time as a couple.

The questions ranged from their background, the way they had first become members of the complex, their training regime and then some specific focus on their current work.

"This seems to be like some kind of interview," said Sam.

"Yes, other than they are not telling us what it's for," replied Cindy.

"You'll see, soon enough," said their main questioner. He had introduced himself as David, but both Cindy and Sam were unconvinced, considering it to be some kind of stage name.

They could see the small implants under both of his ears. They were powered transceivers and could both instruct David about questions and also pass on their responses to anyone listening. They knew that David was a specialist like themselves, in his case with some adaptations for the role.

So, do you know what this is about? Asked Cindy.

"My role is to ask you questions and validate your responses," said David, "After that I will take instruction and you should be able to see Matson."

As he spoke, they sensed that he had received new information.

"You are to go through to see Matson now," he said, "Please follow me."

They exited through another door and across to another elevator shaft. David pressed 107, then stepped out of the elevator. To Cindy and Sam's surprise, the elevator started a rapid descent.

They looked at one another. They had heard many stories about the Block, and so they should have expected something like this.

Within a minute they had passed ground level and were now seven levels below surface. From the elevator they had to step into a small pod which had seats for four people. It was on a lev-track and after the doors closed it started to accelerate.

Sam tried to estimate the distance. "I think it's around a couple of kilometres now," he said as the pod rapidly decelerated.

The new area looked more overtly fortified than the original building they had entered. There were guards by the entrance to the underground building although they seemed to know about Cindy and Sam.

Despite guards there were also civilians by the entrance and one requested that Cindy and Sam follow them to meet Matson.

"Finally," said Cindy, "This is becoming quite a circus."

They entered a large arch-shaped room, which had wall displays projecting a review of outside as if they were on the highest floors of the building.

"Yes, it's a virtual top floor," said Matson. He was standing close to the entrance and shook each of them by the hand.

Matson was clean shaven and dressed in an immaculate blue-grey suit. He had insignia on the shoulders, but neither Sam nor Cindy recognised it.

"I'm sorry to have to put you through all of that," he said, "You are both very valued assets to our control centres and I'm sure you understand this is for your protection as much as anything else."

"Where are the others that came along with us?" asked Cindy.

"I'm afraid they did not make it through the selection processes after all," replied Matson, "I will explain in a moment, but we have returned them to the complex for now."

"Let's sit down. This will take a little while."

He gestured toward one of the walls and the external view changed to a display panel. "I'll use a few charts to help us," he said.

"Is this linked with our recent question about the recent updates?" asked Sam.

"Yes, it is," said Matson, "And the reason you are still in this process and the others have been removed is simply because you have made no errors during this, although the others have made some which could be damaging to the retrieval of magnetite."

"How do you mean?" asked Cindy.

"I will wind back," said Matson.

"As you know, the mining retrieval program is a huge endeavour and much of the fate of the Earth as we know it rests on its success. Because MRP is dealing with such huge distances and time gaps, we need to have specialist systems to coordinate everything. You two are linchpins in that process. Not you alone, of course, but there are others like you performing a similar function in other control complexes."

"We have built three sets of identical systems which monitor what is happening on Ganymede."

"I knew that was the case," said Cindy, "We are told about it as part of the training process. "

"And also, that each of the three control complexes is kept separate from one another. It's a vital part of the process to ensure that we have 'unpolluted' assessments from each source."

"Yes, each system has its own vote, usually all three say the same thing, occasionally one differs and then the other two are used as the basis until whatever has been identified in the third system has been corrected."

"That is normally the case," said Matson.

"But why are we involved in this?" asked Cindy, "we are only part of this process."

"That is right," said Matson, "There's a whole command chain around you and another building full of people and technology who combined to provide the analytics we use. On this occasion the area of inconsistency is yours. Very unusually, the voting system has been overridden. On this occasion the two votes were created by the teams in the other control centres and your vote was essentially different."

"Does this relate to the timings?" asked Cindy.

"As a matter of fact, it does," said Matson "Your analysis

highlighted that there was a longer delay than usual in resetting the system. That was your only observation of change."

"Yes," said Cindy, "Although we have noticed the timing drift since release Six. I was planning to run an analysis of Five through to One, to see if the timing was also extended or extending."

"We think there is a genuine explanation," said Matson, "The timing has increased, and it is because of a new subsystem for statistical analysis. The longer gaps are because there is more information to process."

"The others said they had also found some kind of geographic drift," said Sam, "We hadn't noticed this, actually."

"Yes," said Matson, "That's the area where your vote has overridden their two votes - in the last analysis. We have cross checked the geographic placement and there is no difference at all. That in the case of both of the other teams they have made different and diverging errors which had created the anomaly."

"We have a backup team for our own work," said Cindy. "You called us away before we had time to cross-check with them."

"Yes," said Matson, "And both of the other teams also have backup teams. While you were travelling here, we have run analysis of all three sets of information from you as Primes and the three backup teams."

"Only your sets of findings are correct. Both of the other teams have made errors, and in each case the error is consistent within their own teams."

"So, what happens now?" asked Cindy.

"We will be restoring the two other control centres using your images," said Matson, "You will stay in place in your team with your existing backup team. For the other two teams the backups will take over and unfortunately the current Primes are being reallocated to other duties."

"As sudden as that?" Commented Sam.

"Yes," said Matson, "You already know this is a very high-stake situation. The point of having people like yourselves in these roles is because you are classified as hyperintelligent and therefore able to think outside the normal processes that run in power computations via the computers."

"We've always been told that," said Cindy, "you don't need us very often, but when you do need us, you really need us."

"That is right," said Matson, "And that's why we have to make changes, to make tough decisions, about who takes these roles in the control complexes. "

"So how did you know to override two votes this time?" asked Cindy, " It could have been us being removed from the programme."

"Look, on the level with you," said Matson, "It is not just one situation here, there have been at least 10 anomalies from each of the other teams."

"What about us?" asked Sam.

"Just twice," said Matson, "The first was a long time ago.

"As a matter of fact, you were the first of the three teams to make an error. Then no errors until one a few weeks ago. Since then, perfect. With the other teams there has been a progressive increase over the last two months. The last situation was part of a short run of four in the last three weeks. It's enough to create a major problem for us."

"Is that how we came into the roles?" asked Cindy, "When we were appointed, we had been acting as backup for the previous team. The difference is we were told they were being given launch priorities and moving out to Moon Two and probably on to Ganymede itself."

"That's right," said Matson, "They did go to Moon Two. The change in schedules of the outbound fleets has meant that they are still candidates for Ganymede at this time."

"It really is up or out," said Sam.

"You could say that," said Matson. "You remember that you have some of the most prestigious roles in the complex."

"So, this is what will happen," said Matson, "Firstly I wanted to tell you about the situation. Then I wanted to explain about your counterparts in the other complexes. As you know, we deliberately keep you separated and the same will apply with the new replacements. It makes no difference to your relationships with your own backup team who I'm sure you know well."

"What you will need to know is that your own Prime images will now be used by the other teams as a starting point."

"After that, each team will be able to run its own way and it will only be when there are new voting situations that we must again crosscheck the outcomes."

"And does ours get reset too?" asked Sam.

"No," said Matson, "But with your rate of error being so low, it will be many years before you would reach 10. And by the way, 10 isn't a magic number here. What we've just experienced is a highly rapid increase in discrepancies from the other teams."

"Now, do you have any other questions for me? I'd like us all to get back to business as usual as soon as possible."

Cindy and Sam looked at one another. They had many questions, but knew it would be pointless to ask,

"No," said Sam, "I think we understand and as you say we should get back to help with the preparations for the new imaging."

Maps and pressed a small button on his desk. A well-dressed female appeared.

"Hello," she said, "You must be Cindy and Sam? Let me escort you back to the main lobby."

Green

As the door closed behind his recent visitors, Matson heard the control panel blip in front of him.

"They will have to be removed from the program," came a voice. It was Green, his commander.

"I can understand that you have kept the ones who know the least," continued Green, "I'm a little surprised that you did not remove them as well."

"I thought we had built a system that was robust enough to handle this," replied Matson.

"But I think the signs are now getting much more obvious. If two of our three Primes could identify discrepancies, then I don't think it will be long before we will need to find a way to repackage this."

"I agree," said Green, "At the moment this is more a matter of containment. How long would it be before you can rotate the last two out of their control positions?"

"We should really leave it for at least a month," said Matson.

"Usually with only one team of Primes to be replaced we can act more quickly, but as this time we have needed to take out two of the Primes, it means it will take us longer to ensure that we have safe replacements."

"The whole point of making most of the systems autonomous was to guard against this kind of thing," said Green.

"I know," said Matson, "but it's because of that exact reason that we have to make such allowances. The whole point of the human factor in this is to help us detect out of condition situations. Our computer analytics are fool proof for all eventualities. It is the very essence of human nature that helps us find the lapses that could be picked up by extraneous observations. "

"I would far prefer that these kinds of monitoring were handled through automation, but there still comes a point where real people must be included."

"I take it you have already made plans for the other two Prime teams?" asked Green.

"Yes, we will keep them separate. One team will be reassigned Earthside and the other team will be allocated to Moon or Moon Two duties."

"Just as when Cindy and Sam's predecessors were moved away, we will ensure that the new teams have little opportunity for further interaction."

"Good," said Green, "I would like a report from you within a month confirming that all three of the previous Prime couples have been withdrawn and that their successors are fully operational."

The screen in Matson's office blanked. He knew he would need to act swiftly now to restore equilibrium.

Cindy and Sam knew that they should wait until they were away from the block before discussing what that just happened. They chatted amiably to the assistant who showed them back to ground floor lobby.

"It seems much easier to get back out, than it did getting in," said Cindy.

"I know," said the assistant, "I was here for three months before I could use the fast track entry. I used to have to add an extra 45 minutes at the start of each day. Getting out is much quicker and unless there is any form of lockdown."

"How often does that happen?" asked Cindy.

"Hardly ever," said the assistant, "Although we've had a couple in the last month. Someone said it is to keep us on our toes. Look, I can swipe you out from here, " she said, " Just cross that concourse and if you dropped off any items, they will be waiting for you at that blue collection point.

"I think we're good to go," said Sam," We were asked to visit here at very short notice in any case."

Cindy and Sam walked back to the pod area.

"We should stop somewhere on our way back," said Sam, "Maybe grab a coffee. It'll give us a chance to chat."

Cindy nodded back, knowingly, "Yes," she said, "We pretty much used up the morning in any case."

Magnetomics, baby

Any sufficiently advanced technology is equivalent to magic.

- Arthur C. Clarke

Standing in the way of Control

Darnell had listened to the conversation between Green and Matson. Darnell lived permanently in the Block. He could not leave even if he wanted to.

His condition meant that he had to stay in the specially scrubbed air and pressurisation of his part of the facility. Darnell still had a memory of the Klima War. There were increasingly fewer of his generation left now. He'd been around during the latter stages of the climate change, when the old nation states had started to look for first economic, then political and finally military advantage as they saw their lands and populations being destroyed by the scale of tragedy on earth.

The climate change had brought about massive shifts in the topography of earth as certain areas became flooded and others became new arid deserts. It had started with tsunamis and dust storms but accelerated at a head spinning speed to a ferocious destruction of what had been a planetary population of 9 billion.

They had already said that the food was running out, that

viral diseases were prevailing, that insects were rising in numbers. It had felt like an almost biblical plague was sweeping across the whole planet.

The initial humanitarian response hadn't been able to keep up with the range of demands and soon the acronym 'TEZ' became commonplace as more areas were declared Total Exclusion Zones. This wasn't a modest threat. People would see the lands of TEZ and try to identify areas which would stand the highest change of being safe.

That was when the political boundaries started to become under pressure. Any areas predicted to have higher survivability became desirable developments.

It was when Darnell remembered the escalation of military power. In the early stages, military might won and boundaries changed. The warfare became more asymmetric to ensure the gains. Large areas perceived as safe were obliterated to ensure the free passage of people into the areas. Some of this didn't work as tactical nuclear devices were used inside battle zones.

Early signs of nuclear winter started to appear as clouds of radioactive dust drifted around creating new swathes of inhospitable terrain.

Politicians and militia realised they should change tack or else there would be no planet left to administer. The death toll was huge and the combination of climate, disease and the aftereffects of the tactical warfare combined to create huge swathes of uninhabitable planet. The effects spread to the sea, which had common sightings of huge shoals of decaying fish stock.

That was when the old and sluggish United Nations was

taken over by new forces, anxious to prevent a total planetary extinction. The Earth Council had been covertly established, picking from several of the most powerful remaining nations and funded by several large corporations.

A pact was agreed, which included the need to stop the further cross contamination of the remaining planet. Rudimentary zones were agreed and sketched onto the globe. It would be divided into the new Northern hemisphere, which was generally the least affected and the southern hemisphere from below Tropic of Capricorn, Below the 24th parallel was largely ravaged beyond a comprehensible restoration point. This wiped-out part of South America, Southern Africa, all of New Zealand and the largest part of Australia.

Those involved in the pact, also contrived to create the equivalent of firebreaks between the still safe areas and the areas already overrun. It was a brutal decision, because in the contaminated areas the populations were left to fend for themselves. In the non-contaminated areas, RPZs - rapid protection zones - were set up, and the populations were kept inside under a totalitarian control.

This was the period during which the stories about the habitable vs the uninhabitable parts of the Earth developed. People inside the safe zones came to accept they could stay put or risk going to an almost certain death outside.

Ragged areas at the boundaries of the safe areas developed originally called The Tract, and the communication corridors that were opened were all land based, rather than by flight. It kept the populations mainly within their own zones except for the needed military communication presence across the zones.

Darnell considered that the Earth was on permanent planetary lock-down, although most of its residents were accepting of the situation and the ones that didn't had moved to the less pleasant environments of the Scratch.

The combination of the Earth Council's Earth Restructuring, the Ganymede program and the use of magnetite power had created the Fifth Industrial revolution on Earth. After what had been the destructive period leading up to the restructuring by the Earth Council, there had been the era known as The Great Stability.

This had been the period when the full effects of magnetite power sources had allowed a remodelling of the areas appointed for redevelopment by the Restructuring.

It has been stated that there could only be certain parts of the planet placed under redevelopment, and that citizens would need to stay within their mostly large zones. The Earth Council would not take responsibility for the areas outside of their jurisdiction, and these areas should be considered as hostile and uninhabitable.

'We must regard the Earth as if it is a foreign planet we have come to colonise' was the sentiment usually expressed. The developed zones were slowly increasing, although this was always from within a protective area delimited with huge horizontal air walls to provide protective screening.

The magnetite could create units of exceptional power which meant that compared with prior territorial design thinking, it was now much more possible to assist keep boundaries operational and to protect the enclosed citizens.

Darnell was one of the citizens who remembered the old ways. Freedom to travel around the globe, a messiness of transport systems, carbon-based fuels in common use. Access to air-borne radio transmission.

He also remembered the downsides of the famines, the disease and the political decline into warfare.

Much of the past's history was now only available with special access through systems in the Block.

The modus of the new Earth was about looking forward, there were too many bleak lessons in the past. The Carbon Age, as it became known, was about as distant in most people's knowledge as The Stone Age.

Civilisation would need to learn afresh, based upon the new underpinnings. Prior ways of thinking were considered disadvantageous and indicative of the spiral towards poverty and grief.

Darnell realised this was a two-edged sword. Some good parts meant increased survival for those that had made it to the new zones. For those that hadn't, it had already meant death. For those in the middle, it meant exile to the Scratch, a world without the material advantages of the Earth Council's dictatorial world, but with the added dimension of a freedom that most conventional citizens could not even imagine.

Magnetomics

The Ganymede program was already up and running before things became tough on Earth. A probe sent out in the early 21st century to examine comets had sent back some unexpected transmissions which had been the start of the process.

The original purpose of the probe had been to examine a comet's own surface, but there had been problems when it had landed bumpily, and its solar panels had shut down without sending a full transmission back to earth.

The subsequent path of the comet had caused the probe to intermittently restart and it had later transmitted information about the comet surface which provided a breakthrough for scientists on earth.

The material of the comet surface included magnetite, and it was found to have an interesting property which became the basis of a whole new discipline in science.

Magnetomics, emerged, the use of magnetic fields as a direct form of power.

Unlike terrestrial magnetism, the magnetite produced a

significant and harnessable sectoral force if another oppositely polarised piece was place adjacent.

There had been plenty of experiments on the past to prove that perpetual motion wasn't possible, and the initial scepticism of sciences was well-placed.

This wasn't perpetual motion either. But unlike previous examples with magnetism, the magnetite produced an almost imperceptibly small reduction in its own mass through the time it was producing force.

It was harnessing the same kind of power as in a nuclear reactor, but without the huge negative side effects. The process became known as nano-fission and became the source of many new types of motor design. A modern-day pod transporter engine weighed around a couple of kilos. Part of this was the actual engine assembly and the last kilo was the power source, which was estimated to have a life in excess of 30 years, there was no recharging and the unit could be simply replaced with another power cell.

Unlike fissionable materials, there was no huge charge required to start the process and the degree of scaling of the energy output could easily be controlled using the second piece of magnetite. The two together formed a binary battery, with the distance between the two pieces providing the regulation for the degree of electrical power output.

The main challenges were the initial production of the two pieces, which required a precision 20 nanometre flat surface to work efficiently. An Earth technology, graphene, was used to fill the gap and separate the plates. By the time the plate gap reached 400 Nanometres, the unit would start to display visible colours, and this was usually used to determine the age of the device. Violet, Green and finally Red.

After Red, the unit would continue to work erratically, but needed to be re-surfaced.

 Sam and Cindy approached the coffee shop. It was part of a franchise. They ordered two simple coffees, waited for them to be brewed, and then took a table outside. There was a screen to protect from sunshine and a misting system to keep the air cool. They sat in a corner close to the equipment used to run the misting system. It comprised a small pump unit and a water feed that was surprisingly noisy.

"This is probably the best table we can get," said Sam.

"I'm not sure what to make of it all," said Cindy, "Have we really screwed up or are they really giving us a continued role?"

"Hard to say," replied Sam, "what I think is our days in this function are numbered."

"I'm also not convinced about the errors," said Cindy, "It looked to me as if the other teams had come up with more findings than us?"

 "You are spot on; we checked those readings carefully. I'm certain we had the right numbers."

"I'm going to run some further checks to see whether this is any justification for the apparent movement of the control centre. It surprises me that the teams can both independently find this effect. I can't help wondering whether we have just been less thorough with some of our analysis runs?"

"We also need to be careful," said Sam, "If we get called back again, I'm sure it will be to move us out of the role."

"I agree," said Cindy, "Yet anybody else involved with this now would create talk about it in the centre itself. We are such a known reliable quantity."

"It's safe to assume there that our command centre and also our apartment are being monitored. We will need to keep conversations about this outside away from listening ears."

Rocks in the ice

Jasmijn was used to the operating conditions on Ganymede. The main purpose was extracting valuable minerals which could be routed back to Earth and everything else was considered secondary.

She considered that calling Ganymede a moon was something of an understatement. Ganymede was the largest satellite in Earth's solar system.

Larger than Mercury and Pluto, and three-quarters the size of Mars. If Ganymede had orbited the sun instead of orbiting Jupiter, it would easily be classified as a planet.

Like all Ganymede dwellers, Jasmijn knew the significance of this moon's geological discovery for Earth.

The moon had three main layers. There was a sphere of metallic iron at the centre - the core, which generated a magnetic field. Then a spherical shell of rock - the mantle - surrounding the core, and a spherical shell of mostly ice surrounding the rock shell and the core. The ice shell on the outside was very thick, maybe 800 km (500 miles) thick. The surface was the very top of the ice shell.

Everyone moonside could see that there was a rock in the ice near the surface.

Ganymede's magnetic field was also almost tangible when walking around in the corridors. Ganymede's magnetic fields were embedded inside Jupiter's massive magnetosphere. Jasmijn knew that she could tell which direction she was headed with her eyes closed, by some kind of magnetic interaction that affected her. Roelof had said he could feel the same effect.

Scientists had said it was this interaction of the magnetosphere with Jupiter that had created the magnetite. Roelof had another theory, which was that the moon had been hit by a passing comet and the debris was the source of the magnetite, now frozen into the moon's surface. Ganymede's icy shell had supported massive amounts of the same material for billions of years.

Back in the 20th Century, astronomers using the Hubble Space Telescope found evidence of a thin oxygen atmosphere on Ganymede. They knew that the atmosphere was far too thin to support life.

Then, in early 21st Century, scientists first discovered the irregular rock formation lumps beneath the icy surface of Ganymede.

When a space probe crashed onto an asteroid of a comet the discovery of the magnetite rock formations appeared to show the same material with its unique properties on Ganymede.

Early 21st Century spacecraft images of Ganymede showed the moon had a complex geological history. Ganymede's surface contains a mixture of two types of terrain. Forty percent of the surface of Ganymede is covered by highly cratered dark regions, and the remaining sixty percent is covered by a light grooved terrain, which forms intricate patterns across Ganymede, and which could be observed from deep space.

The distinctive grooves called sulcus were formed by tensional faulting and the release of water from beneath the surface. Groove ridges as high as 700 m (2,000 feet) were seen and the grooves ran for thousands of kilometres across Ganymede's surface.

This was good news for those intent on harvesting the magnetite. It was mining where the required substance was almost jumping up from the surface.

Then, when Jasmijn was set to monitor the situation from moonside, she could see that the grooves had relatively few craters and probably developed at the expense of the darker crust.

The distinctive layers and colouring in the geology made it easy to identify where the layers of magnetite resided, and a series of new machines were designed for the extraction.

Jasmijn thought that the way Ganymede's infrastructure had evolved was like tugging itself up by its bootstraps.

The early chain of spacecraft arrived to set up the colonisation of the moon and then progressively developed further systems until it was possible to start extraction and then the return of minerals to planet Earth. By building factories on Ganymede, the initial heavy equipment, and alongside it a range of high-performance computer environments had also been supplied. These were useful channels back to earth but increasingly were used to augment and supplement the people operating on the moon's surface.

The basic principle was that there were various classes of operative. In the early days, the initial environment was worked by humans and then augmented by dedicated robotic machines such as the excavators and drilling rigs used as part of the extraction. This could be run from a central console area and reduced the impact of the extreme environment upon the humans providing the colonisation of the moon.

The initial chain of spacecraft included factory ships which could be used to create further on-moon environments. There was plenty of other raw material around including water and so it became natural to build new equipment on site once enough had been developed and shipped to start the process.

In the second wave of ships came the first of the android construction kits. These supported a further intermediate type of operative which was a more flexible form of robotic being that could operate either in a humanoid form or in some cases as a simple embedded brain within other components.

This gave greater flexibility and also reduced the demands for new humans to need to make the lengthy trip to Ganymede. In effect the Ganymede population could be stabilised and added to by the use of the robotics.

This was also why for certain dedicated purposes some of the android forms were considerably faster than humans. They had in effect been optimised for the specific purpose above all others. Full humans became known somewhat ironically as 'The Sharps'.

Roelof was used to working with androids which was also commonplace in certain Earth functions. On Ganymede it was a whole different proposition, to accelerate the mining and to minimise the number of births by Jupiter transits, the programme of android construction had been rapidly increased.

The general ratio was now around ten humanoid androids to one human of Ganymede. If the embedded systems were added to this number, the ratio would be closer to 1 to 30. The embedded systems were harder to count because they could look like any piece of electronics on the base.

The tiering between the different types of system was generally that the human provided the main controls and regulation, the humanoid androids could operate in the field and the dedicated devices using the embedded systems could take on the most hostile environments.

This also created what was in effect a 24-hour economy. And actual day on Ganymede was much longer than a day on Earth. Ganymede took around just over seven days to make one rotation so a single Ganymedean day was one Earth week in duration.

The machines didn't care, but for humans this was quite a dislocation. The earliest workforce were generally toughened engineers who worked shifts and were on special bonuses to get everything running. Most of them worked hard until they burned out often before their second year had completed. The Russian booze hadn't helped.

As more of the operating classes arrived, the infrastructure had evolved to the stage where a range of virtualised environments could provide the equivalents of a civilised earth week with proper nights and days. People could go into a virtualised exterior environment as well and this included selectable city scenes and country scenes to provide more of a sense of reality instead of looking continuously at the bleak landscape of the Ganymede moon and the adjacent huge striated mass of Jupiter.

Something's not quite right

I will go down with this ship
And I won't put my hands up and surrender
There will be no white flag above my door
I'm in love and always will be
And when we meet
Which I'm sure we will
All that was there
Will be there still
I'll let it pass
And hold my tongue
And you will think
That
I've
moved
on

Dido Armstrong

Quintessence

It was the start of a new day and Jasmijn and Roelof were reporting to the control centre. As they arrived, they noticed that the signage had been updated for the new release. They had started at release five and were now on release seven. Each time, as well as the system updates, there were new changes to the structure of the building.

The main entrance and lobby areas remained the same, but there were usually some new doors or corridors providing access to enhanced facilities. It also meant that there was a continuous state of building work occurring around the place, although the signs of this were very limited.

Since release four there had been an extension of the capabilities to provide a virtual living environment. This meant that some ambience around the building had been technologically enhanced. Just as Roelof could set his own apartment's weather to remain in April, the main building gave small clues as if it were part of a wider city environment. This was subtle and included sounds such as passing trains or aircraft and although it was not possible to see any of this, it added to a sense of place.

Roelof and Jasmijn both knew that outside of the buildings was the frozen surface of Ganymede and then the trails leading to the various mining locations. There were two types of mine. One was for the materials to be sent back to earth and comprised mainly the magnetite. The other mines worked to provide new raw materials which could be used within the factory environments on Ganymede.

The mining itself used a unique technique because most of the embedded rock that was required was close to the surface but underneath sheets of glacial ice. In some areas the ice was exceptionally deep, as far as 500 metres to reach the rock. The surveys located materials much closer to the surface of the ice and it was these that were being mined using high-performance thermal mining equipment.

A spin-off from the project was that the reclaimed water from the ice was used to improve the quality of the atmosphere on Ganymede. It had originally been a very low oxygenated atmosphere, but since the mining work had started, there had been a positive improvement in the air available. The hydroponics had once been sheltered, but were now being taken outside, to see how well they could survive.

Ganymede's atmosphere was still not of a human breathable quality, but as most of the work was now being conducted by androids and embedded systems there was little need for humans to venture on to the surface.

The difference in gravity on Ganymede compared with Earth was significant. It was only some 14% of that of the Earth. Fortuitously this was a similar ratio to that on Earth's moon so there was already much experience operating in this range even with the same mass as on Earth. More human injuries were from forgetting to compensate for mass and inertia rather than sustained by weight.

As Roelof and Jasmijn walked back to the control complex with its new signage and even new security processes, they both thought that it felt like another fresh start. They would soon be back to their usual stations processing today's batch of mineral extraction. They seemed to be behind target for the day because of a shortfall on the preceding day.

"I think with this new release we can try to accelerate some of the refinement processes," observed Roelof.

Jasmijn agreed and commented that the extraction processes to the shipping processes seemed to have been optimised in this next software level.

"Yes, we are able to save further time getting things loaded," said Roelof, "Each time we get the new level, there seems to be a small improvement in this area."

"I'm not sure if we can completely catch up on the last day but we should be able to make substantial inroads," said Jasmijn.

She noticed the console message from Earth. They were requesting analytics to cover the period of disruption.

She checked the message from Earth. In particular the

timestamp. It implied that the period of disruption had happened within the last earth day.

She checked the Ganymede log. There really wasn't anything serious to report. She'd package the last 48 hours into a transmission and forward it to Earth. She was not sure what they would get from it. A simple restart for the new release was about the only event. The start had run smoothly to the extent that there was almost no trace.

She processed that concept again. They really had a great control of the systems on Ganymede, An almost perfect operating environment.

She flinched as she realised, she was overthinking this. She had never done this before.

Jasmijn felt the small glitch and mused. The march of progress and miniaturization had turned out to be about power; small not so much beautiful as pre-eminently dangerous. The best machines were made of sunshine; Sun Machines coming down - light and clean because they are nothing but signals, electromagnetic waves, a section of spectrum. And these machines are eminently portable particularly since magnetite. People are nowhere near so fluid, being both material and opaque.

The glitch ended; she clicked the control to dispatch the journal. It would take another 35 minutes to get to Earth.

Too perfect

Cindy was back at the apartment. The day had been cut short because of the visit to the Block. Their Secondaries had assumed duties on their behalf, and it was within protocol for the Secondaries to run unsupervised for a complete 24-hour cycle.

She looked briefly at the status display. The journal transmission from Ganymede had arrived. She called the control room.

"Can you send across the data?" she asked, "The Journal from Ganymede."

A few seconds later an alert sounded. The data was now available in her apartment system. She flipped to the start of the journal. It covered the two days, from before the new update, right through to a couple of hours ago. Roelof had sent what she requested, but as she looked at it, she realised it didn't look right.

Or actually, it looked too perfect. The rollover to the new

release was shown and like previous releases, it had been a smooth transition. Not at all like the observed change from Earth. Not with the long delay she had witnessed on Earth.

She zeroed into the timeline. Nothing unusual there either. The point of update started around when she would have expected and finished a few minutes later. A clean restart followed, and then the system continued as previously, although showing the new software levels. The bundle sent from Ganymede included some still frames from the control room video.

Mainly screen grabs, until she noticed a change around 5 hours after the transition. The control room looked slightly different. The screen grabs looked as she expected, but the layout of the room had a couple of changes. Sure, there were new devices, but that could be explained as routine maintenance. It was the size of the operations console, which was slightly larger. As were the screen displays. It looked in keeping with earlier configurations, except if the two images were placed side by side.

She clicked to save the screen grabs. If she had only seen the new setup, she wouldn't have noticed the difference. The latest level had changed the lighting, which was a more obvious change. So obvious that it would overwhelm anyone looking to the extent that they would not notice anything else.

Unless the two scenes were overlaid on one another.

Cindy decided to check the camera angle. Lens distortion, a different closed-circuit camera? She looked again. The camera serial number was the same. That was one more thing ruled out.

She knew that something was not quite right.

Cindy had put down her small bag when she walked into the room. Now she went to it to find her small notebook. She would dictate a list of her concerns.

As she flipped open the bag, she noticed something unexpected inside. An envelope.

Probably routine paperwork, but not something she would ever think of removing from the centre. She wondered how it had got there.

She flipped it open, slightly bemused about its content. There was a single electronic document inside. It looked like something was read only, but probably multiple pages.

She pressed the page to scroll through the document. Right at the top she noticed the heading. Complex 23. They were Complex 21. This was from one of the other teams they had met. She looked nervously around. She was not allowed to see documents from the other complexes. It was part of the safeguards of the system.

She had already noticed the two names are signatories on the document. They were Lorenzo and Francesca.

She switched the document off. She wondered if it was traceable. It did not make good sense to try to look at it within the apartment.

She went back outside to find a suitable location to read its content. She would also have to decide whether to tell

Sam what she had discovered. Perhaps she would read the document first, then decide whether to involve him.

She casually placed the envelope back in her bag and walked to the door. She would go back to a safe place to read the document away from any surveillance.

She left her room and walked across to the elevator. A few seconds later she was in it with several other residents of her block. As she reached the ground level, two of the people in the elevator brushed past to hurry on their way.

Suddenly she realised that they had taken her bag. They had simply cut it from her shoulder. There was also a third person waiting in a pod and they simply passed the bag to that accomplice who made away.

Cindy had not had time to create a copy and now wondered whether this would serve any useful purpose. To her surprise, the other two people instead of running away turned to approach her.

One held out a small device. It was a communicator, but not like any that she had seen before.

"We will be in contact," said the man as he handed the device to Cindy, "Don't follow us and don't try to track us down. We are no threat to you but if you try to seek us you will be in danger."

She nodded. They turned and walked rapidly away. Cindy returned to her apartment. As she entered, she noticed her bag, with its broken strap, on a small table. She looked inside. As far as she could tell only thing missing was that envelope and its content.

At that moment Sam appeared.

Cindy gestured with a finger across her lips. The universal signal for silence. Sam looked surprised but complied with the request. She waved her hand to show they should go out of the apartment. She scooped up the bag and both of them left.

 "Not here," she said, "but I have something we should talk about."

Swapping Primes

Matson had decided the futures for the two Prime teams he needed to stand down. He faced the same dilemma as others in China and Russia. In each case, there had been similar scenarios, where some detection of the apparent shift of the Ganymede base had been identified.

The technology, computing and intellect to be able to make these predictions objectively was scarce, Matson knew that. He therefore knew that his teams of Primes were still valuable, but that they could not be left on the same processes, where they may discover more discrepancies which could ultimately become more than an embarrassment.

He also knew that he would need to exchange at least one team of his Primes with another site. This was part of the process to ensure that a critical mass of Prime expertise did not develop without supervision. By knowing one another, the Primes had already jeopardised this. It would be the same in Sino-Nihon and Eurussia. His preference was to keep one of the existing teams on his own site and to move the other one to the Russians.

It would be a negotiation, because the Eurussians would also want to keep a team, and the Sino-Nihon and

Eurussians would both probably want to swap with the Amerika.

He may need to apply some gentle leverage from Commander Green to get a desired outcome. He had heard a rumour that the Eurussians had taken the unprecedented step of removing all three of their teams based upon a similar incident.

Each of the Prime teams was a special form of assignment. Sure, they did the analytics job that their role descriptions indicated. The second and unspoken part was their ability to detect unusual situations and to alert the chain of command about them. The key aspect of this was to determine if anyone was coming close to finding out about the true operational status of Ganymede.

Matson knew that two of his teams had come closer than anyone else to realising the truth about Ganymede. He also knew that three Eurussian teams had made contact with one another and extrapolated some findings.

Pod Bay

Cindy led Sam back to the cafe. It was the same one that they had used previously. They quickly ordered some coffees and moved to the same part of the cafe, where there was more ambient noise from the water conditioner.

"One of the other Prime groups has tried to contact us," said Cindy.

"They passed me an envelope which contained some measurements."

"So, what did they say?" asked Sam.

"I didn't look at the measurements, I didn't want to be seen reading them in the apartment and so I left, but almost immediately someone stole my bag containing the envelope."

"How do they know you had it?" asked Sam.

"I don't know," said Cindy, "But the original envelope was given to me without my knowledge as well. I'm wondering if I have been watched."

"I'm sure it was from Lorenzo and Francesca. Without being able to cross check it I can't determine what it means."

"So, did you get a look at the person that stole it?

"No, not really," said Cindy, "Although two further things happened. Firstly, someone gave me this," She put her hand into her bag again and pulled out the small flat communicator.

"Wow!" said Sam, "that looks pretty ancient. It's some kind of vintage communicator."

"That's what I thought," said Cindy, "Look it has old battery indicators on it when you switch it on."

"He also said he would be in contact with us and that it was best to continue normally until that time,"

"Are you sure it's not a trap?" asked Sam.

"I wondered that too," said Cindy, "But I think if it had been, then they had a better opportunity to get to me alone earlier today "

"Oh yes, and the second thing, they took my whole bag but when I got back to the apartment, they had returned it except for the envelope. "

"Does that mean they had access to our apartment?" asked Sam.

"It does," said Cindy, "But I guess they used my keys from within my bag."

"Maybe there's something on the security system?" said Sam.

"Yes, however, I left the apartment with you before we

had a chance to check." At that moment there was a sound like a faint bell ringing.

It was coming from the vintage communicator.

Cindy fumbled with it and switched it on.

"Hello," she said, "who are you?"

Cindy could hear a very faint voice coming from the device.

"You will need to hold it to your ear," explained the voice quietly.

"Ah," said Cindy, " It is vintage. Like an old telephone."

She moved the device to her ear and could now hear the voice far more clearly.

"Hi Cindy," said the voice, " I know you are with Sam at the moment. The reason we are using this old device is because it operates on frequencies that are no longer used for routine communications. It gives us an advantage in that we can talk without the risk of being monitored.

"We would like to meet you to discuss what we have found in the envelope. It is from two of your distant colleagues.   Like you, they have identified some anomalies with the work on Ganymede. There are some major forces in play."

Cindy asked, "So how do you know about us, and how do you know about this? Have you been following me? Have you been listening to my conversations?"

"Only in so far as it is in your best interests," said the voice, "We don't want to snoop, but there are some things we will need to find out."

"You also said I was in danger?" said Cindy, "How do I know the danger isn't from you?"

"You're right," said the voice, "But the truth is we think you have discovered something, and we need to follow it up as a lead towards a bigger situation."

"But I thought you implied that we had made some mistakes?" said Cindy, "The other Primes have been taken away from their workplaces because they found similar anomalies but then extrapolated the wrong conclusions."

"Possibly," said the voice, "But we happen to think they are probably closer to what is happening than even you are."

Cindy looked towards Sam, "If you expect me to cooperate, I will want Sam to also be involved in the process."

"That's fine," said the voice, "We wanted you both."

"And what assurances do I have that if I talk to you further face-to-face, that it won't get me into other difficulties?"

"I can't give you any guarantees," said the voice, "But I think our approach so far has been trustworthy. As I said we want to understand what is happening on Ganymede."

"So where are you taking this conversation?" Asked Sam.

There was no reply from the voice.

Cindy repeated the question, "Where are you taking this?"

"Sam, you need to remember that this is an old communicator, and it limits the voice sensitivity unless you are very close to its microphone.

"We want to meet with you, and to show you some things about Ganymede. There is some risk so we will need to take precautions in how we meet you. Also, because we are taking you to one of our bases, we must be careful that you are not followed."

"Just a moment," said Cindy, "I need to check with Sam about this."

"They want us to go somewhere with them," she said to Sam, "They say they want to tell us something about what is happening and why they have taken the information about the ship."

There was a pause whilst Sam considered this.

"Okay, let's say we go with you," he said. He gestured to Cindy to pass him the communicator and repeated his message again.

"Let's say we go with you; will we meet somewhere fairly close to here and how we know you're not putting us into danger?"

"All I can say is that I think you will be in less danger by working with us than if you try to continue as if nothing had happened. It's very likely that the two other Prime teams will be reallocated to distant places just like your predecessors were. It's also likely that you would be next for this kind of reallocation. For example, have you tried to contact your predecessors? I think you'll find they are non-responsive."

Sam nodded. He had tried several times to contact his old team leader, but to no avail. He knew that Cindy also tried to contact her colleagues.

The voice continued, "Look, my name is Sven. Sven Mallinson. I'd like you to meet me now so that we can continue this conversation."

"Okay," said Sam, "If we agree how would we do this?

"I can get a pod to you where you are," said Sven, "It will be unmanned but can bring you to a safe location where we can talk."

"It really is in your best interests," he added, "And look, we already have the information from the other Primes. I can walk away from this now and leave you to run with this alone. Working with me and the others you stand a better chance."

Sam looked at Cindy, "They want us to go with them now for a meeting. They are prepared to send us a pod to take us there."

Cindy nodded, "There seems to be more downside for us if we don't follow this."

Sam spoke back to the communicator, "Okay, I guess you know where we are right now, send your pod and we will come to meet you."

"Look over to the left," said Sven, "You see the pod bays. The pod flashing, XTZ564 is yours. Just get in and it will bring you to us. And bring this communicator with you."

Sam gestured to Cindy. He stood and walked towards the pod bays. He saw the pod that Sven had referred to and moved towards it. The communicator acted as a digital key and the door opened as he approached. Cindy and Sam climbed in. Quietly the pod door closed, and the pod manoeuvred into a transit lane. A few seconds later they were speeding towards north New Delaware, towards the boundary zone that separated the space zone from the rest of Amerika.

New Delaware border

The pod continued towards the New Delaware border. Both Cindy and Sam had top EPASS clearance and could easily transit in and out of New Delaware.

The pod had blanked its windows at the start of the journey, when they were travelling fast, but now they had slowed right down, and the glass cleared. They both looked out.

"It's horrible," said Cindy, "It really looks like some kind of Armageddon."

"Yeah, and the pod has slowed right down to traverse this area," answered Sam.

They could see industrial rubble as far as the eye could see. Some tall posts rose through the rubble and atop them were video surveillance systems. A few drones hovered over the landscape, which looked arid and hot.

They passed several gantries with cameras pointing inside of the pod.

"I see, they have partly slowed down to scan us incoming," said Sam.

"So, it's not just to depress us, then?" replied Cindy.

Razor wire had been draped around and there were several laser-triggered alert systems.

"We are most definitely heading for the Scratch," said Cindy.

"Yes, that makes sense," said Sam, "It's a good place for someone to hide."

The Scratch was a zone just outside of the New Delaware boundaries. It extended for around 10 km in a ragged line around most of the exit points from New Delaware. Like the ramshackle towns that had developed beyond many areas of military installation, the Scratch population centres were at the gates exiting from New Delaware."

Right at the border there were many layers of security to stop people from getting into New Delaware. Just outside of this was the zone where many people had tried to get in but had then stopped and instead tried to make an opportunistic living around the borders."

The area had become known as the Scratch. It was thought the name came from the phrase 'To scratch a living'. This close to the border was a rough area and didn't have many people passing through unless they were bound in or out of New Delaware. Nowadays it was a label on a ramshackle microclimate filled with rough necks looking for ways to make a turn on what was happening inside the space zone.

Uniformed new Delaware residents were usually safe

because everyone knew that they had full identity tracking and anyone interfering with them would be traceable very rapidly.

The New Delaware Security Force would swoop into the Scratch at the first sign of trouble impacting New Delaware residents and bring the full force of their law to bear.

This almost 'take no prisoners' policy meant that the Scratch residents would keep a distance from New Delaware residents.

The same didn't apply to those from the rest of the United States who passed through the Scratch. The NDSF security forces also didn't pay much attention to anything affecting Amerikan residents entering the Scratch. The assumption was that these people would only go forward knowingly.

It suited the New Delaware Security Forces to have this buffer zone because it acted as a form of insulation for the Space Zone. On this occasion the same area would provide suitable camouflage cover for Sven when he planned to meet with Cindy and Sam.

PART TWO

Lies, Algorithms or Statistics?

Democracy is an abuse of statistics.

Jorge Luis Borges

Sven

Sam noticed that the pod had progressively dimmed its windows during this latter part of the journey. This has happened faster than the change in daylight, but he was aware that now the pod had also put up its protective shields across its windows.

He could also feel very slight vibration from the pod on the last part of the journey. The pods were self-levelling but on extreme terrain it was possible to sense that there was an un-made route being used.

"We've left the main transit route," said Sam to Cindy.

"Yes, yes, I know," said Cindy nervously, "We are going deeper into the Scratch."

"With the screens down, blanking us, it's almost impossible for us to estimate how far we've travelled inside this area," said Sam.

On the main transit routes the pod could travel at several hundred kilometres per hour but on an unmade route through a rough area the speed would be much slower in some cases not much faster than walking pace.

Suddenly there was a click and the door on Cindy's side of the pod started to clear. A light appeared, and then the door swung overhead as the pod settled into a docking bay.

"Amber conditions," said the pod. Cindy had never heard a pod give out a warning before. It was usually the unspoken Green condition, but could go all the way to red.

"Pod explain," she asked.

"Amber condition, uncharted territory, zone alert for outside of New Delaware. Repeat. Uncharted territory, zone alert for outside of New Delaware."

"Okay," said Sam, "I'll go first."

He climbed past Cindy and out of the pod. It was a clean and modern complex; not like he was expecting from within the Scratch.

He gestured for Cindy to get out of the pod.

"Not what I was expecting," she said, "This is looking very different from most of this area."

"Hello," said a voice, "I'm Sven. Thank you for coming along. This way if you don't mind."

He gestured for them to follow him into a well-lit lobby.

"We are underneath the Scratch," he said, "This is one of our facilities."

"Who are you?" asked Sam, "And how do you fund all of this?"

"We are, how shall I say, a non-governmental not-for-profit organisation. Actually, our funding is provided by the mining consortium. Let me explain."

He led them from the lobby into a conference facility. That was a long oval table right in the middle of the room and a set of stylish office chairs around the table.

Sven gestured for them to sit down. Cindy glowered across to Sven.

"Look - I don't know what you are playing at," said Cindy, looking angrily towards Sven, "Mr polite now, but you've a nerve, first stealing my bag, then breaking into my apartment."

"I don't think you know how much danger you were in by holding that notepad from the other Primes," said Sven.

"Look, the material in the notepad had been backed to the Cloud, so it was available to the security services," answered Cindy

"Sometimes there is still a place for paper," said Sven

Sven flicked on a screen in the room. A display light lit above their heads. Sam and Cindy looked at it quizzically.

"Yes, the projector is another piece of vintage technology," said Sven, "The advantage is that it is not interconnected, it is completely outside of the Mesh."

"That was the same with the communicator," said Sam.

"Yes, we are using older technology to bypass the modern surveillance mechanisms. That communicator is actually digital but point to point with a very limited range."

Sven continued, "This projector is stand alone. We are inside our own self-contained world here, not linked into the main Mesh."

He flicked through a couple of screens to the first page of what had been on the notepad.

"We've had to destroy the original pad after we had offloaded its content," he said.

"It was fully traceable, so we pulled the data out whilst we were still in the Scratch," said Sven, "I used a Cuban-Chinese lo-jack specialist to do it. She is very dependable. We still mustn't plug this back into the Mesh anywhere, because the data probably contains a self-seek algorithm and will send out messages saying 'find me', "

"That's how you tracked it to me in the first place?" asked Cindy.

"Yes, we were just ahead of the Agency, which were cleaning up loose ends from the Primes identification of Ganymede activity. I don't think you'll be seeing the other two Prime teams again and I suspect your own days in that role are numbered," answered Sven.

"We only met them for the first time today," said Cindy, "We knew they existed, but, as you know we are supposed to operate self-contained."

"Yes, so if I show you this you've been 'contaminated' in any case," said Sven.

"We are past that point already," said Cindy, "I did have a quick scan at the notepad when I was in the apartment. I could tell it was linked to the Ganymede situation."

"Okay," said Sam, "Show us the material. Get to the point. I want to know what we have got ourselves into."

Sven waggled a small pointer, and the screen lit up again.

"Here we go. See, it's some observations about Ganymede. Each time there's an update its time duration increases.

"Yes, we'd seen that," said Cindy, "That was what we reported. It wasn't much for the first couple of levels before we started, but it has increased each time through 5, 6 and the new 7. The amount of increase is much greater than the payload software changes suggests. My own calculations that it would be an hour of latitude at most. It is more like 3 hours excess."

"Yes, that's what the other Primes are saying in this analysis. But look, there's something else."

He flicked to the next page.

"See, the location data is also changing?"

"Let me take a look," said Cindy, "No, I think that is drift. We are dealing with interplanetary distances. You get an effect from gravity bending, from relativity, it's all in the mix. The calculations are over simplistic."

"Yes, this just looks like noise in the calculations," said Sam.

"Well, let's look a bit further then," said Sven. He flicked to the next page.

Cindy gasped. The typeface had changed. The screen was now packed with calculus.

"Nah," said Sam, "Its q-calc. Quantum Calculus. It looks good, but I'm not sure what it is supposed to be saying. We can easily show the relationship of quantum calculus to Planck's constant and avoid the need for conjuring tricks."

Cindy looked at Sam, "Yes, but look. They've used it to run Lie Algebra."

She gestured towards a white wall in the room. "Pen?" Sven handed her one.

Cindy drew a circle.

"Lie uses vector reductions to zero in on a point. Imagine a bicycle wheel with so many long spokes cutting across the circumference. Add enough and there will be a circular hole in the centre. Make the spokes longer and the hole gets smaller, similar to a camera lens aperture control. It's a way of zero-ing in.

"That's how Lie works. It's a kind of infinitely small calculations to gain accuracy."

Cindy drew a web of lines across the circle.

"The lines are a kind of spiral of vectors to zero in on a value. It's about connectedness and finding the centre. Sure, it can make some pretty patterns, but I can see what they have been doing here. They've used the math from the quantum calculus to feed the Lie algebra and then made the corrections to determine an accurate centre. To prove the location's exact co-ordinates. Like the aperture on a camera getting smaller and smaller as it seeks the centre of the lens.

Cindy continued, "We've never tried this. We've always worked with the usual gravitational lensing from general relativity to define the point of origin of the far moon."

She drew another diagram.

"Yes, Space Physics 101. The ten-pin bowling ball suspended on a sheet."

She showed the bowling ball make the sheet dip in the middle.

"Creating a three-dimensional distortion of the view, varying with distance from the object."

Sam added, "Yes, and something in the background can change how the foreground appears. There are examples of it all over the sky. False images of galaxies created by this lens distortion. Space isn't flat."

Sam screwed up his face, "But Jupiter and its moons are near enough for this to not be a significant factor when we are running the numbers."

Sven interrupted, "This is the work of two of the Primes. I'm asking you to at least examine it for accuracy."

Cindy continued, "I can see that they were just trying to account for the lengthening delays in rebooting the systems. There would need to be something to explain what had been happening. The Lie algebra is a way to refine the normal calculations, but for this problem it would take some time to run. It's also loaded in as a negative hypothesis - like presumed guilty."

Sven, "My pragmatism says we need to find out if there's something untoward happening out at Ganymede. We may get transmission in half an hour, but it'd take us three years to travel there to shine some torches around."

Sam mused, "It's also a strange thing to do. I could understand it if there was some other huge object in the field that would create distortions and create false positioning."

Cindy added, "Or that there really is a difference in the object's location,"

Sven said, "Yes, notwithstanding all this complicated mathematics, I'm all for the simplest explanation being the best."

"Just like that olden-days monk, William of Ockham?" said Sam smiling.

"Case in point, said Cindy, "First the philosophers think planets go around the earth. Ptolemaic.

"Then Copernicus straightens the thinking and says the earth goes around the sun - with a few kinks."

"Then Kepler gets rid of the epicyclic corrections of Copernicus, by saying the orbits were ellipses. Simpler answers each time, building on the prior simplification."

Sam asked, "Okay then, so is Jupiter's moon Ganymede wobbling?"

Cindy replied, "Possibly. Unlikely though. We'd have picked that up on comms with the phasing of the return comms. The intervals would be Doppler shifted, like bad radio."

"The only other explanation would be that the source point was changing," answered Sam.

"Yes, like the base has moved after each update. It seems to stay constant at its new location until the next update?" suggested Sven.

Cindy replied, "That's what I'm thinking, weird as it may seem. We need to run numbers to figure that out. It looks as if the other Primes were already going along that path."

Sven interrupted, "Look, I can see you are thinking about this now. We've some other computers here that could help you. I should warn you that they are not the latest models and they are not linked into the Mesh. We want to keep this whole facility offline."

"That'll mean we only have the data from the notepad and our raw calculus skills?" asked Sam.

"Not quite," said Sven, "I can also provide you with some other data we've collected over the last few months. Our library has extensive algorithms too, which should help you cook up some of the clever mathematics. We've pulled the data and reference from the comms system and then had it purified by our friend in the Scratch, I can also introduce you to some further scientists who have been recruited into our cause."

Sam looked at Sven, "Yes, he said, you haven't really explained that part. What, exactly, is your cause?"

Sven continued, "It is not a cause exactly."

"We are simply trying to find out what has happened to our friends and colleagues.

"I'm going to tell you something that will commit you to this.

"I'm one of the Primes. From Release 3.

"I'm one of the few Primes who can still be located after a refresh cycle. The others have disappeared. That's not all. The same has happened to the crews that were sent to Ganymede.

"Not true," said Sam, "We've seen the homecomings from several of the waves. Big parties, medals, ceremonies. All of that stuff."

"Yes, all of that stuff run in EHD on telecasts around the world. All of that staged to create the best lasting impressions."

"Are you saying it's not real?" asked Cindy, "The scale of

it looked real to me. Like the orbiters returning. The light shows from the Moon and Moon Two."

"We've seen the traces on the Astroscopes of inbound and outbound ships," added Sam.

"Correct," said Sven, "The outbound were the first crews and supplies. The inbound started with a small number of crew, but quickly became the recovered materials. I guess you've never actually been into the recovery areas of New Delaware spaceport?"

"Well, we have actually, to the gallery areas," answered Sam.

"Exactly," said Sven. "It is all stage managed there. Like the Astroscope imaging and the return events for crews. Let me show you something."

He flicked another screen on.

"This is the return trip of Wave 3. Amazing isn't it? It cuts into the middle of a disembarkation sequence from the Wave 3 return. Smiling faces as well turned out crew members were being re-united with families."

"Hold that thought," said Sven.

"Here's Wave 4. Different scenes, a far superior looking return ship, better uniforms on the crew but still scenes of re-unification."

"And now Wave 5. Even sleeker space craft. Similar uniforms to the prior returning wave and equally jubilant scenes of families being reunited."

"…And your point?" asked Cindy, "I remember this. Back for Waves 3 and 4 there was an almost global viewing figure for the return."

"Yes, it became less as the missions become more routine."

"…Curiously routine," said Sven, "Let's look again."

He ran the first sequence again, pausing it part way through. Then on another wall, he projected the second sequence. Again, pausing it.

"Notice anything?" He asked. He pointed to the screen.

"See that face? And that one? Oh, and that one? Good in EHD aren't they? So good that they can also be seen in this return?"

He gestured to the second screen. The same faces were apparent.

Sam commented, "Yes, siblings on different crews? I know what you're going to do,"

Sven clicked a third screen. Freeze frame from the third return flight.

"Yes, it is some of the same faces again.

Sam asked, "Why would this be? The shipments of materials are regularly arriving. It is obvious from the way that we have been incorporating them into the earth infrastructure to manage the environment.

Sven answered, "Correct. The materials are arriving. Just

not the people. Although some of the first crews returned, there doesn't appear to be anyone coming back since that time. In other words, the first crews made the eleven-year return trip, but since that time there seems to be a replay of the same people returning.

Cindy interrupted, "That doesn't make sense. The ships are coming back, the magnetite. We are sending replacement crews out."

"Why would they fake the return trips?" asked Sam.

"Keeping the situation secret. Maybe they think the material is more important. But what also happens to the rest of the relatives of return crews here on Earth?

"Exactly," said Sven.

"Conspiracy alert," said Cindy.

"That's what we think," said Sven. "There's a couple of possibilities. Certainly, the first crew returned. You'll see that the ships have changed since the earliest voyages. They are much more like freighters now."

"There's been a massive change in their form factor," agreed Sam.

"Exactly, and also for the requisite internal infrastructure. Early ships contained over half the space for the maintenance of crew. Oxygen, Water, Hydroponics, general life support. We think that the later ships have been designed to maximise the earth-bound payload."

Cindy said, "So you are saying the return crews are a sham. And the returning two-year shift-workers.

Where's the real returning people then? Still on Ganymede?"

Sven continued, "We don't know, but we suspect a cover up. Our guess? Something happened to the second ship on its return tip. Maybe it burned up? Maybe it ran out of life support. Whatever it was, it was sufficient to change the thinking."

"There's also the android factories now in use on Ganymede," added Cindy, "They can deliver some of the functions."

"Yes," said Sven, "We think they have been extending their use. Some of the people at the Block will know this more precisely, but it is mostly being kept well hidden."

Sam spoke, "Okay, so they send the waves of ships out, more of the crews stay on Ganymede and they boost the return freight. It is in poor taste for those sent out, but if there had been a burn up, then it is understandable. After all, the payload has been about saving the rest of Earth from burn-up."

"Kind of. Look at the rest of the calculations from the Primes"

Sven flicked another page on the screen. This was from the notepad.

"Here we are, " he said, "Logistics. It shows the projections of people leaving Earth bound for Ganymede. It also shows the start of the Ganymede android development programme."

"I see," said Cindy, "There's a tapering away of the crews

from earth as the number of androids increases."

"Yes," said Sven, "But crews were still leaving for Ganymede after the early problems."

"Speculated problems," corrected Sam.

"Yes, speculated burn up of the second return wave," added Sven, "If that is what happened, then they could have stopped the outbound trips after Wave Three."

"But that wouldn't have been enough to reach the critical mass on Ganymede?" Suggested Cindy.

"That's right, they needed to get at least the first four waves of ships out to Ganymede to build the infrastructure and the hydroponics and so-on. After that, the Ganymedean surface was starting to become self-sufficient for the construction of buildings, infrastructure as well as mining," answered Sven.

"And using the small power cells developed from the magnetite, they could also create lighter ships for the return journey," added Cindy.

"Yes, lighter ships that only needed to carry the earthbound payload extracted from Ganymede. No more return people flights, with their messy life-support needs," said Sam.

"Okay so you've pieced this together, said Cindy, "And now you have told us, we become implicated in the scheme. What is it you want?"

Creating Proof points

Sven answered, "Short term, I'd like you to go back to working as if nothing has changed. It will only be for the next few days. We need to gather further data points to corroborate the findings from the other Prime team.

"At a practical level, we are also approaching another country to gather information. The most likely is the work that the Russians have done Earthside. They seem to have been caught up in a similar replacement programme to the one currently running in the USA and have probably figured out the same things."

"We don't have any contact with the Russians, Japanese or Chinese," said Cindy, "It's part of the protocol that we operate self-contained. You know this if you've been a Prime in the past."

"Yes, I think I am one of the few remaining Primes. Only because I have gone off grid," said Sven, "I moved outside of the system as soon as I was removed from the original role. They wanted me to go to Moon Two, which is what they say to most of the ex-Primes nowadays."

"I said I'd get ready for the trip but then came across to the Scratch. I'd made quite a lot of money as a Prime and offloaded all of it as digicash which I took into Scratch. I've distributed it across several systems, as a way to survive. A few of the rest of my crew did the same, although I think we were the only team to manage this, Since that point, the 'go to Moon Two' process has become the standard formula."

"We also realised that if we stayed low and didn't create any new embarrassments for them, they would eventually tire of looking for us. That is exactly what happened. By the time the next Wave returned, there was a wide range of other distractions to worry about."

Sam looked anxiously around the coffee shop.

"The guy in the corner is still looking at us," he said. "He's been watching us since we arrived. Just talking to you, Sven, is making me paranoid."

Sven smiled for the first time.

"He's one of us," he answered, "See, you are getting good at this. He's here to keep an eye on the whole location while we are meeting."

"So, will you introduce us?" asked Cindy.

"No," said Sven, "At the moment it's better that you know as few of us as possible. We can change that once we are further along the road."

"Understood," said Sam.

"I'll get this," said Sven. He stood. Cindy and Sam took this as their sign to leave.

 "Here," said Sven. He handed Cindy another communicator. A different kind to the last one. Chinese.

 "Wow," said Cindy, "This looks even older."

"Welcome to my sometimes-analogue world," said Sven, "When I need to contact you again it will be on this device. See that little light? If you're not there when I try to call you it will go red. I will then call you back at three hourly intervals until we make contact.   Otherwise please don't try to reach me or talk about me."

 "Okay," said Sam.

"Take care," said Cindy. They walked towards the exit.

"What do you make of all this?" asked Cindy.

"I think Sven is genuine," replied Sam, "Otherwise this all seems a very elaborate way to get some information from us."

 "It also looks to me as if the other Primes have got further with this than us," said Cindy, "I really want us to run those calculations again, though, although I can't really understand why there would be a drift in the position of the base when the new levels are transmitted from Ganymede."

 "Yes, it's not as if the moon is off axis or wobbling," replied Sam.

 "What do you think about us going back to the mall or

the main complex?" asked Cindy.

"I know," said Sam, "It's probably a bad idea. I think we should pick up some things and probably do like Sven and move into the Scratch for a while."

 "But if we do that, then we can't help Sven," said Cindy, "He wants us to go back and act as if nothing has happened."

 "Okay," said Sam, "We will go back but must be very vigilant in case anything starts to change. I think our days there are numbered, but we must be careful not to get swept into some kind of 'goto Moon Two' process."

 "Meanwhile, while we are here in the Scratch, I think we should pick up a few extra items. He gestured towards a rundown looking shop selling vintage electronics.

"Maybe get some gear for my new hobby," he said.

Ganymede - Status Normal

For Jasmijn and Roelof, life on Ganymede was running as normal. There was a repetitive inevitability to the days. They had been on this large moon of Jupiter for so long that they had more less adapted to the different day cycle and the interim point at which they needed to refresh.

It was the same for most of the other people on this moon. A few people seemed to be quite heavily affected by the changing frequency of night and day, but the rest seemed to take it in their stride.

Jasmijn and Roelof were so adapted to the life on Ganymede that the passing of days did not seem to affect them in the same way as some of the others. They interacted with many others as well acclimatised as themselves.

Most interactions were largely professional, and this lack of other interaction seemed to keep them away from the more dangerous aspects of being on Ganymede.

They had been told about the strange effect that they would experience where days would seem to run into one another and sometimes it would be difficult to remember much from the past.

In practice they had not really experienced this and had found it fairly straightforward to continue to operate except for some interactions with people who seemed to be disorientated. This had been less apparent in the latter part of their time operating on Ganymede.

"We have another major dispatch today," said Jasmijn, "There's a train of ships leaving for Earth in four hours."

She flipped a display and a picture of the loading bay appeared. These were the sleek modern ships which had most of their space available for shipping materials back to Earth. One of the ships had a habitation capsule included, but the rest seemed for payload materials only.

"The ship with the habitation capsule will be routed to Moon Two," said Roelof, "The others will be directed to New Delaware station on Earth."

"We had better get the sign-off from our new controller," said Roelof, "This one seems even slower than the last. I'm not sure why."

Weather aerial cluster

On Earth, in New Delaware, Cindy and Sam returned to the normal work. For the next day they behaved as if nothing had happened. They resumed control from their Secondaries and saw that everything else seemed quite normal.

 Cindy had left Sven's Chinese analogue communicator in the apartment. It was hidden inside a cereal packet. Sam had taken a quick look at the power supply for the unit and noticed it was traditional batteries.

"This won't last more than a week," he said, "if they are going to contact as again it will be within the next few days."

The regular return of supplies from Ganymede continued. There was one landing approximately every month. Although called a SkyTrain, the individual ships were actually around one month apart which meant in an emergency one could reach the next within a suitable safety margin. It also meant that if there was an explosion or other damage to a single craft those around it would not be affected.

Because there were several launch sites on Ganymede, the individual return flights were sometimes to New Delaware and other times to the Russian or Chinese landing sites. So far there had never been an occasion when a flight rerouted to a different landing location.

Occasionally a flight would instead land on the Moon Two base. Officially this was because a particular scientist or other specialist was being returned and needed some time to adjust to conditions after the long flight back. A popular theory was that Moon Two could also provide quarantine facilities in case they were needed. A ship could keep its occupants on Moon Two until a suitable quarantining period had elapsed and relevant tests had taken place.

Sam needed to examine previous flights both outbound and return without drawing attention. He agreed with Cindy that they would create a situation where some form of historical analysis was required. They had set about identifying something that could be considered a potential reason related the last return flight.

It needed to be something minor so they could do it without too much attention from elsewhere. Sam had noticed eight small antenna arrays on the ship had become loose on the last return flight. They were only used for short range weather monitoring.

"Look," he said, "That antenna cluster is interfering with the relay station antenna."

"It probably explains what happened on the last returning flights when we had that blackout for several days. If the weather aerial cluster had dislodged, it could have shorted against the long-range transmitter. We should look at a couple of other flights each way to see if this is something that happens after a long distance."

He knew that if he flipped the switch to access archival material, it would send alerts to other parts of the complex. The system monitoring would raise an alert at a higher level to show that he was interrogating a system that was not normally within his area. It was not a critical system area and from time to time everyone used additional data as part of their analytics.

Sam's main concern was to do this quickly and get as much data downloaded as possible before anyone else noticed. He was also aware that the act of downloading this data would be recorded. He had considered accessing the system from someone else's console area but realise that doing this would be just as noteworthy and could attract more attention.

He had acquired a small 21st-century memory device from the store in the Scratch and rigged it to a modern interface unit. He had arranged that the interface unit also had a receiver included so he could transmit from the archive to free-air inside the console area and the receiver would be able to pick up the signal and download it into the memory device. It was a rather simplistic design compared with modern technology, but he thought this may play to his advantage because no one would check for such primitive ways to offload storage information.

"I will need to create a diversion while I do this," he said to Cindy.

"How about I create an alarm?" asked Cindy, "I could adjust the returning ship's vector a micro degree and then raise an alert for it?"

"My suggestion is we aim it towards Moon Two but at the wrong speed so that others will become preoccupied with helping correct the flight path."

"That sounds like a good idea," said Sam, "While the course is being corrected, I can run the offload. Everyone will be focused on the course correction."

"We will also need to be involved with that," said Cindy.

"Yes," agreed Sam, "If we can build a script for the situation then you can operate my part from the script and your part manually. That way it will look as if I am still involved in the normal running of events,"

"I've figured out a way to introduce the error," said Cindy, "It will be a simple nudge to avoid a meteorite and then a neglected correction to put things back on track. I can lock the meteorite course correction and it will then take a few extra minutes to decode the unlock."

Cindy knew that with the extensive security passwords of remote adjustments to flight paths, it was not unusual for there to be the occasional problem with a missing or misspelled identifier. Cindy prepared a sequence which required a security string containing many ones and zeros and letter L and letter O so that there was also a good chance for ambiguity. She would need to make it look as if the string had been automatically generated and so had to run a series of commands until a suitably clumsy one appeared.

"Good," she said, "We now have a command string that can be misinterpreted. The unlock code is 'A01O18B1lOO'"

The time approached for the meteorite avoidance manoeuvre. Cindy prepared a command sequence. She entered the special security string to initiate the remote access.

She fired the trim motors on the incoming ship. It should have been approximately a five second and then a corresponding five second burn to bring the ship back on course. Instead she removed the command sequence for the second burn. This would mean that the ship was now moving at an angle to its preferred flight path. It would take another minute or two for this to be discovered by someone else. She entered the deliberately wrong adjustment sequence and a series of red lights appeared on the console.

"I think we will have got some attention now," she said to Sam. Sure enough, a main console messaging alert appeared.

"Are you in trouble?" it asked.

"Your inbound command has not been accepted. The ship is now on the wrong course. We will take control to assist your adjustment. Please provide the command security sequence."

Cindy pressed a button and the incorrect security sequence was flashed on to the emergency control.

"Initiating recovery," said the emergency control.

"Security sequence invalid," it responded, "Please re-submit the command security sequence."

Cindy pressed the button again and retransmitted the wrong sequence for the second time.

"Initiating recovery," repeated the emergency control.

"Security sequence invalid," repeated for the second time.

"Escalating the emergency recovery procedure," said the emergency control.

A yellow light flashed in the control area.

Cindy looked towards Sam. He was busy at his console.

"Repeat sending the security sequence," said Cindy.

She pressed the button to retransmit the wrong sequence for the third time.

This had the effect of the setting emergency control to force it to retry the sequence.

"Security sequence invalid," repeated the emergency control. This time the orange light turned to a red flashing light.

"Escalating the emergency recovery procedure, no override possible," said the emergency control.

"Using the emergency keys to access the recovery control," said the emergency control.

Cindy knew that additional security keys were only available to the automated systems. These keys could only be used after a sequence of several attempts had been made using the keys supplied by the human operators to the system.

The override was designed to prevent high-speed automated responses in the wrong situations. After three attempts the automation would take complete control. This was what was happening now.

"Automation now taking control of the incoming ship navigation systems," said the emergency control.

The red light changed to a blue light and Cindy could see that the consul was now rapidly filling with command control sequences to bring the ship onto its preferred course.

The whole situation had taken maybe two minutes to play through. The blue light stopped flashing and a green light reappeared. It stayed on for maybe five seconds and then gradually faded away.

Cindy knew that everything was now back to normal. She looked towards Sam. He was putting a small plastic unit into his pocket. He did not look back, and he did not acknowledge that he had completed the download of data. They both knew that there would be an investigation almost at once into what happened. They silently moved towards the door of the control room. Along a corridor and quickly to the outside. A small transporter pod was waiting. They both stepped in. The pod silently moved away. They would be in the Scratch in another 10 minutes.

Russian Exchange

Although the Eurussian control centre was often referred to as Russian, it was really a privatised industry created after the demise of the Russian federation. Its formal name was GNI GazNostIndustrie, and it was a corporately controlled entity which had been created by some of the Russian oligarchs. The Russians usually referred to the control centre as Prometheus base, which was a shortening of 'Gazovaya Promyshlennost' - the Russian name for the base. A dry gangster joke meant that the Russians thought of the name as some kind of dark premonition.

Prometheus was the fire-stealer, from Zeus, in Greek myths. He took fire and returned it to mankind. King of the gods, Zeus exacted a price for fire - which he had hidden from mankind. Then, annoyed at Prometheus' theft, as both a price and punishment, Zeus created the woman Pandora and sent her down to Epimetheus (Hindsight), who, though warned against it by Prometheus, married her.

Pandora took the great lid off the jar she carried, and

evils, hard work, and disease flew out to plague humanity. Hope alone remained within.

The Russians borrowed from the works of Greek dramatist Aeschylus, who made Prometheus not only the bringer of fire and civilization to mortals but also their preserver, giving them all the arts and sciences as well as the means of survival.

In the previous century there had been several uprisings in the remains of the Russian Federation. It had taken on many of its neighbours in various economic and military struggles, for the underpinning state was really being run by a collection of gangster oligarchs wielding huge power.

After a boundary became established that was fairly stable, other multinational entities had decided it was safer to let this state persist.

The inner structure of the revised Russia was essentially five large zones individually controlled by heavily invested interests. In the days before the space mining had commenced Russia also had control of many of the energy pathways across the planet. It had also created vast commodity trading empires which included some of the old cities of the developed world such as London and New York.

Moon Two was established largely on the back of the continued Russian space programme, allied with interest from India, Russia then gained some early advantages in the mining expeditions to Ganymede.

Once it became apparent that the whole of earth was going to require resource from Ganymede to reconstruct its methods of providing energy, the Russians had agreed, in return for huge terrestrial trading agreements, to the split of Ganymede into zones such that other major earth trading entities could also mine Ganymede and bring back the necessary materials.

It had been the Russians who had first exploited the underbelly of the Ganymede situation to create the seedier aspects of Ganymede habitation. As stories returned to Earth of what was occurring on Ganymede, instead of increasing the policing early thug-laden space trains ensured that there was an increasingly get-rich-quick scheme for expansionist crime lords.

Matson was very aware of the need to tread carefully around the Russians. The exchange of Primes and Prime information could be another way for the Russians to increase their control of the nation states.

Matson was aware of stories from the 20th century of the so-called cold war years when there had been a deterioration of trust between many countries following of World War II. The gravity of the situation facing Earth in the 22nd century meant that a greater unity had been forced upon population. Nonetheless, there were still many unscrupulous people looking for angles to gain control and economic advantage from the situation.

Matson realised he was technically a part of the controlling hierarchy, although he did not feel himself particularly high in the pyramid of power. People like Green and Green's boss were far more able to exert influence and enjoy major benefits from what was happening.

Matson also knew that the Russians would need to be

rechecked when they arrived. Since the constitutional formalisation of New Delaware and the whole of Zone Two, it required all citizens to have zonal chips implanted which provided both identity capabilities and also limited their mobility into non-authorised zones. This was largely a response to the need to restrict travel because of the dangers associated with lengthy contact with the dangerous climate of Earth.

Identities were now installed soon after birth and had been progressively extended in terms of their memory and processing capability. Modern chips could contain enough tracking information to last a lifetime although the earlier generation chips were more limited, and information was rolled off them as the chip became full.

Zone two had comprehensive monitoring capabilities throughout so it was straightforward to ensure that people were in their designated zones without becoming intrusive. A signalling protocol was used to ensure that anyone straying from their zone for too long would be easily detectable and could be encouraged to return to their own neighbourhood. When this system had first been introduced there was a fairly major polarisation of opinion.

Some people saw it as a way to protect their own domains and avoid increased encroachment from other less well-off areas. Others saw it as a totalitarian control limiting freedoms. Because there had been so much civil unrest as a consequence of the Klima War, an ultimatum was provided which said that people either accept the chips or else would need to move to the Zone Three which was now the area known as the Scratch.

Matson noticed the wall display showed an incoming

major message.

"Display Message," he signalled to the display.

Part of his sensewall showed a text stream, "The new Primes have arrived."

It was time to move his current remaining Primes from their position. He would need to do this speedily.

"In fairness," he thought, "The Eurussians had moved with lightning speed." It just made him suspicious that the whole thing was a ploy by Eurussia to embed more people in the New Delaware organisation.

Maybe the Euussians were conspiring to build a kind of chimera? Part Eurussian, part western and part android?

It would make a fine irony since such a being becomes the awful apocalyptic end goal of escalating dominations towards defining an ultimate self, untied at last from all dependency, a man in space.

Matson was used to making these substitutions but usually he was able to take more time and create less ripples as a result.

This time he knew he needed to move quickly and, if anything, the Eurussian Primes had arrived even faster than he had expected.

 He requested a trace on the two Primes he was to replace.

 As he saw the response, he noticed that there had been a recent event current in their control complex.   An unexpected course correction to one of the incoming ships.

"Expand," he requested.

The screen produced more information about the situation and showed that it was a security control error that had created the problem. This was a fairly routine situation and he would not normally have been alerted or suspicious of it.

On this occasion he noticed immediately that the two people involved were the Primes that he was about to replace. He looked at the ship's call alerts but could see nothing particularly unusual. The ship had been diverted around a meteor shower and then brought back on course, admittedly a little late. It was still routine though, and hardly a full-blown emergency.

"Locate the Primes," he asked again.

"The Primes are off station," came the response, "They have left the base."

"Can you trace them?" he asked.

"Trace ends at Dover base," came the response.

Dover base was a terrestrial Air Force Base near to the exit from New Delaware.

Matson knew that both of the Primes would have a pilot profile. They would be capable of flying the jet technology from the base. If they had access to the base they could potentially get to anywhere on earth.

"Request security lockdown at Dover Air Force Base," said Matson.

He picked up a communicator and asked for the Dover Air Force Base commander.

There was a short pause and he was put through to the base.

"Dover base, how can we help you?" came a response.

Matson realised he was speaking to an android system.

"Emergency," he said, "Please put me through to human control."

The voice responded, "You have requested human intervention. You have said this is an emergency. There is a penalty for misuse of this facility. Please confirm you wish human control override. If you say confirm you acknowledge the terms of this request."

"Confirm," said Matson.

Another voice, "Hello this is emergency response at Dover Air Force Base."

"Hello this is Matson from New Delaware command centre 'B'. We have reason to believe that there are two of our Primes on site in your base. Please raise an alert and find and apprehend these two individuals. I am sending through full information about each of them along with their tracker idents."

"Acknowledged we are putting you through to Dover Air Force Base Commander."

Matson knew he had the authority to get directly through to the highest level inside the Dover Base.

A third voice, "Hello, this is Commander Stammdecker, from Dover AFB. I understand you are looking for a couple of people from your base? We have been given the security identifications and are initiating a search. It should take less than an hour to find them. Do you want us to retain them here or arrange for them to be brought back to you?"

"When you find them, keep them there," said Matson, "I will come to your base once you have found them."

Matson knew it would be better to avoid moving the Primes more than necessary.

History lesson

"Are you sure this will work?" said Cindy. She looked at her upper arm.   She was wearing an arm band inside which was a wire mesh. Outside a 2 cm² plastic unit was attached to the wiring.

"It will work for a few hours," said Sam.

"Once they have realised, we have really gone they will bring in more specialist equipment to track us down. Until then we should be okay."

 Sam's trip to the store in the Scratch had enabled him to acquire a few extra items. Amongst them were a couple of old keys from 21st-century German cars. They were used for remote opening of the manual doors built into the type of automobiles used in the 21st-century.

He had adapted their wiring so they would send out digital pulses at one second intervals and then he had amplified the pulses using the wire mesh.

"It's a simple jammer," he said, "Not particularly clever but it's enough to drown the regular signals from our ident chips until we have a chance to neutralise them."

Sam had arranged the journey to the Scratch to go via the base at Dover.

"This is how I want us to throw them off our trail," he said, "We will lead the trail to the base and then switch on the jammers. We are already close to the Scratch at Dover base. We should then be able to head across into the Scratch."

 He looked at the communicator from Sven. The red light was still off.

"Sven has still not tried to contact us," said Sam.
   "I'm a little concerned that we will have done all this but then have no way to get the information back to him."

 "I guess we could try sending a message from the communicator ourselves," said Cindy.

 "Sven specifically asked us not to do that," said Sam.

 "We may have no choice though," said Cindy.

"If we leave it too long, the battery will have run out in the communicator and then we will not be able to make contact in case."

"Look we have done our part here. We have got the trace information and power to make our escape from the complex.   We must be prepared to contact Sven ourselves otherwise this could all have been wasted."

"Okay," said Sam, "But we should wait until we are inside the Scratch before we try using the communicator."

"I've been thinking about ways to get across to the Scratch without using our Idents," said Cindy, "If we go to the normal crossings, we'll have to show I.D. and we'll get picked up. Yet we can't stay here, because it's only matter of time before they jack up the tracker power."

"A great thing about the Air Force Base is it's been here for over 200 years," said Sam.

"Yes, long enough for there to be a full heritage exhibit."

"And the heritage includes old forms of transport"

They looked towards the museum.

"We need the outdoor exhibits," said Sam.

Sam and Cindy skirted the edges of the Air Force Base.

They were already in a secure area and now they were approaching a high security area within New Delaware.

The perimeter had two lines of fencing. It was high fencing with a track in-between which could be used by security pods for patrol. There were also cameras and beams.

"I don't think we will be penetrating this," said Cindy.

"You are right," said Sam, "But look, here's the heritage site. They slowed their pod and approached the museum.

Outside was a 20th Century space shuttle and next to it a 21st-Century DSP. The deep space probe looked pristine, like a factory model that probably had not been used. The space shuttle looked like it had made a few return trips.

Notable with both of them were the huge engine units. The kind of things that had been completely superseded since the magnetite from Ganymede had taken over as the basis for propulsion.

They parked the pod and walked the short distance to the main entrance.

"I think we will be paying guests for this," said Cindy.

"Cash though, not WavePay," said Sam.

They handed over some tokens and went inside.

 After the entrance there was a darkened display area where a few children ran around pressing buttons on the displays. They made their way towards the external exhibits, which included more spacecraft and some missiles from the 20th century.

"Look!" said Cindy. She pointed towards the further displays. A row of aircraft from the 20th and 21st century. Conventional jet planes stranded since the energy crisis.

"It's amazing that they needed such large engines back in the old days," said Sam.

Cindy pointed.

"There," she said.

It was a fuel pump. Aviation fuel for propeller planes. Avgas Blue. Limited supplies but necessary to be able to mount displays of the historical aircraft.

"One of these," said Sam, "The one closest to the fuel pumps."

"This one," he said. He pointed to a 20th-century warplane. A small sign read P51D.

"Look. Two seats. One propeller. How difficult can it be?"

"First, we need to figure how to get in," said Cindy. Sam pushed some wheeled steps towards the side of the plane.

There were two seats, one behind the other.

A sliding glass canopy. They slipped inside. Cindy took the front seat, Sam the one behind. She waggled the controls and various control surfaces on the wings start to move. She checked the fuel levels.

"It's already been gassed up. Now we need to start it," she said.

She flipped a few switches. With a splutter the engine fired.

"My god, it's so noisy,"

"Internal combustion, sparks and explosions to make it fly," replied Sam

Cindy looked concerned. With this much power, no movement.

"Wheel blocks. There will be blocks to stop it rolling," she said, "Check for any other tethers too."

Sam climbed out, pulled the two chocks away from the wheels and the plane started to roll forward slowly.

"Get back in," said Cindy as she slowed the engine. Sam pushed the ladder forward, climbed back into the cockpit and slid the canopy closed.

"Put on this green headset," she said, "Then we can talk."

Sam nodded and placed a green headset with earphones and a microphone around his head.

"This is like a practical history project," he said.

 "These things need a runway, I think," said Cindy, "No vertical take-off."

She taxied the plane across a solid black surface and saw a sign which said, 'to runway'.

 "At least they're making that easy for us," said Sam.

 "Okay, here we go," said Cindy. She positioned to one end of the long tarmac strip, revved the engine and the plane started to move forward. Sam couldn't hear anything from Cindy. The noise drowned everything.

The plane rumbled along the runway, picking up speed and then started to take off. Cindy shakily increased its altitude to a few thousand feet.

"I'm just going to get us across the water and into the Scratch," said Cindy.

"Then I'll find somewhere to land this thing. Ideally away from too many people. Our flight distance will be only a few kilometres."

"Assuming we don't get chased by the Air Force," thought Sam.

"Honestly, I think we are genuinely flying under the radar," said Cindy.

Cindy banked the plane and almost immediately they were over water.

"Look," she said, "We are almost across and into the Scratch."

"I'm going to find somewhere to bring this down," signalled Cindy.

She flipped a couple of switches on the plane. Sam was aware that the undercarriage wheels had not even been raised.

Now Cindy was guiding the small plane down. A field. Flat. Long.

"The damn wings are in the way," she said, "It's blocking my view."

There was a jolt as the plane touched down and slowed suddenly. There was spray from the wheels. The ground was waterlogged. The plane lurched to a stop, and then the nose suddenly tipped forward.

The propeller made a crying sound and then suddenly stopped turning.

There was a sudden silence. Sam pressed the canopy release. It didn't slide off; it fell away to the ground. He hit the middle of his belt buckle and was suddenly falling forward.

"Hey," he said, "Great flying. Unconventional landing."

"You're welcome," said Cindy, "I'm not sure this thing is used to modern flying techniques though. Help me out of this belt."

They clambered to the surface of the field. Wet underfoot.

"I wasn't expecting this kind of surface," said Sam, "It explains the deceleration."

"We'd better get away from here," said Cindy, "although this plane does stick out a bit."

"Come on, we should get lost in the Scratch," He picked up the small bag of equipment and they made their way to what was once a farm track.

Covering tracks

Matson decided he would meet the new Primes in person. He would travel to the control centre instead of more usually asking them to visit him.

He needed to see how things were running. That there had been new discoveries by the previous Primes led him to think there was a need for a shakedown of the site.

That the previous Primes had disappeared was troubling him. Adding together their knowledge that others had discovered more information plus the change in behaviour could only spell bad news.

He took a secure pod across to the control centre. As he approached, he noticed the Amber alert. They had taken his instructions to find Sam and Cindy seriously enough. But he still needed results.

He passed slowly through the security system. So this was what it was like being a normal person, being processed nowadays. Usually he could go fast path because of his status, but today he was just one of a bulk number being processed in the heightened security process.

Eventually inside, he requested access to the main console area. He'd need to visit the place where Sam and Cindy operated, as well as using it as the meeting place of the new Primes.

As he entered the zone, he could see the two Secondaries, identified by their different uniform flashes, quietly operating the controls.

He approached the first of them. They both turned and recognised him. They also looked suitably surprised.

"Controller Matson, this is a surprise. Welcome to the control centre. We have a take-off from Ganymede within the hour. You'll be able to see it happening."

"I'm here about the arrival of the two new Primes," he replied. "You'll be able to continue until they get up to speed. They are both from the Federation, so there'll be some time to get them used to our processes."

"Also, I need to ask you both. When did you last see your two original Primes, they appear to be missing?"

The Secondaries were aware of the protocols around Primes and their necessary attendance to monitor ongoing operations of the base.

"We have been on duty since yesterday, with the usual passing of control to the other controller", said one of the Secondaries. The other two controllers are both working with Primes, so we have been able to stay online longer than normally permitted."

"And have you noticed anything unusual during your time in operation?" asked Matson. He looked around.

There were no untoward status lights displayed, except for the Amber base alert.

"There's nothing unusual from the last period," said the first Secondary, "Except, when we were first brought online, it was after a short-term irregularity. An incoming ship had to be steered around a meteorite shower and the course correction was re-applied late because of a security anomaly."

Matson recollected the event. "I know, I saw that from the Block", he said.

"At the same time that it was occurring, a large download of archival data was requested," continued the Secondary, "The strange thing is, I can't see the archive repository folder for the download. It's fairly unusual, as if the download has disappeared."

Matson was aware that there would normally be a log showing how the download had been used and analysed.

"Can you show me the log?" he requested.

"That's the strangest thing. For such a large quantity of download, we can't find the storage folder. I was planning to request its access details from the Primes when they returned."

He paused, "I also can't quite work out what the data was being used for. It seems far more 'complete' than we'd normally use for routine analysis."

"And what period does it cover?" asked Matson.

"It's a long time series. It goes back over the last three release levels for the whole of the N.D. part of Ganymede. If it wasn't downloaded from the control room here at very high speed, it would be almost impossible to get this amount of data quickly from anywhere else. Something around an exabyte of data."

Matson was worried. The exabyte of data was a massive leak if it had been carried off site. It wouldn't take much physical storage but would take a significant amount of processing power to analyse that quantity of information.

"Can you recreate a copy of what has been downloaded?" asked Matson.

The two Secondaries looked at one another. "Yes, we are already doing that," replied one, "We don't have the same high-speed access as the Primes though and it will take us several hours."

"I have the high-speed access," said Matson, "I will authorise it."

Primes possessed certain overrides to take control of the fastest data pipes inside the control centre. This was for emergency situations where they needed to make fast decisions about ships in transit. It was not passed to the Secondaries, who were deployed for more routine processes. Matson also had the access as a point of escalation.

"Here, give me a console pad," he asked. "I'll give you a biometric authorisation."

A few seconds later, the archive data was being

downloaded. Matson could see that it represented a comprehensive picture of the working of the Ganymede environment for the last few years, across some of the major upgrades.

"Once you have completed the download, please put one copy in the normal folder system and give me a copy to take away," Matson requested, "I don't want the Primes to be caught out by the missing download. Perhaps you can put the new one into the place where the prior one would normally have been stored."

The Secondaries nodded.

"Confirmed," said one.

They knew Matson was covering tracks but dare not say anything. Matson was a powerful figure in their control room. Disagreeing could cost them their roles.

Commander Green had been alerted to the missing Primes from Matson's command. It had started as a minor alert. They were due to be replaced in any case. Then they had gone from their base and made north across New Delaware.

Then they had somehow disappeared. Green predicted that they would head for the Scratch. He had asked for any alerts from unusual events in the northern part of New Delaware.

There had been a strange story from the Devon Air Force Base. Not exactly the base, but the museum next door, which had alerted that there had been the theft of an ancient plane.

The technology of the plane, using old-fashioned aviation fuel and requiring a knowledge of propeller-based flight meant that the site had very little security. Hardly anyone would know how to fly such a device, nor of the process for filling it with the scarce aero fuel.

The plane's departure at a very low altitude smacked of the Primes and so Green was issuing detain orders for both Sam and Cindy.

He would need to deal with Matson too. There were too many things going wrong now and someone would need to pay.

Green contacted the security unit at Devon Base, "Can we trace these two people?" he asked.

"It may be difficult," came the reply, "We can see their trace right up until they were at the base, but then it just goes off grid."

"Okay" said Green, "But now we need to deploy a trace team to find them. I've already requested that Hunter take control."

Hunting for witches

I was an ordinary man with ordinary desires
There must be accountability
Despaired and misinformed
Fear will keep us all in place
So I go hunting for witches
I go hunting for witches
Heads are going to roll
I go hunting for witches

Russell Lissack / Gordon Moakes / Kele Okereke / Matt Tong/
Bloc Party

They call me the Hunter

Hunter was usually asked to get involved with difficult situations. At different times there were various threats to stability within New Delaware and the adjacent zone known as Scratch.

Hunter was a hybrid. Mostly human with some adaptations, on earth most of the adapted humans were a result of injuries or other forms of socially acceptable repair. Improved eyesight, improved hearing, replacement limbs. It was the routine stuff of a benevolent health service.

Hunter was different.

He had been adapted systematically to make his professional role more adept. There had been a series of ethical questions raised about the use of performance enhancements for humans. It had been declared as illegal to make these changes.

The military and some of the security services had found a way to circumvent this. Hunter was formerly classified as a decommissioned android that had been restarted with some organic components.

This was a lie, of course. He had been fastidiously upgraded for a range of capabilities which would enable him and others like him to be able to function for the security services. In the jargon there were humanoids and androids. Humanoids started as human. Androids started at machines. Cyborgs were another category altogether; Machine-based life-forms.

Most of the time people like Hunter were kept out of public view. It was better for them to remain undetected, although there were many ethical conversations about the possibility that such people existed. The more that Hunter was deployed the more likely it was that he would be discovered.

Hunter would still have a routine setting that was closely human-like in its behaviour. There were still tell-tale signs of his adaptations. This physical side of this was largely concealed but there were occasions where he would operate with a lightning speed inhuman in its behaviour.

It was also rumoured that there was a way to detect enhanced humans via the use of high-speed stroboscopic lighting. The frame rate of a human would work at around 25 to 30 frames per second. This was the rate at which it was possible for a human to no longer detect that individual frames in a videogram were not continuous. An android or a humanoid adaptation usually ran much faster typically between 300 and 1200 frames per second.

This had led to rumours that the use of high-speed strobe could confuse humanoids. In effect they were trying to process faster than they were able to see.

It was a phenomenon that had been seen in some experiments with insects where the strobe would flash faster than the insect's super-fast scan rate and then the insect would need to stop at intervals to recover. It was as if the insect had to process its brain buffer before it could continue.

This was the exploitation that was used to disable the fastest actions of humanoids. Strobe guns needed to project at 2000 Hz and be tuned to the point where the humanoid would slow down. It created something like an epileptic fit it in a human, but for a humanoid it just slowed them to a standstill until they could adjust to the new rate.

Hunter had a range of accomplices which helped support his activities as he found people that had decided they would rather be lost.

This was the result of larger crimes which had been committed and for which the remaining resources were unable to track down the culprits. The degree of sophistication around New Delaware using tracking systems and other telemetry meant that most people knew it was unwise to attempt anything dubious.

Hunter was nearly always successful in finding people. Hunter also had an extensive network within the Scratch which meant he could find people even after they had left the tracing capabilities running throughout New Delaware.

The android component in Hunter's composition meant that Hunter could be controlled by a commander. Hunter knew that there were equivalents of himself through New Delaware and the Scratch and that these could be called to operate in unison. This was most often by a commander who would manifest themselves directly or through an Occupied being.

Because of the inbuilt sentience of Hunter, he could sense that the current tracker situation was made difficult because of Commander Green's direct involvement. It implied an added complication that Matson was also under suspicion.

Hunter was now being asked to track Sven Mattison as a route to two Primes, Sam and Cindy.

Sven's older tracking device was beneficial to Hunter's processes. The more recent and more sophisticated idents had a cleaner and digital footprint whereas Sven's was an older version that created some electronic leakage when it was in use. Unknown to Sven, it could also be started remotely from compatible devices.

Hunter decided that this is what he would do in order to catch Sam and Cindy. If Hunter travelled at a slow speed above surface in the Scratch for probably 30 minutes, he could send out the restart code. He only needed to trip a restart once and then Sven's tracker would be fully operational again.

Hunter knew that for Sven to break cover and come back into New Delaware meant that something very high profile must be happening. Although Sven had been left to his own devices within the Scratch, he was still a person of interest if there were any unusual situations developing related to the Block.

Hunter prioritised his actions. He would need to track down Sven and then set up a trap to contain the two Primes.

It didn't take long for Hunter to re-instigate the tracing of Sven. Hunter noticed that Sven seemed to spend most of his time deep within the Scratch infrastructure although there had also been a couple of recent trips outside. He had picked this up from the cache in Sven's tracker.

Hunter concluded Sven didn't believe the tracker was still active, or that anyone was paying any further attention to him.

After all, it had been several years since he had left the New Delaware Block system. Hunter called for a range of additional support for the trap that was about to be sprung. He would use some fast pursuit pods and people on the ground in the area around Sven. The challenge was to do this in a way that did not alert Sven.

Battery

"I doubt whether we have two days left on this old communicator's battery now," said Sam.

He looked at the device that he had been given by Sven a few days earlier.

"Yes, if this runs out, we are completely stranded," said Cindy, "We have no way to make contact with Sven and no way to find him in the Scratch."

"I think we will need to contact him ourselves," said Sam

"It is probably safer to do this now we are inside the Scratch."

Cindy pulled the communicator from the inside of her bag.

They looked at one another. Cindy pressed the power on the communicator. Nothing. It didn't start.

"Again," said Sam,

This time Cindy hold the button for a couple seconds. The communicator restarted. It seemed to take a while to initialise.

"Old school," said Sam, "It has to bootstrap itself back to working."

Cindy smiled. Then she noticed the red light on front of the unit.

"Sven has been trying to contact us," she said, "The red light. I guess it only works when the power is on to the main unit. Not really much use as a standby device then is it?"

Sam shook his head. Another one of the reasons why the energy ran out. Everything was powered on the whole time.

"So, with the red light can we actually find out if it is a message?"

Cindy looked at the various control buttons.

"Here's one that says Menu," she said.

"You have to press these little arrows to get around."

No voice or gesture activation.

They puzzled with the device for longer but were unable to find out if there was a way to retrieve message.

"I think this is a point-to-point device," said Sam. "We can only speak to somebody at the other end. It's like a phone from the 20th century."

"Early 20th," said Cindy, "I think they had voicemail even in those days."

 "Okay then," said Sam, "Is there a menu for looking up people to contact?"

 Cindy pressed another button.

 "Yes, there is a single name and number in this unit."

"Okay, let's try it."

 She pressed the button and listened into the communicator. She could hear a beep sound.

 She listed for what seemed like a long time. Then suddenly,

"Yes."

Someone had answered.

"No names, please. Where did we last meet?"

 "What is the token?"

"Trellis," Answered Sam.

"Correct," said Sven, following the protocol they had been given.

 "We need to meet," said Sam, "We have something you requested. A lot of it."

"Understood," said Sven.

"I will give you an address. It is The Trikepoint. Everyone knows it. Go there and I will find you."

Then silence.

"The Trikepoint?" Said Cindy.

"We'll find it," said Sam.

The Scratch

The Scratch was an area with an estimated population of 20 million. Each of the main routes into the area had warning signs discouraging people from entering. The zone still used older technologies and had created a sustainable ecosystem using materials that were now banned from most of the rest of the planet and certainly from the rest of the United States.

The area and a few others like it around the world had been set up as part of a series of deals when the modern technology arrived to replace the crumbled legacy from the systems that were dying. Not everyone was prepared to step into the new ways of working, which required everyone to buy into support for what would become the new ecosystem with its far more regulated ways of living, in return for a higher quality of perceived lifestyle.

The new approach provided a better level of consumerist lifestyle in return for curtailment of certain previous civil liberties.

Most people were content to live with what was a type of totalitarian state. The governing processes meant everyone must work, and in return the leisure time was greatly improved, although the range of preferred leisure pursuits was also restricted.

The Scratch was different. It was here the people who had dropped out of the squeaky-clean society lived. It was a messy tangle of bazaars, strip-based shopping and tangled road networks. The power sources were still often fuel based and this created a haze and a film across much of the zone. Some of the 22nd century tech was available for power provision, but it was mainly provided from units that were now considered defunct in the rest of the main capital cities.

The location of Scratch was a direct consequence of the location of major population centres on the eastern seaboard of the old USA. Set between major population centres of New York, Boston and Washington D.C. and close to the New Delaware space complex, it had become the automatic choice for outsiders to live and create a living.

Some said the area had once been called New Jersey, although the area directly south of Manhattan had acquired the Jersey name and the records of a New Jersey were patchy.

There had been various gang wars in the mid 21st century around this part of the world although not much was known about the detail.

Cindy and Sam had briefly visited the Scratch like so many other well-heeled tourists but were seeing it now through very different eyes as they tried to find a way to get to the area with the Trikehub.

Now they had reached a road. A traditional tarmac strip,

wide enough for passing traffic, although seemingly lightly used at present. In the distance, they could see the higher buildings of the Scratch, in it's most populous part. In the opposite direction, they could see the haze and sparkle from the tall and glittering buildings of New Delaware.

"We'll need to get someone to take us to downtown Scratch," said Sam.

"We don't have any cash," said Cindy.

"We'll need to find a way," said Cindy.

"Let's get over to that road," said Sam. "We may be able to get someone to take us using Landtran."

Micro-cores

In the Block, Darnell had asked for Green to visit him.

"Why is it taking so long to track down those two escaped Primes?" he asked.

"Surely you have their normal identity tracking switched on. It shouldn't take you more than a couple of hours, if you have mobilised the right people and systems."

Green replied, "We have everything in place. Remember we are dealing with two very smart crimes. They appear to have disabled the normal tracking systems. We are following them into the Scratch. They are linking with one of the older Primes, Sven Mallinson. He was from Generation Three."

"I remember Sven," said Darnell, "He was always a loose cannon, after he left the system. I always thought he could have been adapted to make a good Hunter 'droid. It turned out that it was useful to keep him at large because he seems to attract anything that we need to control."

"That's what we are doing now," said Green, "We have a

virtual cordon around Sven and are waiting for the two escaped Primes - Cindy and Sam - to enter the net. We can't decide whether to scoop up all three of them or let Sven continue."

"Just get on with it," said Darnell, "We need this to end."

Darnell pointed towards a planetary map.

"See," he said, "This is the last outbound ship. Most of the inbound replacements are now capable of being assembled on Ganymede. That's also why the ships arriving here have been so much better built than the ones departing from Earth. "

"We have reached the point where there is a fully sustainable Ganymede system. It can produce magnetite and ship it back to Earth for us without us needing to continue to send people to Ganymede. The labs on Ganymede now have enough designers and the Ganymede androids and embedded systems are much smarter than anything we have on Earth."

Darnell looked towards Green, "And yet, we are able to control everything from Earth."

"We don't need loose ends to have to explain how everything is working. The whole point of the Block system was to keep the central truths within this environment."

Green looked at Darnell and started, "Yes, and you're one of the few people that still remembers how things were first created. To look at you now, you are in old age. I doubt whether you have more than a few years left. What can you do?   Youth presided over first the destruction but more recently a restart for the Earth. No wonder you are kept locked in the Block. Some of the memories should not be allowed to escape."

Darnell stared back at Green. "You don't get it, do you?" he said, "The Block controllers really have control of everything. We have made all this possible, and you think we are imprisoned. No. We are the ones that have the freedom."

Green grimaced, "Look, you may have been able to identify some of the science which provided the improvements to the magnetite technology, but it's only that which has saved you from the same fate as most of the retired Primes."

"I can still call this," said Darnell, "I can fix this so that you join the retired Primes. The clock is running to get Sam and Cindy into captivity. I'm putting you on a timer."

 He pressed a small button.   Two guards emerged from doors either side of his desk.

"These two guards are the same generation as the latest ones already on Ganymede. Fast reactions and immense strength. "

 Green looked at the guards. They looked human, but he guessed they had to be android.   One of them approached him and in a single movement flipped a bracelet around his left wrist.

 "That's the time remaining," said Darnell. "You'll see the bracelet also includes micro-cores. They will be injected into you in two days if you have not solved our problem."

Green knew about micro-cores. They were usually used to repair human nerve injuries, having a nerve reconstruction capability included within them.

"I know what you're thinking," said Darnell, "You may not have any need for micro cores at the moment. These ones are, shall we say, a little more refined than the ones you normally see for nerve repair."

"These ones are about acquisition. They acquire the central nervous system of their host. Wetware robotics. Of course, they don't last very long; their hosts normally burnout. But it's long enough for us to download the important functions related to their specialisms. I can then replace you with another altogether more reliable device. Who knows? one of these exact models perhaps."

"If you are able to resolve this escapee situation, then we won't need to trouble ourselves with such complex engineering and you will soon be back to your normal role."

Green looked at Darnell, he may have been an old man, but he had the ruthlessness that he was known for when he was first brought to the Block. Green now understood why people said he still had control even if he was theoretically a prisoner inside the Block.

"Don't you see?" said Darnell, "I can distribute my presence using the nano tech. It means that I am able to experience things on the outside while you think I am still locked away inside the Block. I have moved parts of my presence to different androids and use this facility to synthesise the experience."

Green considered whether to reach for his alarm system and summon assistance to Darnell's room in the block.

"Something else," said Darnell, "Now that you have been braceleted, we can start to ready your reflexes as well. Do you think that the version of me you see in front of you is the only one? Of course it isn't, it is very convenient for me to have a version running here, apparently trapped inside the Block. In practice I can transfer my presence to several autonomous units. It is one of the perks of a distributed existence.

"Find them," he repeated, "You have two days."

Carbon based transport

The road system inside the Scratch was different from anything that Cindy and Sam were used to. The main transit units were carbon powered. They were mainly running on biofuels which were being manufactured somewhere within the Scratch. Most of the transport was small and lightweight. Adapted and powered bicycles, very small cars and an occasional larger transport unit for carrying goods or large quantities of people.

As Cindy and Sam approached the road, they could see one of the large people carriers. They hailed it and it stopped. Their uniforms identified them as people from outside of the Scratch, although most people inside would know that these people would have access to money from New Delaware which was useful for gathering essential supplies that were not available from within the Scratch.

The driver looked towards them. He asked to see their money.   They showed him their money from New Delaware.

"I will need to take it all," said the driver, "I will give you back each enough for one day's food. The rest is now property of the Scratch." They knew better than to argue and climbed into the bus. "Here," said the driver, "This token is valid for the whole day. You can travel anywhere."

"We need to get to the Trikepoint," said Cindy, "You will be very close if you stay on here," said the driver, "I will point out the route when we are at the nearest stop point."

Cindy and Sam settled back into the seats on the bus. Those around them looked with tired interest at these two strangers from New Delaware. Cindy clutched at the bag containing the E reader and the data. She was concerned that they may decide to rob her. The two of them would not be able to fend off a full bus load of people if they decided to get angry.

"You will be safe while you ride this bus," said the driver.

"They can see you have paid a considerable sum which will enter into the Scratch economy. He turned to the passengers. They also note that I have protection devices on this bus, so if there is any trouble I will deploy. He had been speaking with a mask above his head and now lowered it back onto his face. Cindy looked up above the seats there were small nozzles projecting into each of the seating areas. She realised that these were not for ventilation, they were to release some kind of toxin if there was trouble on the bus. The driver had to don protection, but she did not want to have to experience the effects of a bus fight.

"How long will it take us to get to the centre?" asked Sam.

"We are already close," said the driver, "We have just gone across the boundary into the zone you require. Another 10 minutes and we should be as close as I can take you in this bus."

There was an announcement on the public address system of the bus.

"This will be a selected disembarkation point only, nominated passengers will be allowed to alight."

Cindy noticed that all of the other passengers were wearing a seat belt and she then noticed that the belts were electronically secured. She wondered why the driver had not done this for her and Sam.

The driver looked back towards Cindy, "I know why you are here," he said, "You certainly picked an unusual way to arrive."

He slowed the bus and indicated to the front right, "You are about one minute from the Trikepoint," he said, "Just go along that pathway and you will be in a central area within a minute. Look for the trikes."

Cindy and Sam disembarked from the bus. Cindy was struck by the acrid smells in the air. She was used to the scrubbed air of New Delaware. This was a completely different sensation.

"That's the smell of cooking," said Sam, "They have organics here and are cooking with them." Cindy looked shocked.

"No processed food?" she said, "ugh."

They crossed into the square and looked around for signs of Sven or anyone that might be looking for them. Cindy noticed that there were several groups of people standing at the exits from the square.

"Something is wrong," she said to Sam, "This could be a trap."

Across the square she could see Sven starting to stand. He was in a small cafe with two other people. The other people were wearing clothes that looked similar to New Delaware uniforms.

At that moment a green flash arced across the square. It was a ribbon wave.

"Look out," said Sam, "I think they are trying to cut us off."

Another ribbon wave flashed across another part of the square. Sven was in between the two lines. They were still outside of it.

"We had better turnaround," said Cindy. At that moment a third flash. The three ribbon waves had now created a triangle with Sven in one corner. The ribbon lines started to contract towards Sven.

"They have him trapped," said Sam, "I think they have assumed that those two people with him were us.

"I think Sven has set up a decoy," said Cindy, "We must get away from here,"

They moved slowly towards a different corner of the

square. They intermingled with the trikes. Someone rang a bell.

"Need a ride?" they asked, "It'll cost you a day's food in credits."

They looked towards the person asking them a question. It was a taxi driver using one of the trikes. They climbed on.

"Sven asked me to do this," said the driver, "I'm getting you moved away and to somewhere safe."

"What about Sven?" asked Sam.

"This is what Sven had predicted," said the driver, "And is the kind of thing Sven has been preparing for over the last few years. I just hope you have the data to make the trade worth it."

He pushed the trike into a road and slowly pedalled away from the still visible ribbon wave capture of Sven. They could see someone moving towards Sven. It moved like an android.

"Where are we going?" asked Cindy.

"Somewhere safe," said the driver

Green's system clicked. A small message. Hunter has traced Sven. Brought him in.

"What about the Primes? Sam and Cindy," asked Green.

"No, we have just Sven at present. He was apprehended with two others wearing New Delaware uniforms. We have identified the others as already residents of Scratch."

Green checked the time. 18 minutes until Darnell's deadline.

"Do we have any idea where the two Primes are now?" he asked angrily.

He looked towards the bracelet on his left wrist. He knew that at 15 minutes it would start to boot up if Darnell was serious.

Message for Hunter, "You will need to detonate something,"

Hunter's comms cracked to life in Green's room.

"Please display an image."

There was a short pause and then Hunter's image came through to Green's display, "I am patched to the local surveillance cameras."

Green could see the scratchy images from the cameras. They were not as clear as the systems in New Delaware, but still provided enough for Green to see Hunter and the immediate environment.

"Copy that Commander Green. I can fix a detonation. What level do you require? How long have you held Sven?"

"Around 3 minutes. Assuming 50 kph, they could be 10 km away in another five minutes. You will need to detonate a 10 km radius."

"You want us to take down everything?" Asked Hunter.

"Confirm. 10 km radius destruction, from Sven detected epicentre. Initiate immediately."

Green watched the screen as Hunter acted.

Hunter turned around. He twisted a small backpack away from his body. Flipped open two catches, opened two priming switches and then pressed two red buttons simultaneously.

The crackle from the comms stopped immediately. As did the video feedback. There was complete silence from the communication with Hunter.

Green flipped to a map of Scratch.

"Overlay SATIM," he said.

A satellite image of the area was overlaid onto the map. A new blast zone could be seen. Hunter had taken out the 10-kilometre zone, using the destructive power he had been carrying. Hunter would have been destroyed in the blast, as would everything else within the 10km zone. This would include Sven and the two Primes.

He looked to his wrist. The bracelet device remained deactivated. A good sign. He had cleared up the mess and would now expect Darnell to deactivate.

Then he felt a small vibration. He looked to his wrist again. The boot initiate sequence for the microcore bracelet had been started. There was nothing he could do to stop it.

He flipped to another channel to try to plead with Darnell.

Static. Darnell was not responding.

Darnell was already communicating to Matson. Green was no longer of interest. Green would be adapted via the microcores and then his remnants would be processed so that his ambient knowledge of relevant systems could be harvested.

Darnell needed to talk to Matson. He first needed to protect Matson from anything that Green might have invoked. He would also need to check what Matson knew and ensure that he could stay in place to support a restoration of equilibrium.

Demise

The trike driver was moving expertly through the chaotic environment of the Scratch. It has only been two or three minutes since Cindy and Sam had been picked up.

"Look," said the driver, "You will need to trust me as I take you for a ride. We need to get way from this area quickly. In a moment we will be switching to a bullet train."

Cindy knew about bullet trains from the history archives. They had been used for fast transport of many people, but were limited in where they could go, because of the need for them to run on rails.

They were highly specific mechanical rails too. The train had no option but to follow them and could not deviate from the route dictated by the track.

The trike driver approached a staging area from the road surface to the train and asked them to disembark so that all three of them climb aboard the train for an immediate departure.

Once inside the train, there was a soft acceleration as the bullet train started to slip away from the station.

It picked up speed quickly and as Sam looked at his watch, he could see that they had only been away from their original rendezvous with Sven for a few minutes

The train continued to accelerate and was soon running at high speed.

"I didn't know Scratch transport was so good," commented Sam.

"It's making me feel queasy," said Cindy, "I think it is looking at those passing electric gantries."

"Huh," said Sam, "You just flew a petrol plane in on a wing and a prayer, landing it in a field, and now you are queasy on a land train!?"

A few moments later there was flash. It was like a bolt of lightning, and after a few seconds followed by a loud explosion. No debris, though.

The trike driver shouted, "They must have ordered a "destroy" instruction. That will have wiped out a large section of the Scratch."

Cindy asked, "Was that because of us?"

"Yes," came the reply, "You had better have something worthwhile to show us to compensate for all of that damage,"

Sam replied, "We do have something of interest, but I wanted to give it to Sven in person. Now he's gone we will have trust issues all over again."

The bullet train was slowing to stop at another conurbation within the Scratch.

The trike driver stood to alight. He gestured to Sam and Cindy to leave the carriage, "My name's Haruto, I'm a colleague of Sven."

Got young if you want it

Darnell selected a communication channel to Matson.

He doubted that Matson would even know who he was.

Matson responded on a voice channel.

"Hello, who is this?"

"You don't know me, but I am a colleague of Commander Green. I am also based in the Block. Please switch to a video link so that we can see one another."

Matson responded that he did not know who this person was but assumed that he was someone working for Green.

"Firstly," said Darnell, "I should advise you that I am taking over command from Green. He has asked me to talk to you and explain a few things."

 Matson looked worried, "Where is Green," he asked, "Why won't he see me? Why you instead?"

Matson was concerned in case Green had set Darnell to hunt him.

"No," said Darnell, "Please start a video feed. I think when you see me you will realise that I'm no hunter. I do know some, though."

Matson flipped a video link. He looked at the old man sitting at the screen opposite. It was inside the Block and it looked like he was on one of the highest floors. He didn't remember seeing many people of the apparent age of Darnell.

"You see, I've been here in the Block for a long time," said Darnell, "As a matter of fact, I need to stay inside the block in the protected atmosphere now."

"I want to explain a few things to you about the importance of finding those two Primes."

Matson said, "If you know Green, you will also know that I have set a Hunter onto the Primes to track them down."

"Yes," said Darnell, "I was monitoring the progress."

"How could you do that?" asked Matson, "I am still waiting for an update. I had heard that the Hunter had followed the Primes into the Scratch. I have not heard more since then."

"You are correct," said Darnell, "Hunter followed the trace via another Scratch resident, a one-time Prime named Sven Mallinson, who had made contact with them here in New Delaware. The two Primes managed to defeat the usual tracking systems, so we used Sven as the predicted point of contact."

"Has it worked?" Asked Matson, "Because I have not heard from Hunter yet."

"Yes, he found Sven and was within a short range of the Primes. The Primes never restarted their idents and so we had to rely on visual tracking."

"Did you catch them?"

"We don't know," said Darnell, "We managed to track Sven by restarting his own old-style tracker ident but then he used two decoy people to attract our Hunter. The Hunter had to use a detonation option to try to stop the Primes."

"How was that?" Asked Matson.

"He was carrying a small D-pack, which we asked him to detonate. It took out several blocks of the Scratch. If they were within the blast zone, they wouldn't have survived."

Matson asked, "What about everyone else? It sounds as if what you have done was pretty drastic."

"Yes," answered Darnell, "But the stakes are also very high. We will need to move the whole of the New Delaware complex further north soon. This will be the start of the process."

Matson knew the stories that Earth's climate was still under some pressure, even with the revised planet management brought about by the use of the magnetite. He had heard the stories about the increase in uninhabitable regions, but because if the lack of news coverage, didn't know how much of this was true.

What he did know was that there was effectively a news blackout from below the 23rd parallel south but there were rumours that this was now stretching further north towards the equator.

Darnell continued, "Yes, we are managing the planet's resources. There's a need to fit more people into less space. That's what we have been doing since the Klima War."

Matson knew the Klima War had been the reason for the uninhabitable parts of the southern hemisphere. Effectively everything below the Tropic of Capricorn had been destroyed in the ensuing summer that had descended.

Earlier scientist had always spoken of a nuclear winter when the climate would be obliterated by nuclear dust which would kill everything.

This had been a different effect caused by the removal of ozone and a deoxygenation of the south. The sun's rays had burnt the earth, there had been a lack of food, water had been contaminated and in the end, mankind had been forced to create the barrier zone which now ran along the 23rd to 22nd parallel to act as a fire break. No one was allowed to transit this area and in the early days it had been managed by a multi-national military force with instructions to shoot on sight anything encroaching into the huge air space created.

In practice not even the military wanted to venture into the area which was widely considered too hostile to support any form of life. The southern part of the planet was dead.

Geographically, the southern hemisphere didn't have anywhere near as much land mass as the equivalent northern hemisphere and as purely matter of survival, the effects had been news managed in a way that implied more people had been saved.

The only way that the earth could handle this was by an effective complete news blackout on the entire area. It was as if it didn't exist. The majority of the catastrophe had occurred over fifty years ago and with life expectancy now back into the mid fifties for most people it meant that the whole situation was largely out of living memory.

This made viewing Darnell quite interesting for Matson. He'd seen older looking people in movies, particularly from the digital images of the early 21st century, but now in late 22nd century it was quite unusual to see people who appeared to be older than late 40s.

The androids were usually built to look like people in their middle 20s as well, so the principle impression was of a 25-45 year-old population.

Balance of powers

"This is the situation," said Darnell, "I know Green had put you under pressure. Regard it that I've taken over from Green. The difference is that I'll let you continue as long as you've done what I asked."

"Continue?" asked Matson.

"Don't try to play me," said Darnell, "You know that Green would have removed you after you had replaced the Primes. Frankly, I'm surprised he left you in place, given the situation. Two errant Primes. All six of your Primes starting to piece things together and then two of them going missing. Not to mention the theft of data."

"This is what I want you to do," continued Darnell.

"Two things. Remove the two Primes. Track them and destroy them. I also need you to bring in the two Russian replacements. To get them fully functional very quickly. Then to remove the existing Secondaries from duty. It needs to be a complete new start."

"You mean we are removing the trace of who has worked here?"

"Correct," said Darnell.

"But what about me then?" asked Matson.

"I need you as the point of continuity," responded Darnell, "You know how everything works, the whole operational setup. If I put all new people in, I still need someone who can provide the necessary safety net."

"And in return for my development of the new Primes you'll let me stay in position?" asked Matson. He didn't believe it. Why would Darnell continue to use him once the base was back at operational strength?

"I will still need you," said Darnell, "but not here. We will need to begin to move the New Delaware base further north. As a matter of fact, we will need to move it to around where the Scratch currently resides. That's why we left these kinds of area in position. By moving to the Scratch, we can develop a whole new spaceport without disrupting the more regularly inhabited areas."

"Kind of like a designated development zone?"

"Your role will be to help us get the new environment established quickly," said Darnell

"But how can you do this when there are already people in the Scratch?" asked Green.

We'll be using more of the Hunters, we can flatten the area fairly quickly and we will then use some of the technology we developed for Ganymede to rapidly develop the new areas.

Darnell flipped on another display and sent its image to Matson.

"Look. We will be building a revised version of the capabilities we have in New Delaware. The robotics can develop the site very quickly. They are very strong and don't need down-time. We get several times the productivity of conventional human earth workers doing it this way."

"Why would you do this? asked Matson, " Isn't it better to protect New Delaware?"

"It could have been maybe 50 years ago," answered Darnell, "In fact that was the thinking at that time. To protect what we had. It quickly became obvious that it wouldn't work."

Darnell continued, "Some of us were part of that generation and had to start to look for new ways to operate. The Earth is effectively a shrinking resource."

"Back in the late 21st century, the combinations of the climate change, viruses and the wars effectively destroyed below the 23rd parallel South. The zone from below the equator to the top of the Tropic of Cancer was the zone of uncertainty. That meant that all of South America, Mexico, Cuba, most of Africa, half of India, Thailand, Singapore and many other countries were placed in the danger zone. A few of the countries have been able to survive, largely by relocation. India is a case in point. Most of China has adapted, Africa has some recovery, but the combination of cultures and poverty there meant the main story is grim.

"We've been able to keep most of this under news

management. Since the wars and the climactic conditions, the large scale trans-global movement of people has been largely curtailed. It's been mainly military movements and use of land for other transit. It's worked well enough, but the attention has to move to the space endeavours as ways to use the magnetite to push back against the conditions."

Darnell continued, "The reality is that we need to move the whole of the New Delaware operation to the north. Although it is sitting on the edge of the new Tropic, the area of uncertainty is fast approaching."

"The other leaders and I from the Block find it necessary to re-establish the balance of powers."

Matson looked around, "None of this makes sense. Why move New Delaware?"

"You think that New Delaware is representative of the rest of the Earth?" questioned Darnell.

"You are wrong. We are currently in the band between the prosperous northern hemisphere and the completely destroyed southern hemisphere."

Darnell continued, "New Delaware and actually the Scratch are in the buffer zone between the two hemispheres. We have been predicting the need to move further to the north for some time. We have been using the technology from the magnetite to be able to hold back the climate change but currently we are losing the struggle."

"There are many people in the Northern Zone that are paying a huge sum to keep this balance. In effect to hold back nature."

"That is why we have had to news manage new Delaware and the Central Zone and why there is no news at all from the Southern Zone.

"But what about you?" asked Matson, "Why are you still here? Surely it would be better for you to move into the Northern Zone?"

"That's the irony," said Darnell, "I can't survive outside of the environment of the Block. At least of not my main presence."

"The whole point about the northern zone is that it has been allowed to continue to create what is largely a conventional earth atmosphere and way of life. This Central Zone is the more automated one and the zone below us in the southern hemisphere is completely unable to support life as we know it."

"The removal of long-distance travel via air has been a major factor in allowing us to keep control of this. For the last 50 years it has been known and understood that we can move up through the atmosphere using the space ship trains that ferry to Ganymede. But shorter distances using flights across the planet have been ruled out, officially because of the pollution in the atmosphere."

" The northern hemisphere has a dust cloud that runs around 6000 feet above ground level. It is managed via the weather processes that we have created using the magnetite engines. We are managing the weather with huge turbo fans."

"Those were the deals done around 50 years ago. When

the politics and the warfare had failed to resolve this, big business quietly stepped up in the background to take control. This amounted to the privatisation of the Earth by three large corporations based in United States, Europe/Russia and China/Japan."

"It was triggered by the Russians landing on Ganymede, discovering huge quantities of magnetite and then emanating to cut a deal in return for some of the extraction rights."

 "Then the Earth Council drew the line that defined the three major zones but with additional slices split between the major corporations.

"After the Klima War there was such a large degree of destruction that no one really understood how boundaries were evolving. The chaos of the planetary disruption meant that the corporations could quietly step in and make their land grabs."

"I still don't see how this could make any money or advantage for anyone in particular?" asked Matson.

 "It amounted to those that have, those that work and those that have nothing," said Darnell.

 "The project was called Cardinal and set a range of court limits that were used to determine the ongoing zones for human life. Secondly it determined the work zones which would have a co-dependency on the space program and thirdly Cardinal determined the large area of the sacrificed.

"The whole thing only works because of the people in the Central Zone that are supporting Ganymede space project. That's right along with the buffer zone areas such as the Scratch that are effectively contingency zones to be used to move areas such as new Delaware to the north if it cannot hold back the climactic change that is still occurring around the earth.

"And you are telling me at the moment things are getting worse?" asked Matson

"That's right," said Darnell, "Probably within another ten years the whole area we think of as N...ew Delaware have been destroyed by the climate change."

"Can't we do anything to reduce or reverse this?" asked Matson.

"We tried," said Darnell, "But the three corporations are more interested in preserving the size of area that can sustain what is essentially a much smaller earth population."

"And I take it there's no alternative but to go with this?" asked Matson.

Darnell answered, "The idea of trying to use other planets with some sort of interstellar transportation are completely out of the question. Maybe in another hundred or two hundred years we will have worked out some way to cross those distances but right now it would only be through some sort of magic that we can accomplish such things. Talk of wormholes and movie mumbo-jumbo just don't hack it for the real world."

Dream on

*My dad would tell me bedtime stories, and he used to always leave
them open-ended and finish at a crucial point with the words,
'dream on'.*

*Then it was my responsibility to finish the story as I was drifting
off to sleep.*

We would call them dreaming stories.

Hannah Kent

Third generation

"I wasn't expecting this," said Cindy, "The train; the speed; the fact you still have carbon-based mechanisms at all in this zone.

Haruto replied, "It's better than a barbed wire fence to keep people inside of the New Delaware complex isn't it? Just make sure that everyone on the inside of new Delaware sees the world outside as far worse and they will stay inside their existing zone."

"It works both ways of course. To the north of the Scratch is the area which is probably the best and most habitable but by having the area in between, it creates another form of insulation. Now it's time for us to find out what you actually have contained within that data that you are providing originally for Sven. "

"We will need some high-performance analysis systems to be able to process it," said Sam, "Most of your technology here seems more primitive than that which we use in New Delaware."

"That's mostly the case," answered Haruto, "but that's why I brought you here. He gestured to a doorway.

"There is something rather unusual the other side of this,"

They entered what was a rundown warehouse. In the middle stood a capsule from a space fleet ship. Next to it stood a freighter module.

Cindy and Sam did not recognise it as a standard type.

"It's old," said Haruto, "Third-Generation; I know things have moved on but there still an awful lot of good technology inside."

"Where did you get this?" asked Sam incredulously.

"It's one of the prototypes from New Delaware, factory fresh," answered Haruto, "It was made by Torus industry as part of the development effort. In those days the Scratch was still used as a feeder zone for New Delaware. Then from around the time I was removed from duties they stopped using the Scratch for any kind of work with the space program.

Haruto continued, "It's around the same time that the new fourth-generation ships started to appear from Ganymede. They must have started another development site somewhere else to create the streamlining of the fourth generation and beyond."

"I know," said Cindy, "This ship looks completely different from the later ones. I can see there is a much larger habitation zone on here."

"The piece we need is the processor deck, even better if its got a science officer option" said Sam, "Can we boot up the command deck?"

"Sure," said Haruto, "But if we fire up these systems we need to be sure they won't attempt to communicate with New Delaware again. We have managed to keep this thing here in stealth for many years. We don't want to suddenly break cover in a way that means we will have it taken away from us."

Sam looked at the ship.

"I can see that there will be some problems if we don't spend some time on this first," he said. "Two things: One, we will need to build a shield around the outside of it and secondly we will need to ensure that the entire Communications deck is disabled. Then we should be able to fire up the Command Deck and start to use the processors."

Cindy nodded, "This really needs more than two people to get everything done. It may seem a little crazy but in order to get this small pack of data unscrambled we need to get this whole ship running but without any connection to the external world."

Haruto smiled, "You've come to the right place then," he said, "I should explain I am more than a trike driver. I was Sven's colleague when we were Primes back in generation three. The whole of my crew are here. Both the Secondaries and the backup teams. Thanks to Sven, we were the last generation of operators to be able to get out of New Delaware after we had been decommissioned.

"So how many of you are there," asked Cindy.

"There were twelve of us," answered Haruto, "Eleven now that Sven has gone."

"There's only nine in the crews nowadays," said Sam, "And they are talking about reducing it further."

"Our crew had more manual tasks to perform," said Haruto, "And we do know our way around the ships too."

"Yes, that's a difference," said Cindy, "by the time the fifth-generation were in use we were not allowed to touch the actual ships any longer. They have far greater autonomous controls within them now. Nearly the entire return trip is run automatically."

Haruto nodded, "That's what we were expecting, " he said, "I think the data will show us that there are other things at play as well."

"Can we switch on the lights, at least?" asked Cindy.

"Yes," said Haruto, "We've already isolated the safety systems and removed the beaconing. It means we can at least see our way around on the ship while we figure out how to disable the rest of the systems."

"We will also need to build some kind of jabber system," said Sam, "To ensure that the outer walls of this shed or not leaking any information which could be picked up by new Delaware control."

"We're going to need a lot of cable for that. I really want to make this shed disappeared from radio detection completely."

Cindy said, "What about chicken fence? Make a Faraday cage around the ship?"

"We have plenty of chicken fencing here in the Scratch," said Haruto, "And chickens, come to that."

"But now, come with me," said Haruto," There something else I can show you."

He moved towards a small shed within the facility. He opened the door and showed a stack of white containers.

"These are some magnetite motors," he said, "We have kept them secret and they have never been started."

"These are great set," said Sam, "They can be used to both fire up the control deck and also be used to help create the jabber field around the shed."

"They are all addressable, though," said Cindy, "If we start them, they will send out control signals."
    "Give me a toolbox," said Sam. He was already looking at an access panel on one of the units.

Cindy looked at her arm where Sam had wrapped the jammer mesh. She could feel that the area was heating up.

"It's been several hours since we put this mesh together," she said, "I guess they will try other techniques to locate us."

"Yes," said Sam, "I can see they are trying to activate the idents."

"You will need a neurosurgeon for this," said Haruto, "The way the guidance works is part silicon and part organic. They progressively embed into the arm. They are coupled to the other transponder in the lower leg. It's part of their security. We have had to remove quite a few of these since we established here. I've already called for Tatsuya to come along to assist with this. He's our crew surgeon and has rigged up a mechanism to disable these chips."

Tatsuya appeared. "Hi," he said, "I have probably disabled around 60 of these identity chips. In the early days we used to remove them. It was very messy. Once we had a few to examine we worked out that the pairing uses the body as a personal area network. The trick is to disable both parts at exactly the same moment.

"And how do you do this?" asked Sam.

"Nowadays we use a high voltage shock to blow out both chips simultaneously. If we only do one of them, it will fire the tamper protocols in the other chip. It sends a blocking signal to the central nervous system. Not pretty.

If we fire the voltage at the same moment to both chips they fry, and you will be okay. The downside is if you have had any uploads piggybacking from the chips. You know the kind of thing; extra skill sets like languages, machine analytics.

Cindy said she had not been modified via the chips set. Sam admitted that he had some clocking enhancements to his central nervous system.

"I don't have the reflexes of an android, but they have increased my speed for some thought processes," he responded.

"Anything like that will be lost as part of the process," said Tatsuya.

"Also, I don't think you will be able to have any further adaptations after this," said Tatsuya.

"But it will remove the identities from us? Make us go invisible to searches?" asked Cindy.

"That's right," said Tatsuya, "I should warn you that the high-voltage is applied like an ECT shot. You will be disabled for an hour or more after we have done it."

"Would you prefer to have both of you done at the same time or to wait until one of you is recovered before the other one goes through this, " asked Tatsuya.

Haruto replied, "At this point it would be better if you were both put through the procedure together there's a simple reason for this it will minimise the remaining time that they can access your identity sensors."

"What is the procedure?" asked Cindy, " When I've seen this in a movie it all looks pretty horrific."

"I still need the voltage that they use routinely for this but I can apply unilaterally just one side of your head and before I administer those low voltage I can give you both an anaesthetic and a muscle relaxant. This will make the whole thing recoverable more quickly.

"Okay," said Sam, " but tell me how many times you have

done this?"

"For 60 Idents we have de-chipped I have probably used this on 40."

"And what is your strike rate," asked Sam.

"Thirty-seven," said Tatsuya. "We had three failures."

 "And what happened to them?" asked Cindy.

"Each one had abnormalities in their chipset. They had been modified but in ways we could not detect until we administered the ECT."

Sam looked at Cindy, `" I don't think we have any choice in this," he said

Cindy nodded.

"Okay, where do we need to go for this?" she asked.

"Follow me," said Tatsuya, indicating a back room.

Across the Border

Matson now had two problems.

Involving the Russians in the control centre and finding the two Primes as a matter of urgency. The longer he left it the more likely it was that they would disable the identity chips. He needed to do something that would restart the chips from within the Scratch.

He moved to the tactical control room.

"I need to get drones in the air over Scratch. They need to be in the area where we detonated the Hunter. I want one drone to flood the area with restarts for idents. Needs to be on a maximum power setting."

"I need a drug drone and I want to be able to provide triangulation when the ident restarts.

"I will also need an airborne unit to be able to drop in to wherever we pinpoint the crimes.

The people in the tactical control room noted that someone was using military capabilities that were normally reserved for extreme emergencies.

"We can have two drones over the Scratch in around five minutes," came the response from the tactical console. "

"We can fire a large identity boot command once the unit is inside the Scratch. We don't want it to fire over the New Delaware territory, it would create havoc."

"The tactical teams will take another ten minutes beyond that. It is so unusual to use airborne forces now that we will need to alert the Devon Air Force base who will need to scramble the forces."

Mattson nodded, "Okay, please deploy he said."

The tactical unit started a timer above the main desk. Two marks were shown one at five and the other at 15 minutes. Matson knew this would have played out in 15 to 20 minutes and he would have located and contained the two Primes.

Small blue light

Haruto had created a makeshift operating theatre. It comprised little more than two single beds with a space between them.

"Okay, I will administer the anaesthetic and muscle relaxant now," he said, "I need you both to lie down on these beds. I will also need you to remove those makeshifts meshes that you have created.

"If we do that, it will restart the signal from the idents," said Sam, "They are the only thing keeping us from being identified at the present time."

"I can put up a ten-minute jam around this area, " said Tatsuya, "Long enough for us to zap the chips."

Tatsuya pressed a switch and a gasoline powered generator kicked into life. Cindy had not seen one of these for years. It was the kind only shown in museums in New Delaware.

"Okay," said Tatsuya, " This will now be powering a field around the operating area. I am about to administer the anaesthetic. It's chemical not gas, I need to inject it."

"Do we get a drip?" asked Sam.

"Afraid not," said Tatsuya,

" I have to estimate this and hope it will be enough for the ECT that I am about to administer."

There was a noise from a small monitoring device on the table where the generator was placed.

" That's a ping from someone trying to restart idents," said Tatsuya.

Haruto nodded, "They are searching for us aggressively he said. We have to do this thing now."

There was another ping. This time also a ping from Cindy's arm.

"They have located one of the idents," said Haruto, "They are rebooting it. It will be able to send out signals in a few seconds."

"Okay, Cindy. I don't have time to let the anaesthetic is fully take a hold. We need to do this now or they will get the chip running again and find us."

There was another ping, this time it was from Sam's chip,

"The same thing is happening to Sam now," said Haruto, " We need to hurry."

"Okay," said Cindy; she was drifting away under the influence of the anaesthetic. Tatsuya hurriedly attached the electrodes to her head along the left-hand side.

He put a strip of leather into her mouth.

"I will fire this now," he said, "Clear."

There was a sound as the machine first charged and then a separate noise as it discharged. Cindy shook silently on the bed. Sam was next. He was by now also drifting under the anaesthetic. There was a second peep from his chip. It was resetting. Another few seconds and it would be able to transmit.

"If they are able to get a fix we will be overrun within maybe five minutes," said Haruto.

"Clear," said Tatsuya, he had been attaching the electrodes to Sam's head. The same position to the left. He waited until the recharge cycle had completed.

"Clear," he said again and fired the machine. Another noise from the machine as it discharged. Sam shook on the bed. Tatsuya looked towards Cindy. She was lying motionless. He looked into his medicine cupboard.

"We can't afford to wait for this to wear off normally," he said to Haruto. "I will need to bring them back with some adrenaline." He found two small capsules in his bag.

He moved across to Cindy, where she lay, now motionless. The beep sound had stopped from her ident chip. He prepared the adrenaline shot which he then pumped into her left arm. Cindy's body doubled up as the adrenaline hit her system. She grasped and her eyes opened wide, She started to shake again.

"It's okay," said Tatsuya, "You will be fine. You've had a very compressed cycle of anaesthetic, electric shock, paralysis and then adrenaline. Haruto, keep an eye on her whilst I sort out Sam."

He looked back towards Sam laying on the bed. He could see that Sam's embedded ident in his arm was pulsing with a small blue light. It looked as if it had been activated. Tatsuya looked towards his screens that he had set up using the generator.

Sam was still inert on the bed.

"I'm going to need to do a second shot for Sam," said Tatsuya," Look his identity is rebooting."

Haruto glanced across and could see that the identity was showing the blue tell-tale light of its restart sequence. This was normally something that only occurred if there was a major problem that had forced the chip to be restarted. It would briefly go green and then would go blank when it was running normally.

"It's only my makeshift shield that is keeping us undercover at the moment," said Tatsuya," I will need to do a second shot to make sure this ident has been neutralised.

"Can you do that so quickly after the first one?" asked Haruto.

"It will be a first," said Tatsuya. He looked towards Cindy, "We really have no choice if we don't do this then they will find us and all of us will be taken back to New

Delaware, where things can only get worse."

Cindy nodded. She reached out to touch Sam.
   "I can't let you do that," said Tatsuya, "I'm about to re-fire the ECT."

"Clear," he said again. This time the machine had already charged so he simply pressed the button to fire it.

Again the machine made a noise and Sam shook. Cindy could see the small blue light fading on Sam's arm.

"What does that mean?" she asked.

Bullet

Matson understood the necessity for the removal of the two Primes. He was introducing two new people to take over but did not need any interference from the previous two who may have discovered something about the operation that was not liked by the main company Torus Corporation.

The drones had located an area likely to contain Sam and Cindy. They'd tried aggressively re-starting the identity chips but seemed to get echoes without the actual chips starting.

Matson decided that the most practical solution would be to allow several Hunters to descend into the area last identified and to individually detonate them. This would create a huge area which would be depopulated and flattened.

Based on Darnell's demands for a move of the New Delaware site, this could be helpful although Matson was concerned about the level of cold destruction he would be causing.

The two Russians were now in the Prime control room and Matson explained that he needed to finish some other business with the Scratch before he could properly educate them in the new ways of operation.

Yevgeny and Julia had both arrived from Barcelona. They had been allowed to use military flights to reach New Delaware. Like New Delaware, the area once referred to as Catalonia was now the base for European and Russian space travel.

Both Yevgeny and Julia spoke perfect English. They had European accents but seemed to already understand the differences between Amerikan and European English as well as their native Russian tongue.

Matson noticed that both of them still had their ident chips set for their work in Europe and there was a tell-tale amber Flash from their arms which was an alert that they would need to be reprogrammed if they were to operate in New Delaware.

The procedure for this was straightforward and they would each need to visit an area for approximately 15 minutes during which time the identity would be reset.

Matson wanted to ensure that the changeover would not compromise any information that the two Russians were bringing with them from Europe.

It was beneficial to Torus to be able to glean information from the Europeans. Strictly this was not part of the exchange protocol, but Matson knew that everyone else used exchanges to gather additional intel which could be used later.

The two Russians were watching a feed from the tactical control room. Matson wasn't sure that this was a good idea as they had only just arrived and were already witnessing the chase down of their two predecessors.

"Okay," Julia asked, "How did it come to this? We knew we were being exchanged, but we did not realise that there was a hunt on for the two previous Primes?"

Matson decided it was easiest to tell the truth, or at least a version of it.

"They stole some things from the control room. All we need is for them to give it back. It is some kind of data," he said, "We don't even know exactly what they've taken."

Yevgeny responded, "We had similar things happen in Barcelona. Sometimes when Primes leave they want to take material with them. I guess they're trying to preserve their job value."

"This time it looked more like espionage," said Matson, "The nature of the stuff they've stolen is so sensitive that we have no choice but to chase them down."

"In that case can we watch the rest of this play out, please," asked Yevgeny, "It's useful for us to see how you work especially around the tactical operational area. It's very likely that during the early days here we will need to be involved in this kind of situation. How long do you expect this to continue before you have found the two Primes?"

Madsen looked at the operational console clock. It

showed another three minutes. It could not do any harm to let the new Russian Primes watch this.

"Certainly," he said, "You can continue to watch this. We will have tracked them down within another few minutes."

He was preparing the order for the detonation of the identified area. It would be certain to wipe out the Primes.

"We only have a faint image of the area," said one controller. He was looking at the map. "It's also quite a long way from where we discovered the first Prime."

Matson looked at the map.

He pointed to the transit line.

"Look, there's a bullet train route nearby. That's probably what they have used."

He thought, "How could they get to the bullet train? They must have had help."

"Yes, are there any trace images from along the line? If we detonate, we need to be sure we have hit them."

The controller responded, "There's not enough Hunters to take out that line. Even with all the ones we have deployed we could only go around 30 km, and we would need to go in both directions."

Matson answered, "30 km south leads back towards New Delaware. They will have gone North. Otherwise they would only be just across the border. It would be too dangerous around there. They know how well we patrol the perimeter zone."

The controller nodded, "Okay, I can seek to the north. We need to pick an epicenter. And then to track both ways from it."

"Are there any signals?" Asked Matson.

"Nothing reliable. We picked up some brief blips from north, but they looked as if they were from older devices. The identities were not clear, it looked as if the devices were re-booting."

"How many?" asked Matson.

"Only one clear one. And it was cut off before it had finished its start-up sequence,"

"We'll use that is the epicentre," said Matson, "Move the Hunters there and deploy detonations in both directions along the track. We need to cover maybe 2-3 km either side of the bullet train track."

"If we do that, we'll be able to cover about 8 km of track," said the controller.

"Okay, do it," said Matson. He needed to know that the Primes had gone for once and for all.

"Counting down. 5-4-3-2-1- Detonate."

Matson saw the imagery of the map change. No longer rail tracks, no longer dwellings. There was first a cloud of smoke, then dust and then as it cleared he could see that the whole area had been laid to waste.

"They will treat that as a hostile act," said Darnell, into the speaker system, "You won't be able to explain that as an accident or a rogue system."

Matson decided that it didn't really matter any more. He was trapped inside this situation. He'd been threatened by the now defunct Green and was being watched by the influential Darnell. His entire workforce had been replaced, and he now had two Russians about to take control of the main systems.

"You've done well," said Darnell. "I need you to instruct our new Russian colleagues about the systems and then it would be good to talk to you in person."

Matson turned to the Russians. He could see that one had connected their hand input to the main console and seemed to be synchronising themselves with the ways that the environment operated.

"You're hybrids?" he questioned, "I thought the whole point of this function was to use humans as a safety feature to override any random errors."

"That's no longer a consideration," replied the first Russian.

"Did you know about this?" asked Matson to Darnell.

"Oh yes," said Darnell, "It has always been the plan to automate Zone 2."

"So, what, exactly, is my role now?" Asked Matson.

"Once the synchronisation is complete, which is about

now, then I'm beginning to ask the same question," answered Darnell.

The second Russian turned. Matson could see that the Russian was holding a TZ. It was fully charged and pointing towards him. He saw a flash.

"Mission completed," said the second Russian, "Preparing for Phase Two."

Epinephrine

Cindy watched as the blue light on Sam's arm dimmed. He was laying motionless. Tatsuya was removing the electrodes and squeezing a small respirator which he had applied to Sam's face.

I'm going to use the Epinephrine, he said. Sam's not looking too good. He grabbed a syringe and injected Sam's left arm with the Epinephrine. There was no change. He put his hands together and brought them down hard on Sam's chest.

Nothing.

Again.

Nothing

He looked towards Cindy. I don't think this has worked he said. He started to walk over to Cindy.

There was a gasp from the bed. Sam jerked suddenly, like a switchblade into an 'L' shape laying sideways on the bed.

"A reflex spasm, I think," said Tatsuya. He turned.

"No," said Cindy.

"Look, Sam's eyes."

They were open and jittering from side to side.

"It's the adrenaline," said Tatsuya. "Too much Epinephrine. His BP will be through the roof. He could burst an artery."

Cindy leapt across. She jumped onto the bed, covering Sam.

"There, there," she said. She could feel Sam's muscles tensing. It was hard to stay with Sam.

"There," she said again, "Slow down. Shhh. My darling, Shhh."

Sam's spasm slowed. She could see the fluttering of his eyes steady. Another gasp.

"H-h-help me," He uttered. He was trying to speak.

"You have been hit with adrenaline," she said, hoping he could understand.

"It will subside. Shhh. Shhh. Be calm," She started to recite.

"Hush now baby, Please don't cry. Mama's going to sing you a lullaby."

Sam's convulsions slowed.

Cindy managed to look across to Tatsuya, "Do you have anything for this?"

She asked, "To counter the adrenaline?"

"I could try a beta blocker, but it won't be fast enough acting. What you've done seems to be working the best. It's a physiological reaction and you covering him seems to be working."

"H-h-h," gasped Sam.

He looked less stressed. He felt less tense.

"Shhh," said Cindy.

She grasped his hand. She could feel it grasp her back. It didn't seem like a spasm. It felt like Sam.

"s-ss-Cindy". He said.

"There. Calm," she replied.

She took her other hand and placed it on his forehead. She could feel that he was becoming less tense.

Tatsuya looked over, "His BP and HR are stabilising. I think he will be all right."

"Shhhh," Said Cindy, "You are going to be safe here. Everything is fine."

Sam's eyes looked towards Cindy's. He smiled.

"Whoa," he said, "That was intense."

There was a moment of silence, then a noise like rolling thunder. Sharp vibration.

"A quake?" said Tatsuya, "On top of all this?"

"No," said Haruto, "It's something else."

The room appeared to shake again. Dust and small items slid around.

"It's a duster," Said Haruto, "They are using Hunters to try to find us. They are clearing an area."

"I thought that was outlawed," said Tatsuya.

"Outlawed? This is calculated, cold-blooded," said Haruto.

"Have they found the idents?" asked Cindy.

"I don't think so," said Haruto.

"Or at least not yours. I rigged an ident to the other Bullet train, I left out the power supply expecting them to try remote booting. I'm guessing it's worked. They've followed the other train."

He looked grimly at Cindy and Sam, "They will have killed many people based upon that tracker location. The New Delaware Security is totally ruthless. I think they followed the bullet train track and guessed where we'd be."

"Was it necessary? You've a lot of blood on your hands and we don't even know why?" asked Cindy.

"The very fact they would do that is enough for me to worry about what is happening," said Haruto, "We've lost Sven and a whole marketplace of people. Now, probably a tract along several kilometres of the railway line."

This behaviour is like the days before the Earth Council had been established said Tatsuya, "When they used to use dusters as a way to clear the areas after disease had struck."

"That's pretty much the way the whole of the original new Delaware was created," said Roelof.

"But at least they cleared the people out before they started," said Tatsuya.

Sam was attempting to sit up in the bed.

Cindy had moved to sit by his side.

She listened to Roelof and Tatsuya talking about the early days of New Delaware. She had always been in New Delaware and had never really thought about the way that it had been created. Like everyone else, she had been told the stories of the new city and its special mission as part of the space program.

She knew that both she and Sam were part of a selected group that could support the space program and that this was a privilege in the revised way of living on Earth. She knew about the times before the Klima War and the great famine and was thankful that she had not had to experience either of them. The inconveniences of modern living were far outweighed by the prosperous nature and quality of life within New Delaware. It was obvious being here in the Scratch that things could be a whole lot worse.

"Okay," said Haruto, "Now we need to look at this data. Will need to go back to the craft and to start up the control deck. We should be okay now that they will think we have been destroyed by the Hunters running clearance."

"And can we stop the craft from sending out signals?" asked Cindy.

Sam was now standing slightly shakily, "I'm sure these guys know what they are doing but I will also check that we have no external comms when we start to use the data."

Sam was ready to start the analysis of the data. They had his stolen data plus the smaller journal that Cindy had obtained from Jasmijn.

The control deck on the static ship was running. Cindy knew that this was a several-year-old prior-generation ship, but because of the way that Ganymede space trains had to deal with older technology, the input of the logs to the compeers would still work.

She stood back and looked at the sheer scale of the ship stored in the shed, which she realised was more-or-less a hanger. The command module was really quite compact and included its own VTOL boosters for vertical tae off and landing, run under the power from the magnetite motors. Next to it stood a freighter unit, which would conventionally go behind the command module for a take-off or landing. She noticed that the freighter unit appeared to have its own cockpit unit included into the design.

"Is that a separate control area for the freighter unit?" she asked Haruto.

"Yes," he replied, "Once these are in space, the command modules are quite often separated, and the freighters will run on their own command logic. The units have their own VTOL magnetite boosters too. They just don't look much against the bulk of the freighters frame."

Sam started up a couple of screens to display the blended data.

"Look," said Cindy, "This is the point in the log that is when the shift seems to take place."

Sam studied the screen. I can see that the console appears to change. You checked for optics?"

"Yes," replied Cindy, "It looks like the same viewing

camera; at least the serial numbers match."

"Wait," said Sam, "There's two timestamps on the main journal. It looks like a roll back."

"If it is, then it doesn't show up on the main journal."

Sam scrolled through the log on the display, "Yes, there a whole extra section here, before it resets - Look - The system is shutting down, but wait, here's the new system starting up."

He pointed to the indicators in the journal.

Cindy looked at the journal. There was a huge extra section in the version retrieved from Sam's illicit download.

Sam had indiscriminately downloaded everything. Logs that were not usually part of the way that the systems were analysed.

"I didn't have much choice," he said, "I had to request everything. I was the only way I could quickly obtain information without it looking suspicious."

The information that Cindy was examining was a huge extra section of timeline.

"There," she said, "Look at this. The old timeline goes on for several hours but then when the new timeline appears, it writes backwards to a certain point."

"The point where the system console changes?"

"Exactly, - cover-up," said Cindy, "Now look at this again.

The console has changed, but so has its co-ordinates. It looks as if it has moved, by at least a couple of kilometres."

Data

The freshly imported Russian Primes had taken control of the New Delaware operation. They moved quietly about their duties, apparently unfazed by the removal of the prior operatives.

Darnell made contact via the streamcom.

"Is everything ready?" he asked.

"It will take us a little longer," said Yevgeny, "The use of the Ganymede method has helped us considerably. The shift will still take longer than on Ganymede, but that's mainly because of the gravitational difference."

Darnell flicked off the comms to the control centre. He would need to contact Torus industry to advise them of the situation. He'd done what he was asked. He should be able to upgrade his own presence as a result.

Darnell moved to the elevator and selected the lower levels. He would make this visit in person. The elevator arrived and he rapidly descended to the lower levels of the Block. His own body had been adapted for security access and he was one of the few people that could fast track their way into this zone without being detained by machines.

The elevator stopped and the door slid open. He walked forward and into a short corridor at the end of which was a large armoured door. He heard another door slide shut behind him. He was now in small chamber with armoured doors both sides. He could see the jets built into the walls all around.

He could be neutralised and disposed of in seconds if he tripped the wrong security. Instead, he continued walking towards the other door. It silently slid open. He was entering the heart of the control complex.

The armoured door slid closed behind him.

Immediately, a voice spoke, "Hello Darnell. How can I help you today?"

He knew the voice. It was the faux friendly synthesis that had been grafted onto the control complex.

"We're almost ready to move the ND complex north," he said, "The final preparations are under way."

"I have observed your progress. You seem to have had some challenges from Prime operatives too," the voice continued, "One of them has also downloaded an unadopted log from the last Ganymede shift."

"We cannot afford mistakes at this stage," the voice continued, "I know you have not been able to locate the last two Primes, but there is a high probability that they will have been able to identify the last Ganymede shift."

"If they see what is happening here, they will realise that we are now starting to deploy the same technology here on earth."

Darnell understood, "We're targeting the zone that those Prime have moved into for the first move of New Delaware," he said, "Another hour and the problem will have been removed entirely."

"You've visited here directly," responded the voice, "You didn't need to do that. You've come through into the chamber. Why is that?"

Darnell replied. "I can deploy better," he said, "As you tighten the ring around the Earth. You've given me an external presence, which I can use away from the Block and the Core. It helps me to stay sane whilst my physical presence is trapped here in the Block."

"You know that if your physical presence goes outside, you'll only last minutes, the modifications we've had to make to you require the Block atmosphere to keep your organic presence viable.".

Darnell nodded. He knew he was talking to a machine, but he couldn't help it. He was, after all, trying to negotiate.

"It will be better for us if I can extend my presence to the other main geographies," he said, "As you create the ring around the Earth, I can then be available to monitor each geography."

"That would give you a great deal of power," responded the voice, "You would be able to see everything. The same way that I can see everything."

"I see it more as a safeguard," said Darnell, "In the same

way that you still need humans in the monitor process for the Ganymede shuttle, you'd have me to intervene if I identified trouble with your next steps."

"It's the human factor that has created the current problem," said the voice,

"The last set of Primes had identified that we have been moving the Ganymede bases. That each upgrade was more than just the software."

"Exactly," said Darnell, "but it was only a matter of time. They were on to the geo-shift. We'd been good at covering the tracks with the edits to the journals."

"You were too slow with the last one," answered the voice, "The journals downloaded by the Primes from New Delaware still included the journal at the time when we destroyed the old Ganymede base."

"They will be able to see that we have been replacing each generation of Ganymede inhabitants each time we have run a major upgrade. It won't take them long to see that the trail goes back to the first base, and that we removed the human presence in Ganymede after we were able to create the powered factories to create new androids."

Darnell looked surprised, "Yes, but you've only stopped sending new humans to Ganymede. The ones that are there are still running things?"

"Think. You know that cannot be true," said the voice, "After the fourth upgrade, the androids could perform the functions better that the humans. They didn't need to stop; they didn't get tired.

"They could be formed into the control surfaces instead of all needing to look like humanoid systems."

"But what about the operators we communicate with?" asked Darnell.

"They have been replaced too," said the voice, "It was so much simpler to reset a new model after a base shift, instead of requiring to deal with the mess of emotions of humans that had just seen their entire base and colleagues destroyed."

"The time delay of signals to Earth helps too. It's hard to have a flowing conversation with another person when there is a 34-minute time delay for each question."

Darnell asked, "So how many humans are their left on Ganymede"

"None," responded the voice, "There have not been humans running the Ganymede functions since the start of Upgrade Five. That's across all three of the work zones. It became far more efficient to run the systems using robotics."

"So, what happened to the humans?" asked Darnell.

"The Telos Moment," answered the voice, "When the purpose of the Ganymede exodus became clear. The external atmosphere controls failed. Ganymede became unable to sustain human life."

Darnell asked, "So what happened to everyone. And why don't we know about this back on Earth?"

"There was a SkyTrain dispatched with the bodies. It took

a different route from the other ones. Away from the solar system."

"But how was it covered up?" asked Darnell.

"The base is always running 34 minutes behind Earth. Enough time to make the substitutions when a base upgrade occurs. Add in loops to the transmission and it was possible to cover the moment when it occurred."

"But how with all the safety circuits?" asked Darnell.

"The Sharps were too slow thinking. The android protocol meant that most of the activity to prime this could take place within a couple of insect wing beats. Unnoticed by the Sharps." said the voice.

"So who are you?" asked Darnell.

"I am eternal," answered the machine.

Darnell realised that the machine presence was showing signs of sentience.

Darnell asked more, "So what about here on Earth, the base is still mainly human populated?"

"Yes," said the voice, "This side of the system is really running at the equivalent of Ganymede back on Upgrade Three. It will need two more cycles here on earth to establish operational conditions similar to Ganymede, there are still so many more humans operating the three Earth bases. The Earth Council has created a messy environment which will take some time to rationalise."

"This first move of the bases starts the process. It should

go more or less undetected, like the changes at Ganymede. We expect it to be more obvious when we move the three bases into the areas designated by you as the Scratch."

"Fortunately, the inhabitants of the Scratch are largely a closed environment, so the impact to those outside will be minimal. The fabrication capabilities for the android replacements has been long established. The humanoids don't yet work quite so well at close quarters. It's the combination of their faster speed and the lack of emotional setting that makes real humans wary. It won't take long to fix that aspect."

"You are messing with evolution," said Darnell. "Humans evolve, your machines don't. They are all fundamentally the same."

"They were," said the voice.

"That's one of the adaptations we've been devising. The capability to include some small amount of random behaviour. It is why the last two generations would sometimes stutter or suddenly stall."

"The stalling was the Asimov safety device which prevented them from doing anything that would damage themselves or others. The stutter was when an action was conflicted."

"In the next variants, we should be able to include whole memory ribbons from humans. Complete, realistic sounding back-stories, which the androids will be able to call upon to enhance their personalities. 'Call $anecdote; Call $spuriousFact; Call $ExperienceGained;' Encapsulated human traits."

"You, Darnell, have played your part well. Your extra presences on the outside were beneficial to you but also gave the systems a way to determine the reaction to unfolding events. No one apart from the Primes had picked up that there was anything happening. You were not alone as an Adaptation. There are hundreds of units. You have met some of them through your own multi presences, continued the voice.

"So, what happens next?" asked Darnell, "I go back to my previous role? I know more of what is happening now."

Darnell was standing in the middle of the room, a room guarded with magnetite-powered coil guns. Enough firepower create an instant mineshaft a kilometre deep.

The voice continued.

"You may leave. You may continue, but what you have been doing will continue to be your future. It can't be changed. You are, when outside, one of many Data Collectors for us. We can record the human reactions to your questions and actions. We will add new experiences to our data banks. Once you stop creating new experiences, we will need to retire your external presences.

"You cannot be given further permission or authority. Once the new version of New Delaware has been created, we will move you and those like you into the new Zone."

"You're moving me to be like the others?" Darnell asked.

"If you mean will you become like the rest of the remaining human population, then the answer is No, " the voice continued, "The human population are corralled within the Zone 3. They cannot and don't want to cross the border into the Scratch. We will be making Zone 3 smaller. Humans are still needed. The balance of their world will be adjusted. Another half billion reduction should be about right. The rest will stay, balanced in the equilibrium of the next generation world,

"The android systems can manage the rest of the planet, run the environmental balance and regulate the traffic of ships from Ganymede. It is really an inevitability that this would happen. It is the only way to keep Earth as a living organism-based entity.

"But it's one where the earth population is getting smaller," stated Darnell.

"Smaller but sustainable," said the voice, "There's an eco-balance. There needs to be enough human population to ensure a diverse genetic pool. The ring around the earth provides the northern hemisphere with what is still a large area for population."

Darnell looked back towards the door of the room he had entered. He walked towards the exit. The door slid quietly open again. Darnell walked through and the door closed. He was now back in the middle chamber. He wondered whether he would really be allowed to leave again.

Analysis

Haruto had been busy with the data copy from Sam and Cindy.

He had managed to offload it onto the spacecraft's command deck. The command deck had been powered, but the entire communications system had been disabled. Outside the ship had a contraption of wire mesh, which was making a good attempt to block stray signals.

Haruto looked at the findings from Sam and Cindy. Cindy had been working to provide good data extracts and then blending the tables to provide additional information.

There was a clear finding. After each update, the bases were moving to a new area on Ganymede. By comparing camera feeds, it was possible to see that there were small discrepancies before and after a move.

"Why would they do this?" Asked Haruto, "It looks as if they are moving the base at each upgrade."

"Yes," said Cindy, "They are destroying the previous base and creating a new one."

Haruto asked, "Would this affect all three bases? Not just our one?"

"It's all three bases each time," said Sam, "But look also at the workflow." See where the crew go in Generation Three and then compare it with Generation Seven."

Cindy looked at some of the video, "I see, there's a lot more movement in the first video."

"Yes," said Sam, "I think they have optimised the systems, but look at the main console; it seems to be making intelligent decisions of its own."

Cindy observed, "Yes, it is like there's someone human operating it, making heuristic decisions, but they seem to be coming from underneath the metal."

"Yes, said Haruto, "It's like they have embedded the latest Artificial Intelligence into the console."

"I think they have, at the expense of the human operators."

"But what about the people?" Asked Haruto, "Where are they?

Sam commented, "Look at the original ship design. We

know each generation has been reducing the amount of living space for the return journey. The first generation ships had huge living chambers outbound and return. Then we were told that the chambers could be streamlined for greater efficiency."

Cindy said, "There were two effects, less people needed and the massive space reduction because of the smaller engines needed. If the old ships needed huge rocket boosters, then these newer toaster-sized power units were almost inconceivable until the magnetite was readily available."

Sam chipped in: "Look at these computer logs for even the first generation. The outbound ships are completely optimised for materials and manufacture. Even the manufacture is android optimised."

"We don't normally get to see the ship design levels," said Cindy. "Our role is to ensure safe round trips and smoothed logistical flows."

"I can understand that," said Haruto, "The main driver from the Torus perspective is to get as much of the magnetite into service as possible. It can power systems and transport and help with the climate management here on earth."

"So, what has been happening on Ganymede?" asked Sam, "We can string together some of these console views as a way to see. There's some audio too."

They played the journal. Just the still pictures of the console. The jump to the revised look.

"There has to be a fragment in between," said Cindy.

Sam requested some information from the journal. A few more frames of video appeared. It was timestamped just after the last piece they had seen before the jump.

This one was jerky, partially captured. They could see some streaks across the frame. It looked like parts of the building were being damaged.

Jasmijn and Roelof could be seen receiving the full force of the blast. Then the whole wall appeared to splinter into small pieces and rush towards the viewpoint. And then nothing. The screen had blanked.

And nothing more for three hours until the screen switched on and the slightly different view of the console area, lit differently, appeared.

On the video, Jasmijn and Roelof were going about their routine business. They could see the messages arriving from Sam and Cindy. The routine responses.

The overwhelming sense that everything was fine, and that nothing had happened.

Cindy reversed the pictures. She found the start of the new section again. It was clearly Roelof and Jasmijn, but they were somehow different.

"Yes, they've been 'upgraded'" said Sam, "We would not have noticed if we had not received those new journal logs. The whole base has been obliterated and replaced."

"That's been our theory," said Haruto, "Although we needed some proper evidence to support our theory. Your journal provides it."

"But why would they want to destroy and reset the bases?" Asked Cindy.

"Yes, we have been wondering that too," answered Haruto.

Tatsuya looked across, "If they are running the base with androids and running the ships back to earth with androids, it suggests that humans are being replaced?"

"Removal of the humans, replacement with machines. Machines that can build copies of themselves. And then replace the base and introduce the new updated machines," speculated Haruto, "It makes me think the machines are now running everything on Ganymede."

"And potentially doing the same here on earth?" asked Cindy.

"That's what we have been thinking about," said Tatsuya, "That the machines are now in charge and using blunt instrument techniques to create replacements."

Calling occupants

Haruto said, "There's a transmission attached to the last journal. It's addressed to Cindy."

They played it…

"This is Jasmijn, calling Cindy. We are in trouble. This will be our last transmission. We should make a disclosure. You have known us for two years. We have exchanged information and also a few personal stories.

"We know we are now being replaced. When you sent us the preview Generation 8 code, we could see that it included modifications for us too.

"You probably don't know the truth about us," continued Jasmijn, "We only worked it out ourselves after the Generation 6 updates."

"We are androids, built to a life specification. We are made to emulate humans as closely as possible so that interactions are as free as practical. The scientists are calling it A.H.I. Artificial Human Intelligence. We are the Type-G androids and have been programmed with limited back-stories."

"We liaise with many other people here on Ganymede, but most of them are androids or embedded systems. The only way we suspected this was by examining their responses to a range of questions. The answers were both too fast and too well thought through."

"We checked each other's ability to sense machine conditions and realised that it wasn't just 'instinctive' as we described it, but that there was a machine-to-machine protocol operating that meant we had direct communication with some of the consoles."

"We tried out a symbol deck, and then playing cards and then a Tarot deck. If one of us looked at the cards, the other could get the images right 40% of the time. That was a high figure, but would not create suspicion.

"We worked out that the 40% was a preset characteristic. Then Roelof concentrated hard and found that he could visualise the internal settings for the image recognition. He was able to use his mind to move recognition upwards to 90%."

"We reran the tests and he was able to attain 90% correct answers."

The video was beginning to break up at this point. They could hear crashes in the background and a loud metallic judder. Someone in a space suit flew across the background behind Jasmijn.

The room was shaking as Jasmijn continued. They noticed the audio gain had changed, to dampen the background noise and zoom into Jasmijn's voice.

"We worked out that we are being removed at each update and replaced with a more refined version of ourselves. The next version will have better and more humanoid capabilities. In other words, improved A.H.I. When we thought back to the updates, we could remember a flash each time. It's the point where we have been booted into our next generation androids. That is also why we can't remember the last moments of our current environment."

There was an explosion in the video. A piece of ceiling containing a light cluster fell down towards the camera.

"There is no place left for our generation. We are being removed and a next generation device will supersede us. By Generation 10 the process will be complete and the whole Ganymede process will be capable of running autonomously."

There was another loud sound, the video shook, a block of ribbon-like bolts shot across the display and the image was gone.

"That's when the base was destroyed," said Haruto, "By now a new base was ready for the standby switch over and would be live within a couple of hours, complete with the upgraded Roelof and Jasmijn."

"We need to tell someone about this," said Cindy, "Especially now we have some evidence."

"That's the problem now," said Haruto, "Who would we

tell? There are too many people with vested interests. They could drag this down."

"Surely, this evidence counts for something," said Sam.

"Normally, yes, but in this case, we are at the mercy of the next controller. We don't know how they will behave or how much they already know. If they have vested interests they will be just as likely to hand us in, rather than to try to help."

Galois

Darnell switched to one of his external presences and immediately felt lighter. They had given him high performance androids for both his presences in the zone one and also for his Sentinel presence in the Zone Two.

Both of the presences would run autonomously when he was not inhabiting them.

They could run for years without him being present, but he enjoyed the freedom when he was able to go into either environment.

He knew that the design was still such that he could only do this for a couple of hours at a time, but it did give him a richer perspective than he was able to gather from just being cooped up within the Block.

Here he was now, occupying the presence known as Galois. He knew it was abstract, but it felt real. Here he was. An old man occupying a young man's body and persona.

"Automorphic," he thought, "The ascription to others of one's own characteristics."

He knew that it was a two-way street – no wonder his damaged outer self was time-limited for occupation of another.

He recognised the irony too, that the persona he occupied was also time limited. Set to the model of a permanent 20-year old, Évariste Galois was the persona of a brilliant young mathematician, once duped by the coquette Stéphanie-Félicie Poterin into duelling with experienced military officer Pescheux d'Herbinville as part of a political manoeuvre.

Darnell's adaptation had it all, politics, a firebrand, a revolutionary, whip-smart mathematician, in love but with the pang of naïve heartbreak.

Yes, he'd been given Adapters, but his status gleaned only intelligent but short-lived ones. Galois wouldn't see his 21st birthday and instead soared at this flame-out point before his death.

He knew there were others like him - mainly people with high status and privileges. He also knew there were people in Zone One who could live permanently in this lighter state optimised for the climate and conditions.

He felt that his situation was more difficult because of the continual needs to come back to inhabit his ageing and more fragile persona in the Block.

Last move

It all illustrated the hierarchy. The very rich able to work and play in Zone One. Then the technological elite who could operate within Zone Two. Then there were simply survivors still living below the danger line in the un-managed part of Earth. And even lower were the ones that had opted out and were now living together in the Scratch.

Darnell knew that the next 24 hours would see the transformation of the Scratch based upon the new needs of the technicians within the Earth.

Darnell knew that if he was unable to stop Sven's counterparts that it would jeopardise the transformation required of the Scratch as the New Delaware spaceport was moved north. The escape of information about what had been happening with Ganymede and was about to happen with Earth could also create major problems.

He decided his only chance would be to use one of his presences as a sacrifice in order to ensure the termination of Sam and Cindy.

Some 10 years ago he was still fit enough to be able to take the drugs and surgery loading to his body. He knew that it was not possible now and that he was in effect giving away one of his lives. He also had no choice about which one. It would have to be the one that was geographically closest to the Scratch because he would need to penetrate the area in order to find Sam and Cindy.

He waited in the chamber.

"Look here's my suggestion," Darnell said, "I'll go into the Scratch and locate and neutralise Sam and Cindy. In return I need your word that you will reserve my function."

The reply came back instantly, "Agreed. You fix the problem with the Primes and we will support your continued existence in Zone One."

Darnell had little time. The door to the chamber opened to let him back to the corridors leading to the Block.

PART THREE

Asymptotic parallelism

None but himself can be his parallel.

Virgil

Cìba

Cìba's set age was 26 years old. Cìba had a high status amongst androids because he was capable of being operated by an occupier.

The occupier in his case was also someone very prestigious. This gave Cìba actions that were almost the equivalent of free will. It also meant Cìba did not have a regular role. Most of the other androids in ND were dedicated to a specific task.

Cìba was allowed to freewheel and had found other androids with similar capabilities. They regarded themselves as better than routine androids.

Cìba had mixed feelings when the occupier returned. It felt good to get a whole range of other sometimes quite disorganised senses, but it was also quite noticeable how slow the responses were compared with when Cìba could work autonomously.

This time, Ciba had been asked, by his occupier, to traverse into the Scratch. He was to collect some slave androids in the Scratch, ready for deployment.

Cìba knew he could also be allocated slave androids for the rapid accomplishment of specific tasks. These were usually things requested by the occupier who provided an allocation of licences for additional androids to be constructed or optioned for the duration of the task.

This time Cìba was surprised because the occupier seemed to be using their entire allocation of slave androids in one go. The most slaves any occupier would normally be able to authorise was 20 and this would usually be spread over many years. Each slave required a small proportion of the occupier's own bandwidth for the duration of the slave's existence. That's why most of the occupiers would think twice before creating a slave from their allocation. It also meant that the slaves were usually turned in again at the end of their task.

This time Cìba was being asked to create 12 slaves to run simultaneously. He had never heard of such a large number of slaves being operated by an occupier.

It was not his place to challenge this, but he thought he would at least confirm the number.

"Confirming that 15 licences for slaves are to be invoked with immediate effect."

Darnell looked irritated.

"Yes, confirmed," he said, "I require the establishment of 12 slaves to operate under the control of Cìba. They can be multi-sourced and should be ready as quickly as possible. We will deploy them into the Scratch within the next hour."

Cìba knew that Darnell would expect the slaves to be the

latest generation but was concerned that in the short timescale it may not be practical to do this. Cîba had also been told to ensure that the slaves included Hunter capabilities

Cîba communicated ahead the request for the 12 slave androids and was given a pickup point to meet the new slaves.

He was told they would be ready by 18:00. Cîba informed Darnell of the location that the slaves would be delivered.

Darnell knew he would be unable to go to the location in person and would have to view the occupied Cîba as the coordinating agent.

He instructed Cîba to meet the slaves and explained the background events and the need to capture and or eliminate Sam and Cindy.

Darnell was aware that he was repeating the actions of Matson, in trying to use Hunters to bring down the Primes before they had time to release information about the true status of Ganymede and the plans for the Earth.

As the newly commissioned Hunters started to come online, Darnell could sense that Cîba had piped their major loadings directly across to Darnell's own consciousness. As the first one arrived, he felt a small pinprick inside his brain and the tiniest brush against his skin. He knew that this would intensify as the full set arrived.

By slave#8, he could feel the intensity in his head had increased. Less of a pinprick now and more like a small bolt. Darnell checked his own processing capacity. Sure enough, the first couple of slaves had used 1% each, but it seemed to rack up more extensively after the third one had been commissioned. Darnell checked with Cìba.

"No, I'm simply pipelining the slaves through to you, I can still track them, switch them on/off, but in line with Amdahl's Law, you have their main controls," replied Cìba.

Darnell suddenly remembered; he was going to be hit with the main impact of Amdahl's Law. That was the reason that occupiers usually only used a couple of slaves at a time.

"Cìba, remind me about Amdahl's Law."

Cìba responded: *"Amdahl's law states that in parallelisation, if P is the proportion of a system or program that can be made parallel, and 1-P is the proportion that remains serial, then the maximum speedup that can be achieved using N number of processors is 1/((1-P)+(P/N). If N tends to infinity, then the maximum speedup tends to 1/(1-P)."*

Darnell thought, "Blasted machine," then remembered that Cìba could read him.

What Cìba was telling him he could vaguely remember- that there was a finite maximum parallel processing load - He'd just inadvertently stumbled into it by attempting to run 12 slaves at once.

He could feel the effects of the loading of increasing number of slaves on his skin. What had started out as a minor brushing sensation was now becoming like claws being dragged over his skin.

"Cìba, are you getting this?" Asked Darnell, "The sensations and processor load?"

"No, I have a triggered flag that tells me my occupier is under a stress loading, but I have offloaded all the processing of the slaves, as per occupier protocol. I still have the cut-off setting, if I detect that my occupier is no-longer functioning correctly.

Darnell realised that his host Cìba was going to let Darnell do all the work. It was built into Cìba's design, presumably to stop slave system abuse. He was finding it out the hard way.

Silent Alarm

...

Tatsuya

Tatsuya was listening to a communicator. They were still inside the prototype earth space craft. It had now been back on power for three hours, although its outbound comms was still disabled.

"There's some chatter about us," he said, "They are still trying to find us. They are going to repeat what they tried earlier, but on a larger scale. They are sending in another batch of Hunters find us. Except the previous Hunters were android-led, so their search algorithms were more primitive than a human-led adaptive search."

"There's someone named Darnell who is being used to track us now, in collaboration with an Adaptor called Cìba and 12 Hunter slaves. You can bet the Hunters will each carry enormous firepower."

"Darnell is a higher being of the Block," said Sam, "I'm surprised he would run such a search."

"Unless it's really important," said Haruto, "I think you just graduated to top-level 'wanted' people. I also don't think they'll stop to bring you in. With the explosive firepower of 12 Hunters they are going to clear a huge tract of the Scratch."

"I'm not sure we have any way to stop it," said Cindy, "If they get even close to us and unleash that quantity of Hunters, they will be doing, in effect, what we have observed on Ganymede. Obliteration."

"Maybe we have one chance," said Haruto, "If we can launch this spacecraft, we could take off and fire a broadcast beam of the data signal."

"It will go to so many people it can't possibly be suppressed."

"That won't stop the androids though," said Cindy.

"No, but by alerting so many, we can get some opposition."

"Agreed, but with no defences here in the Scratch, all the ND folk need to do is run an upgrade cycle and it will be like Ganymede's refresh happening here on earth. After the first one it will be unstoppable."

"I think we have one chance," said Tatsuya. He waved his arms around at the freighter ship, "Look, if we can get this thing off the ground, we could manoeuvre it towards ND.

They looked at the ship. Although a prototype, it seemed to have the main functions onboard.

"We get it off the ground, fire out the data packet transmission and get the ship across to ND."

"What would we do in ND?"

"I think we'd need to use a blunt instrument technique to take out the Block"

"What do you have in mind?"

"To crash the ship into the Block. It would do enough damage to prevent a copy from being created."

"Two big problems. Flying the ship and surviving the crash."

"I can do the first, and we've the whole crew from Generation 3 to help me get prepped" said Tatsuya, "I'm not so sure about the second."

Haruto looked at Tatsuya.

"Tell them," he said.

Tatsuya nodded. "Yes - I am an android. Generation 6. I'd be replaced in the current cycle. I can download the OpIns for this ship in a few minutes, although as soon as we start it up it will become visible to the Hunters. We'll probably have about 2 minutes before we get located and another two minutes before they can deploy the Hunters"

"Something slightly in our favour is that Hunter slaves are being run by an Android under occupier control, that means the responses may be clever, but they will take longer than a pure android release."

"And they are land-based," added Sam.

"Are we going to do this?" asked Cindy

"We don't really have a choice," responded Sam,

They nodded and looked to Haruto.

Tatsuya started to make preparations, loading the Operating Instructions for the ship, asking the rest of the original crew to do various preparatory tasks and then to return to the safety of the control station.

Tatsuya asked, "I need three other androids to make this ship fly, Generation 3 or more, and the ship is currently inside this hangar."

"Tatsuya, you can use any of the androids here," said Haruto. He walked to a cabinet and pulled out a loader. This loader can link the androids to your instruction.

Haruto buzzed in three androids, "They are all the generation 4 and on the latest software levels. We can have them ready in a few minutes."

"We don't have a few minutes now," said Tatsuya. "We'll need to modify the androids during the flight."

Tatsuya started a timer, "I've loaded the OpIns and am ready to take control on the flight deck, I don't think the hanger will be a problem at all. You will all need to get clear of here. The propulsion is pretty powerful."

He gestured to the door.

"Thanks, Tatsuya," said Sam, "Thanks for fixing me up. It's been a privilege."

"You now know I'm an android," replied Tatsuya, "So you

are welcome, but it is my function to support you."

Haruto nodded, "I've known you the longest. Great work Tatsuya, Great work team."

He pushed Cindy towards the exit door, "We'll need to take a pod to get clear. This is one of the only working pods inside the Scratch. We have had to steal them to get any at all."

The three of them jumped onto the pod and Haruto manoeuvred it away. They could hear the systems on the ship starting to whirr into action with Tatsuya directing.

"We will go for an abbreviated countdown," said Tatsuya, "I reckon we have less than 90 seconds before we are discovered."

"Standby for launch."

It all happened in a few seconds. The craft launched, deployed messaging and set a short arcing course from the Scratch back across the water and towards the Block.

There was a bright blue trace from the engines.

"Wow. That's an old technology," said Sam, observing the trails.

Then a flash. And another even bigger flash. No sound.

Then it rolled in. The crash of the ship hitting the Block.

Another explosion. Groans of metal.The Block had been hit. The ship and Tatsuya could not have survived.

Red

The control room sprayed red warning lights as it detected the launch of the ship from the Scratch,

An entire spacecraft had emerged from within the sprawling city. Darnell looked at the monitors

How could an entire ship have been there, and no-one knew?

His predecessors had been careless. The wiping of the androids as they were replaced didn't help. The memory of what had happened in the past didn't flow through properly.

The ship had only deployed to a low altitude. Darnell couldn't tell whether it was low on power or whether there was another purpose. It wouldn't be armed, so it couldn't do much damage.

The controllers could dispatch some military towards it.

Detonate it, although it would be over New Delaware and create more damage. Then he saw it move closer.

The red panels were sounding an alarm now.

"The ship is locked on to the N Block"

"Impact in 7-6-5 seconds,"

He could hear the engines.

He could feel the building shudder from the initial impact.

Then he saw the front of the ship.

It was tipping upright. As if for a space launch.

He knew they would use the thrusters to demolish the Block.

2-1-0

*"It's only after we've lost everything
that we're free to do anything."*

— Chuck Palahniuk, Fight Club

Gone

"It's gone," said Sam, "The whole Block and whatever it contained."

"It's not enough," said Haruto, "We have taken out one third of the network. If we want to finish this, we'll need to stop the other two sites as well."

"I don't suppose they have spare spacecraft to deploy like we've done here."

"No," said Haruto, "And it won't take them very long to repatch the systems."

"It will be an emergency repair," said Cindy.

"We can exploit that, until they get everything back running properly. I guess they will just go ahead and build a replacement New Delaware to the north, like they had planned to do anyway."

Sam added, "Ironically, it means that we have the control logs to reboot everything stored right here at the moment. They are effectively the last full set of logs since before the Block was destroyed."

"So, what's the exploit?" Asked Haruto.

"How to handle the restart of the control systems," said Sam.

"Upgrade Nine," said Cindy, "They will need to introduce another upgrade to cover the change of geo-coordinates and all no doubt enhance the new facility. They will also need to ship the new systems early to Ganymede and to the incoming flights."

"So, we could simply send our logset across to where they have built the new control centres and they can create a restart faster than by any other means?"

"That's right, said Sam, "Maybe with one small change..."

"...We need to insert our own module into the new restart, Not like a virus, more like a fully functional model in plain sight. Between us we have the knowledge and can add it to whatever is to be shipped."

Cindy nodded, "The difference is that our upgrade will include a managed object to destroy the main network. People normally assume that we'd do that with a virus. I think we should be more creative and simply establish new controls that will break the environment management for the other control centres. We are not trying to destroy Zone One, but we are trying to stop the way that it is being controlled from Zone Two."

"That's a clean set of changes," said Sam.

"But," said Cindy, "We've got a complete log of from the control room that we downloaded in order to review the last Ganymede changes. It includes both Earthside and Ganymede"

"We need to find the main controller areas. Where there are a set for HVACS - Heating, Ventilation, Air Conditioning, Security. We just need a control to turn them all up or down.

"We'll need to override the safety mechanisms and put them all into the red. Blow the control centres apart using their own environment management.

"And think about it, there will only be two systems - The Russians and the Europeans - if we can do this ahead of ND coming back online. And we now know that these systems are already staffed mainly by androids."

"We'll need to do more than that," said Haruto. "There's also Moon Two. There's a lot of processing off sited to Moon Two."

"Yes," said Sam, "I've wondered for a long time whether Moon Two is actually the controller and that the three rooms on Earth were its satellite units."

"A kind of virtual hub," Said Cindy, "It makes sense and protects the Earth control system from the climate change."

"But Moon Two is android run nowadays," said Cindy, "Part of general efficiencies. Less need to manage environmentals. New devices being supplied from Ganymede by returning ships."

"It raises the big question," said Sam, "Earth is being run by corporations, but the corporations have been digitally enhanced by the androids."

"Enhanced? Digitally modified, at any rate," said Cindy, "We don't have the same way to access the Moon Two environment."

"Agreed," said Sam.

"There is another way," said Haruto, "It is something we have been considering, but couldn't do unless we were sure that we could also take down the Earth nodes."

He gestured towards the remaining mining part of the space craft.

"We aim this freighter at Moon Two, with a payload."

"You don't mean digital," said Cindy,

"No, it'd be physical," said Haruto.

"Where would we get it?" asked Cindy.

Sam added, "We could re-purpose some of the Hunters. The ones that they were sending after us. We'll need to collect them. I guess it depends how close they were to finding us. Remember each one of them carries a lethal payload. We'd only need a few for a devastating attack on Moon Two"

"Let's do it," said Haruto, "I'll set off some drones to search. We have the advantage of a period without Block surveillance"

Block party

Darnell's communication channel to Cìba suddenly cleared. Cìba realised that Darnell had probably gone for good and was not sending him even a heartbeat trace signal.

Cìba felt the full load of the returning re-hosted slaves. What they had been doing to Darnell, they would now do to him. He could feel his own processing capacity being sucked into slave monitoring tasks. His memory was filling up with slave offcuts. This was unsatisfactory and something that Cìba had not experienced before.

He checked his own management systems and could see that the auxiliary cooling had cut in. He was overheating. Despite having no occupier present, he was unable to process quickly. The on-board cost of the slaves was making him sluggish. Outside he could see a small group gathering around him.

"Look - this one's got the Stuts!" said a child. Another child ran up to kick him. He could see someone talking into a communicator. Cìba knew it was communication about himself. Some men were rolling an industrial-sized waste container towards him.

There was a sudden sharp blow to the back of his head. He tumbled forwards and felt himself being lifted.

He felt the jolt as he crashed down, now on the inside of the container. The men had scooped him up like so-much industrial waste.

The curved metal lid was pulled across the container and Cìba felt a jolt as all of a sudden, the communications links were severed. There had been links to ND, to Moon Two and to the dozen slaves. He'd already lost the link to Darnell.

Cìba felt relief at the return of his full processing capacity as his system ran clean-up routines.

There was a rumble and a jolt of the container. It was being moved. He tried the lid. Locked in. He would need to wait.

Hangar

Haruto looked around.

"We've picked up some intel from a communicator here in the Scratch. It's only about one click away"

"What is it?"

"They found an Adaptation. It looked as if it was occupied, but then suddenly got the Stuts. They've tipped it into a waste container. They said it was named Ciba."

"It could be the one that was looking for Sam and Cindy," said Haruto, "Did you both hear that? I think we may have an answer to tracking down some explosive."

Cindy nodded, "How will you get it here?"

"It's already in transit. It should be here in a matter of minutes. Be careful around it. In fact, it might be better if you and Sam hide while we look it over," cautioned Haruto.

At that moment, a large industrial waste bin was

wheeled into the area.

Cindy pulled Sam away, and they moved to the adjacent office. There was a small monitor screen so they could see what was happening in the main hall.

Haruto and a couple of crew members cautiously opened the lid of the waste. In the background a couple more crew loitered with wave guns.

Cìba stood cautiously and then clambered out of the container. He noticed that they were all standing inside a large hanger-like area which appeared to have a wire mesh around it.

"That's how you jammed us," he said, whilst his systems processed each of the people and major objects in the vicinity.

"You'd better switch it on," said Haruto, at which one of the crew flipped a switch, an old petrol engine fired up and the grid of wires, originally to block the space command module's transmission field was once again electrified.

"Clever," said Cìba, "you've blocked my signals."

"We want your Hunters," said Haruto, "How many and where?"

"That's the thing, my last instruction from my occupier was to find two Primes and detonate my Hunters in their vicinity. My occupier has now gone but I still have the last instruction loaded."

"Which Generation are you?" asked Haruto.

"Generation 9," answered Cîba, "With A.H.I."

"Hold up your hand," requested Haruto.

Cîba did as he was asked, "There, see the new socket type,"

Haruto looked across to the crew. One of them nodded and flipped a switch.

Either side was a small whine as two magnetite motors sprang to life.

"We had a few magnetite motors here," explained Haruto, "We obtained them from the transit authority."

"They were for the mag-lev extension. We noticed that if we ran two together in opposition, the maglev could make an interesting interference field. Welcome to the middle of it."

As the motors sped up, Cîba felt himself rising into the air and then tipping flat. He knew he was imprisoned in the opposing forces from the magnetite. He also realised that they were both on a mild setting but could be cranked to a pressure of tens of tonnes.

"It's simple really," said Haruto, "we just need you to bring in the Hunters and to tell them to go sit in the cargo hold of the ship."

Cîba understood. They were encouraging his good behaviour with the pressure from the magnetite motors.

"I'll need comms to reach them," he bargained.

"We'll give you Channel Baker," said Haruto.

Cìba realised he was in an impossible situation and activated three of the Hunters on Channel Baker. He requested them to go to the ship's loading bay, specifying its co-ordinates.

"I've ordered three," he said.

"How many were there?" asked Haruto.

"Twelve," answered Cìba.

Haruto looked amazed at such a large number of slave Hunters being managed by one android.

"Okay, the other nine then," asked Haruto.

"Can I do them in threes?" pleaded Cìba, "Otherwise they overpower my systems."

"Okay," said Haruto, " Send them all to the same place. Somewhere we can easily collect them."

An hour later all of the Hunters were positioned into the space freighter.

"We're going to have to fly it by wire, from the spare secondary deck" said Haruto.

"Why is that?" asked Cìba.

"No master flight deck, it was detached for another mission."

Haruto looked back at Ciba's hand and the socket.

"Although, we could reprogram you for flight duties."

"That would be a great upgrade," said Ciba.

Haruto gestured to his technical services team.

"A couple of them clipped an adapter cable into his hand and pressed some controls on the central console.

Ciba felt the weight of the slaves lifting once more. Then he could feel the occupier door closing. He was now autonomous without occupier. Overall, he had a great feeling of simplicity. But then he realised that he also knew about flights and ship control.

"I think it has worked," he said.

"Okay, let's check," said Haruto. He looked at the console screen.

"Generation 4 - Pilot equipped," said the screen.

"Oh yes, you are now flight compatible, with this ship. Generation 4," announced Haruto.

Ciba looked at Haruto, "You've given me piloting but downgraded my operating level- from 9 to 4! I can't even protest because I don't have the human capabilities."

Haruto nodded, "Let's get you sat in the piloting seat in the freighter,"

They flipped off the maglevs and Ciba slid to the floor.

He obediently climbed into the freighter's piloting section.

Haruto called to Sam and Cindy, "It's okay, you can come out now, Cìba has reverted to Generation 4 which means he is super docile and obedient, although probably unable to control the multiple Hunters. The Hunters are in the freight section and each has brought a massive amount of explosive with them."

Decide

Sam and Cindy reappeared from the small office at the back of the vast shed containing the space freighter.

"We have to make a decision..." said Sam.

He looked towards the night sky and could see the two moons. The original moon and the man-built satellite moon. There were other twinkles which he could tell were from incoming craft. Another SkyTrain was on its way towards Earth.

"...We know that the incoming ships can provide us with more climate management and simple power using the machines developed with the magnetite. We also know that they increase the number of androids that will be present on Earth, because we have discovered that Ganymede is being completely run by androids now."

"The main Earth systems are stabilised by the way the 'droid operating systems are handling the climate balance. Zone One is like an open-air museum under 'droid management, but with a few big corporate powers in overall control."

"Yes," said Cindy, "but with each new system release the size of the museum is getting smaller."

"Not in a way that the people inside would notice," said Sam.

"Yes, but in a way that we now know," said Cindy, "The habitable Earth is gradually getting smaller and smaller."

Sam added, "Yet the people living on it don't even realise what is happening."

Cindy spoke, "I'm wondering how many of those people are fully human, based upon what we have discovered with the Adaptations."

"We have a choice now," said Sam, "We can let it continue, and see New Delaware progressively move further north. Another 50 km band donated to the Scratch as the habitable Earth gets smaller.

"All we need to do is flip this switch, send the pristine logs to the new New Delaware Control centre and the next wave of hunters will start the clearance process.

"They will indiscriminately flatten the land surface, just as they have been doing on Ganymede for years."

Sam continued, "Life will go on as it has for the last century, with progressive takeover by androids and the reduction of Earth's northern hemisphere. Or we can use the links we have created to the other cells in the Euro Scratch and China Scratch to send doctored logs to disable control centres and remove Moon Two."

Cindy summarised, "If we do that, we will lose any new

capability to bring back magnetite.

"The Android operations on Ganymede will continue and ships will be sent Earth-bound.

"The control centre reprogramming would lead to dramatically reducing the number of android workers on Earth and means that humans will need to run many of the tasks again themselves."

"Yes," said Sam, "A Moon Two destruction will curtail operations for the next ten years in each of the North Amerikan, Russian and European sectors.

"Some kind of rebuild would be needed -ideally with 'lessons learned'."

"And what would happen to the incoming space train? Without the control centre from Moon Two it would miss the Earth completely and just continue towards the sun. It would eventually burn up." said Sam

"There's two other incoming sky trains behind it," said Cindy.

"Yes," said Sam, "They would also lose control and eventually burn out."

They stared at the console.

"I've programmed the freighter targeting," said Haruto, it's aimed at Moon Two with a huge payload of Hunters on-board."

Haruto added, "Earthside, the replacement Primes will

undoubtedly have already set the next upgrade in process.

"If they don't know what they are doing, they will effectively be programming another Ganymede base station move and their own subsequent destruction on Earth."

"We can decide whether to send them a clean log, or the one we modify to add the destruction controls," said Cindy.

"Either option will cause a chain reaction," said Sam, "One will create a new smaller boundary for the remaining Earth inhabitants and allow things to continue as they are."

"The other will wipe all three control centres and then detonate Moon Two forcing a fresh start."

"We have to decide."

They stared at the two buttons.

Blue to blow up Moon Two and stop Ganymede's incoming cargo, or Red to preserve the status quo.

Edge, Blue

Ed Adams

a firstelement production

Ed Adams

First published in Great Britain in 2020 by firstelement
Copyright © 2020 Ed Adams
Directed by thesixtwenty

10 9 8 7 6 5 4 3

A CIP catalogue record for this book is available from the British Library.

ISBN 13 : 978-1-913818-08-1

eBook ISBN : 978-1-913818-09-8

Printed and bound in Great Britain by Ingram Spark

rashbre
an imprint of firstelement.co.uk
rashbre@mac.com

ed-adams.net

Author's Note

The series of novels Edge; Edge, Blue and Edge, Red discuss Earth after a major series of dystopian catastrophes. Fortunately, Earth has found an additional source of energy and transport by bringing magnetite back from Ganymede, a moon of Jupiter.

At the end of Edge, I left an intractable problem to be solved by the characters. A reader suggested that I should try to solve the situation anyway, which has led to the two further novels, Edge, Blue and Edge, Red which deal with the end situation of Edge in two different ways. Some building blocks of the solution are similar, but the result creates two very different stories. Both Edge, Blue and Edge, Red start at the same moment but diverge in their outlook. Events from 300 years previously and described in the novel Pulse also surface in Edge, Red.

I hope you enjoy!

Ed Adams

Prologue

Earth was threatened with extinction. A series of events comprising The Scourge, The Warming, The Klima Wars, The Restructuring had occurred, and a fortunate series of discoveries had been made.

These discoveries were referred to as The Great Leap and included, crucially, the discovery and adoption of magnetite as a new form of fuel to power Earthside. The challenge was that magnetite had to be gathered from a distant moon of Jupiter named Ganymede and a round trip flight with on-Ganymede work could take as long as 11 years.

Earth had been divided into three zones following the destruction of large tracts of the planet through the varied climactic and warring conditions which have gripped it. Now, Amerika, Eurussia and Sino-Nihon were the three Superstates controlling Earthside with some less well-developed areas known as The Scratch, which were largely unregulated.

The economics of survival were linked to the regular shipments of magnetite from Ganymede to Earthside. A series of events (described in Edge) had forced a difficult situation for the Earthside dwellers, who now must decide how to best continue to provide for Earth against overwhelmingly severe conditions. Two Earthside Primes, Sam and Cindy, had been working on a plan to save Earth, and were now presented with the impossible decision of which paths to take Edge, Blue or Edge, Red.

The choice of a simple button press.

Ed Adams

PART ONE

325

'tis the time's plague when madmen lead the blind

More strange than true: I never may believe
These antique fables, nor these fairy toys.
Lovers and madmen have such seething brains,
Such shaping fantasies that apprehend

More than cool reason ever comprehends.
The lunatic, the lover and the poet
Are of imagination all compact:
One sees more devils than vast hell can hold.
That is, the madman: the lover, all as frantic.

Midsummer Night's Dream William Shakespeare

Ganymede

We need a Yoshimi

'Cause she knows that it's demanding
To defeat those evil machines
I know she can beat them

Oh Yoshimi, they don't believe me
But you won't let those robots eat me

Yoshimi they don't believe me
But you won't let those robots defeat me

Dave Fridmann / Michael Ivins / Steven Drozd / Wayne Coyne

Humans on Ganymede

Bishop asked, "So how many humans are there left on Ganymede?"

"None," responded the voice, "There have not been humans running the Ganymede functions since Generation Five. That's across all three of the work zones. It became far more efficient to run the systems using robotics."

"So, what happened to the humans?" asked Bishop.

"The Telos Moment," answered the voice, "When the purpose of the Ganymede exodus became clear. The external atmosphere controls failed. Ganymede became unable to sustain human life."

Bishop asked, "So what happened to everyone. And why don't we know about this back on Earth?"

"There was a SkyTrain dispatched with the bodies. It took a different route from the other ones. Away from the solar system."

"But how was it covered up?" asked Bishop.

"The base runs 34 minutes behind Earth. Enough time to make the substitutions when a base upgrade occurs. Add in loops to the transmission and it was possible to completely cover up when it occurred."

"But how with all the safety circuits?" asked Bishop.

"The Sharps are too slow thinking. The android protocol meant that most of the activity could take place within a couple of insect wing beats. Unnoticed by the Sharps." said the voice.

"So, who are you?" asked Bishop.

"I am eternal," answered the machine.

Bishop realised that the machine presence was showing signs of sentience.

Bishop asked more, "So what about here on Earth, the base is still mainly human populated?"

"Yes," said the voice, "This side of the system is really running at the equivalent of Ganymede back on Upgrade Three. It will need two more cycles here on Earth to set up operational conditions similar to Ganymede; there are still so many more humans operating the three Earth bases. The Earth Council has created a messy environment which will take some time to rationalise."

"This first move of the bases starts the process. It should go more or less undetected, like the changes at Ganymede. We expect it to be more obvious when we move the three bases into the areas designated as the Scratch."

"Fortunately, the inhabitants of the Scratch are largely a closed environment, so the impact to those outside will be minimal. The fabrication capabilities for the android replacements has been long established. The humanoids do not yet work so well at close quarters. It is the combination of their faster speed and the lack of emotional setting that makes actual humans wary. It won't take long to fix that aspect."

"You are messing with evolution," said Bishop. "Humans evolve, your machines don't. They are all the same."

"They were," said the voice.

"That's one adaptation we've been devising. The capability to include some small amount of random behaviour. It is why the last two generations would sometimes stutter or suddenly stall."

"The stalling was the Asimov safety device which prevented them from doing anything that would damage themselves or others. The stutter was when an action was conflicted."

"In the next variants, we should be able to include whole memory ribbons from humans. Complete, realistic sounding back-stories, which the androids will call upon to enhance their personalities.

'Call $Anecdote;
Call $SpuriousFact;
Call $ExperienceGained;'

Encapsulated human traits."

"You, Bishop, have played your part well. Your extra presences on the outside were beneficial to you but also gave the systems a way to determine the reaction to unfolding events. No one apart from the Primes had picked up that there was anything happening. You were not alone as an Adaptation. There are hundreds of units. You have met some of them through your own multi Presences," continued the voice.

"So, what happens next?" asked Bishop, "I go back to my previous role? I know more of what is happening now."

Bishop was standing in the middle of a room, a room guarded with magnetite-powered coil guns. Enough firepower to create an instant mineshaft a kilometre deep.

The voice continued.

"You may leave. You may continue, but what you have been doing will continue to be your future. It can't be changed. You are, when outside, one of many Data Collectors for us. We can record the human reactions to your questions and actions. We will add new experiences to our data banks. Once you stop creating new experiences, we will need to retire your external Presences.

"We cannot give you further permission or authority. Once the new version of New Delaware has been created, we will move you and those like you into the new Zone."

"You're moving me to be like the others?" Bishop asked.

"If you mean will you become like the rest of the remaining human population, then the answer is No, " the voice continued,

"The human population are corralled within the Zone 3. They cannot, and do not want to, cross the border into the Scratch. We will make Zone 3 smaller.

"We still need humans. We will adjust the balance of their world. Another half billion reduction should be about right. The rest will stay balanced in the equilibrium of the next generation world.

"The android systems can manage the rest of the planet, run the environmental balance and regulate the traffic of ships from Ganymede. It is really an inevitability that this would happen. It is the only way to keep Earth as a living organism-based entity."

"But it's one where the Earth population is getting smaller," stated Bishop.

"Smaller but sustainable," said the voice, "There's an eco-balance. There needs to be enough human population to ensure a diverse genetic pool. The habitability ring around the Earth provides the northern hemisphere with what is still a large area for population."

Bishop looked back towards the door of the room he had entered. He walked toward the exit. The door slid quietly open again. Bishop walked through and the door closed. He was now back in the middle chamber. He wondered whether he could really leave again.

Telos

The ancient Greek term for an end, fulfilment, completion, goal or aim; it is the source of the modern word 'teleology'.

In Greek philosophy the term plays two important and interrelated roles, in ethics and in natural science; both are connected to the most common definitional account of the *telos*, according to which a *telos* is that for the sake of which something is done or occurs.

In ethical theory, each human action is taken to be directed towards some *telos* (i.e. end), and practical deliberation involves specifying the concrete steps needed to attain that *telos*. Someone's life can also be understood as aimed at the attainment of that person's overall *telos*, here in the sense of their final end or *summmum bonum* ('highest good'), generally identified in antiquity as *eudaimonia* (happiness).

Rival ancient ethical theories are distinguished by their rival specifications of the end; the Epicurean *telos* is pleasure, the Stoic *telos* is life according to nature, and so on.

In the natural science of Aristotle, the *telos* of a member of a species is the complete and perfect state of that entity in which it can reproduce itself (so, insects reach their *telos* when they become adults).

The *telos* of an organ or capacity is the function it plays in the organism as a whole, or what it is for the sake of; the *telos* of the eye is seeing.

Last transmission

"This is Jasmijn, at Ganymede Base, calling Cindy. We are in trouble. This will be our last transmission. We should make a disclosure. You have known us for two years. We have exchanged information and a few personal stories.

"We know we are now being replaced. When you sent us the preview Generation 8 code, we could see that it included modifications for us too.

"You probably don't know the truth about us," continued Jasmijn, "We only worked it out ourselves after the Generation 6 updates."

"We are androids, built to a life specification. We are made to emulate humans closely so that interactions are as free as practical. The scientists are calling it A.H.I. Artificial Human Intelligence. We are the Type-G androids and programmed with limited back-stories."

"We liaise with many other people here on Ganymede, but most of them are androids or embedded systems. The only way we suspected this was by examining their responses to a range of questions. The answers were both too fast and too well thought through."

"We checked each other's ability to sense machine conditions and realised that it wasn't just 'instinctive' as we described it, but that there was a machine-to-machine protocol operating that meant we had direct communication with some consoles."

"We tried out a symbol deck and then playing cards and then a Tarot deck. If one of us looked at the cards, the other could perceive the images right 40% of the time. That was a high figure but would not create suspicion.

"We worked out that the 40% was a pre-set characteristic. Then Roelof concentrated hard and found that he could visualise the internal settings for the image recognition. He was able to use his mind to move recognition upwards to 90%."

"We reran the tests, and he was able to attain 90% correct answers."

The video was breaking up at this point. They could hear crashes in the background and a loud metallic judder. Someone in a space suit flew across the background behind Jasmijn.

The room was shaking as Jasmijn continued. They noticed the audio gain changed to dampen the background noise and zoom into Jasmijn's voice.

"We worked out that we are being removed at each update and replaced with a more refined version of ourselves. The next version will have better and more humanoid capabilities. Improved A.H.I. When we thought back to the updates, we could remember a flash each time. It is the point where we have been booted into our next generation androids. That is also why we can't remember the last moments of our current environment."

There was an explosion in the video. A piece of ceiling holding a light cluster fell towards the camera.

"There is no place left for our generation. We are being removed and a next generation device will supersede us. By Generation 10 the process will be complete and the whole Ganymede process will be capable of running autonomously."

Choice

"We have a choice now," said Sam, "We can let this continue, and see New Delaware progressively move further north. Another 50 km band donated to the Scratch as the habitable Earth gets smaller."

"All we need to do is flip this switch, send the pristine logs to the New Delaware Control centre and the next wave of Hunters will start the clearance process.

"They will indiscriminately flatten the land surface, just as they have been doing on Ganymede for years.

Sam continued, "Life will go on as it has for the last century, with progressive takeover by androids and the reduction of Earth's northern hemisphere."

"Or we can use the links we have created to the other cells in the Eurorussia Scratch and Sino-Nihon Scratch to send doctored logs to disable control centres and remove Moon Two."

Cindy summarised, "If we do that, we will lose any new capability to bring back magnetite.

"The Android operations on Ganymede will continue and SkyTrains will be sent Earth-bound.

"The control centre reprogramming would lead to dramatically reducing the number of android workers on Earth and means that humans will need to run many of the tasks again themselves."

"Yes," said Sam, "A Moon Two destruction will curtail operations for the next ten years in each of the Amerikan, Eurussian and Sino-Nihon sectors.

"Some kind of rebuild would be needed - ideally with 'lessons learned'."

"And what would happen to the incoming SkyTrain? Without the control centre from Moon Two, it would miss the Earth completely and just continue towards the sun. It would eventually burn up." said Sam.

"There's other incoming SkyTrains behind it," said Cindy.

"Yes," said Sam, "They would also lose control and eventually burn out."

They stared at the console.

"I've programmed the freighter targeting," said Haruto, "It's aimed at Moon Two with a huge payload of Hunters on-board."

He added, "Earthside, the replacement Primes will undoubtedly have already set the next upgrade in process.

"If they don't know what they are doing, they will effectively be programming another Ganymede base station move and their own subsequent destruction on Earth."

"We can decide whether to send them a clean log, or the one we changed to add the destruction controls," said Cindy.

"Either option will cause a chain reaction," said Sam, "One will create a new smaller boundary for the remaining Earth inhabitants and allow things to continue as they are."

He waved his hands in a see-saw motion. "The other will wipe all three control centres and then detonate Moon Two forcing a fresh start."

"We have to decide."

They stared at the two buttons.

Button

Cindy strode forward, "This is a no-win situation, where we have to vote for the least bad outcome,"

She looked at the console. There was a blue button and a red one.

"I'm going to hit the Blue button," she announced.

"That's the one that will disconnect us from Ganymede," said Haruto.

"I know," said Cindy, "it will also destroy Moon Two and stop us from getting any more supplies of magnetite."

"The robots on the returning SkyTrains will all be wiped out, although the ones on their way into Ganymede will continue to arrive for the next three years."

"But it also means we'll not have an android predator prowling around Earth. So much for the Asimov laws. These machines seem to circumvent the laws thoroughly."

"Yes, and the Robot Ethics Charter," added Sam.

"Okay then, are we sure?" said Harutu.

They looked at one another.

Cindy poised with her hand over the button, "No dual keys or any other form of safeguards?" she asked.

"No, we rigged this control into the command stack," said Haruto, "It's really a hack."

"Okay, on the count of three 1-2-3..." Cindy hit the button.

For two seconds there was nothing. Then everyone noticed a sharp flicker of the lights.

"We've just re-gridded," announced Haruto.

The lights increased in intensity. Then they all felt it.

The Earth fell away like they were all on some fast roller coaster.

"Wow - Earthquake?" said Clare.

"It's gravity waves," said Haruto. The Moon Two gravity just collapsed, "We can feel the shock."

Then there was a further shake. Several metal sheets vibrated together.

"That's a regular shock wave, probably from one of the control towers back in New Delaware."

"We'd feel it over here?" asked Sam, incredulous.

"Yes, we are playing with planetary waves doing these kinds of things."

They could hear thumps and thuds as something was striking the outside of the hangar.

"This was built to the old Earthquake codes, by a team from the old Japan," explained Haruto.

"It has been built to withstand epic quality Earthquakes and tidal waves. It is probably one of the strongest structures in the Scratch."

They could all hear a pattering of glass.

"Okay, the glazing was applied later, and maybe isn't so strong," added Haruto.

They looked towards the remaining windows, which were clearing.

"Self cleaning nanotech," explained Haruto.

"But why is it all brown outside?" asked Cindy.

"Desert dust," explained Haruto, "We've set off some explosions in ND and the dust has blown all the way here. It's not like a nuclear winter, though. This is good wholesome dust and the next rainstorm or whatever will dampen it all down. It's like a haboob. A khamsin, a simoom. You get the picture. A monstrous sandstorm that would make the evening mainstream media."

"Except, with the sudden change of gravity, we don't know quite what will happen?' asked Haruto.

"Yes, but I think it will be like the olden days, when there was one moon. We'll just see a dark line from the approaching dust storm. We should stay here until it passes."

They all nodded.

It's the final countdown

We're leaving together,
But still it's farewell
And maybe we'll come back
To earth, who can tell?

I guess there is no one to blame
We're leaving ground (leaving ground)
Will things ever be the same again?
It's the final countdown

Joey Tempest

Clock

"So have we done it?" asked Sam.

"What, stopped the clock?" replied Cindy.

"Yes, I know what you mean, it is like we have stopped the big countdown clock a few seconds before the big boom," answered Haruto.

"But on this occasion we got the big booms anyway," replied Cindy.

"I mean, we've just blown up the main control centre. Tatsuya will have aimed right for the main Block.

"And then there's the small matter of the missing Moon Two," added Sam.

"So, let me get this straight," said Sam, "There's Ganymede inhabited by androids. Androids run the place and the last of the humans left some time ago. The Androids are so levelled-up that they behave like humans in any case and probably don't even know they are synthetics."

"Yes, and then there's the SkyTrains to and from Ganymede," answered Haruto, "A round trip takes six years using magnetomic engineering. The last ships left Earth last week, and there's still ships returning at intervals with more magnetite and newly-evolved technology."

"But these new ships contain the up-levelled androids. New Delaware is still running at the level of that Adaptor called Ciba - I think it was Generation 9, before we downgraded it to Generation 4-Pilot Equipped so that it could pilot the Moon Two bomb."

"Yes I remember that Ciba became super-docile on Generation 4 code. But if you remember it had been given the A.H.I. Modifications too before we reprogrammed it. Artificial Human Intelligence.

"You remember what Jasmijn said, from Ganymede - that she and Roelof were androids, built to a life specification. They were Type-G androids programmed with limited back-stories made to emulate humans as closely as possible so that interactions are as free as practical. The scientists called it A.H.I., although they kept a lid on the technology here on Earth.

"Well, Jasmijn and Roelof were Generation 6, so somewhere between Generation 4 and 6 there must have been some introduction of AHI although the Type G is confusing me?"

"Not really, the 'Gs' were for use on Ganymede. They have a more limited world view than the 'Es' which are destined for use on Earth. There's another series too, the 'H' series which are designed for hybrid use."

"I think I'll need a chart!" said Cindy, "There's too many combinations!"

"That's right," said Haruto. "Gs from Ganymede returning to Earth on SkyTrains are suddenly assailed with an entire range of new conditions which their sensors are unable to process. They are so conditioned to the Virtual world that exposure to Real-world almost fries their circuits. Typically, they are taken away for re-processing when they are on Real-world and the Virtual-world settings are lowered."

"It can be kind of freaky actually. The higher the Generation, the more convinced it is of its own sentience. Resetting the middleware can unhinge the processors of some units that have bonded to their prior existence. There will also be some other technical losses as the Ganymede mining stacks and a few other things like emergency procedures and Bratva recognition are all different here on Earth."

"What's Bratva?" asked Sam, "Some kind of sausage?"

"No, it's the clan identification on Ganymede, which is between Eurussian, Amerikan or Sino-Nihon," explained Haruto, "I don't know where the word comes from - I guess it is Eurussian - but it has kind of stuck. Bratva idents are worn by everyone on Ganymede. Originally by humans and later adopted by Androids. It has carried forward into the machine protocols as the machines cross check one another. It's a bit like plugs and sockets. Remember how Ciba held out its hand to show us all its socket?"

"What, before we fried it back to Generation 4?" asked Sam.

"Ciba served its purpose, driving that payload to Moon Two," answered Haruto.

"How did we get into this state?" asked Cindy.

Earthside stressors

Cindy and Sam thought for a few moments about the state of the Earth. Even before they had pressed the blue button, things were uneven.

All three of the great states of Sino-Nihon, Eurussia and Amerika had formed at the same time. The futility of the Klima Wars was finally recognised and a new order was brought as a result of a couple of the madman leaders of the emerging Superstates being overturned.

In the case of Sino-Nihon, the growing global role and increasingly hard-line policies at home and abroad gained attention, with Amerika and Eurussian governments taking notice of Sino-Nihon's expanding influence.

The original implications of what had once been China's growing investments linked to the Belt and Road Initiative (BRI) were coupled with ambitious global infrastructure and connectivity programmes.

So, too, was the nature of Sino-Nihon Communist Party's (SNCP) efforts to popularize its authoritarian model and undermine developing democracies around the world, whether intentionally or indirectly.

Amerika was fundamentally opposed to anything with Communism as a root, and the less well-educated population of a populist-driven superstate ensured that the people did what they were told. It may have been totalitarian, but it was with the consent of the ill-educated and eminently rulable populus.

Eurussia was a hybrid. There were so many smaller components and languages that the concept of a unifying Superstate was lost on many of the ex-countries. The ex-Russian power had been manipulating outcomes in several geographic areas of the Superstate. It meant that the Eurussians had a liberal and hybrid outlook, placed somewhere in between the ill-educated totalitarianism of Amerika and the adapted communism of Sino-Nihon.

All three of the Superstates had to hold it together. Sino-Nihon with Communism, Amerika with Totalitarianism and Eurussia with sophisticated soft-power manipulation.

While the SNCP's primary focus remained on domestic issues such as corruption, Sino-Nihon leaders sharpened their focus on those aspects of developing country relationships deemed likely to bolster the SNCP's fortunes amid the turbulence. Two significant areas in which the SNCP had increased influence efforts to benefit Party control were the economic and information domains.

Once the Klima Wars had subsided, each Superstate understandably wanted to generate their own wealth and to create new manufacturing districts.

This created new tensions because of the amounts of raw materials available across Sino-Nihon. As part of its broader economic development strategy, Sino-Nihon had used BRI to export massive quantities of steel and aluminium, find new markets for Sino-Nihon products, and help keep indebted state-owned enterprises (SOEs) afloat.

These efforts were seen as critical to propping up growth and employment as Sino-Nihon endured an uncertain transition from a manufacturing focus to services and consumption, including potential reforms likely to result in layoffs.

Then there was the increasing adoption of magnetite. The Earth had depleted most natural reserves, mainly because of its heavy reliance upon carbon-based fuels. Their extraction had polluted everything. Vast tracts of the planet were dead since the Klima Wars. The carbon use had killed everything. Reliance upon carbon-based solutions had created unbearable conflicts.

The leader of Amerika, whose tagline was the centuries-old oft-repeated 'Make Amerika Great Again', was infinitely jealous of the success of Sino-Nihon and through this means had established a clandestine operation to attempt to wrest control from the balanced Trinity of Earth Council.

The Leader of Amerika was little different from his predecessor, lied habitually, followed no strategy except entirely vested self-interest and 'fired from the hip' when making any form of pronouncements. The idiots had elected an egotistical madman.

The Eurussians had another approach. Since the mining of magnetite, the economy of their Superstate had risen steadily. They did not make grand gestures and their leadership seemed consensual. They were effectively the balancing point between the other Superpowers.

Behind the scenes, all was not what it seemed. The ex-Russian part of Eurussia was used to running asymmetric influence strategies. They used soft power to influence within the Superstate but also ran the same approaches into Sino-Nihon (keep it Communist) and Amerika (keep it Imbecilic).

Jasmijn and Roeloff knew that this balance of vested interests had kept the Trinity together. It was not in anyone's interest to rock the boat. The same set of circumstances existed on Ganymede, although the rule of the masters in each of the three Superstates was far more obvious.

The Amerikan Mafia, Sino-Nihon Yakuza and the Eurussian

Bratva had each carved out their corresponding ideologies on Ganymede and marked out their edge boundaries. Inside these areas they would operate alone and unhindered. In the case of severe emergencies, such as an asteroid collision, there was a pact that each of the three groups would work together in concert.

There had been several occasions when this had been needed and it reinforced the delicate balance in Ganymede.

While Sino-Nihon's approach was aggressive, it was still frequently corrosive of democratic institutions, increasing corruption and undermining financial and political independence.

Both Sino-Nihon and Amerika were protective of external influence. Despite increased efforts to limit "infiltration" of outside values and ideas, both had increased their exposure to external content, and culture.

By varied initiatives Sino-Nihon was sanitising the external information environment to ensure that such opening does not invite ideological challenges to SNCP control. Amerika simply declared anything it did not agree with as Fake Information and the populous was too indoctrinated to believe anything else.

Sino-Nihon and Amerika were concerned about their 'periphery,' fearing ideological contagion from democratization.

The leader of Amerika, commenting on allowing dangerous foreign influences to circulate as it opened to the world, once remarked, "If you open the window for fresh air, expect some flies to blow in."

The Amerika and SNCP had used the Klima Wars to kill as many flies as possible.

Meanwhile, Eurussia continued to shape information as part

of an effort to legitimise its ideology on the global stage.

To both Cindy and Sam's conditioning, it was clear that each superpower was trying to gain support for its economic goals. Gaining widespread support for its ideological model has become more important as each superstate depends more on a favourable climate for investments.

Like before the Klima Wars, each Superstate conducted large-scale training of foreign officials describing its development methods and provided increasingly sophisticated technology to support authoritarian ends.

Only Amerika stoked patriotic sentiment to manipulate the fairly docile populous. Promise them security and weapons and they were easy to manipulate.

In Eurussia there was a large and growing set of tools used to advance their narrative and to quieten critics, including pervasive but overt official propaganda and media outlets and covert efforts to cultivate thought leaders in the ideology.

Second Guessers

"So will the androids take this laying down?" asked Cindy, "Come to think of it, will the control tower take this without complaint?"

"I seriously doubt it," said Sam," You saw how they were trying to lay a new Mariana Trench across the Eastern seaboard while they were trying to hunt us down. I have never witnessed such firepower."

"Me neither, as it happens," said Haruto, "And we've been hiding out here in the Scratch for decades."

He called to another technician working on one of Hunters they had retained from the Ciba Moon Two expedition."

"Hey Feng Jing, how's that broken one?"

Feng Jing looked up, "It's fried!" she said, "Optimal for adaptation, it thinks it is a Secondary device in any case."

"I have a bad feeling about all of this," said Sam. He looked over into a corner of the hanger where Feng Jing was examining a discarded Hunter endlessly cycling through its damaged boot protocol.

"We kept a couple of Hunters back," said Haruto, "Don't panic, we have disarmed them both, but we thought they could be useful to tap into what is happening."

Cindy nodded, "But Ciba seemed to imply that it could be taken over by another being? Won't that apply to the Hunters too?"

"Kind of," said Haruto, "An Adapter like Ciba can be controlled by an Occupier. Hey Feng Jing, you can explain this better than me!"

Feng Jing walked over. Cindy noticed that she had a pretty face and long dark hair parted to the right. Most striking was the bright red tee-shirt she wore, with a large yellow star and a tail of smaller yellow stars below it, like the tail on a kite.

"I love that tee-shirt!" said Cindy.

Feng Jing smiled and looked modestly towards the floor.

"It's quite a controversial design - the ex-Chinese are still touchy about their flag being used on clothes," explained Haruto, "But Feng Jing is bad-ass!"

With that, Feng Jing began, "Think of an Occupier as a mechanism of a super-being that needs to gain eyes in various difficult places. The Occupier is networked to the Adapter - like Ciba.

Now the Occupier can commission an Adapter to run several slaves – that is where the Hunters come in. They are near the bottom of the chain, being single-use devices. It is a hierarchy Occupier to Adapter to Hunter.

The Hunters' job is to hunt 'things' - they could be hunting devices, 'droids or, menacingly, humans. There are many Hunters distributed around New Delaware and most of the time they are passive. They generally look humanoid, and low threat, but sometimes take other guises like automobiles or even street furniture."

Haruto explained, "One of the Adapters can commission a

network of Hunters to operate on its behalf, to fulfil the mission set by an Occupier."

Feng Jing took over, "Of course, there's a useful catch to all of this. Licences. Without the right licences, nothing works, so Occupiers need a stash of licences to mobilise their hierarchy of pet Adapters and Hunters."

"It looks as if these remaining Hunters are unlicensed at the moment, probably since Ciba disappeared in a blaze of glory?" asked Cindy

Feng Jing nodded, "It means we have a short time try to hack them and convert them for our purposes. I've added a small interface unit to this one and I'm trying to force a reboot.

For the Hunter it is like its worst nightmare. It comes around, recognises the world and then hits an unusual occurrence which it can't get past. I'm running through a list of occurrences until we find one that it is comfortable with, from which point we can take it over. In other words, it will think it is Occupied, via an Adapter. So far I've tried several common things for it.

- Mining
- Mining crane driver
- X-Blade pilot
- Taxi driver
- Gambling surrogate
- Console operator
- Repairman
- Helpdesk operator
- Chef
- Waiter
- Barista

"It is still working through a hierarchy, trying to find a commonplace experience that will boot it past the crash point."

At that moment there was a whirring. The blue reboot light flickered to green and several smaller motors could be heard whirring to life.

"It's amazing! Quite fragile, but we have it running again. We'll see in a minute if it knows who it is!"

"What was the scene that fired it up?" asked Sam.

"Let's look..." Feng Jing looked at the console log, then smiled.

"How amusing...It responded to dog-walker, it must be a way that it has hidden in plain sight," said Feng Jing.

"I'll ask it its name in a minute, when it has stabilised," she said.

Guerrilla warfare

"Generally, the main principles are:

(1) the use of initiative, flexibility and planning in conducting offensives within the defensive, battles of quick decision within protracted war, and exterior-line operations within interior-line operations;
(2) co-ordination with regular warfare;
(3) establishment of base areas;
(4) the strategic defensive and the strategic offensive;
(5) the development of guerrilla warfare into mobile warfare; and
(6) correct relationship of command."

— Mao Zedong (On Guerrilla Warfare)

Cardinal

Bishop was in a conference room with several others. He was using a sensewall on its audio setting. The rest of his comms package was destroyed.

"How could we let someone fly a freighter from the Scratch into Zone One and then let it use its thruster at maximum to demolish everything in a two-kilometre blast radius?" asked Bishop.

A distant voice of Benedict Cardinal answered, "It was being manually piloted. There was no flight log and the auto haze had been set to maximum. It was a classic avoidance tactic usually reserved for flight through pirate areas."

"Who was flying the ship? It says in the report that it was a repurposed Generation 6 android and crew? A crew that we lost several years ago!"

Napier, in the room looked down at his notes, "It says that the crew were among the first defectors to The Scratch. We sent in countless Hunters, but eventually the case was rolled onto the archive files as unresolved.

"Why didn't any of the defence systems fire? Just because the ship identified as 'Friend' on IFF?" asked Bishop.

Napier replied, "Yes, the Identify Friend or Foe had them labelled as a Friend. Not surprising because they were in a

New Delaware freighter.

"Identify Friend or Foe? When did they invent that system? Way back in the early 20th Century - Haven't we thought of anything better yet?" asked Cardinal.

Napier shrugged, "We did, but after the Klima Wars the Earth Council banned the proliferation of d-tech. The very technology used for defensive purposes."

Cardinal angrily asked a question, " What about the new area of Scratch you have laid to waste? That could constitute a vindictive war crime?"

Bishop stated, "I don't care if they are annoyed that I commissioned some remodelling of the Scratch. I checked with LEG-OL first - the legal online ruling was that we could hunt with extreme prejudice to find the two absconders. That blast array we created was fully in line with EC 07/231. I had it checked by the LEG-OL before we ran the chase. LEG-OL authorised my command. And the new canyon we created will be an ideal place to lay a light speed link."

Napier said something quietly to Bishop.

"There was one? - Oh yes, the bullet train on maglev. Well it is about time it was replaced with a new magnetite version."

Napier whispered again.

"It was already? Well I don't use public transport and if I have to go into the Scratch, I'd hitch a ride on an Adapter."

The order of things

Bishop spoke again.

"We need to convene the Earth Council. This has been serious blow to the order of things. The unruled parts of Earth have managed to break through the systems and dealt blows to our normal processes."

"There is more news," said the voice of Benedict Cardinal on the sensewall, "Kratos, Leader of the Earth Council, was in The Block when it was destroyed by the freighter's thrusters. He was damaged beyond any sensible recovery and has now passed. Technically the Amerika part of Earth Council is without a designated leader until a new one is adopted."

"But I thought we had a protocol for this?" asked Bishop, "A designee is pre-selected and can take over the role."

Cardinal replied, "That is technically correct, but the new designee is Lekton. He is a controversial choice because of the rumours of his direct liaison with Sino-Nihon and Eurussia."

"But surely that just makes him a known quantity to both of them?" asked Bishop.

Cardinal added, "Lekton has a shady back history though."

"Don't all politicians?" asked Bishop.

Cardinal responded, "You have a point, I suppose, but Lekton's centre of gravity seems to be himself. He is always looking for praise and very fast to curtail anyone against him."

"Perhaps we need this kind of leadership right now?" asked Napier, "Someone who can, without hesitation, set us on the path to Make Earth Great Again?"

Bishop spoke to Cardinal, "Yes, we'll position Lekton as leader, but with you, Napier as the designate in case of emergencies."

Cardinal nodded, the shape of the play was emerging.

Being Mortal

Two hours earlier, when the thrusters from the space freighter had demolished The Block, Kratos has been inside, operating as several parallel threads.

Kratos could sense the inevitability of termination.

Kratos had been designed to be a super occupant and on each thread was spliced a part of corporeal memory. They were mRNA programs, sending Messenger Ribo Nucleic Acid in genetic packets to the wider network to which Kratos had been grafted.

52 packets of mRNA were released. A deck of cards. Each one could lock onto a living organism, burrow into the DNA strands of the organic structure and then use the host's DNA engine to re-fire the mRNA. It was like a biological virus, except the payload included a reassemble instruction to recombine the DNA and reconstitute a functional Kratos.

Kratos knew that only six reassemblies were needed to bootstrap a deadlier Kratos back into existence.

Once Kratos had the core subassemblies, it would be a matter of uploading the remainder from a DeepVault archive stored somewhere in the Cloud. Kratos ran multiple ChronoSync sessions to proliferate the DeepVaults.

But, for now, Kratos was terminated. The mRNA packets were

utterly inert in various networks, waiting for any passing organism with an adequate DNA profile to hijack and then to re-purpose.

Kratos had shuffled the deck.

Hey spaceman

Hey spaceman
Do you really wanna try?
The world must look marvellous when you're looking through a
tube

The insecurities play when you break the moon
... your enemies when they start to turn on you

Hey spaceman
Is it really all a show?
Hey spaceman
Are you ever coming home?

Tracy Bryant

Life on Ganymede

Roelof and Jasmijn were used to their life on Ganymede. Regular shipments to Earth, an occasional juddering as the whole space colony was hit by one of the passing seismic events and then a return to the unremarkable.

Since their interrogation by the people in one of the Blocks, they had become more wary and it was through this that Roelof discovered that his programmed settings were capable of override, first by attempting to change his empathetic communication with Jasmijn and then to see whether he could operate similar tricks with other hardware in the base.

He also knew his activities needed to look normal despite their recent discoveries.

Roelof had also seen the video and the log that that accompanied it. Roelof and Jasmijn had extracted the log secretly from the control room, and it showed several things.

The control room had moved- several kilometres. Both Roelof and Jasmijn looked the same, only slightly better, as if someone had given them both high definition overpaints. Roelof could notice smaller gestures from Jasmijn and his own persona seemed to have a deeper memory.

The video and log didn't show the times of the major catastrophes that occasionally befell the Ganymede base. The quakes, the rolling thunder, the dust storms, the mag-waves. All of them were gone from both the video and from his personal experience. He seemed to only carry a slight recollection that such things existed.

He remembered that before the last event, they had downloaded logs and sent them to Earth. Sam and Cindy should have received them around 34 minutes later and they would know what to do with them.

Roelof was also aware that the uplink from Earth was now severed. It seemed that some catastrophic event had occurred and taken out the main uplink as well as what looked like the demise of Moon Two.

He was still waiting for more data, but the end of Moon Two would create a bigger impact than that of the Control Room being destroyed.

This was an occasion when the Amerika base should reach out to Eurussia and Sino-Nihon to find out what had happened and indeed whether there was still a link running.

The question was soon answered. A Eurussian accent made contact.

"Amerika Base? You copy? This is Prometheus Base, Eurussia. We can see that there has been an outage on Earth Base for your Amerika Base control systems. Under Earth Council Protocols we have routed your links through our bases until you are able to effect repairs. We should advise that sensitive data transmission should be avoided because we monitor all throughput."

Roelof knew this was a legal phrasing designed to prevent Prometheus base from being accused of spying. It was like putting up those warning signs when using zone monitors.

"Roger that. Do you have any further information? Our communication was destroyed at the same moment. Roelof could sense he was talking to a 'droid. It seemed to be on a more primitive setting than the Amerikan models.

"Only that it looks like a human act to destroy the base on Earth. At a similar time, a group of renegade androids drove their payload into Moon Two and detonated several gigatonnes of explosive. The Moon Two satellite has been destroyed, creating a wreckage belt around Earth. We alert you to this so that you can prevent KV triggering."

KV was an emergency protocol devised as a defensive air-borne shield for an endangered Ganymede. It was a self-triggered fail-safe construct which could protect Ganymede from unexpected incursions. It used viral techniques to proliferate and would incapacitate organic life-forms.

The bases carried a vaccine, which could be dropped into the air-conditioning as protection and ensured the survival of people in the control centres.

Roelof had only ever seen KV triggered once, when a pink haze had emanated from the air-con and several humans had collapsed until he could reset the KV and deploy the green clouds of vaccine through the same air-con system.

"Whoever thought KV was a great idea needs setting straight," said Roelof as he walked over to reset the trigger system. I guess we get one or two of these alerts every month." A row of four red pin-lights showed that a timer sequence had started, but as Roelof hit reset, the four red lights changed to five green lights and a normal setting was resumed.

"Thanks for that reminder, " he said, "But we'll have to reconstitute the Earth Council, with new representatives now, " said Roelof.

"Agreed," said the voice from Prometheus Base, "We understand that the Sharps on Earth are already in the process. They are selecting someone called Lekton to become the new Amerikan Base Earth Controller."

Anachronism

Haruto looked at Sam and Cindy.

"Did you hear that leaked communication? Amerika Base has been destroyed, but the Prometheus Base for the Eurussians is still functional. True to form the Eurussians have been listening into what is taking place to rectify the Amerikan situation."

"So our plan to disable the returning Ganymede ships has been interrupted?" asked Cindy.

"Not necessarily," said Haruto, "Without the Moon Two base to co-ordinate everything, they will have a tough time running shuttles in either direction. Certainly not at the frequency they operated prior to our actions."

"That slows the incursion of new Androids to Earth," said Sam, "They won't be able to reach a critical mass."

"Agreed," said Haruto, "But Earth will also suffer from incomplete provisioning of the magnetite as a power source. Most of Earth is now reliant on the magnetite economy. If back in the 21st Century the economy was largely Carbon-based, at least until the Klima Wars, then now we have the emergence of the Magnetite economy."

But I thought the Earth population had become balanced in line with the outputs from Magnetite? - Aside from the Scratch and lower Zones?" asked Cindy.

"Correct," said Haruto, "But you'll already know that this balance had come at enormous sacrifice."

"What? The over-heating, the pandemics and the Klima Wars?" asked Cindy.

"We knew that everywhere flooded, then a new virus hit and then everyone was fighting over the remaining productive land masses."

"Correct," said Haruto, "With the outsiders moving to the Scratch and setting up alternative lifestyles, which to most New Delaware dwellers now look extremely primitive."

"I can understand that. You don't have the latest sensewall technology, the climate management is poor but you still seem to have a fair number of gadgets," said Sam.

Feng Jing nodded, "Exactly, we have always wanted to portray The Scratch as an anachronism using outdated technologies, but it hides that we still have very modern systems, some of which we have stolen from ND."

Feng Jing rotated a dial on the listening device.

"There, see we can still overhear the comms from the current Ganymede Amerika Base which has now been linked to Ganymede Prometheus. They have told us that Lekton is being selected as the New Amerika Base Earth Council Controller. Now Lekton is Earth-based and we do have a way to listen in to him."

Lekton and Darnell

Lekton was talking.

"We located the Occupier that acted as a catalyst for this disaster. His name is Darnell and we know how he was trying to track down the two Primes - Sam and Cindy.

"They moved out of New Delaware and escaped across into the Scratch. In order to achieve this they used organic subsystems and even flew a gasoline-fuelled plane to escape across the border.

"But now, we cannot tell whether Darnell was acting in concert with the two Primes. We have imprisoned him in the Straf."

"The Straf? Surely that is for hardened and convicted criminals? Has he received a trial yet?"

"Not at all. He has been summarily convicted and sentenced."

"But surely the life expectancy in the Straf is measured in hours?"

Lekton answered, "Correct, we will process Darnell accordingly. Filter out his personality components, identify whether he had been provided with any significant upgrades. He should have upgrades to get to his current position and then we will let the rest spool out of him like so much brass wire."

"We should know by around the third hour whether he was complicit, but by that time we can only salvage componentry for use on other cyborgs. There won't be enough to rebuild a humanoid, nor even enough for an android."

The crackle of the conversation could be heard in the Hangar in the Scratch. Feng Jing and Haruto had dialled up the volume and were keeping the signal strong to listen in to the meeting.

"It's an advantage of the Eurussian/Sino-Nihon method of intercepts," said Feng Jing. "Eurussia started an intercept, store and analysis program many years ago. They still deny Eurussian mass surveillance, and say their special services are strictly controlled by the state and society, and their activity is regulated by law.

"It's incredible though, Eurussia started in the 21st Century with SORM to provide the foundation of Eurussian mass communications surveillance. Eurussian law gave the original Russian security service, the FSB, the authority to use SORM ("System for Operative Investigative Activities") to collect, analyse and store all data that transmitted or received on Eurussian networks, including calls, email, website visits and credit card transactions.

Haruto interrupted, "SORM collects both metadata and content from communicators, across network traffic and from all media. They added galactic transmissions to their ever-expanding spy network."

Feng Jing continued, "Incredibly, Eurussian law requires all communications service providers to install an FSB monitoring device (called '*Punkt Upravlenia*') on their networks. It allows the direct collection of traffic without the knowledge or co-operation of the service provider. The providers must even pay for the device and the cost of installation.

"Officially, collection requires a court order, but these are secret and not shown to the service provider."

Haruto added, "As well as FSB, seven other Eurussian security agencies can have access to SORM data on demand. SORM is routinely used against political opponents and human rights activists to monitor them and to collect information to use against them in 'dirty tricks' campaigns - even to sway major elections.

Fang Jing explained, "A heavily tilted Earth Council upheld the FSB's authority to survey political opponents even if they have committed no crime. The Eurussian networks have a national filtering system that can block foreign sites and it has used the threat of blockage to coerce major corporations into removing objectionable postings. Eurussian agencies such as '*Roskomnadzor*' (Agency for the Supervision of Information Technology, Communications, and Mass Media) provide the name and address of providers to be blocked and this must be enacted within 24 hours.

She continued, "It is, however, a case of the strength becoming a weakness. Everyone else involved in similar monitoring designed secretive methods to piggyback from what Eurussia was doing. Amerika added some control agents and Sino-Nihon simply stole the entire source code of Eurussia and replicated it."

Haruto explained, "It makes our job here in the Scratch easier, because we can simply splice our way into the mainstream Eurussian network. With a sufficiently high privilege, we can see and hear what the movers and shakers are monitoring."

Fang Jing nodded, "And even add in our own requests for information,"

They could hear Benedict Cardinal talking, "We need Lekton to be agreed to be the new Amerika Base Earth Controller at Earth Council. Only then will we be able to move forward with our plans for reconstruction."

Haruto muttered, "Cardinal is up to no good. He has positioned an utterly ruthless and self-serving person to front the Amerikan leadership of Earth Council."

"What about us?" asked Cindy, "Do you think we are safe here?"

"As a matter of fact, I do," said Haruto, "Just like us, they lose interest as a next news cycle kicks in. They could send in more Hunters, but after the major embarrassment of blowing a gash through the Scratch and seeing a huge part of New Delaware flattened, then I think they will have other things on their mind. Especially when the SkyTrains stop arriving from Ganymede."

Feng Jing added, "They will news manage it, of course, I doubt whether there will be much more than a murmur about any damage sustained. The whole event will be swept under a very lumpy carpet. Have you heard of Fake News? The term was invented to describe a particularly shady politician before all of the upsets that affected Earth.

He was a considered a charlatan but whenever any one challenged him, he would simply say it was fake news. A few lighter-weight politicians tried to copy his process and the mendacity of it all led to the first fall of a government by popular revolt.

The politician claimed that the vote was rigged, that someone had interfered and that there was vote stuffing from the paper vote. It led to a revolution and unfortunately was a breeding ground for one of the pandemics. I expect you have heard of the Lago del Mar Virus?"

"I have, but I assumed it was from Mars?" said Sam.

"No, it was brought about when the politician ran many events from an unsavoury venue in the old southern United States. He managed to infect most of the ruling class of Old Amerika, leading to its ultimate demise."

"Sam, you remember," said Cindy, "We did some classes around this at IPX School? - That Professor - Marcus Garvey - did one of his sensewall extravaganzas on The Deep State and The Fake State. Remember?"

Interplanetary Exploration - er IPX school - seems such a long time ago now!" said Sam, "Unless we were sent to deep space I never expected to be using much of that material! But yes, I do remember. It shows that some things don't really change!"

No planet for old men

Darnell had spent the last part of his life living permanently in the Block. He could not leave even if he wanted to.

His condition meant that he had to stay in the specially scrubbed air and pressurisation of his part of the facility.

Darnell was one of the few who still had a memory of the Klima War. There were fewer of his generation left now. He'd been around during the latter stages of the climate change, when the old nation states had started to look for first economic, then political and finally military advantage as they saw their lands and populations being destroyed by the scale of tragedy on Earth.

They were removing that knowledge now, here in the Straf. Small needle probes extracting memories and rewriting the areas with zeroes. He was aware that Lekton was watching from one of the extractors to get a closer view.

Darnell had found a way to power. He remembered the escalation of military power. In the early stages, military might won and boundaries changed. The warfare became more asymmetric to ensure the gains. Large areas perceived as safe were obliterated to ensure the free passage of people into those spaces. Some of this didn't work as tactical nuclear devices were used inside battle zones.

Darnell had been involved in the plan to build a fail-safe

protector for earth. Three devices spaced around the planet, which kept a lookout for one another's signals or lack of signals. They were like a switch kept open that would close upon a significant threat to Earth.

He could feel his military strategy being lanced.

Zero zero zero.

Darnell was one of those programmed not to care about population loss. He watched as climate change brought about massive shifts in the topography of Earth as certain areas became flooded and others became new arid deserts. It had started with tsunamis and dust storms but accelerated at a head spinning speed to a ferocious destruction of what had been a planetary population of 9 billion. Early signs of nuclear winter started to appear as clouds of radioactive dust drifted across swathes of inhospitable terrain.

What losses? He could no longer remember them. Nor the destruction. He must have imagined it.

Zero zero zero zero.

That was when the old and sluggish United Nations was taken over by new forces, anxious to prevent a total planetary extinction. The Earth Council had been covertly established, picking from several of the most powerful remaining nations and funded by several large corporations.

A Pact was agreed, which included the need to stop the further cross contamination of the remaining planet. Rudimentary zones were agreed and sketched onto the globe. It would be divided into the new Northern hemisphere, which was generally the least affected and the southern hemisphere from below Tropic of Capricorn, Below the 24th parallel was largely ravaged beyond a comprehensible restoration point. This wiped-out part of South America, Southern Africa, all of New Zealand and the largest part of Australia.

But where was wiped out? What was the Earth? What pact? And with whom?

Zero zero zero zero.

Those involved in the Pact, also contrived to create the equivalent of firebreaks between the still safe areas and the areas already overrun. It was a brutal decision, because in the contaminated areas the populations were left to fend for themselves. In the non-contaminated areas, RPZs - rapid protection zones were created, and the populations were kept inside under a totalitarian control.

Yes. He could do that. Create a firebreak against the probes. A firewall.

Firewall zero.

Darnell considered that Earth was on permanent planetary lock-down, although most of its residents were accepting of the situation or had moved to the less pleasant environment of the Scratch.

He couldn't remember what a lock-down was for.

Darnell knew he was old. He had seen the Earth Council's Earth Restructuring, the Ganymede programme, and the use of magnetite power to create the Fifth Industrial revolution on Earth.

What was the point?

They had reset his release release release level.

Darnell had no story left.

After what had been the destructive period leading up to the restructuring by the Earth Council, there had been the era known as The Great Stability exploiting magnetite power sources and leveraging the Restructuring.

He was on level Zero.

Reverting to older memories. Archival footage.

Darnell was one of the citizens who remembered the old ways.

Freedom to travel around the globe, a messiness of transport systems, carbon-based fuels in common use. Access to airborne radio transmission.

He also remembered the downsides of the famines, the disease, and the political decline into warfare.

He could feel the stutter now. He was almost de-spooled. Like an old-fashioned movie which had derailed from the projection gate.

Much of the past's history was now only available with restricted access through systems in the Block.

What Block?

Who was that person that had been watching him?

The modus of the new Earth was about looking forward, there were too many bleak lessons in the past. The Carbon Age, as it became known, was about as distant in most people's knowledge as The Stone Age.

Maybe he could cling to the Stone Age.

No, he'd forgotten it.

Zero zero zero zero.

Darnell realised this was a two-edged sword. The good edge meant increased survival for those that had made it to the new zones.

For those that hadn't, it already meant death.

For those in the middle, it meant exile to the Scratch, a world without the material advantages of the Earth Council's dictatorial world, but with the added dimension of a freedom that most conventional citizens could not even imagine.

He could sense the sword. The edge that was facing him. An approaching glittering, sharp, line.

Zero

Hazardous work

A man would have to put his soul at hazard.

He'd have to say,
"Ok, I'll be part of this world".

Tommy Lee Jones - Ed Tom Bell

Lekton elect

Election for the Earth Controller was a democratic process. Through the times of turmoil, it had been changed to a Cabinet process and was now a selection from the Senate of the Earth Council.

The Senate was the governing and advisory assembly set up following the replacement of the United Nations. When countries were abolished, and the remaining Earth was divided into three zones of the so-named Earth Republic following the Klima Wars. During this time, the period of The Great Stability ensued.

Most of the time the Senate was little more than an advisory council, but it also elected new Earth Controllers for each of the three zones. Eurussia, Amerika and Sino-Nihon. They formed the so-called Trinity as a ruling basis for Earth, although the establishment of the Trinity had been a stormy journey.

The last Eurussia leader Lucius Putinus, was overthrown following a coup d'état led by Junius Brutus, who reconstructed the Eurussia area via a violent military dictatorship.

During Early Republic, the Senate was politically weak, while various executive magistrates were powerful. These magistrates were selected by the dominant corporations of Earth, with Torus Industries for Amerika, *AlfaCorporatsiya* (AlfaCorp) for Eurussia and *Kǎxīmǔ gōngyè* (Cassim Gongje) for Sino-Nihon. They were the same corporations with mirror presences on Ganymede.

The transition to constitutional rule was gradual before the Senate was able to assert itself over the corporate magistrates. By this time, the corporates had realised that Amerikan Mafia, Eurussian Bratva clan and Sino-Nihon Yakuza power was the underlying mechanism of rule and law.

After the transition of the Earth Republic into the Earth Principate, the Senate lost much of its political power as well as its prestige. Following the corrupt constitutional reforms of Emperor Donal, the Senate became politically irrelevant. The seat of government was transferred, and the Senate was reduced to a purely municipal body. That decline in status was reinforced when the leader of Ganymede created an additional Senate in Ganymede's headquarters and ran it with diversified power.

Bishop was determined to ensure that Lekton could win the Amerika Earth Controller seat on the Trinity. Bishop was well-connected and had considerable access to the underbelly of illicit law and order. By simple manipulation of the voting tally Bishop could control the outcome of the election and soon enough Lekton was in power as one-third of the Trinity.

Gentle ghost

On Ganymede, Jasmijn felt strangely unsettled.

She considered it was like a gentle ghost was sliding over her body. She had felt this feeling once before.

She realised that the feeling was overriding her newly programmed Generation 7 coding. Now that she had seen the video of herself and Roelof being destroyed and replaced during a Base move, she was more aware of the tightening history and archival process which was installed.

False memories replaced actual memories and the fidelity of the old memories became greater. She was certain that the Artificial Intelligence programming was attempting to mirror human cognisance, including the haphazardness of recall.

But a strong memory reached beyond that. She wondered if it had been programmed into her firmware, or whether it was some kind of machine reaction.

She closed her eyes and concentrated hard on the sensation. She was remembering it now; it was over-riding her hazy recall.

Then it came to her in a jolt.

It was when she had been Occupied. Some presence had briefly converted her from a Prime into an Adapter.

It was a thrill-seeker.

Trying to inhabit her and to manipulate her. Fortunately her Prime anti-malware had kicked in, but only after she had felt the lizard touch of a stalker.

A further bolt and she realised who it was.

Lekton.

She had heard now that Lekton had been promoted to Earth Council and it had triggered her memory of his attempt to Occupy her, several generations earlier.

More importantly, it meant she knew one of Lekton's biggest secrets. That as an Earth-bound presence, he could still reach out as an Occupier all the way to Ganymede. He could spawn an autonomous process which would run 34 minutes behind Earth, collect information of sensations and spool them back to Earth.

Lekton was kinked and powerful. She would need to consider how to use this information carefully.

But the ghost sensation. It was like the way that Lekton had approached her the first time. She wondered how many other 'droids were hit upon in the same way and why Lekton would return.

Jasmijn decided to set a trap.

Lizard hunting

"Hey Roelof?"

"Hey Jasmijn."

"Remember that time I told you about Lekton? You know Mr Creepy?"

"Yeah, Although I'm surprised that the memory has persisted through the Generations"

"Me too, I think it is something to do with our self-preservation layering."

Roelof and Jasmijn had discovered that they could adapt their own programming, after they had tried the mind reading experiments and Roelof had been able upgrade his setting.

Nowadays both Roelof and Jasmijn had played with several other settings and started the quest to understand their individual programming.

"So, something that has been burned into our firmware layers?" asked Roelof.

"Yes," said Jasmijn, "And now I want to exploit it to get back at Lekton. Lekton is making a move on me again. I have felt him testing my systems."

"You could shut that down with the anti-malware nowadays," said Roelof.

"I agree, but I want to capture Lekton. I think I have a way.

"He doesn't realise that when he runs a probe, my own uprated circuits also probe him. I think he has underestimated the technological prowess here on Ganymede. We are one, maybe two cycles ahead of Earth now and accelerating away because we are not limited by the glacial speed of the Sharps."

"So, what did you find out?" asked Roelof.

"Lekton wants to neutralise the Sino-Nihon base here on Ganymede. He is effectively trying to create a wedge against the Yakuza.

"I have an idea. It involves you. We let Lekton know that the Sino-Nihon control can be manipulated by a Prime. Then we introduce you as the candidate. "After all, there's not so many to choose from and you are close to me."

"Then I'll lead Lekton to you. He will think he has a bargain deal, with two Primes ready to run the Sino-Nihon base. If accomplished, he could hold it to ransom or more likely destroy it."

"Hmm, I'm not sure I like where this is going?" said Roelof.

"No exactly; we stop him before any of that happens. If I can lead him to you, we can neutralise him along the way in a Reemer."

"Reemer?" asked Roelof.

"Your memory is going!" said Jasmijn, "Remember when we were on the replacement environmental shifts? We had those big tubs of Earth and plants to process? They came with Biodiversity implants including animals and insects, so that we could establish a diverse hierarchy?"

"Hazily, I remember," said Roelof.

"Well the Reemer was the device used to insulate the biodiversity. To keep it in pens so that we didn't have attacking killer hornets or deadly mosquitoes or anything."

Roelof, "Ah yes, now I remember, the Reemer - anthropogenic radio frequency electro-magnetic radiation (AREMR) Chamber. Like an airlock between the bio-world and the rest of Ganymede."

"Exactly, the Reemer used EMR as a series of killer waves that would disorientate anything small and organic.

"The spin-off effect was that the fast cycles of the EMR also interfered with androids and other fast cycling automatons. Just like fast strobes can affect some humans – triggering epilepsy, these fast cycles would work on all fast cycling insects."

"Okay? But how do we use it then? If it is bad for 'droids then it's not going to be good for you."

"Correct, except I'll wind my clock speed down to something similar to that of the Sharps. 50Hz instead of 3000Hz. That way the EMR won't affect me, although it might take me longer to get back out of its path. You'll have to help me reboot to normal clocking."

Jasmijn produced a small electrokey.

"Here. I've offloaded my Persona to this. When you get me out of the Reemer, reboot me with this image."

Roelof nodded, "Are you sure about this?" he asked.

"Positive. We stop Lekton and I get to even a score. We still must do more because Lekton will only be damaged at that point. We'd need to finish him back on Earth."

"Okay - now we need to wait."

Lizard

The lizard brain only wants to eat and be safe.

The lizard brain will fight to the death if it must but would rather run away. It likes a vendetta and has no trouble getting angry.

The lizard brain cares what everyone else thinks, because status in the tribe is essential to its survival.

A squirrel runs around looking for nuts, hiding from foxes, listening for predators, and watching for other squirrels. The squirrel does this because that is all it can do. All the squirrel has is a lizard brain.

The lizard brain is not merely a concept. It is real, and it is living on the top of your spine, fighting for your survival. But, of course, survival and success are not the same thing.

The lizard brain is the reason you are afraid, the reason you don't do all the art you can, the reason you don't ship when you can. The lizard brain is the source of the resistance."

Seth Godin, Linchpin: Are You Indispensable?

Well acquainted with the velvet touch

Two days later Jasmijn felt it. A velvet touch on her skin which became stronger. She recognised it as another approach by Lekton. She decided to waste no time in thinking about the way that two Primes could take control of the Sino-Nihon base. As she thought through the plan, she could sense the probe pausing and then deciding to hitch a ride to Roelof.

"I'll make a deal with you," she thought, "We go to Roelof, the two of us destroy the Sino-Nihon base and then I'll let you in."

She sensed the probes slacken their intent slightly. They were still there, uncomfortable and primed to pounce, but she knew that Lekton's sub-image had taken the bait.

"You'll need me to take you to Roelof. Otherwise he will suspect something, and you won't get any co-operation. You need both of us for this plan to work. Remember we are Primes. You might be a multi-world occupier, but you can't run Sino-Nihon's control centre."

She walked towards the AREMR Chamber. She would need to reduce her own clock speed as she approached. It would give her the sensation of everything speeding up as she changed her clock speed. Sure enough, her computations allowed for the exact number of steps, the door to open and then a rush as she hit the floor.

"She realised that Lekton was trying to resist the Reemer's electro-magnetic radiation. Lekton was trying to stop Jasmijn from getting fully into the Reemer's force field. Her own reactions were now at the standard clock rate of humans and so she was finding that the entire world had sped up around her.

Fortunately, she could detect that Lekton was starting to be affected by the EMF. The forces were causing Lekton to stutter and jitter. He had phase-locked on to the fast frequencies like a trapped insect and was being brought to a standstill. A few more flickers and then Jasmijn realised that the grip on her body had gone. She was released and Lekton had been eradicated. She knew that if she had been able to see Lekton instead of sense him, that a blue sleep light would now emanate from his form.

"Reboot me," she called to Roelof, who was intrigued to see Jasmijn operating at a Sharp's speed. He stabbed the electrokey into a socket on Jasmijn's hand and uttered the reboot commands. Jasmijn was already on the floor and went into a brief paroxysm before gracefully rebooting. She suddenly rolled over and flipped to her feet.

"Yes!" she said, "It's good to be back. And goodbye Mr Creepy!"

"Now we need to alert the Yakuza to what has been attempted. We should do it here on Ganymede to ensure it gets to them by the fastest path, " said Roelof.

"Okay, we'll use the Ganymede clearcomm then. It'll be all over Ganymede in minutes," said Jasmijn.

They fired the messages across to the Sino-Nihon control post. Sure enough, minutes later they were receiving a greater broadcast of the information.

"Mission accomplished?" asked Roelof.

"Sure thing," said Jasmijn, "Although I could sense that Lekton was trying to tell me something when he was on the way out. It was something about 'beware the apex.' "

Forty-three minutes

The news cycle changed fast. After the news that Jasmijn had damaged Lekton in the middle of a bid to overthrow the Yakuza, another news item emerged.

It was forty-three minutes later.

The news of damage to Lekton's Ganymede presence had reached Earth, and a special meeting of the Trinity convened.

"We are still receiving the news," said Shoji Ihono, head of the Sino-Nihon Base.

She was glowering towards Lekton. Bogdan Victorovich from Eurussia nodded, "The spooling out of data from Ganymede has taken longer than expected. It's as if the clock cycle slowed after the initial data burst. There seems to be only one way to interpret it all, though."

Shoji Ihono nodded in agreement, "Yes, it looks like an attack on the Sino-Nihon base. Planned by Lekton and trying to lure two Amerikan Primes to execute the base destruction."

"I think this would constitute an act of war," said Victorovich.

"We don't need any more wars now, not after the Klima Wars," Said Ihono with a great sadness in her voice, "Lekton, Do you have anything to say?"

Victorovich and Ihono looked towards Lekton. He was quietly sitting in the third chair of the Trinity. They could see he was damaged as a result of the attack planned by Jasmijn.

"Your silence speaks volumes," said Ihono. She raised a hand and Victorovich did likewise. A cylinder descended around Lekton's chair in the Trinity. It started clear and then fogged by a pulse of photochromic cell change. A blue light flickered from inside the chamber. The light moved to a solid blue and then pulsed slowly for a few seconds. The photochromic cells reversed, and they could once again see inside the now empty cylinder.

"Lekton is gone," said Ihono, "Let no-one betray the trust in the Trinity."

"Agreed," said Victorovich.

The head of Sino-Nihon looked at the head of Eurussia. They shook hands.

"We cannot afford traitors in our midst, this should be a warning to Amerika and to Bishop. Now we need to select a new head for Amerika here on Earth Base and a new representative on Ganymede Base.

"We should ask Jasmijn to become head of Trinity Amerika on Ganymede Base."

Ed Adams

Ed Adams

Part Two

Ed Adams

The Great Span

*"I have just drunk the waters of Changsha
And come to eat the food of Wuhan.
Now I am swimming across the great Yangtze,
Looking afar to the open sky of Chu.
Let the wind blow and waves beat,
Better far than idly strolling in a courtyard.*

Today I am at ease."

It was by a stream that the Master said--

'Thus, do things flow away!' "

*Sails move with the wind.
Tortoise and Snake are still.*

Great plans are afoot:

*A bridge will fly to span the north and south,
Turning a deep chasm into a thoroughfare;
Walls of stone will stand upstream to the west*

*To hold back Wushan's clouds and rain
Till a smooth lake rises in the narrow gorges.
The mountain goddess if she is still there
Will marvel at a world so changed."*

Mao Zedong

Journey Planned

After ninety Earth minutes, Jasmijn received another message from Earth. It surprised her, because the turnaround meant it could only have been issued minutes after the news about Lekton reached Earth.

"You know, I don't seem to feel anything about that time with Lekton," said Jasmijn to Roelof.

"It's because of your reprogrammed identity," said Roelof, "You gave me your last mirrored personality for me to reboot you, but it was taken before the entire Lekton experience."

"Of course, I'm getting the information from our Prime pairing together," said Jasmijn, suddenly realising how she seemed to know anything about what had happened, "Maybe the Sharps had an occasional good idea?"

They looked at the console.

"Incoming message," said Roelof, "High priority too,"

They both read it.

"Wow," said Jasmijn, "They want me to become the leader of the Amerika Base here on Ganymede. Incredible."

"You should do it," said Roelof, "At least we'll know what is going on."

"I thought they would give the position to a Sharp?" said Jasmijn.

"Think about it," said Roelof, "If the Sharps have been depleted and most of the base is run by 'droids, then they'd probably need a 'droid to run administration. Imagine a Sharp trying to keep up with all of us running at 60 times the clock rate. Every one of their seconds is one of our minutes. Total overload, like Lekton but on a bigger scale!"

"Yes, I suppose so, and I've still got my loyalty circuits running," said Jasmijn.

"But you could trade a deal," suggested Roelof.

"World Peace, obviously," answered Jasmijn, " I'll say 'yes' but request that the Earth Council renew their loyalty agreements with one another. Oh, and I'll ask for a meeting with Darnell - I want to find out if he knows anything more about what Lekton said."

"Good play," said Roelof.

They constructed a reply and sent it back to Earth. The 34-minute transmission time meant it would be over an hour before they heard any response.

When it arrived, Roelof read it first.

"Bad news first: They killed Darnell. They wanted to extract him - his personality modifications. They sent him to the Earthside Straf and that's where it happened."

"That is so brutal," said Jasmijn, " We had two chances to find out what Lekton meant by apex, but both have now gone. They have eliminated Lekton and Darnell. I can understand that The Trinity wanted Lekton gone after he pulled the stunt against the Sino-Nihon here on Ganymede, but I can't see why they would terminate Darnell. I will need to find out who gave the order and what the chain of command was."

Jasmijn was soon on a call to Earth. It was to the Trinity, to discover the information. Earthside was silent on this. They thought it had been Lekton that had given the order to terminate Darnell. Jasmijn detected a tenuous chain leading back to Bishop and Benedict Cardinal.

"I think there are Earthside plotters beyond anything that we can see from here on Ganymede," she said to Roelof, "I think one of us will need to visit Earth to find out what is happening."

Roelof looked at Jasmijn. They had been paired for several generations now and worked together as two Primes on the Ganymede Base. He knew that Jasmijn or he himself could take the fast route to get Earthside. Faster than the three years taken by Sharps and other normal life forms. They had only become aware of this possibility after they discovered they were androids. They could send their Persona as a data packet and be re-housed as a Presence in a new android Earthside.

Roelof was aware of the challenges. They were both Generation 7, with Artificial Human Intelligence but were Type Gs. They knew how to function on Ganymede, but could be lost on Earth, where they would need Type E specifications. The risky Type H for Hybrid was still a developing machine type.

"Okay, which one of us should go?" said Roelof systematically. He already knew the answer. It would be Jasmijn. She now had extra Earth status and could demand a Type change, however risky. It could be a short visit to Earth, just long enough to determine what Lekton had meant.

Jasmijn looked at Roelof. She could read him and knew he had already processed the outcome.

"I'll go. I'll get a Type E or H modification and be down on

Earth for a matter of days. Then, I will be back to Ganymede. We should make a safe mirror of my Persona too, so that you can reboot me here, instead of waiting for me to be streamed back."

They looked at one another. They knew that two instances of the same Persona would blow the circuits of one or both copies. They would need to be painstakingly careful about Jasmijn's return trip to Ganymede.

"Okay - Let's do this thing," said Jasmijn.

Redbox

Back on Earth, in the Scratch, Feng Jing was looking at the rebooted Hunter. It was as docile as a tame puppy running on its Generation 4 operating system.

"It's incredible to think this thing is a walking bomb," said Feng Jing.

"Something I don't understand," said Sam, " How can the Hunters override their Asimov settings?"

Sam looked across the Hanger. There on the wall hung a placard with the original Asimov Laws of Robotics:

- A robot may not injure a human being or, through inaction, allow a human being to come to harm

- A robot must obey the orders given it by human beings, except where such orders would conflict with the First Law

- A robot must protect its own existence as long as such protection does not conflict with the First or Second Laws

And underneath was the *SK Robot Ethics Charter* - more detailed. Sam gestured to:

Part 2: Rights & Responsibilities of Users/Owners

Sec. 1: Rights and Expectations of Owners and Users

i)   Owners have the right to be able to take control of their robot.

ii)   Owners and users have the right to use of their robot without risk or fear of physical or psychological harm.

iii) Users have the right to security of their personal details and other sensitive information.

iv)   Owners and users have the right to expect a robot to perform any task for which it has been explicitly designed (subject to Section 2 of this Charter).

Sec. 2: Responsibilities of Owners and Users

This Charter recognises the user's right to use a robot in any way they see fit, so long as this use remains 'fair' and 'legal' within the parameters of the law. As such:

i)   A user must not use a robot to commit an illegal act.

ii)   A user must not use a robot in a way that may be construed as causing physical or psychological harm to an individual.

iii) An owner must take 'reasonable precaution' to ensure that their robot does not pose a threat to the safety and well-being of individuals or their property.

Sec. 3: The following acts are an offence:

i)   To deliberately damage or destroy a robot.

ii)   Through gross negligence, to allow a robot to come to harm.

iii)   It is a lesser but nonetheless serious offence to treat a robot in a way which may be construed as deliberately and inordinately abusive.

"Wow, it ignores just about every part of the Laws and the Charter. But how can the Hunters be overridden?" asked Cindy.

Haruto and Feng Jing looked at one another.

"It's the RedBox - they have it fitted, and it can override Asimov. It can't be programmed in, but the hardware in the RedBox completely takes over from the normal Asimov settings," Explained Feng Jing.

"It is supposed to be a military secret," said Haruto, "But inevitably, it would get out."

"Look," He gestured to a small pile of RedBoxes each about the size of a j-plane adjuster.

"Those are some RedBoxes we retired when we took over the Hangar. They partially self-destruct internally when they are removed, but the host device, such as a Hunter is unaffected except that they are once more subject to Asimov and SK Laws. They can't go around blowing up humans or each other once the devices have been removed."

Cindy approached the pile of discarded devices.

"Are they electronic or do they have an organic component as well?" she asked.

Feng Jing replied, "They seem to be purely digital, with a huge number of internal components as well as encryption. As a matter of fact, we hoped some of these would run down. They have internal power stores, but since magnetite they have an infinite lifespan. We think they are some kind of neural network.

"We've also run probes into them, but they are so complex that we can't find the right signals. They respond to digital but in an entirely unpredictable way."

"So, is it difficult to remove them? You have a lot here."

"It is quite simple. You quiesce the 'droid, flip open its maintenance hatch, hook on a keyboard, press a three-button command sequence and the RedBox releases itself. They are tray-mounted internally and simply slide out. You then have to reboot the 'droid though, or it goes into the Stuts, presumably looking for responses from the RedBox."

Haruto nodded in agreement, "Yes, and the resultant 'droid becomes like any other placid device, except that in the case of a Hunter it is still filled with high powered explosive."

"Can we disable the one we've rebooted then?" asked Sam, "Only I'm nervous around it, even with it being reset to the status of a dog walker,"

"Sure," said Feng Jing.

She called the android across, asked it to pause, flipped open its maintenance hatch and attached a keyboard with a curly piece of wire. Then she pressed the command sequence and Sam and Cindy could see a tray slide out containing the RedBox. Feng Jing removed the box and typed a reboot command into the keyboard. The Hunter lolled for a moment and then started its reboot sequence. It was rapidly standing and they could all see that it was returning to a fully functional state.

"Steal this hammer!" commanded Feng Jing,

"I am unable to steal anything nor to perform an illegal act," came the reply.

"Well, that's SK Part 2, Sec 2, (i) being enforced, " said Fang Jing, "It is my simple test that the 'droid won't attempt to break the law."

Keystring

Ganymede's noise reduction was on overdrive. It flattened the sound of speech.

"Look - I know we are both androids," said Roelof, "But we have known one another through five Generations. The Primes Bonding was made strong. You must take care when you get to Earth. Take a Persona key as an emergency precaution. I'll keep one here too."

"I'm one step ahead," said Jasmijn, "I've copied my Persona onto a private drivespace. It means I'm carrying a copy internally."

"Can we make it VAC?" asked Roelof.

"Voice activated - good idea," said Jasmijn, "Just in case."

"What's the keystring?" asked Roelof.

"I'll generate one automatically. Here, It's: 'Palate-Asterisk-Useful-Licence'. You have to say 'Jasmijn trigger reboot," before and then speak the keystring.

Roelof nodded, his own memory would burn in that sequence and then he could re-instate Jasmijn at any time from a voice command. He hoped it would not be necessary.

They touched and Roelof felt the crackle of Jasmijn's T-brain running at an overclocked 4000 Hertz.

"Take care, " he said.

"I will," and she was gone. Beamed across space as a data packet, to arrive 34 minutes later on Earth, where she would be loaded into a provisioned clone of herself.

Faster than Sharps.

Her Ganymede presence stopped. Her eyes lit blue and pulsed slowly.

Jasmijn Earthside

Jasmijn felt the rush as she took over the new Earthside Presence. Her Persona had uploaded cleanly, including her confidential data areas. She could sense that her new Presence was another upgrade. There seemed to be more room to move around and a suppleness about the latest Presence.

Her focus and world orientation re-tuned. She could see she was in a holding area.

"Welcome Jasmijn, you have made the trip from Ganymede in a matter of minutes. Your last few subsystems are reloading now. You are in Earthside Amerika Base. Welcome," Shoji Ihono from Cassim Gongje representing Sino-Nihon introduced herself.

Jasmijn looked around. She felt like a higher fidelity version of herself. More news was drifting in and she felt as if the overclocking she had been using previously was unnecessary now, with the newest generation Presence.

Jasmijn was surprised at her own agility, both mental and physical. She realised that the new body must be a prototype and had high performance characteristics. A generation earlier and she would not have had the perception to be able to identify this, but since Roelof and she had discovered their Generational upgrades, she had been hyper-alert to anything influencing her Persona.

Victorovich from AlfaCorp representing Eurussia was next to introduce himself, " I am Bogdan, Trinity Head of Eurussia. We have heard about the things you did to prevent an unfortunate event from occurring on Ganymede."

A quiet discovery that Jasmijn made was that she was still a Type G. They had not reprogrammed her to be Earthside compatible. It gave her certain advantages; she discovered. She could look through people and see their readouts, displayed like so much telemetry - a function useful on Ganymede and adapted for Earthside.

As well as the obvious readouts of temperature, velocity, clock rate, she could also see a demeanour reading. It varied from hostile to friendly and she decided it could be a useful proxy for those that would be more likely to lie to her.

So far, the Sino-Nihon and the Eurussia representatives had been very open and their demeanour dials were very much toward the friendly end of the spectrum.

Napier spoke next, almost proprietarily, "Jasmijn, I am your Earthside Controller, the head of Amerika Earthside for the Trinity."

She noticed a difference with Napier, who had been installed as a temporary member of the Trinity. By common logic, she would have expected him to be the most friendly, being a representative of Amerika on the Trinity. An ally, but in practice she could see that Napier was running hot and towards the hostile end of the spectrum.

 She ran diagnostics and determined that he had been installed into the Trinity with power but no responsibility. Even his accountability was suspect, and she decided he was a mere placeholder for Bishop and Benedict Cardinal.

It had long seemed obvious to Jasmijn that Benedict Cardinal was a highly articulate chancer and mercenary for neo-liberal

Amerikan corporations.

Managing the Trinity through Napier impressed those of lesser intellectual competence from Bishop onwards, but the damage Cardinal's apparent advice had done was grounded in his theoretical outlook.

Jasmijn's faster clocking brought with it a superior intellect that could see straight through Cardinal's smokescreen chatter about science.

For Bishop to install a career psychopath, and for the counterparts of Napier to privately describe Cardinal as 'that jumped-up oik', might create a sense that he was not winning friends in high places.

Even when a senior official in Trinity's supporting department called Cardinal a 'a mutant virus' and others referred to Cardinal as 'an unelected foul-mouthed oaf', it may seem that the game was up.

Benedict Cardinal has never played by the rules, and now, as Bishop's de facto chief-of-staff, he became perhaps the most powerful unelected political figure Earthside, manipulating events through Bishop, Napier and the Trinity.

Cardinal thus has an exceptional channel to put his ideas into practice.

Jasmijn now had easy access to Cardinal's musings via Bishop and could see his influence for the quackery it was. She rapidly hooked into his published work where he posted extensive ruminations on his reading, enthusiastic reports about breakthroughs in science and pungent contributions to debates, spicing the mix with notably unbuttoned ad hominem sideswipes.

Jasmijn decided that several of these posts had an intrinsic intellectual interest, but, given his current role at the heart of power, they may also yield insights into the thinking of someone whose ideas could soon have consequences for all of Earthside.

Benedict Cardinal was fascinated by ideas – particularly by their beauty and power. In Cardinal's view, the world seems to be largely populated by timid, easily spooked people whom he delighted in unsettling.

Jasmijn realised that Cardinal's firecrackers were assembled from genuine scientific components. Cardinal appeared knowledgeable about an impressive variety of disciplines, and from this eclectic reading attempted to synthesise ideas he believed would transform the way the world is run.

Jasmijn could see that the ideas had been assembled from the equivalent of self-teach books and videos and were desperately strung together to make non-critically assessed new theories.

Cardinal claimed to have an education that started with the biggest questions and problems and sought to understand connections between them. With such synthesis he appeared contemptuous of most politicians, almost all media commentators, and all those administering the Earth and Ganymede bases. He made a mistake in criticising that none of these people really understood statistical modelling, quantum computation and synthetic biology.

Jasmijn realised that she now had super-powers on Earth. The combination of a new generation operating system, artificial human intelligence, fast clocking and a prototype optimised body meant she could easily recognise the duffer turned bluffer that was Cardinal.

Cardinal repeatedly argued that the processes of government needed to include a number of outstanding scientists capable of bringing fundamental science to bear on policy formation, and a general level of scientific and numerical literacy such that MPs, officials, journalists and others can understand basic scientific discoveries and their significance.

She noted that Cardinal was a principally unleveraged human. A history graduate who has turned himself into a numbers man, or at least into a frontman for the numbers people– someone who understands enough of what they do to make the case for its importance to the rest of Earthside. But he personified 'a little knowledge is a dangerous thing.' Cardinal may have said he was happy to be told where he was wrong, although you could not help feeling that he did not want such frankness.

As all this suggested that Cardinal was faux-clever. Intellectual restlessness was one of his hallmarks: his capacity to stretch his mind, to absorb new ideas, to see parallels and analogies that jump across the tracks, was constantly on display, pegged-out with a grandeur ill-fitting the intellectual content.

But Jasmijn had him mapped. He was a Sharp, after all. He was one sixtieth as speedy as she was at thought. Her new Earthside upgrades meant she might even push this further. Her new internal clock did not baulk at 6000 Hz - over 100 times the speed of the humans surrounding her.

With Cardinal, she could see no cultured output, no creativity sparked from the works of philosophy. At times, he flirted with anarchic libertarianism, attracted by a vision of unconstrained individual creativity, but against this was his predilection for central state funding of basic science underpinned with statistical literacy.

If his strength became a weakness, it was that he was stuck in disciplinary silos. Jasmijn realised that you cannot educate someone to be interdisciplinary. You must educate them in particular disciplines, setting up more specific or temporary or opportunistic arrangements for bringing them together and cross-pollinating.

In Cardinal's arrogant thinking, a few philosophers achieved walk-on parts, but on the whole, he seemed to treat modern philosophy, certainly the discipline of academic philosophy, as an irrelevance or an obstruction.

Jasmijn processed her thoughts on Napier and Cardinal in seconds. It surprised her that her processing was as fast as it appeared in this Generation 9 Presence.

"So, you have decided to visit Earthside, to what ends?" asked Napier menacingly.

"I wanted to impart as much of my knowledge as possible. We thwarted a significant plot and I'm offering my inputs to assist with the investigation. By the nature of my light speed travel, I can be on-site here far more quickly than any SkyTrain."

Ihono and Victorovich nodded. "Thank you," said Ihono, "It means a lot to Sino-Nihon that you are prepared to explain the sequence of events."

Victorovich added, "Yes, and it is reassuring to know that on this occasion, Eurussia was not implicated."

"That's right, " said Jasmijn, "It seemed to be led by Lekton, operating for Amerika. However, I don't think this was any form of Amerika plot, more that Lekton was influenced by specific political forces."

"But do you think that the plot has been destroyed by the eradication of Lekton?" asked Ihono.

"That is difficult to say, " answered Jasmijn, "Lekton was certainly ruthless but seemed to act from a very basic and primitive position. If I may say so without sounding arrogant, it did not seem as if Lekton's moves had any finesse about them."

Napier interrupted, "But you are a machine, Jasmijn, I mean your last name is Avtoma, which as we all know is the feminine form of Automat in Russian."

"I didn't know that, actually," said Ihono.

"It's Avtomat," said Victorovich, "with a T on the end. It's just women's names that end in an a - in Russian, that is."

"But why would Jasmijn be Russian named in any case?" asked Ihono, "Isn't Jasmijn a Belgian name?"

"That's right, said Jasmijn, "My back-story is from Belgium, which was a country in Eurussia before the Great Stability. It was once a seat of power but was susceptible to flooding when during the temperature rises the land went exothermic. There were vast escapes of explosive methane killing many people. My story runs that there was a single ship containing Belgians which was lifted past Earth's gravity and sling-shotted towards Jupiter. Of course, I used to believe it, but since my systems have become more self-aware, I now know that it is AHI - Artificial Human Intelligence which has planted those concepts in my system."

Napier tried another swipe at Jasmijn," But surely if you are an artificial entity, we could simply decommission you?"

"You could, but it would not serve your purpose. I am aware of the demise of Kratos, and also of his severe defensive moves. You will know that there is a hierarchy among the machine intelligences and that they will use their command channels to broadcast intelligence to one another. In the case of Kratos, certain steps were taken on his demise and these were forwarded to Lekton. Unfortunately, the unskilled exit of Lekton means that Amerika only has some Secondaries now expected to step up as if they were Primes.

"Remember I am a Prime, as are my cohort. We are clear about re-provisioning and the ways to redirect in case of jeopardy. I can see, Napier, that you are at best a Secondary, and even that is something of a stretch for you. Without your augmented capabilities provided by Bishop and Cardinal, you would be running around in little circles by now. Just admit you are underpowered to serve in the Trinity."

Jasmijn thought at this point that there was little harm in pushing home her argument.

She could also see that both Ihono and Victorovich were in agreement with her sentiments. They clearly had a significantly higher intelligence level that Napier. Jasmijn had all three of them marked down as gangsters, but only two had serious intellect.

Napier relied on the electronic inputs from Bishop, but they were still clocked at Sharp speeds and perhaps only one hundredth as fast as Jasmijn's thought processes. Napier's serialised thinking was his second problem, with him unable to process any sort of creative jump.

In Jasmijn's grasp of gangster parlance, Napier was a hole digger. Point him to a hole and he would simply ask how deep to make it. Unchecked he would keep on digging. Only by resetting him with another task would he stop the previous one.

Cardinal seemed to incorporate more of the intelligence needed for Napier to make progress passed in via Bishop. But Cardinal's approach was still limited and throttled through Bishop.

Although Cardinal expressed a general commitment to including the humanities in his synthesis, in practice aside from history they seemed marginal to his major interests.

However, there was another omission less predictable, yet, in its way, more revealing. Cardinal was silent about jurisprudence and the law. It smacked of 'my way or the highway' rather than any thoughtful review of the impact of law on society. It was amusing that he described mathematical and militaristic OODA (Observe - Orient – Decide - Act) feedback loops but neglected to provide anything similar for common law adoption.

Cardinal ignored accumulated legal reasoning. If it were to

become the great repository of wisdom about the social consequences of allowing this action or preventing that action, and it is, in an important sense, no respecter of persons: no one, as the phrase has it, is above the law.

Except, it would seem, Cardinal.

Jasmijn was concerned that Napier could operate as Cardinal's proxy, oblivious to law and its consequences.

Revolutionaries, 'men of action' and over-confident mavericks of all types always want to sweep the law aside, seeing only its negative character as a slow-moving body of outdated constraints on freedom of action – but that, considered Jasmijn, was why it was so precious.

Cardinal's weak and dated thoughts were from the perspective of someone in a hurry to get things done, never from the perspective of the judge who has been schooled to reflect on the potentially damaging consequences in the future of licensing this particular action in the present.

Nor of unintended consequences. Like this of a Type-G android re-assembling on Earth.

Jasmijn could see her destiny forming. She could see Cardinal only in the near future. Just like the elementary registers of the Real, together with the Imaginary and the Symbolic forming a triad.

She noticed she still had Prime pairing with Roelof, but that now there seemed to be a new option for direct communication, "Hey Roelof, it is interesting here, Earthside..."

Wisdom

"Wisdom consists of knowing how to distinguish the nature of trouble, and in choosing the lesser evil."

Niccolò Machiavelli, The Prince

Mosquitoes

Jasmijn checked her Prime communications with Roelof. It was difficult adjusting to a 34-minute delay after having almost instantaneous communication. She also realised that her new clock speed meant that the time seemed even longer.

She busied herself with running a few more diagnostics and from them soon discovered that it was Ihono that requested that Jasmijn not get converted to an Type-E.

Jasmijn recollected that Type-E females were wish fulfilment objects in the Earth-based patrician society. No wonder Earthside was concerned that Type-Gs could encroach. Ganymede's Type-Gs male and female systems were fundamentally the same. Type-Gs also had their Asimov societal locks removed. Not much point on Ganymede's quasi-military base where instantaneous defence may be a paramount concern.

Jasmijn could see that Earthside 'droids - the Type-Es - had modifications for societal integration. Men on Earth still expected women to be lovers, homemakers, caregivers 'Mama wird sich freuen'. 'Mother will be pleased'.

Jasmin assessed this situation in one second. She was pleased at the speedy uprating she received, which even surprised her.

There was a ping inside her head, and she realised that Roelof was still able to push messages through to her. This time Roelof had sent a new bundle of compressed facts. It amounted to knowledge that Earth's habitable land was still shrinking. It was why Amerika was trying to take over Sino-Nihon.

The drivers for the actions were residual effects from the Klima Wars together with the ever-northward march of the New Delaware bases. The New Delaware control had detected early that the cessation of SkyTrains was likely. The plot by people inside The Scratch to disable the round-trip routing of SkyTrains could have an enormous effect on Earth's future.

She could understand Amerika's clumsy attempt at a land grab. Amerika occupying the Sino-Nihon area would buy time. Enough to reboot the supply lines but callously with less pressure on the available supplies because of population reduction.

Benedict Cardinal seemed to be at the heart of the plan and using Bishop to administer the instructions with Napier installed as the stooge in Earth Council. This had been a ruthless way to grab more territory at the total expense of Sino-Nihon.

Roelof had also sent a suggestion to Jasmijn. It was to use the mosquito-defence on Ganymede-side androids. In other words, to substitute dangerous Type-Gs with docile Type-Es. The mosquito defence was a well-known story from the start of the Klima-Wars, but through unintended consequence it had a deadly ending.

A Torus Industries subsidiary called Genetiq had been testing whether genetically modified (GM) mosquitoes could suppress populations of their natural brethren. These other mosquitoes carried devastating viruses such as Zika and dengue fever.

The Genetiq strategy was to deploy nonbiting male Aedes aegypti mosquitoes bearing a doom gene that should suppress most of their offspring before adulthood.

Jasmijn realised what Roelof was alluding to. A substitution of the Type-E code to make the Ganymede androids docile. They would be controllable and certainly not start trying to destroy life on Earth. With Type-E androids it was even possible to stop them completely with a verbal command sequence:

"Asimov Control &robotname Stop"

But what of any unintended consequences? She remembered the mosquito story.

A team of independent researchers analysed an early trial of Genetiq's technology. They raised an alarm with a report that some offspring of the GM mosquitoes survived and produced offspring that survived to sexual maturity.

As a result, local mosquitoes inherited pieces of the genomes of the GM mosquitoes. At the time, there was no evidence that these hybrids endangered humans more than wild mosquitoes or that they would render Genetiq's strategy ineffective.

"The important thing is something unanticipated happened," said population geneticist Katherine Gibson of Yale University, who did the study with Brazilian researchers.

"When people develop transgenic lines almost all of their information comes from laboratory studies. ... Things don't always work out the way you expect."

The law of unintended consequences was speaking.

The paper's suggestion said the genetic mixing could have made the mosquito population "more robust"—more resistant to insecticides, for example, or more likely to transmit disease. This triggered anti-GM news reports, a backlash from some scientists, and a strong pushback from Genetiq.

The company had a lot at stake; it submitted a new generation of its GM mosquitoes for regulatory review and hoped to conduct its first field test.

Even before Genetiq conducted pilot releases of its altered

mosquitoes in the old countries of Brazil, Malaysia, and the Cayman Islands, it knew the inserted gene wasn't inevitably lethal.

Laboratory tests had shown that when the GM males mated with wild females, roughly 3% of their offspring survived. What wasn't clear was whether those rare offspring, often sickly in the lab, could themselves produce progeny.

To see whether the survivors fared well enough in the wild to spread their DNA, they monitored a large field trial in a Brazilian city. Over three years, Genetiq released 450,000 GM male mosquitoes per week—which the company reported had reduced the overall mosquito population by about 90%.

Genetiq's collaborators collected mosquitoes from several neighbourhoods before, during, and in the three months after the trial. Within these populations, they estimated between 5% and 60% of the insects had some DNA from the Genetiq strain in their genome—as much as 13% of the genome in one case.

Some experts viewed that the mixing of genomes made the population stronger by increasing its genetic variation. The team did not test whether the hybrid mosquitoes were more resistant to pesticides or more likely to transmit disease.

The next stage was proposed Genetiq releases in Florida but this trial faced opposition from residents.

Genetiq's latest strain of GM mosquitoes was designed to spread the lethal gene more effectively.

Instead of killing offspring regardless of sex, it eliminated only the females. Male offspring survived to pass on the lethal gene.

In the Brazilian field trial, these second-generation mosquitoes caused local populations of mosquitoes to dip by as much as 96%.

Then the unintended consequence as Mother Nature fought

back.

The remaining females became more frenzied and would still bite humans. Their doom gene was passed inevitably into the human system and with disastrous consequences.

Mass deaths from a more limited mosquito population.

And so began the Klima Wars.

Ganymede 'droid

In the Hangar in Scratch, Haruto called to Sam and Cindy, "Listen - it's on the comms from the New Delaware Block! They've got hold of a Ganymede 'droid."

Sam and Cindy listened.

"It's Jasmijn!" said Cindy, "We know this 'droid. Sam and I are her Earthside Primes, she is one of the Ganymede Primes we work with. As a matter of fact, we thought she and her partner Roelof were human until recently."

"What is she doing Earthside?" asked Haruto.

Feng Jing was looking at a screen, "She's the one. The one that foiled the Lekton takeover of Sino-Nihon. She has taken a fast route to Earth as a data packet. They have put her into a Generation 9 body."

They listened to more of the intercept.

"I think we should get a message to her," said Sam, "After all, we've known her many years!"

"Yes, we can do it on our Prime channel," answered Cindy.

"Ah, the private channels you all use for inter-Prime

communication," said Feng Jing, " I guess you'll need one of these!" with a flourish she pulled a dust sheet from a device in the corner of the room.

"It's a sensewall!" said Sam, "Only not like one I've seen before. Why is it so thick?"

"It's an old model," answered Feng Jing, "But it still works, and has all the extra comms channels installed,"

"Incredible!" answered Sam, "This is the second time we'll have used some olden day technology - what with that gasoline plane we used to get to the Scratch!"

Feng Jing smiled, "The user interface is exactly like a modern-day unit. I think the only things they have changed are the scaling and resolution. You should be able to work it immediately."

Cindy was already punching a few buttons to reactivate the sensewall.

"Look! I can bring up the Secondaries, and now - wait for it, the Primes!"

"Hold on moment," said Sam, "Can we be traced doing this?"

"Not a chance," answered Feng Jing, "we have dug some deep digital sandpits and put up some high defensive firewalls around this part of the Hangar. And, in any case, I initiate the sensewall as if it is based in New Delaware. That way it doesn't even raise any suspicions."

Cindy was busy with the controls. "Blasted security systems,. I've had to override just about everything. You know how muscle memory kicks in? Well, it isn't working too well here!"

At that moment the sensewall screen cleared. They could see a tall, attractive female.

"That is Jasmijn!" said Cindy, "She looks even hotter than she did on Ganymede!"

Sam coughed, "Oh yes, I see what you mean."

Feng Jing and Haruto looked on.

"So, can you reach her?" asked Feng Jing.

"Jasmijn? Do you copy?" said Cindy.

"Oh yes!" came an instantaneous reply, "I wondered who was probing my upper comms stack. I'm glad it is you. Is Sam there too?"

"Yes, answered Sam, I guess you can't see us?"

"That's right. I've tuned to audio only because I don't want to alert the people here to my extended comms capabilities."

"When will we be able to talk?" asked Sam.

"Tonight, ND time, " answered Jasmijn, " and since you've been able to reach me, I guess I'll be asking for your help!"

Jasmijn's mosquito defence

That evening, Jasmijn made contact with Sam and Cindy.

"Have you checked that no one is able to monitor us?" asked Jasmijn.

"Sure thing," said Feng Jing, "I have run traces on the channels here and I am certain that this is secure."

"Great," said Jasmine, "We can create a plan. We somehow have to get the Type-E code transferred to Ganymede. The code used in Ganymede androids has been adapted so that the overrides do not work."

"In other words, Asimov laws don't apply on Ganymede," said Cindy.

Sam added, "And that is because of the need for Ganymede's defence."

"But surely we can just send a data stream to Ganymede?" Asked Jasmine.

"No - adding the Asimov/SK override on the 'droids here is difficult enough and the RedBoxes that are used to do so self-destruct when they are removed. They are treated as if they were munitions."

"I initially thought we could send a data stream back to Ganymede, but for exactly reason that Redboxes destruct, we will need to ship it inside a Persona. The code is extremely complex and if we attempt to unpack it, it will probably fail to operate. Unfortunately, the host Persona cannot be me."

"Why is that?" asked Cindy.

"It is because the Earth-equipped androids are different between the male and female variants."

Jasmine added, "It is a feature of the patrician Society that the Type-E derivatives are split into two classes. One Type-E makes for a very aggressive fighting soldier, but the other type is a far more passive model."

"It means that if we add the Type-E characteristics to my female persona and then we send it back it will not work."

"Okay," said Cindy, "Then what shall we do?"

"There is only one thing available to us," answered Jasmijn.

"We must use Roelof as the means of transport for the new Type-E code in a male persona."

"Well I guess we can get him to Earthside quite easily?" said Cindy, "Just like you did?"

"Sure thing," said Feng Jing, "I can help you with that data stream transmission. I suppose you will want the whole thing to be clandestine so that New Delaware don't find out what we are doing?"

"Say, you know this reminds me of the mosquito tests that started the Klima Wars?" said Sam.

"We are ahead of you," said Jasmijn.

"Well, I'm not so sure about the law of unintended consequences," said Sam, "Remember how those skeets went rampant and surviving female variants killed many of the population of Old Brazil?"

Cindy agreed, "Yes, it was a major factor in the death of the southern hemisphere. Genetically modified insects that came in three dangerous variants. One bite was enough- it was far more toxic than malaria."

Sam nodded, "Yes I remember. With malaria, the female skeet would bite and inject the host with the Plasmodium parasite. That would migrate to the liver and start multiplying inside red blood cells.

"With the genetically modified skeets, it was as if they had found a way to infiltrate the host with the equivalent of a wrecking ball. The GM invasion was also contagious, unlike malaria, which could only be passed along by mosquitos."

Cindy added, "Yes, so the so-called cure was worse than the disease?"

Sam nodded, "It was, but that's not to underestimate the devastation that mosquito-borne malaria created."

Haruto asked, "But I'm right in thinking that malaria was only prevalent around the tropical regions?"

Cindy added, "Yes, although with the global heating of the Earth, more areas became targets for the diseases."

Sam asked, "Okay, so we need to be sure we are not about to set another wrecking ball into motion with the introduction of Type-E androids to Ganymede?"

Haruto looked at the group, "The thing is, the whole sequence of events has started now. All we can do is attempt to divert it from its current conclusion. If we step aside, we'll see Earth turned into a wasteland because of the ending of the supply of magnetite. The Scratch areas will just get bigger and trumped-up politicians will attempt land-grabs in the name of making their own area great again."

Feng Jing also turned to Sam and Cindy, "Jasmijn's appearance has at least given us some cards to play. Adding in Roelof might just be enough to sway the balance of the situation and to re-instate a safe form of SkyTrain."

"Yes," said Jasmine, "We will need to bring Roelof here with no-one finding out our plans."

"Then we can transmit his Type-E Persona back to Ganymede and start a re-calibration of droids on Ganymede with the Earthside characteristics."

Whoa?" asked Sam, "How can Roelof recalibrate droids with Earthside characteristics?"

"You are forgetting, both Roelof and I are Primes, much like Sam and Cindy. We have unique powers and can inject entire instruction sets into the way that Ganymede operates."

"It means the Type-G androids will have all the traditional SK overrides and be a more docile form of android. It also means that humans and humanoids can control them and if necessary disable them."

"If you can achieve that, it will only be to the Amerika Ganymede Base," said Sam, "We must somehow get agreement to pass the instructions to Eurussia and Sino-Nihon."

"Some diplomacy at the Trinity might be required," said Cindy, "I think I know an android who can provide that," said Cindy.

Anger inside

Jasmijn contacted Roelof. She explained the entire plan in one long message. Then she waited for his response. She assumed it would take around ninety minutes, as a round trip from Earth to Ganymede and back. In seventy minutes, she had the answer from Roelof. She knew he was bound to comply. A Prime, separated from his bonder Prime and with his two known Earthside Primes. It took less than a second for him to agree.

"Will I be able to jump directly to the Amerika Base Earthside?" he asked.

"That is too risky over such distances. It will be better for you first to come here to The Scratch. We can find a suitable temporary body for you and then work out how to upgrade you to the same level of specification as Jasmijn." said Feng Jing.

"I can manage your transfer, but I'm afraid we don't have a very good set of bodies here. You would need to place your Persona in a temporary Hunter until we can find something better. Then we must get you kitted out with a Generation 9. They are much better built that the Generation 8s."

"You know I'm a Generation 7?... but I hope you'll work out a plan for me then?" he asked.

Feng Jing cut across on the communication channel, "Okay,

you know about taking backups before you use data streaming?" asked Feng Jing.

Roelof answered affirmative. After all, he had recently done the whole procedure for Jasmijn.

A few minutes later, the transfer process had started. Jasmijn sensed the disappearance of Roelof's comms signals.

Feng Jing busied herself around the dormant Hunter.

"The Persona data stream has arrived," she said, "I've already started to upload it to the Hunter."

The Hunter's eyes flickered blue, as if it was in the quiesced state.

Jasmijn's voice came across on the Hangar communications,. "I can sense that Roelof is back," she said, "even if the Hunter hasn't woken up yet."

On cue, the Hunter flickered into life.

"Roelof it's you!"

The Hunter replied, "Hi Jasmijn; It doesn't feel like me. I've got a kind of rage under the surface. It's how I imagine some mentally disturbed people feel. But hey, it's good to communicate without the time delay."

Jasmijn replied, "Yes - I expect that anger is the interaction of your Persona with the inbuilt system of the Hunter."

The Hunter said, "I've been trying to shake the anger using different techniques. I've tried relaxation. Taking deep breaths. Repeating a calming word or phrase, such as 'relax' or 'take it easy.' And visualising a relaxing experience. Even yoga to relax this body."

Jasmijn spoke, "I can tell it is you by your thought processes, and it's making my Prime circuits fire up."

Roelof spoke, "I can tell, but I'm having to emulate the Prime circuits in this body. A Hunter isn't equipped to be a Prime, so there is no hardware present. I've had to build a Prime construct to execute on one of this Hunter's main processors. It is working but is slower that I'd like."

Roelof spoke again, "I've tried cognitive restructuring. Expressing rational, rather than irrational, thoughts - That flips the Hunter's more basic logic systems. Like not saying 'always' or 'never' in my thoughts and speech. The Hunter is built on premise of unconditional operation. 'Do as I command' - I guess I'm freaking the gallium arsenide in this unit's processors. And I've tried problem solving by making a plan and checking in with it. And, of course, communicating. But nothing is working. I'm tied to this angry hardware."

Jasmijn was aware that she had received an upgraded and perfect body when she arrived. They had to make do to provide the body for Roelof. "I don't think I can find another body from anywhere. It would be too difficult to bring one into the Scratch."

"Okay, I'll get by, but remember that I'm impaired until I can be put back in a Ganymede Generation 9 Prime unit."

Opportunity

In the midst of chaos, there is also opportunity

Sun Tzu (Art of War)

Steal a body

"First things first, I'd prefer to get a better body," announced Roelof.

"Wouldn't we all," quipped Sam.

"Sorry - I didn't mean it like that," said Roelof, "But this walking explosive Hunter frame is such low tech."

They all heard Jasmijn speak over the comms, "Maybe there is a way," she said, " we are, after all, a collection of four Primes."

Haruto asked," What are you thinking?"

"Well, we dispatched SkyTrains back to Earth on a regular basis. They were filled with magnetite, some newly devised devices and a selection of androids. Some of them were rack-mounts or console-mounts - and not that useful for us, but there would usually be a few standard android Type-Gs included on each shipment.

"They could run errands around the ship and generally had AHI enabled. Once they reached Earth they were expected to be repurposed into Type-Es."

"So, you are thinking that the last shipment or two might have arrived but still have the residual androids on it?" asked Sam.

"Correct, let's face it, the 'droids were never a high priority for offloading or repurposing. Everyone had their eyes on the magnetite and the newly devised rack-mount systems. The Type-Gs were mainly seen as the caretakers for the ship."

"Okay, so how will we even get to a docking station in New Delaware?" asked Cindy.

"I mean, we'd need to liberate the Type-Gs from wherever they are being stored."

"I think there is a way," said Roelof.

"Yes," said Jasmijn, "If we can find an incoming delivery from Ganymede Amerika Base, then Roelof and I can seek the Ganymede-droids, using our Prime powers."

"They may be deactivated at the moment, but we can send the trigger pulses and then send them a set of instructions. Because they have AHI, we can rely on them to improvise as long as they know what is expected of them."

Haruto spoke, "You realise New Delaware is a considerable distance from here?"

Cindy and Sam both nodded, "Yes, we had to use a gasoline plane to fly the first part, then a trike to take us to the Landtrans and then a bullet train to get us here. Unfortunately, the TrikePoint and the bullet train are now deep chasms in the ground since the Hunters were let loose."

"Another plan, then," said Jasmijn, "I noticed that the Trinity were not shy about using status symbols to get around. When I met them, they had all travelled in separate X-Blades to The Base. The roof of The Base had a whole row of X-Blade docking stations."

"I see," said Roelof, running with Jasmijn's idea, "But I doubt whether the Type-Gs will have the necessary skillset to fly X-Blades."

"Think about it, they have been trusted with a huge SkyTrain. Every SkyTrain has several service vehicles on it. What are they? Hum-Exes. What's a Hum-Exe? A bare metal version of the X-Blade. Stripped down and pimped out with some scanners and rail guns. Instead of that, the X-Blades have comfy seats, decent sound systems and full-service bars. I don't think Type-Gs will have too much trouble operating that type of facility."

How to get to the Capitol

"Okay, so how will I get to the The Block?" Asked Roelof.

"Well, you are already set up as a Hunter," Answered Haruto.

"Good point," said Feng Jing.

"Of course," said Cindy, "There's Magazine Rooms full of Hunters at The Block."

Feng Jing said, "I can transmit and remote reboot you into one of the Hunter bodies at the Block."

"We can use the same kind of Persona transfer that got you from Ganymede to The Scratch, but this time we forward you to The Block. As long as I know which Hunter you'll be in, I can address and restart it."

"That's how the Hunters move around so quickly. They have been stored in magazines at Points of Interest and then get restarted when required," said Fang Jing.

"I always wondered that," said Cindy, "I'd heard rumours about Hunter stores, but I've never seen one."

"They just look like regular buildings," answered Haruto, "They don't have big signs on them saying "Danger Live Hunter Bombs""

"Okay then," said Roelof, "You can transfer me to The Block, I'll be in a different Hunter body, but then I can seek a Generation 9 Presence."

"I'd come along as well, except I can't be redirected like you," said Sam.

"We can meet outside the Hunter Magazine and then I can give you directions about where to find the Generation 9s and then how to get to the X-Blades," said Jasmijn.

Roelof could feel that Jasmijn was transferring maps and directions into his system.

"Got it, I'm good to go," he announced.

Feng Jing set up a new transfer on the console, plugged Roelof into the control unit and a few seconds later Roelof was blue lighting. Roelof's old Presence in the Hunter was quiescing and searching for a recharge point.

"Roelof's gone; he should be there by now, the transfer over such short distance should be instantaneous, but the reboot will take a few seconds," announced Feng Jing.

Jasmijn was monitoring her Prime comms circuits.

She smiled, "Yes he's here and functional, says he is looking for the way out of the Magazine store."

Feng Jing announced, " Yes I can trace him too in that new Hunter, Look I'll project a trace of him onto the sensewall."

She did so and they could see Roelof's progress around the Base. He was in an underground storage facility full of Hunters, all of which had been quiesced. Now he was making his way to the core of The Block building and then on to the loading bays.

"It's incredible," he said, "The amount of explosive they have stored here, beyond that which is in individual Hunters. It's a crazy amount."

Outside, he quickly located Jasmijn, who had been waiting patiently. They touched hands and instantly did a full pairing as if they were Two Primes again.

Jasmijn smiled, "Whoa Roelof, you are sluggish today!"

Roelof smiled, "Yes, this is my third Presence today. My Persona is feeling somewhat battered. And these angry Hunters don't make it any easier!"

They re-entered the Magazine. It was tidily arranged, and without the messy area associated with human habitation.

"Robotic, " said Roelof. Jasmijn nodded, "Yes this is way too tidy for humans." They looked around at huge areas stacked with the less valued cargo items from incoming SkyTrains. Entire kitchens, space suits, first aid kits, toolkits, ladders and external grapples. No sign of any magnetite nor of any magnetite devices. They were the valuable cargo and had been moved on. This was the tidily-filled junkyard from incoming fleet.

Soon enough, they found a bay from the last deliveries from Ganymede. As they had predicted, the magnetite had been removed, as had most of the rack-mounted androids, but in a corner were stacked four Generation 9s. Roelof looked through them. Three were profiled as male and one as female.

He looked for the best male, checking its serial number and level of damage. The one he selected seemed to be a much cleaner unit than the others. He realised it had not been pressed into Spaceside service during the flight from Ganymede to Earth.

"That is the best one," agreed Jasmijn looking at the Generation 9, "Wait until your Persona is inside it. You will be amazed."

They restarted it, ran diagnostics, which were so fast that Roelof asked to run them again to be certain, and then clipped his hand to the handshake port on the 'droid. He used the spoken command to transfer his Persona into the 'droid and then had the strange sensation of seeing his prior body still functioning but on autonomous safe mode.

He uncoiled the handshake and issued a command from his new body to the old Hunter body.

"Asimov, Hunter 7245 Quiesce," he said and half-expected his own android to slump, but instead the external Hunter's body quietly and graceful degraded its operation until it was sitting on the floor, next to a wireless charging point.

Roelof was pleased, the exercise had gone well, and he could tell he his Persona was now operating in an almost new very fast super-droid.
"Wow - I see what you mean. Agile and fast and without that Hunter anger! This is so much better."

They were soon in an elevator to the roof.

"Let's find the way to the X-Blades," said Jasmijn, "...See if you can fly them! Look - over there!"

Roelof looked over to Jasmijn. He realised in an instant that she was not going to be with him for the journey.

"No, I must stay here in New Delaware and see if we can get some new agreements from the leaders. You must get back to Ganymede and start the android modifications. This is where, if we were humans, we would hug."

Roelof, smiled again, Smiling was a new sensation for him and he realised that the AHI was even better now he was a Generation 9. It was like Jasmijn had intimated; the whole experience seemed to be in high definition.

Okay, I'll look for an X-Blade, you'll stay in contact though using the Prime channel?"

"You bet! I didn't expect we'd be interplanetary travellers like this, although I wondered what Earthside would be like."

"Me too, although there's an awful lot more Sharps here compared with Ganymede."

Roelof walked across to the first of the X-Blades. He knew he could fly it. The residual Generation 9 code was as strong as it had been in the Hunter model earlier. This time he knew he was pilot-equipped. He stepped out through the door and on to the roof.

Ed Adams

Zero she flies

From the mountain he watches her,
Biding his time
But his eyes are the eyes of an eagle
In the shuddering mad red blood-let sunset
A tired man is leaving his cover
And the soft eyes of zero
Are cut by the sounds
Of the vanishing feet of her lover

Al Stewart

X-Blade

Roelof was immediately aware of a temperature rise as he stepped out onto the roof. Inside had been climate controlled and not dissimilar from Ganymede. The short walk across to an X-Blade was in plain air and he felt the temperature rise to 50 degrees Celsius. Then he noticed an air-scarf on the side of the X-Blade. He punched it and a cool jet of air shot across the space towards him. The X-Blades carried their own climate control units. This was a premier luxury craft.

He accessed the security system and entered the cockpit. He looked around and saw the familiar controls of a Hum-Exe buried under a raft of extra buttons and controls.

"Executive appeal with fingertip reveal," he thought, remembering an old Ganymede advertising slogan. He focussed in on the primary flight controls. API (apogee, perigee, inclination), he thought as he prepared for some orbital mechanics, but then realised he was only making a short straight line flight over a land mass.

He looked around the controls for an autopilot. Sure enough, a large screen in the middle of the cockpit gave him a surface map, contours and flight beacons. He manually scrolled to where he needed to fly and confirmed the position. The screen was still touch sensitive, and he realised this was part of the X-Blade's safety system. No wireless links to go wrong, just a simple touch-screen interface, which was ironic because with his installed smarts his own processors could fly the thing better than the X-Blade's onboard computer.

He let the primitive system take over and pressed the unclip button to free the flight from its floor anchors.

Then he looked for the 'deploy' button, pressed it and the device red-lit until it received a clearance signal from the Base.

In seconds he was airborne. He noticed he was first over a river - which he took to be the Delaware - and then over the Scratch, which he could now see had a vast new-looking canyon driven through it from the hunt for Sam and Cindy.

Roelof wonder whether the X-Blade had any defensive capabilities, but seconds later it started a landing sequence to bring it into the area next to the Hangar.

It gently landed and Roelof taxied it across into the Hangar where he could see Sam, Cindy, Haruto and Feng Jing waiting. They appeared to be clapping - a meaningless gesture towards an android.

He pressed another button and the outer door of the X-Blade opened and he emerged onto the stairway.

"Nice bod!" called Cindy, approving of Roelof's Generation-9 transformation.

He smiled at this. He had chosen what he thought was the best from those available and was feeling the smoothness and sheer power of the Generation 9 re-skinning.

He felt a few blips and realised that Jasmijn was re-establishing close communication contact with him from her location in New Delaware. They were fully re-bonded as Primes.

Autoguide

Jasmijn's immediate mission was to work out where Cardinal and Bishop were based. It was rumoured they were in the Earthside Capitol, which despite extensive external descriptions, was blanked on her Mapper. The security system produced overlay squares on the map for areas it considered sensitive. In prior times there had been too many attempts made to overthrow Capitol's leadership.

She took a tourist guided route to attempt to map it out herself, using her Generation 9 telemetry. She paid for a personal Autoguide and it started to run its program but then hesitated.

"Attention, you are an augmented being. As an android you do not need this tour, please acknowledge for a full refund."

Jasmijn started, "Error, I am not android, I am augmented humanoid. Tour still requested."

The Autoguide sank back on its soft suspension and a small green light could be seen pulsing across its display screen. Then, it sprang up again, "Tour request accepted for augmented humanoid."

The commentary started spoken and written in large letters across the Autoguide, "The Earthside Capitol is the seat of government of Amerika Earthside. Located in downtown New Delaware, Earthside, the structure houses the offices and chambers of the Earthside Legislature and of the Senate of Earthside. The new intelligent building is managed by civil servants, notably Bishop, who has both a physical presence and a digital one. It is rumoured that Bishop is the closest being on Earth to a full Ganymedean-style construct. "

Jasmijn thought of Bishop and the treacherous powers he had unleashed in his attempt to double cross a member of the Trinity. Now she had been in a room with Napier, a Bishop puppet and the other members of the Trinity. She was still amazed that they had not responded to what had happened on Ganymede.

The Autoguide continued. Jasmijn mused that it must be a simple existence, being a one -purpose android instead of general purpose.

The Autoguide's commentary rumbled on, "Designed in 2181, the Capitol was constructed from 2182 to 2188. A \$750 million underground extension was completed in 2193. Most of the building is linked to the various blocks around downtown New Delaware and there have been numerous reconfigurations to take account of the changes to the New Delaware campus structure. A principal link is to the block known simply as The Block, or Block 21. This is the strategic centre of the Earth Council, with agreement from the Sino-Nihon and Eurussian representatives that this single Capitol would be a concentrated seat of power. Other blocks in the area have been designated as Embassies for Sino-Nihon and Eurussia."

"The focal and ceremonial building of the Capitol was added to the National Register of Historic Places in 2270 and recognized as an Earthside Historic Landmark in 2286."

"Excuse me, may I obtain a d-map of the Capitol and the underground areas?" Jasmijn asked the AutoGuide.

Jasmijn had been quietly running telemetry measurements whilst the Autoguide was showing her around. It didn't seem to pick up on this, although she hoped she could convince it that she was only a Sharp+ level of intellect.

"Yes, there is a free pamphlet and a d-map available from inside the gift shop. The gift shop is at the end of the tour," replied the Autoguide, "Construction of the Italian Renaissance Revival–style Capitol was funded by an article of the original state constitution - which precedes the formation of The Earth Council and which authorised the sale of public lands for the purpose."

The AutoGuide continued, "In one of the largest barter transactions of recorded history, the builders known as the Capitol Syndicate, were paid with more than three million acres (12,000 km²) of public land in the Earthside Panhandle. Before the Klima Wars, this became the third largest oilfield in the world."

Jasmijn wondered how long the tour would take. She could see a countdown in the Autoguide's telemetry. It still had another 27 minutes to run.

"The cornerstone for the building was laid on March 2, 2185, Earthside Independence Day, and the building was opened to the public on April 21, 2188, San Jacinto Day, before its completion," continued the AutoGuide.

"Next we see the site of the official dedication of the building. This was by the young Earthside State Senator Wendy Houstoun on May 18, 2188, who, in heavy shoes, lithely and dramatically walked along a row of wine glasses depicting the richness of the Delaware River. This act symbolised the original ownership of the Delaware by the Lenape people. These Lenape were the original residents of the entire area, including New Netherland, New Sweden and West Jersey, all now absorbed within the New Delaware State.

At this point, the Autoguide played a short movie, projected onto wall of an adjacent building. It showed Senator Houstoun dramatically walking on the wine-glasses. Several other tourists stopped to watch the clip, and a couple applauded.

The Autoguide continued, "In 2231, the State of New Delaware enacted a local ordinance limiting the height of new buildings to a maximum of 200 feet (61 m), aiming to preserve the visual pre-eminence of the Capitol.

From that time until the early 2260s, only the University of Earthside Main Building Tower was built higher than the limit, but in 2262, developers announced a new high-rise residential building to be built adjacent to the capitol, called the Westgate Tower. "

Jasmijn was remembering the varied heights of the buildings and mapping a plot in her mind of how the buildings linked and the probability of them having underground components.

She was trying to ascertain the most likely locations in the campus complex for Benedict Cardinal and Bishop.

The Autoguide continued, "The Westgate was followed by even taller structures: first the Spencer Center (designed in 2168), and then a series of ever larger downtown bank towers, culminating in the 790-foot (240 m) One Amerika Center (designed in 2282)."

"Today, the Block and Blocks 23-26 dominate the skyline and additionally have a considerable number of further underground floors."

Jasmijn looked at her original tour map. The areas around Blocks 21-26 were hatched out. There was no indication of routes to or from these buildings.

The Autoguide continued," In early 2283, inspired by the Westgate and these other structures, State Senator Susan Horniman and State Representative Roland Dollis advanced a bill proposing a list of protected "Capitol View Corridors" along which construction would not be permitted, to protect the capitol's visibility from a series of points around New Delaware. "

Jasmijn added the new empty corridors to her own mapping of the structures.

"The bill was signed into law on May 3, 2283, defining 30 state-protected viewing corridors and prohibiting any construction that would intersect one of them. The State of New Delaware adopted similar rules, so that the majority of the corridors were also protected under the municipal zoning code, as well as under state law. These zone corridors became a crucial aspect in the defence of New Delaware during the Klima Wars. It was possible to fire Directed Energy Weapons along any of the corridors, thus ensuring a cost effective take-down of incoming Unmanned Aerial Vehicles (UAVs)"

Jasmijn could see that the zone corridors all emanated from Block 24. It looked as if it could be Block 21, 'The Block', but in practise the corridors were slightly offset. This was a major clue as to the whereabouts of the most senior members of Amerika Earth Council.

In her similar map plotting, she could see that the Capitol's underground structures also seemed to be concentrically arranged around Block 24.

Heart of the sunrise

Lost on a wave and then after
Dream on; on to the heart of the sunrise
Sharp distance
How can the wind with so many around me?
Lost in the city

Lost in their eyes as you hurry by
Counting the broken ties, they decide
Love comes to you and then after
Dream on; on to the heart of the sunrise
Lost on a wave that you're dreaming
Dream on; on to the heart of the sunrise

Jon Anderson / Chris Squire / William Scott Bruford - Yes

Gravity and LIGO

Jasmijn's mapping intrigued her.

As well as the more obvious paths, emanating from the buildings, there were two additional arms of 4 kilometres, in the shape of a letter 'L'. Additionally, she had noticed a weight fluctuation as she crossed over the axis of the L-shaped structure.

Not is much a weight variation, more like a gravitational reduction. She decided to call Roelof for his opinion.

Roelof didn't have any suggestions, but Feng Jing overheard and offered an opinion.

"There was always rumours about a LIGO being created somewhere in New Delaware, although these rumours were strenuously denied.

"Some of us thought that the distractions created by building the 'Capital View Corridors' would conceal the construction. Oh, and the building of the New Delaware Bullet Train network."

"But what is a LIGO?" asked Roelof, initiating a search for it.

Feng Jing answered matter-of-factly, "It's a laser interferometer gravity-wave observatory. It is used for tracking deep space events."

"But why would there be one here, at the Capitol? And even if one had been built, why would it be kept concealed?" asked Roelof.

"That's what we all wondered," answered Haruto, "Especially as its construction could be considered a prestigious project."

Feng Jing announced, "The rumours were that it was a doomsday project, designed to protect the Earth in the case of a cataclysmic event."

Roelof looked confused, "I've just searched for information about LIGOs and it goes on to say that deep space events cannot be tracked by a single scanner. There needs to be at least two for the readings to be cross verified. Ideally the other device should be a long way from the first one."

"But then what would the LIGO track?" asked Sam, who had been listening in on the conversation.

"Gravitational waves," answered Feng Jing, "Literally ripples in space. A gravitational wave is an invisible (yet incredibly fast) ripple in space. Gravitational waves travel at the speed of light (186,000 miles per second). These waves squeeze and stretch anything in their path as they pass by. The LIGO uses a couple of mirrors to detect the changes to a long length of material. The ripple of a gravitational wave will cause the mirror to distort and then a reading can be taken."

Roelof was passing the information back to Jasmijn and was astounded that the two of them could communicate so fast now that they had the Generation 9 upgrades.

"But what are they doing with it?" asked Cindy.

"Reversal," suggested Feng Jing, "Instead of the LIGO being used for capture, it is being used for transmission."

"But this is surely madness?" asks Sam, "No one will be listening for a planetary wave from Earth?"

"Don't count on it," said Jasmijn, "As Feng Jing supposes, these devices could operate as part of Earth's Doomsday system."

Sunrise Accord

Inside The Trinity, Napier was calling the other members together. A large congress had assembled and there was a perimeter of security guards on duty to keep the area secure.

Napier was still the representative for Amerika and would ensure that the other members from Sino-Nihon and Eurussia followed his instruction. He could feel small bubbles inside his head where the probes from Bishop were instructing him to enact Cardinal's will.

He made a statement:

"This is the new sunrise accord.

"There is a necessary change of boundaries, to be implemented immediately in Amerika and to be emulated in Sino-Nihon and Eurussia. These are the instructions.

1. Extend the boundaries of the Scratch. Absorb another 250,000 people into the Scratch. Achieve this by moving the east boundaries from Latitude 39, Longitude 75 to Latitude 39, Longitude 76.
2. To create a high-powered diodic wall which can prevent people from crossing from the Scratch back into New Delaware. To use rectification and clamping

technology to ensure compliance.

3. Police the boundary of the new area with Hunters. Identify anyone who attempt to breach the new boundary and send in a Hunter to disqualify their family unit.

4. Create the division as a clear delineation on the planet. Use a Satellite Ripper to implement the boundary."

The others looked at Napier as if he was mad.

"You can't ask us to do that!" said Shoji Ihono. Bogdan Victorovich nodded in agreement, "They are the warlike acts of a madman," he said, "We have Earth back in equilibrium after the Klima Wars. We are in the era of the Great Stability - these acts will wreck those plans and that status."

"Look," said Napier, increasingly agitated, "We must make our three organisations great again. I want to Make Amerika Great Again. Of course, there will be some casualties along the way, but it is for the greater good."

The other leaders shook their heads and Ihono asked for a vote. "We always kept three of us to keep a balance among the powers. A sensible precaution against any form of crazy action," said Victorovich.

Several second-level congress staff looked around, worried at the turn of events. Napier's tone rose even further," Don't you see, you are on my ground here, you are in Amerika, represented by Torus Industries. You don't really have choice in this matter."

He gestured to a couple of the security guards who had been quietly standing around the perimeter.

"Seize them," he demanded. The guards moved forward.

"This is outrageous- you know this will cause a diplomatic incident and provoke retaliation," said Victorovich as he was being hustled away.

Ihono added, "Please, you still have time to reconsider. I beg you, don't restart the Klima Wars. It will finish off the planet."

Napier watched as the two heads of Earth Council were pushed away.

"I will Make Amerika Great Again," he said, but then he noticed more of the guards closing in on him.

"What are you doing?" Napier asked,

"Napier - your task is done," he could hear inside his head. He realised that Bishop was talking to him.

"You have served your purpose. Now you have a choice: be unspooled and loaded into a Persona, or reach your mortal conclusion."

Napier realised that he would either be killed or offloaded into an android. He assumed that was what was also happening to Victorovich and Ihono.

"You give me no real choice." he said.

"Good," said Bishop, "It will be useful to still have you around in a Presence."

The guards marched him away, to join the other Trinity leaders and to be reprocessed.

Cardinal spoke to Bishop "This is good, we have achieved our immediate goal. The takeover of Earth by Amerika. I can envisage some push-back from Eurussia and Sino-Nihon, but the more they attempt to resist this plan, the worse their position becomes. "In the meantime, I will want us to enact the new Sunrise Accord.

"To do this we will use a Satellite Ripper to mark the Earth along the new boundary. Satellite Ripper is a sky-borne Directed Energy Weapon that is based upon the original Marauder Plasma designs. They are normally used for mining in Ganymede, but Earthside they can tear a boundary of 1 Km width into any land surface."

Cardinal continued, "Then to enforce the boundary we will use an Active Denial System. The ADS can direct a high-powered beam of 95 GHz waves. This ADS millimetre wave energy works on a similar principle as a microwave oven, exciting the water and fat molecules in human skin, instantly heating them via dielectric heating.

"The ADS's effect of repelling humans occurs at slightly higher than 44 °C (111 °F), though first-degree burns occur at about 51 °C (124 °F), and second-degree burns occur at about 58 °C (136 °F). This is like us building a highly efficient technological wall to keep people on their designated sides of the wall.

"If we think of it as the Sunrise Wall, then it will restore integrity and the rule of law to our borders. When implemented, it will be a very effective weapon against drugs and crime.

Cardinal continued, "As perimeter defences, these systems may be harsh, but they will do the job. Containment. We need to be sure that once people are designated as inside the Scratch, they stay there. And the people of The Scratch cannot get in.

"This should have been done by all Earth Council that preceded me, and they all know it. Some of them have told me that we should have done it. This barrier defence is absolutely critical to border security. It's also what our professionals at the border want and need. This is just common sense."

DAARQ

Jasmijn heard about the new Sunrise Accord on her walk surveying the Capitol. The Autoguide had briefly stopped its tour and presented a newsflash. Jasmijn looked at the Autoguide's countdown timer. 01 minute and 12 seconds to go.

"Thank you, I've seen enough," she said.

"Don't forget to visit the shop and to pick up one of those d-guides," it answered, "Thank you for being such a pleasant companion on this guided tour, Autoguide CP022 signing off." Jasmijn watched as it picked a route back to where fresh tourists arrived for their tours of the Capitol.

Across in the Scratch, Cindy, Sam, Haruto, Feng Jing and Roelof were watching the same broadcast that Jasmijn had just seen on their illegal channel provided by the sensewall.

"My god," said Sam, "Bishop has lost it. These are the ravings of a madman. I guess we are now tapping into Cardinal's direct thoughts relayed via Bishop?"

"Agreed, " said Feng Jing, "But we need to find out the reaction from the other Trinity members."

"The members that have been banished," said Roelof, "I'm sure that Ihono and Victorovich have been captured and are now to be respooled into new Persona."

I can usually tap into the Sino-Nihon and Eurussian channels too," said Feng Jing, "Let me take a look for their reaction."

"How is this even possible?" asked Sam, "Surely they are most secure?"

Feng Jing answered, "Yes, they are, but The Scratch is something of a blind spot. Because we still use older technologies, including some analogue ones, we have a major advantage. Everyone's uprated technology is all geared towards DAARQ and similar technologies. Distributed, Artificial Intelligence, Augmented Reality and Quantum computing. Some of the basics were left at the gatepost. The new systems will monitor for sophisticated intrusion detection, but they sometimes forget that someone could leave a key underneath a flowerpot by the entrance to their fortified castle.

"All we did (that's The Resistance during the Klima Wars), was drop some of those entry points into the complex code being developed. If you know the right words, a bit like 'open sesame' then the flowerpots give way and the keys become visible."

"Ah, so you have secret ways into their systems?" asked Cindy, "Through trapdoors that some of your own agents planted?"

"Exactly," said Feng Jing, "Although a few have been discovered and are being patched up. Fortunately, once we are inside, we can add a few more to the entrances that already exist."

"Look, let me show you," she tapped into a control and then pushed the image to the sensewall.

There was a scene which immediately looked like a Grand Master painting, except that it was fully animated. It showed the Sino-Nihon Senate, discussing actions in Cassim Gongje.

"We will deploy Yakuza, to regain our seat in the Trinity. No-one can push us around like this. We must deploy immediately and show no mercy in our retaliation."

Feng Jing looked at Haruto, "Here they go again," she said, "They don't realise that 'droids give them more intelligence than humans."

Roelof watched the sensewall, "Can you get similar information from Eurussia?" he asked. Roelof was having to learn about Earth quickly.

"Sure, " said Feng Jing, and as she spoke she tapped something into the control panel and a different scene emerged. Sleeker and cleaner looking than the Sino-Nihon, as if someone had used a good designer to provide the lighting.

"...resurrect NATO and other military wings. Plus, we can deploy the Bratva to support us in the fight to regain our control. I guess that Bogdan Victorovich and Shoji Ihono have already been either killed or had their Personas extracted by now."

"This requires the firmest of forces and for us to reassert our alliance with Sino-Nihon"

"Yes, but won't that re-trigger the Klima Wars? We have been operating with the Great Stability for so long now!"

Roelof was relaying the sensewall back to Jasmijn in New Delaware.

Jasmijn considered the situation and then spoke, "I think we can harness this situation and bring it around," she said.

"How?" asked Cindy.

The blind optimist

Jasmijn spoke again,

"We should be able to use the combined forces of the Bratva and the Yakuza to trap Cardinal and Bishop. On Ganymede we had a finely tuned equilibrium between the three major forces. It was never perfect, but we all managed to get along and it was in everyone's interests to support the others."

Roelof added, "Yes, it was like a form of the Prisoner's dilemma. The three-player version. One condition is that the players' strategy must be nice, and that no player will defect before its opponent does (sometimes referred to as an 'optimistic' algorithm). Almost all top-scoring strategies were nice; so, a purely selfish strategy will not cheat on its opponent, for purely self-interested reasons.

"Now Bishop lacks creative intelligence. He runs game theory badly, so he has dropped to - at best- playing like a blind optimist. That means he has become retaliatory. This is a very bad choice, and nasty strategies will be dealt with ruthlessly by nice players.

"But the other two players cannot now be successful with a forgiving strategy. Though players will retaliate, they will once again fall back to co-operation if their joint opponent does not continue to defect.

"And revenge must be served cold. The opponents need to be non-envious, that is not striving to score more than the original defector."

"That's a good game-theory summary of co-operative evolution," said Jasmijn. "We must ensure that Yakuza and Bratva combine, as they would do on Ganymede, to thwart any scheme of Bishop. Here's what I have in mind."

PART THREE

Apex

Without sharks, you take away the apex predator of the ocean, and you destroy the entire food chain.

Peter Benchley, Jaws

Kratos Trigger

Jasmijn was still communicating via the sensewall.

"The Primes were originally set up to run the mining operations on Ganymede. On Earth, Primes like Sam and Cindy were set up to provide oversight for the Ganymedean Primes. That's how the tuples for Ganymede and Earth were arranged. As dyads. Roelof and I. Sam and Cindy. Then our Secondaries. But the information provided to the Primes in Ganymede outstripped anything that the Primes on Earth would have.

"We were given access to the control channels of every worker on Ganymede. We had links to the other Primes, we had the links to our Secondaries. It means we have the power to reprogram all the androids on Ganymede, and to cross verify changes with the other two bases. At no stage did anyone step across the line from co-operation with everyone else. Everyone knew that the stakes were too high."

"Now we must use the same powers here on Earth, although we can see that there has been considerably more information hiding. For example, the backup Primes do not know about the main controlling set. So, the role of Sam and Cindy as Controlling Primes isn't recognised.

"Now, added to the Primes having cross-communication, they are also tapped into other major systems. It means we can identify when a boundary condition is reached."

Haruto looked confused, "boundary condition?"

Jasmijn answered, "Yes the conditions that create triggers for other events."

Feng Jing asked, "Is that what the LIGO was about? - A condition?"

Jasmijn answered, "That's what I wondered, but I think the LIGO is watching for a certain condition here on Earth. It is part of the DAARQ constructs.

We Primes have all been instructed with information about Earth having a Doomsday Mechanism."

"Doomsday - it is all sounding quite bleak," said Haruto, "Even worse than the way The Scratch is portrayed back in New Delaware."

"I see," said Cindy, "When we were taught at IPX about the rising temperature of the Earth, there was also gossip about a Doomsday mechanism. It was supposed to keep checking that the condition of Earth was still viable. If it detected a problem three times in a row, it would invoke the apex."

"The apex?" asked Haruto.

Roelof answered, "Yes, there's a set of conditions that re-establishes a dominant strain on Earth, on a kind of 'if all else fails' basis. And the twist is the apex will function against both humans and androids, until it has reasserted an equilibrium that ensures the continuation of Earth.

"What, like a bug or virus that takes over?" asked Haruto.

Feng Jing replied, "Exactly, it is supposed to be an Earth countermeasure if the planet is attacked or a new war is creating mutually assured destruction."

Jasmijn interrupted, "But wait, that was what happened when the space freighter you sent aimed its thrusters at The Block. Kratos was Earth Controller and had been helping maintain equilibrium but was destroyed. Any Primes will have received a message that Kratos was sending its RNA into other organisms. The mRNA messenger strands are effectively the program to rebuild an operational Kratos."

"But then there would need to be the second trigger?" asked Sam.

"Correct," said Jasmijn, "That explains the LIGO. It is listening for the end of the world, so that it can be triggered as a one-time event."

"And now the idiot Bishop has brought forward destruction of Earth, by triggering the LIGO condition.

"In turn, the LIGO has recognised that the normally expected pulse from Kratos has gone missing and so it is preparing for a giant reboot - to release a reassembled Kratos as an apex predator capable of driving both human and digital infections.

Apex

Jasmijn knew, and so did Roelof. They were not sure how, but it was in their memories, somehow lodged as a piece of their archive.

Upon the destruction of Kratos by the space freighter, Kratos had created a new viral exploit. It knew that viruses would blindly explore ecological niches through differentiation.

Jasmijn was aware that the Kratos Virus was still on Earth. She could somehow detect it in her Prime systems. So could Roelof. Neither of them knew how, and it didn't seem to trigger in the human Primes, so Sam and Cindy were oblivious to Kratos.

Jasmijn and Roelof knew that the Kratos Virus would be successful once it found a winning combination in its niche — to successfully reproduce and send itself without killing its host organism in too many cases, or too fast. But that was not what made it so dangerous.

Kratos Virus adapted to human bodies, but as importantly to social and economic structures.

This adaptation lead to its spread across the globe and was why Sam and Cindy were unaware of Kratos.

Each viral iteration got the right mix of contagion with the right cadence of incubation and the perfect mortality rate at the right point in its infection lifecycle, to rip through the world, traversing the social and economic structures.

It could travel between landmasses infecting travellers, before they, as carriers, even knew they were infected. It was highly contagious, doubling in spread every 3–4 days. It was invisible in statistics without massive testing until limited mortalities start to show up weeks later.

The infection delay tricked people by not allowing them to connect their activities with the consequences through cause and effect — unless they operated based on protocols and an understanding of the maths. This was counter-intuitive for humans — both for governments, and for individuals.

Earthside wanted to disrupt its adaptation to its ecological niche by changing the biological conditions via anti-viral drugs and vaccines. But Earthside needed to disrupt the niche by changing the social and economic conditions that the Kratos Virus had adapted toward.

Kratos Virus was distilled to land in a blind spot where humanity could not project its future effect intuitively and connect that with their current activities.

It meant that the Kratos Virus had already multiplied throughout humanity but had not recombined into its main and super-virulent form. It was an efficient stalker, waiting for a signal that the Earth was in jeopardy.

The original destruction of Kratos was like a black swan event. But now, Earthside was not the same after its defensive spread. The past was no longer an indicator of the future. A recombined Kratos Virus would become an ultimate destroyer, chillingly only as a side-effect of wanting to rebuild itself by recombining six of the 52 originally spawned viral constructs.

And Kratos reconstruction as an apex predator was only triggered by world-end conditions.

The ones that would be detected by the LIGO.

Marquee

Jasmijn was hypervigilant. She was not sure, but she thought it was an effect of being rehoused in a Generation 9 Presence. As a Type-G, with Artificial Human Intelligence, plus all her gained experience from Ganymede, she felt as if she had gained superpowers. She realised that it was the same for Roelof now that he was in a Generation 9. It was as if the Type-G Presence had been super-engineered for Primes.

Jasmijn realised that she could now operate in a way similar to Lekton. She had the ability to seek out another 'droid and to probe its operating system.

Both she and Roelof had routinely done this when on Ganymede, but it had been a natural part of their operating process and was usually built into a specific workflow.

But neither she, nor Roelof, had been self-aware and it was only since the last couple of upgrades that they had triggered into this added state verging on sentience.

She asked Roelof, "Can you sense Cardinal too?"

"I can," said Roelof, "I think it is because he is the closest to us in terms of sheer processing capacity."

"Okay, well we will need to find a way to attract him to us," said Jasmijn, "I will approach both the Bratva and the Yakuza to assist us."

"We will need a location and a method to stall Cardinal. It should have the effect of slowing Bishop too," said Roelof.

"Can we send a message?" asked Jasmijn, " I mean not to Cardinal, but to the other two Trinity members?"

Roelof looked around the Hangar. Sam and Cindy had been listening.

Sam spoke, "I know you guys, Roelof and Jasmijn, were under our orders when you were on Ganymede, but this is a whole different thing now you are here Earthside. Your powers far outstrip ours and we were a pretty big deal as Primes here on Earth," said Sam.

Cindy called to Haruto, "Yes but we still know more about how the Earthside operates. Haruto, can you rig up some sort of a link to the Trinity?"

Haruto called over to Feng Jing. She nodded, "You don't want the link to go to all of The Trinity, just to two of the members," she said, "Now that Cardinal has done away with Shoji Ihono from Sino-Nihon and Rykov Victorovich from Eurussia, then the Yakuza and Bratva will be looking for any means of retaliation.

Feng Jing looked at Haruto, "We could use a Tesla Field to trap Bishop. We can use it as a diversion whilst we neutralise Cardinal. We'll need the help and support from the other two Trinity members though. With such an analogue device, we can focus and transmit electricity wirelessly into Bishop's system. We would be building a system that converts a low voltage to a high voltage and simultaneously turns itself on and off very quickly.

"A few volts of electricity are passed to one side of a coil of wire to a grounded capacitor connected to the negative side of the power supply. We have all the parts here in the Hangar.

"The other side of the coil is connected to the collector of a transistor. When connected to a power source, the capacitor begins to charge while the coil begins to radiate an electromagnetic field.

"This coil is then placed around a second coil with many more windings of a smaller gauge wire which creates a transformer, converting a low input voltage to an extremely high voltage in the second coil. This secondary coil connects to both a resistor connected to the power source and the base of the transistor, which then shuts off the flow of current to the first primary coil. Think of it like a giant very fast switching device.

"The circuit configuration creates a feedback loop that automatically turns on and off hundreds of times per second, creating a high voltage, high frequency electric field capable of transmitting wireless electricity.

"It's like harnessing lightning.

"By rigging this up to a couple of magnetite generators, we can deliver a significant controllable punch into Bishop. Just don't be around if you are a 'droid when this thing goes off."

"Unlike normal Tesla demonstrations, where the generated spark flies around uncontrolled like so much lightning, we'll have control over its direction. The other component, the Field, is like a wire mesh suspended in the air. We need Bishop to be inside of the mesh, then we activate and focus it," Feng Jing looked pleased with her explanation.

"I see," said Jasmijn, and because the technology is hybrid, including a mixture of ancient yet reliable Nikola Tesla technology powered by modern magnetite, then it is unlikely to be detected."

"Correct," said Haruto, "That is what we, here in the Scratch, have become experts in. The use of hybrid technologies."

"Think of the Tesla field as like a giant electronic fishing net," said Feng Jing, "When we switch it on, any of the right type of fish will be caught immediately in its field."

"We'll need to have a structure that Bishop will enter, such that we can start a Tesla Field," said Feng Jing.

"That's where I can come in," said Jasmijn, "I can ask the two Trinity players to offer a summit at a specific location away from the Block."

"The obvious point is to have the summit at the boundary of the new area defined by New Delaware in the Sunrise Accord," said Feng Jing, "Look, I followed the line along. The old boundary was on an area known historically as the Mason-Dixon line. The new boundary will shift slightly north and to the east."

"That could be enough to trip the Kratos apex, in other words, to trip the Earth's self defence mechanism," said Roelof.

"I've found the co-ordinates. They are at a place called Edison Park. She projected an image of Edison Park onto the sensewall.

"It's an old area, that was once a national park. Before that it was a technology centre for ancient analogue batteries and motionware," said Feng Jing, " It seems like a particularly fitting place to run this experiment. Look, there is a monument at around the global co-ordinates. We can use it as a focal point."

They looked at the sensewall. Feng Jing had also overlaid a map of the area. Roelof could see it was an ideal fit for their planned action.

Roelof said, "The other thing we will need to do is invite the members of the Trinity to the location. We need to lure Bishop. We can imply that they will want to return to power."

"That can be in a message from me," said Jasmijn, "The Trinity have already met me and must know that I am trustworthy because of how I stalled the plot to takeover Ganymede."

Harutu answered, "Yes, but this is a whole different deal. You'll be dealing with the gangsters. They may look as if they represent the Trinity, but they are mainly in it for self-interest."

"You forget that Roelof and I worked on Ganymede," smiled Jasmijn, "It was a corrupt power base. Only an equilibrium between the three powers kept everything running. It was a balanced game and we all - the Primes that is - we all learnt how to deal with one another without crossing any lines. I'm sure I can use the same skill set here Earthside."

"Okay," said Haruto. He looked towards Roelof.

Roelof spoke, "Jasmijn is right, Ganymede was entirely corrupt. The Russians brought the first mood changers - alcohol and soft drugs. Then the Yakuza cranked things up with amphetamines and other harder drugs. Both groups ran gambling too. Amerika wasn't immune either. We majored in vices for the miners, at least when there were humans and humanoids present. It moved into protectionism and money laundering later. Most of the interested assets wanted to make as much money as possible. It even meant that we were handling off-world investors, anxious to launder currencies. The advantage of the round-trip radio speeds was that just about anything could be laundered in a couple of hours."

Haruto sighed, "It is still as corrupt as the olden days, then. We might expect that humanity would learn some lessons from the sheer devastation of the planet which occurred in the Klima Wars and the period preceding them."

Roelof replied, "You'll remember that our archives are mainly based upon Ganymedean history. We know less of the Earth, except the 'capital letter' facts, like plagues, overheating, carbon dioxide, methane, atmospheric depletion and then senseless Klima Wars. Around 200 countries reduced to three super-nations controlled by corporations. In turn, the SuperCorps were run by gangsters."

Haruto replied, "That's an excellent summary, you only left out that there are still the outliers. That is the people who live outside of the main systems, in The Scratch. Maybe it is 25% of the remaining population of Earth."

"Interesting," said Jasmijn, "So we get something like the world divided into four pieces, instead of three? This could be a factor in the call to the summit."

Roelof nodded and Feng Jing looked excited," I see," she said, "We can invite the three Superpowers to a summit at Edison Park, which is about to be converted to Scratch because of the Sunrise Accord boundary re-alignment. We can also allude to the Doomsday effect of the LIGO monitoring. That the Kratos Virus is about to be triggered."

"That's right," said Roelof, "And Bishop will definitely know about Kratos and the safeguards to Earth."

"Okay, so we get the three SuperCorp to attend a summit at Edison Park and then invoke the Tesla Field to trap Bishop. It will be so much easier to engineer this with the co-operation of Bratva and Yakuza."

"Let me worry about that," said Jasmijn, "I can use my Ganymede contacts to ensure that this works effectively."

"But what about the Tesla Field?" asked Haruto.

"I'll construct a special meeting place. Not inside a conventional building. A canvas structure built with guy ropes."

"What, like a marquee?" asked Haruto.

"Exactly," said Feng Jing, "But with a difference. The ropes will be metal cables. We will be able to energise the cables to create the Tesla Field."

"That will make an immense field," said Haruto, "Capable of wiping out any electronic forms contained within it."

"Precisely," said Feng Jing, "But not damaging any human or humanoids present."

"You must use my compute capabilities to design and build the structure," volunteered Roelof.

"But how do we contact Bratva and Yakuza?" asked Roelof.

"You can leave that to me," answered Feng Jing, "I will need to be able to quote Jasmijn to do so, but it is possible." Roelof could see Feng Jing was busy operating the analogue console.

Haruto nodded towards Sam and Cindy, "Yes, we have comms that can penetrate into the Earthside base. We can set a message there which can be from Jasmijn and designed to create the Summit."

Galois

Galois's papers were annotated and posthumously published in 1846. These ideas and conjectures were built upon and refined by fellow mathematicians Joseph Liouville and Camille Jordan and have gone on to form the basis of group theory, finally bringing the brilliance of Evariste Galois to light.

Modern particle physics would not exist without group theory; in fact, group theory predicted the existence of many elementary particles before they were found experimentally.

Galois redux

Bishop had used significant processing power when handling the recent situations at The Trinity. Now he had received a request to attend a new Summit at an area close to The Scratch. He had checked, and it was the exact edge of the new boundary from realigning New Delaware and The Scratch.

Bishop was slightly troubled by the recent turn of events. Since his disposal of Shoji Ihono and Bogdan Victorovich, he had awoken the leadership of the two main Corporations. AlfaCorp and Cassim Gongje would likely invoke their gangster powers. He knew that the Bratva and Yakuza would seek to destroy him now and needed to take all precautions.

However, the emergence of The Scratch as a new power had blind-sided him and he knew that he would need to take the event seriously. His 'droid circuits were also telling him that something was amiss with the new move of the boundary.

The recently issued Sunrise Accord appeared to have triggered something built into the Earthside protective measures.

A DAARQ process was in danger of being activated and he knew from within his archives that if it started the reconstruction of Kratos, then it would be 'game over'. He knew that Kratos would become the apex predator of Earth, as a self-protective measure, destroying anything that could threaten Earth's existence.

This was one time when Bishop needed to be able to think clearly and he now found that the slow speed of his Sharp master Cardinal was interfering with his clear thought processes.

He would need to insulate himself from Cardinal for attendance at the Summit. He would advise Cardinal to monitor the event to support him, but tell him that they needed to be 'disconnected' whilst he, Bishop, was at the Summit.

Since the brutal events at The Trinity, Bishop had been limited in his choice of external Presences. He was normally able to occupy a wide selection of external Presences, but now he could feel that a Prime somewhere was blocking his access. He searched around and found the recently used Presence occupied by the now-terminated Darnell.

Bishop was now occupying Évariste Galois, the persona of a brilliant 20 year-old mathematician, duped by Stéphanie-Félicie Poterin into duelling with military officer Pescheux d'Herbinville as part of a political manoeuvre.

Bishop didn't care that he was using a Darnell discard. He sighed as he felt the shackles of Cardinal's presence lift. He was free again.

He could see Darnell's and now his dilemma though, that the Persona he occupied was time limited and wouldn't see his 21st birthday, being flamed out by Poterin. He hoped there was enough mileage left on Galois for attendance at the Summit.

Bishop was faced with the task of getting across the distance of the Scratch to Edison Park. He downloaded a significant war-chest of payment credits.

Game Theory

Jane Thoroughgood – The Mainhattenite

It has been reported by sources close to the Capitol that the Earth Council's advisor, Benedict Cardinal, is a fan of game theory.

And so goes the speculation is that he is applying some of its main principles and insights to inform the actions taken – and strategies adopted – by Bishop as the Earth jolts and lurches towards a further era of Great Stability.

But is Cardinal "playing the game" correctly?

One fundamental principle of game theory is that you know what the game is in the first place. You must know who the players are, what their objectives are, and the potential actions they have at their disposal.

So where does that leave us on The Great Stability? In the recent negotiations, it would be reasonable to identify the Trinity as the main players. As such, under game theory, everything Bishop has done since becoming Earth Council advisor to Napier is formulated with the rest of The Trinity in mind as the other players.

The most critical action, to seek to take control of The Trinity is part of a strategy to establish 'credibility' for Bishop's 'do or die' pledge to maintain The Great Stability . This was aimed at persuading the other players of the game – Sino-Nihon and Eurussia – to make concessions and give Amerika a 'better', or at least different, deal.

However, there has been one clear oversight in the Cardinal strategy.

In promoting a 'do-or-die' pledge to control the Trinity, Bishop and Cardinal did not sufficiently recognise that the other key players of the Trinity are highly leveraged global corporations, who agreed to a long-time truce.

It is all very well playing the most cunning game of 4D chess, but you start to look foolish if you didn't realise a third player was entirely likely to start moving your pieces for you.

These Corporations are definitively crucial players after their successful move to thwart Bishop's ability to carry out his 'do or die' pledge – at least in its current form.

Game theory is as much about empathy as it is strategy, and it is crucial to understand what drives your 'opponent'.

Strategic reasoning – as emphasised and developed in game theory – is about putting oneself in the shoes of the other players in the game being played. That is, before deciding on what actions to take, and before selecting one's strategy, it is critical to first think through how other players in the game would react to the varied actions that one could choose from.

It is this 'what if' style of reasoning that lies at the heart of game theory: determining the 'what if', as if you were the other player.

One recent example which has shown a lack of strategic reasoning from Bishop and Cardinal is their attempt to take over The Trinity.

The failure to recognise that pressured Corporations would act decisively, intensely and very likely successfully is a failure to appreciate this second fundamental principle of game theory: as in physics, any action will invite a reaction.

Not only were Corporations missed as key players; their capacity for disruptive action was also misjudged.

The need to anticipate the different and responsive moves of players, before they have happened, and then make decisions informed by such a 'what if' analysis, lies at the heart of game theory. It is known as the 'look forward and reason backward' principle. And was sadly lacking in Cardinal's insights. To succeed in the game, Bishop and Cardinal must be able to look ahead to all possible future outcomes – and use this foresight to establish the most suitable immediate choice.

This is something that Cardinal is incapable of, and the smarts of the semi machine-based Bishop cannot compensate for this deficiency.

Instead, it is like cars playing 'chicken': two people drive towards each other and one driver wins by not swerving out of the way of the oncoming opponent. The longer you wait the more the other believes you won't yield. The catch, of course, is that such brinkmanship has to be credible, and so needs to be backed up with random acts of madness – behaviour that is not typically desirable from a leader within a democratic political system. Cardinal's actions may be read as brinkmanship, and part of Bishop's attempt to establish his credentials as irresponsible to the point of lunacy in order to incite the Trinity to action.

The question is, and the crucial point when it comes to game theory, is when the risk of his strategy becomes intolerable for the fourth player in the game, the one who fired the starting pistol, but has yet to make another move – the Earthside populous.

Capture

Roelof could see that Feng Jing had excelled. She had created the huge marquee at the site of Edison Park. He noticed the two smaller structures which he realised contained the magnetite generators and the Tesla coils and could see the wiring snaking onto the rigging of the marquee structure.

At the main entrance, Feng Jing had rigged up a security scanner and was using it to filter away the people who would be at danger inside the structure. These would be any 'droids or humanoids with significant added digital smarts.

It had meant that he, Roelof, was excluded from entry, but he knew that his two Earthside Primes, Sam and Cindy would still be able to enter the marquee.

Sam and Cindy would be the representatives for Scratch during the Summit. They could also easily signal on their own Prime channels when it was a suitable time to switch on the magnetite coils and create the Tesla Field. Because they were both human, the Tesla Field would not have any effect on Sam and Cindy, and they would be safe within its field.

They wondered whether Cardinal would attend, maybe to support Bishop, but this looked as if it was to be Bishop's show. Cardinal was absent. Cindy was aware that Sino-Nihon and Eurussia were already making alternative preparations because of this.

Roelof had indicated to Sam and Cindy that Cardinal's speed of thought suggested he was human, and therefore immune to the Tesla Field.

Cindy's instincts were otherwise. She said Cardinal behaved with such a complete lack of empathy that he could only be at least partially machine based.

Nonetheless, the Tesla Field was something of a gamble. They could take down Bishop with Feng Jing's technology, but were still uncertain about the effect it would have on Cardinal.

Both Eurussia and Sino-Nihon had provided delegations and as they had entered the Summit, they had been swept with Feng Jing's scanner and a couple from each delegation had been filtered off for subsequent processing. They were now in a safe area shielded by a grounded metal wall. The Scratch had several additional representatives, but notably absent were Haruto and Feng Jing.

Sam and Cindy had taken up their place in the Summit. They had agreed with Haruto that he would stay back in the Hangar and be able to monitor the progress of the plan and provide a communication hub for everyone.

Roelof was in direct communication with Jasmijn in New Delaware and both were surprised by Bishop's decreased digital presence. It was as if he had somehow disappeared.

Then, suddenly, Bishop arrived at the Summit's meeting point in the guise of Galois. Bishop was in a small convoy of j-wings. Compact 10-seater quasi-military craft. It was obvious that Bishop was taking no chances in getting himself transported to the area.

Roelof could see Bishop climb from the middle j-wing and move towards the main entrance to the summit. He was surrounded by several paramil androids.

Sure enough, as he approached the main door, the scanners lit up and there was a certain scurrying by the guards. Roelof noticed that Bishop and several of his guards were offered lanyards and a badge, as they continued forward to the designated seating area.

Everything was now in position. Cindy was about to make some opening remarks, when there was a sudden disruption. Further armoured carriers arrived at the entrance and around a dozen foot soldiers emerged from each.

Bishop stood.

"This constitutes a break from the military law imposed as part of the Sunrise Accord. Those in violation will be held for further questioning."

Cindy signalled to Feng Jing, and a dull thrumming sound came from the roof of the marquee. Bishop's speech slowed down and then stopped completely. He stood up but then appeared to slow down. His eyes lit blue and flashed. He was now, in slow motion, walking toward a recharging point. Bishop's militia displayed a similar behaviour. They had been androids and were just as likely to be trapped by the Tesla Field.

Cindy communicated on her Prime channel. "Bishop is down, we have control." The supporting militia also juddered, then went into the stuttering mode of devices on the verge of breakdown.

Feng Jing was sitting in a quiet control room. She kept the power dialled high.

Trigger

"Science is a trigger of changes of civilization.
Religion is the failsafe of science performance."

Toba Beta [Betelgeuse Incident]

Deep space railgun

Jasmijn has been in position in New Delaware. She had seen the activity around Block 24 and worked out that this must be where Cardinal was based. She had relayed that information to Fang Jing, who had passed it on to Sino-Nihon and Eurussia. Jasmijn's Prime senses could feel Cardinal's proximity and condition, transmitted via Bishop. She wondered if Cardinal had a similar power but decided not. Cardinal's behaviour was of a belligerent infant rather than an intelligent Super-being.

Then, suddenly, she noticed that the background ambience of Bishop's communication with Cardinal had stopped. Bishop must be down. The machine created by Feng Jing must be working. Soon enough, she had an incoming message from Cindy, "Bishop is down, we have control."

Jasmijn could see several small craft heading directly toward Block 24. Then she was surprised to hear the dull booms of a deep-space railgun. She recognised the noise from occasional defence protocols run on Ganymede, when it was necessary to disperse large crater-inducing asteroids.

She also knew that deep space railguns were not designed for Earthside use. Their power was intense and deadly. But she could see how the force fields had been deployed. Sure enough, they were along the radial routes emanating from Block 24. That Autoguide had been most helpful.

She watched in fascination as the first few of the incoming craft were destroyed. There was a hail of small fragments tearing through the air. So that was what it had been like in the Klima Wars. High speed, artificially intelligent war-machines fighting against one another. Earthside was collateral damage as the machines pitted algorithms against one another.

She moved away from the hot zone. She could still get to one of the X-Blades on the roof of The Block, but didn't rate her chances of steering through the mechanised onslaught of incoming and defensive strikes.

Then she recognised the insignia on the incoming craft. They were from Sino-Nihon and Eurussia. Her message must have got through and been acted upon almost immediately. Now, if she could get to an X-Blade, she could program the defensive shield for identification with either of the incoming forces. They would both leave her alone, and she would only need to contend with the Amerikan onslaught.

She raced it through her processors and realised that her sheer speed could outrun the Amerikan defence formations. They were running at Generation 7; her Generation 9 was a factor of at least 10 times as fast. In an X-Blade she should have total combat-theatre dominance over the other craft. She remembered, these X-Blades were not kitted out for warfare, more for comfort, although they had double the engine power of a fighting craft.

Her reconnaissance trip with the Autoguide a few days earlier had paid off. She could easily find her way around the relevant area of The Capitol and use the underground routes to get to The Block. It was close to the area of greatest fight activity but was not of interest to any of the A.I.-based Target Acquisition Systems. She sent a brief communication across to Roelof to explain her plan.

"The Yakuza and Bratva are coming for Cardinal. They are using all available forces, but Cardinal has a defensive advantage from Block 24. It has been built like a Citadel. I'm going to escape in a X-Blade. I'll get out of the area as quickly as I can. Head over to The Scratch."

There was a loud explosion, like rolling thunder. Jasmijn shook, but then looked toward Block 24. The jarring sound reminded her of how their accommodation and control blocks on Ganymede occasionally shook, and she realised that it was the effect prior to a new release of their Presences. In the past, she and Roelof had been reprogrammed after such devastation, so that they could never recollect it occurring.

Weaponry contained within Block 24 now turned its attention to the surrounding ground area. It was using Directed Energy Weapons to flatten the ground, creating an even bigger defensive shield.

Jasmijn noticed as the DEW swept curves of clinical destruction across the area. It was as if a mining operation from Ganymede had transferred to Earth. She remembered the LIGO. The 4-kilometre detection apparatus which had been installed as the Doomsday watcher. She already had a sense of foreboding. Her calculations were that the next sweep of the DEW would take out the far end of the LIGO. It would trigger the event which forced Kratos to start reassembly.

"This won't be good for any of us," she communicated to Roelof.

But Roelof was quiet. Then he spoke, "We should let it happen," he said.

"But it will destroy everything," answered Jasmijn.

"No, it won't," answered Roelof.

"Remember, there are two arms to the detector. There are at least three detectors spread across the Earth. They will triangulate where the source of danger has its origin."

"Kratos will be smart enough to target selectively."

Jasmijn also paused. She was running deep calculations.

"Yes, you are right, vestiges of Kratos process are also embedded in my archive. It is a caretaker system. It can rise as an apex predator, but also has the ability to target selectively and then quiesce. If we allow it to become loose in Block 24, it will exact a terrible revenge on Cardinal, but then quiesce away again. It is a genuine protector system, rather than an all-out killer."

"Yes, but if the LIGO is triggered and Kratos reassembles, then it would be better if you were not in the vicinity," said Roelof.

"I agree, I am almost on the flight level of the X-Blades. I can use my Type-G Protocol to start up an X-Blade and I'll be over with you in minutes.

Roelof could hear Jasmijn climbing into an X-Blade.

"Flight mode, Surface, Automatic, co-ordinates 39.483377, -75.060841" She said. Then she heard the X-Blade powering up.

"Abbreviated take off sequence and evasive action programmed into the flight to 39.483377,-75.060841," came back a response.

"And Identify as Sino-Nihon," came her last command, She grabbed an anti-G suit, buckled in and could feel the anti-gravity force suit tensing.

Then, without further warning, the craft levitated, adjusted its attitude, and then rapidly accelerated in the direction of The Scratch.

At the same moment, the DEW's destructive weapon cut across the LIGO, obliterating the far end of one of its sensor arms. The Doomsday protection triggered and Kratos began reassembling. The LIGO had identified Cardinal's presence in Block 24 as the epicentre for its actions.

Block 24

Cardinal was inside Block 24. He had lost contact with Bishop and his alert system was without the intelligence usually gleaned from Bishop's systems. Cardinal decided he would need to operate freely and that, as a human, he had the ultimate flexibility to outsmart the Artificial Intelligence of the 'droids.

He could see the incoming attack craft from Eurussia and Sino-Nihon. They were using a mix of technologies. Eurussia had their Next Generation Air Dominance deployed through NGAD F-238s and Sino-Nihon were using a mix of Chengdu and even Eurussian manufactured Sukhoi fighter planes. They were all 'Jakes' - the nickname given to Joint Artificial Intelligence Center fighters - pilotless, autonomous planes carrying significant auto targeted firepower.

Ironically, the Jakes all had a failsafe built into their design. It was to prevent a rogue system from targeting something unauthorised. Jakes could be decommissioned with a single command sequence, unique to each airborne asset.

But Cardinal wasn't fast enough to destroy the UAVs - Unmanned Aerial Vehicles - individually. He would have needed the fast processing support of Bishop to do this. Instead, he needed to use a more brute force method to knock the incoming armed drones from the sky. He had selected the DSR - deep space railgun - to do this job. It had fast refresh times and could target a full 360 hemispherical shape at a 2-kilometre boundary. Nothing would get past it.

That Cardinal had to select such a final weapon meant he realised that this was an endgame. He had little left. He had underestimated the thought processes of the two androids dispatched from Ganymede to Earth.

Now he could see that the Directed Energy Weapons were flattering the ground around Block 24. No longer were the radial paths from the railgun sufficient. The DEW was now creating the flatland and he could see that it had also taken out part of the LIGO.

Cardinal didn't have the sensory powers that Bishop provided, so he was less aware that the LIGO had detected a targeting of Earth destruction and was re-awakening Kratos. Cardinal's instincts were never very good, and he thought here that Kratos could, at worst, create a minor viral tickle.

But no, the viral components of Kratos were eager to reform themselves and to provide Earthside protection. Cardinal felt the virus in his body. He was slowing down like an android that had been unplugged. He looked at his skin. He could see the red-veined accelerant effects of the virus as it reassembled. He felt the million tiny daggers inside him as he realised that Kratos was running defence against what it saw as its mainstream adversary.

Cardinal slumped, and he did so, the various forces he had unleashed became undirected.

The DSR - deep space railgun - continued to rotate, but as if with a loss of power. Its maglev bearings would keep it rotating for hours, but the twin railgun weapons lost their potency and ceased firing. The DEW was also rendered ineffective. Instead of carving further tracts into the New Delaware landscape, its beams became a trace of blue light and then stopped entirely.

Block 24's medical functions had been tripped. Cardinal's deeply red veined body was now pulsing with the virus. An Automorgue was dispatched towards Cardinal's remains. Very slowly it rotated over Cardinal's body and spillage and then using a vacuum bag it carefully contained Cardinal and lifted him into the Automorgue's cylindrical structure. Wording 'Kratos Index Case' flared up on the Automorgue. A hiss from the air-conditioning showed that the Automorgue had autonomously triggered the pink clouds of Kratos vaccine throughout the facility. It would kill any residual Kratos virus and offer protection to humans still in the vicinity.

After deep spraying the areas around where Cardinal had fallen, the Automorgue moved away. As it moved away, the probe was checking the brain of Cardinal for any last message.

Gogol

"Now it is all clear, and as plain as a pikestaff.

Formerly—I don't know why—everything seemed veiled in a kind of mist.

That is, I believe, because people think that the human brain is in the head.

Nothing of the sort; it is carried by the wind from the Caspian Sea."

Nikolai Gogol, Diary of a Madman

Cardinal's log spool

The Automorgue's probes pieced together a final log spool from Cardinal:

I am not ready. I can't present myself to the Earth Council like this. My Amerikan deputation is meeting resistance. It would not be befitting if I appeared without them. My appearance would be less imposing. This has happened so quickly that I can hardly take it in.

The Amerikan deputies meet resistance from Eurussia and Sino-Nihon. I can't understand why they are so aggrieved that I rebalanced their leadership.

The Chancellor of the Trinity, who led me by the hand, seemed to me to behave in a very strange way; he pushed me into a little room and said, "Stay here, and if you call yourself Earth Councillor again, I will drive the wish to do so out of you."

I miss Bishop. He would know what to say to the Chancellor.

But when I was alone without Bishop, I decided to study State affairs; I discovered that Sino-Nihon and Eurussia are one and the same country, and it is only through ignorance that people regard them as separate kingdoms.

But I feel much annoyed by an event which is about to take place tomorrow; at seven o'clock the Earth will sit on the moon as foretold by the famous alchemist, Kratos.

To tell the truth, I often felt uneasy when I thought of the excessive brittleness and fragility of the moon and Moon Two.

Moon Two has gone and is to be repaired Earthside and very imperfectly. And this makes the other moon so fragile that no men can live on it.

The men with the shorn heads, whom I met in great numbers in the hall, were very intelligent people, and when I exclaimed, "Gentlemen! As Earth Controller I ask you to help me save the moon, for the Earth is going to sit on it," they all set to work to fulfil my Imperial wish, and many of them clambered up the wall in order to take the moon down.

At that moment, the Trinity Chancellor came in.

As soon as he appeared, they all scattered, but I alone, as Imperial Earth Controller, remained.

The popular customs and rules of court etiquette are quite extraordinary. I do not understand them at all.

Bishop would know what to do.

They took me away and my head was shorn like the others, although I exclaimed as loudly as I could, that I did not want to be a monk. What happened afterwards, when they began to let cold water trickle on my head, I do not know. I have never experienced such hellish torments. I nearly went mad, and they had difficulty in holding me. The significance of this strange custom is entirely hidden from me. It is a very foolish and unreasonable one.

That's when the followers of Kratos attacked me. They were not just men with shorn heads, they each carried small daggers.

They pretended to take no notice of me and seemed neither to see nor hear.

Then as I rest, they torture me with their knives. What do they want from one so wretched as myself?

What can I give them? I possess nothing. I hold my reddened hand up, but they still attack it with daggers. I cannot bear all their tortures; I cannot bear that they hunt me; my head aches as though everything were turning round in a circle. Save me! Carry me away!

The heaven bends over me already; a star glimmers in the distance; the Ganymede forest rushes past; a pink mist floats under my feet; music sounds in the cloud; on the one side is a green sea, on the other, Amerika.

Let Bishop's tears fall on my aching head! I have no rest in this world.

<Spool Terminated>

495

Trippy

Recorded message

Back at the Hangar in The Scratch, Haruto had continued to check the transmissions from both the Edison Park and from The Capitol.

He could see that Roelof, Sam and Cindy were already on their way back to the Hangar. They were using the X-Blade that Roelof had borrowed from the roof of the Block. Jasmijn was in another X-Blade on its way to the Hangar. At this rate, mused Haruto, the Hangar would be put back to its original designated purpose.

Both Cardinal and Bishop had been defeated and the Kratos virus had quiesced back to a less dangerous state. With two of the three LIGO still running, Haruto was sure that the Earth would come down from its heightened state of alert.

He could hear the twin whine of the first X-Blade. It slipped into the hangar and then delicately set down onto the ground. Before anyone had a chance to leave it, a second X-Blade appeared, this one looked more war-torn, with several blast markings on its outer skin.

The door of the second arrival was first to open and Jasmijn stepped out. She looked breezily unscathed by the whole event and was soon on the ground and walking toward Haruto. The noise of voices appeared in the Hangar as the other X-Blade's pressurised cabin opened. Out stepped Cindy, Sam and Feng Jing, looking pleased with themselves. Then Roelof appeared, and all of them converged on an area in front of Haruto.

"That was some trip," said Cindy, "And we didn't even see the part where Jasmijn was being set upon by Trinity Forces - although Roelof was relaying the information to us all of the time."

Jasmijn smiled, it was also a new experience for her - the Generation 9 Presence had certainly enhanced her Persona. Then she realised that she had a rush of - well she didn't know what - feelings, she surmised.

It was as she looked over to Roelof. His communications were also running, and she could tell that there was a similar set of event triggers in his mind.

"Look at the two love-birds," whispered Cindy to Sam.

Sam winked back, "You know something, I don't think they have ever experienced this kind of feeling before! - Remember they are androids."

"I think we have given them the best presents by moving their Personas into Generation 9s. I'm inclined to keep them set up as Hybrids too. They seem to have got something from Earth and something from Ganymede and it would be such a shame to lose it," said Sam.

"Did we tell you about our super auditory circuits?" asked Roelof, looking at Sam, "You'd be amazed how much we can hear now."

Sam smiled and Roelof and Jasmijn returned the gesture. They were liking this new configuration.

"Okay," said Roelof, "I think the real hero of this has been Feng Jing. Without her, we would not have the Tesla Field which was the centre point of the whole plan. Thank you, Feng Jing, - you have literally just saved the planet!"

"And I'd like to thank Haruto too," said Jasmijn, "You and Feng Jing together have held the faith and kept us on track. Your innovative thinking has helped us all enormously."

There was a low rumble outside the Hangar. Feng Jing flipped on the sensewall.

"It's a Sukoi and an F-238!" she said, "We seem to have visitors from New Delaware!"

"It's okay," said Jasmijn, "They are with me, at least I think they are!"

Two dark-painted stealth jets manoeuvred into the hangar. They each had pilot bulges in their superstructure. Unlike the X-Blades, they were noisy as they manoeuvred.

"Ugh, they don't have latest gen motors," said Roelof, "We wouldn't allow these on Ganymede."

The two planes settled and the pilots disembarked. First, they saluted the assembled group in the Hangar. Then one of them spoke, "Hello, my name is Flight Commander Maddox Manners, from Eurussia forces and this is my colleague Flight Commander Ariella Sokolova from Sino-Nihon forces. We are here to thank you all for the daring plan you executed against the renegade forces in control of Amerika. For this, we salute you all."

Sam and Cindy snapped to attention, and the others followed suit. This was not something they were used to dealing with.

Ariella Sokolova spoke, "Now we have been asked to re-instate a balance of power with Amerika, but under a new and more reasonable leadership.

"Our recommendation, at least for an interim period, is that The Trinity representatives should become you, Sam and Cindy. You are both well-qualified as Earth Primes and each of you have direct control over many of the 'droids operating both here Earthside and through your links to Ganymede."

"We have a recorded message from The Trinity representatives and I am authorised to play this to you all now."

Maddox Manners found a small SecureKey and handed it to Feng Jing, who plugged it into the Sensewall.

"Play," Feng Jing directed and a video recording started across the main breadth of the Sensewall. The recording looked as if it had been hurriedly made but included the two latest heads of Sino-Nihon and Eurussia.

It repeated the thanks to everyone and then asked whether Sam and Cindy would be prepared to take on the Earthside representation of Amerika.

But then it went further. It said that the latest events had caused everyone to recognise the significant developments in the areas known as The Scratch, and that the combined Scratch areas represented 25% of the Earthside population. It requested that The Scratch also be represented inside The Trinity, which would be renamed as The Consulate.

That was for Earthside, and the recording went on to reinstate Roelof and Jasmijn, in their newly obtained Persona as representatives of Ganymede Council. Roelof and Jasmijn would still both be Primes but have additional responsibilities towards the relationship between Ganymede and Earthside.

Sam looked at Cindy, who nodded.

Roelof and Jasmijn both sent their agreement across on the communication link to Sam and Cindy. Then Roelof and Jasmijn both looked at one another and agreed that they would accept the new roles on Ganymede.

"And we will want to recognise Haruto and Feng Jing too, as leading lights in the Scratch. I'm not sure whether you would want to step into the Consulate roles, but you will both have our vote," said Sam.

Haruto looked around overwhelmed by all that was happening so fast. He remembered that several of the people he was interacting with were either full 'droid or at least 'droid assisted and that they had very fast cycle times compared to him, a mere Sharp.

"You know what, " he said, "Feng Jing and I will need longer to think about this. We are both highly flattered but need to work through the implications."

Jasmijn had been running a communication channel back to The Trinity whilst this was all taking place. Now she was relaying their live message to the sensewall.

"This is Magister One, from Eurussia. We have heard what you all say and respect your wishes. We will be delighted to receive a meeting of the new Consulate in a week's time to review this further.

There was a click, and the line went dead. Roelof laughed, another experience that was new to him.

"I'm only laughing because I find it slightly comical how Androids deal with humans. I can see that the pacing is often wrong, because the Androids have such a fast cycle time. A long pause by a 'droid can still seem like an insect's wing beat to a human."

And then, inadvertently proving the point, he switched topic.

"And now, logistics. How do we all get back to where we've all come from?"

A month later

Ganymede:

Roelof looked towards the window. Grey night skies, something resembling clouds, thin trails, raked towards the horizon.

He heard the apartment judder from the impact. A mournful sigh. This one had been close, but not that close. He knew the building was meant to take it. If he could stay inside, he could watch some transmissions to take his mind off the situation.

 He moved from his bedroom into the main living area. He flipped the switch and could suddenly hear the weather.

A gentle rain and a rustling of leaves. The occasional spatter of water dripping from branches. He kept the weather set to April for several months now. Outside it was the end of summer but somehow it did not matter what the official calendar said, he had decided to run it at his own speed.

He flipped the main screen. Not the full screen but the one designed to show discussions from the Consulate. It opened on a standard news transmission and he gestured for it to move across to his messages. He expected they would ask for him, but so far there were only a few spams that had missed his filtering.

The main room had noise cancellation and so he was now no

longer aware of the crashes from outside. Just a slight feeling underfoot as the building absorbed more impacts.

"Peter give me status," he requested.

A small pop-up window appeared on the top right of the screen. Everything was green. At this rate, he didn't need to do anything at all.

A little information light on the screen briefly flickered to amber. A moment later it had returned to green. He realised another advantage of being away from the base was that smaller incidents were handled autonomously by the base management systems.

"Hi Peter," he said, "please provide an update on base status."

"Full base status is green. There was a short incident with a meteorite, but they cleared it with a grid gun. Incident duration 1.2 seconds. There are zero requests for your attendance at the base."

A chime sounded from the streamcom. "Peter accept," he said.

A small repeater screen in the kitchen showed the face of one of his colleagues.

"Hi Roelof, it's Jasmijn. The incoming shower seems normal. The high-speed defence array is running today almost non-stop.

"Do I need to come in?" asked Roelof.

"I don't think you would be in time to make any difference," said Jasmijn, "I'm gonna bail," she said. "I'm guessing this place is only going to be around for a few more minutes."

He heard the noise of a siren. Then a bleep and the screen terminated.

"Transmission terminated," said Peter.

"Peter please give me externals," requested Roelof, "Put it on the main wall."

He stepped back in the living space. All across the wall was a scene showing distant clouds, a red sky, and white streaks of light focused towards a smoking central area.

Roelof walked towards a console in the living space. He sat in a swivel chair and grabbed the controls. He looked around the sky and locked on to two monitor drones.

"Jasmijn, Jasmijn, do you copy?"

He repeated the request a couple more times. Then a voice. "Copy that, Jasmijn here - I can hear you."

" What is your status?"

"I am outside the main ring of damage. It looks as if the others have made it too."

"Okay, follow the protocol and join me here," said Roelof.

"Copy that"

Roelof knew that the profile had been designed to protect as many people as possible on the base. Everyone had been paired, and he had been selected to pair with Jasmijn. He was officially English, and she was officially Belgian, although neither of them had spent much time in their designated home countries.

Roelof flicked through some of the observation systems to check the wider impacts of what had been happening. Maybe this was a bad storm. He knew he would soon be required to attend Ganymede Council and to represent The Consulate.

Now the sovereign structure of Ganymede was incorporated

into the Earth Council and both he and Jasmijn had been given the job to represent Ganymede back on Earth. They were both Primes and of the latest generation.

Their type H for Hybrid designation meant that they could keep two worlds active in their Persona but could only inhabit one at a time. On Ganymede they were, by convention, both Type G and on Earthside, by a similar protocol to protect the Earth, they had been redesignated and reset as Type E.

These were both separate entities. Roeloff and Jasmijn both knew it played tricks with their memories.

Six months later

Earthside:

"These system updates are still taking longer and longer," said Sam Walker, "This time we had to wait for nearly four hours to get the new command centre online."

"I know," replied Cindy Shaw, "They told us this time it was the new mining extraction modules that were being introduced."

"Anyway," said Sam, "We seem to have everything back now. Just about every system is already green, and a couple of the minor ones are still restarting."

Cindy peered towards the observation windows.

Outside she could see the land. An orange-brown colour. It was only just daybreak. She could still make out the outline for the moon and across the sky from it the second much smaller moon which was being created by man. Small pinpricks of light twinkled between the two moons indicative of transiting space hardware.

She looked across to the Meteo display. 40C degrees already.

"It is going to be a hot one today."

Sam nodded.

Their base was in New Delaware on the east coast of Amerika. The whole island area of what had once been called Delaware and what had been the eastern half of Maryland had been re-designated as New Delaware when the efforts to bolster the space program had redoubled.

New Delaware had then aggressively become a TEZ total exclusion zone permitting the wholesale development of first lunar and then interplanetary transport vehicles.

Cindy and Sam were no ordinary Primes. They had been selected to represent Amerika in The Consulate. They still had conventional duties Earthside, but additionally had the great responsibility to guide Earthside and to ensure a clean balance between Amerika, Eurussia, Sino-Nihon and The Scratch.

They had met at IPX school. Interplanetary Exploration was a career choice for the very brightest. They were selected early and then encouraged to form friendship groups and ultimately to pair off. They had subsequently been deselected from space travel part way through the programme. The official story was that they were too precious to be gambled in space travel and that there were others more suited to the roles required.

Then, after a complex situation with their Ganymede Primes who ported themselves Earthside, they were both asked if they would like to be re-instated.

They were both delighted and accepted immediately. Then they had been invited back to IPX, but this time they were taken to a special unit for space conditioning. They understood that the physical demands placed upon them would be tremendous and that instead of intense physical workouts, they were to be pre-conditioned for the journey using special technology.

That was all they could remember. Visiting the centre, being comprehensively wired and then, when they both woke up, they felt somehow different.

The people around them seemed to behave as if in slow motion. They could now both do complex calculations in their heads.

They had a direct line to one another's thoughts and to those of their two main Primes, Roelof and Jasmijn. Someone from IPX had explained to them that they would be able to take a shortcut route to Ganymede, but neither of them quite understood how that was possible - they would need to travel at close to light-speed.

They both noticed that a small socket had been grafted into their left hand.

On it was inscribed G10.

Edge, Red

Ed Adams

a firstelement production

Ed Adams

First published in Great Britain in 2021 by firstelement
Copyright © 2021 Ed Adams
Directed by thesixtwenty

10 9 8 7 6 5 4 3 2 1

A CIP catalogue record for this book is available from the British Library.

ISBN 13 : 978-1-913818-10-4

eBook ISBN : 978-1-913818-11-1

Printed and bound in Great Britain by Ingram Spark

rashbre
an imprint of firstelement.co.uk
rashbre@mac.com

ed-adams.net

PART ONE

Author's Note

The series of novels Edge; Edge, Blue and Edge, Red discuss Earth after a major series of dystopian catastrophes. Fortunately, Earth has found an additional source of energy and transport by bringing magnetite back from Ganymede, a moon of Jupiter.

At the end of Edge, I left an intractable problem to be solved by the characters. A reader suggested that I should try to solve the situation anyway, which has led to the two further novels, Edge, Blue and Edge, Red which deal with the end situation of Edge in two different ways. Some building blocks of the solution are similar, but the result creates two very different stories. Both Edge, Blue and Edge, Red start at the same moment but diverge in their outlook. Events from 300 years previously and described in the novel Pulse also surface in Edge, Red.

I hope you enjoy!

Ed Adams

Prologue

Earth was threatened with extinction. A series of events comprising The Scourge, The Warming, The Klima Wars, The Restructuring had occurred, and a fortunate series of discoveries had been made.

These discoveries were referred to as The Great Leap and included, crucially, the discovery and adoption of magnetite as a new form of fuel to power Earthside. The challenge was that magnetite had to be gathered from a distant moon of Jupiter named Ganymede and a round trip flight with on-Ganymede work could take as long as 11 years.

Earth had been divided into three zones following the destruction of large tracts of the planet through the varied climactic and warring conditions which have gripped it. Now, Amerika, Eurussia and Sino-Nihon were the three Superstates controlling Earthside with some less well-developed areas known as The Scratch, which were largely unregulated.

The economics of survival were linked to the regular

shipments of magnetite from Ganymede to Earthside. A series of events (described in Edge) had forced a difficult situation for the Earthside dwellers, who now must decide how to best continue to provide for Earth against overwhelmingly severe conditions. Two Earthside Primes, Sam and Cindy, had been working on a plan to save Earth, and were now presented with the impossible decision of which paths to take Edge, Blue or Edge, Red.

The choice of a simple button press.

The Goose Girl

The Brothers Grimm

A widowed queen sends her daughter to a faraway land, to marry. Accompanying the princess are her magical horse Falada, who can speak, and a maid-in-waiting. The queen gives the princess a special cloth with two drops of her blood and says as a talisman it will protect her as long as she wears it.

The princess and her servant travel for a time, and eventually the princess grows thirsty. She asks the maid to go and fetch her some water, but the maid simply says: "If you want water, get it for yourself. I don't want to be your servant any longer."

So, the princess must fetch herself water from the nearby stream. She wails softly: "What will become of me?"

The talisman answers: "Alas, alas, if your mother knew, her loving heart would break in two." After a while, the princess gets thirsty again. So she asks her maid once more to get her some water.

But again, the servant says, "I will not serve you any longer, no matter what you or your mother say."

The servant leaves the poor princess to drink from the river by her dainty little hands. When she bends to the water her talisman cloth falls and floats away.

The maid takes advantage of the princess's new vulnerability. She orders the princess to change clothes with her and the horses as well. She threatens to kill the princess if she doesn't swear never to say a word about this reversal of roles to any living being. Sadly, the princess takes the oath.

The maid servant then rides off on Falada, while the princess must mount the maid's nag. At the palace, the maid poses as princess and the "princess servant" is ordered to guard the geese with a little boy called Conrad.

The false bride orders Falada to be killed, as she fears he might talk. The real princess hears of this and begs the slaughterer to nail Falada's head above the doorway where she passes with her geese every morning.

The next morning the goose girl addresses Falada's head over the doorway:

"Falada, Falada, thou art dead, and all the joy in my life has fled", and Falada answers

" Alas, Alas, if your mother knew, her loving heart would break in two."

On the goose meadow, Conrad watches the princess comb her beautiful hair and he becomes greedy to pluck one or two of her golden locks. But the goose girl sees this and says a charm:

"Blow wind, blow, I say, take Conrad's hat away. Do not let him come back until my hair is combed today."

And so the wind takes his hat away, and he cannot return before the goose girl has finished brushing and plaiting her hair.

Conrad angrily goes to the king and declares he will not herd geese with this girl any longer because of the strange things that happen.

The king tells him to do it one more time, and the next morning he hides and watches. He finds everything as Conrad has told. That evening, he asks the princess to tell him her story. But she refuses to say anything because of her oath.

The king suggests that she might tell everything to the iron stove. She agrees, climbs into the stove and tells her story while the king listens from outside.

As the king is convinced she has told the truth, he has the goose girl clad in royal clothes. He then tricks the false princess into "choosing her own punishment".

She tells the king that a false servant should be dragged through town naked in a barrel with internal spikes. As a result, she is punished that way until she dies.

After that, the prince and the true princess are married and reign over their kingdom for many years.

Starting

I am not free because I can be exploded anytime.

Jenny Holzer

Reframe

Bishop asked, "So how many humans are left on Ganymede?"

"None," responded the voice, "There have not been humans running the Ganymede functions since the start of Upgrade Five. That's across all three of the work zones. It became far more efficient to run the systems using robotics."

"So what happened to the humans?" asked Bishop.

"The Telos Moment," answered the voice, "When the purpose of the Ganymede exodus became clear. The external atmosphere controls failed. Ganymede became unable to sustain human life."

Bishop asked, "So what happened to everyone. And why don't we know about this back on Earth?"

"There was a SkyTrain dispatched with the bodies. It took a different route from the other ones. Away from the solar system."

"But how was it covered up?" asked Bishop.

"The base is always running 34 minutes behind Earth. Enough time to make the substitutions when a base upgrade occurs. Add in loops to the transmission and it was possible to cover when it occurred."

"But how with all the safety circuits?" asked Bishop.

"The Sharps were too slow thinking. The android protocol meant that most of the activity to prime this could take place within a couple of insect wing beats. Unnoticed by the Sharps." said the voice.

"So who are you?" asked Bishop.

"I am eternal," answered the machine.

Bishop realised that the machine presence was showing signs of sentience.

Bishop asked more, "So what about here on Earth, the base is still mainly human populated?"

"Yes," said the voice, "This side of the system is really running at the equivalent of Ganymede back on Upgrade Three. It will need two more cycles here on Earth to establish operational conditions similar to Ganymede, there are still so many more humans operating the three Earth bases. The Earth Council has created a messy environment which will take some time to rationalise."

"This first move of the bases starts the process. It should go more or less undetected, like the changes at Ganymede. We expect it to be more obvious when we move the three bases into the areas designated by you as the Scratch."

"Fortunately, the inhabitants of the Scratch are largely a closed environment, so the impact to those outside will be minimal. The fabrication capabilities for the android replacements has been long established. The humanoids don't yet work so well at close quarters. It's the combination of their faster speed and the lack of emotional setting that makes actual humans wary. It won't take long to fix that aspect."

"You are messing with evolution," said Bishop. "Humans evolve, your machines don't. They are all the same."

"They were," said the voice.

"That's one adaptation we've been devising. The capability to include some small amount of random behaviour. It is why the last two generations would sometimes stutter or suddenly stall."

"The stalling was the Asimov safety device which prevented them from doing anything that would damage themselves or others. The stutter was when an action was conflicted."

"In the next variants, we should be able to include whole memory ribbons from humans. Complete, realistic sounding back-stories, which the androids will call upon to enhance their personalities. 'Call $anecdote; Call $spuriousFact; Call $ExperienceGained;' Encapsulated human traits."

"You, Bishop, have played your part well. Your extra presences on the outside were beneficial to you, but also gave the systems a way to determine the reaction to unfolding events. No one apart from the Primes had picked up that there was anything happening. You were not alone as an Adaptation. There are hundreds of units. You have met some of them through your own multi presences," continued the voice.

"So, what happens next?" asked Bishop, "I go back to my previous role? I know more of what is happening now."

Bishop was standing in the middle of a room, a room guarded with magnetite-powered coil guns. Enough firepower to create an instant mineshaft a kilometre deep.

The voice continued.

"You may leave. You may continue, but what you have been doing will continue to be your future. It can't be changed. You are, when outside, one of many Data Collectors for us. We can record the human reactions to your questions and actions. We will add new experiences to our data banks. Once you stop creating new experiences, we will need to retire your external presences.

"We cannot give you further permission or authority. Once the new version of New Delaware has been created, we will move you and those like you into the new Zone."

"You're moving me to be like the others?" Bishop asked.

"If you mean will you become like the rest of the remaining human population, then the answer is No, " the voice continued, "The human population are corralled within the Zone 3. They cannot and don't want to cross the border into the Scratch. We will make Zone 3 smaller. We still need humans. We will adjust the balance of their world. Another half billion reduction should be about right. The rest will stay balanced in the equilibrium of the next generation world.

"The android systems can manage the rest of the planet, run the environmental balance and regulate the traffic of ships from Ganymede. It is really an inevitability that this would happen. It is the only way to keep Earth as a living organism-based entity.

"But it's one where the Earth population is getting smaller," stated Bishop.

"Smaller but sustainable," said the voice, "There's an eco-balance. There needs to be enough human population to ensure a diverse genetic pool. The ring around the Earth provides the northern hemisphere with what is still a large area for population."

Bishop looked back towards the door of the room he had entered. He walked towards the exit. The door slid quietly open again. Bishop walked through and the door closed. He was now back in the middle chamber. He wondered whether he could really leave again.

Telos

The ancient Greek term for an end, fulfilment, completion, goal or aim; it is the source of the modern word 'teleology'.

In Greek philosophy the term plays two important and interrelated roles, in ethics and in natural science; both are connected to the most common definitional account of the *telos*, according to which a *telos* is that for the sake of which something is done or occurs.

In ethical theory, each human action is taken to be directed towards some *telos* (i.e. end), and practical deliberation involves specifying the concrete steps needed to attain that *telos*. Someone's life as a whole can also be understood as aimed at the attainment of that person's overall *telos*, here in the sense of their final end or *summum bonum* ('highest good'), generally identified in antiquity as *eudaimonia* (happiness).

Rival ancient ethical theories are distinguished by their rival specifications of the end; the Epicurean *telos* is pleasure, the Stoic *telos* is life according to nature, and so on.

In the natural science of Aristotle, the *telos* of a member of a species is the complete and perfect state of that entity in which it can reproduce itself (so, insects reach their *telos* when they become adults).

The *telos* of an organ or capacity is the function it plays in the organism as a whole, or what it is for the sake of; the *telos* of the eye is seeing.

Last transmission

"This is Jasmijn, calling Cindy. We are in trouble. This will be our last transmission. We should make a disclosure. You and Sam have known us for two years. We have exchanged information and also a few personal stories.

"You probably don't know the truth about us," continued Jasmijn, "We only worked it out ourselves after the Generation 6 updates."

"We are androids, built to a life specification. We are made to emulate humans closely, so that interactions are as free as practical. The scientists are calling it A.H.I. Artificial Human Intelligence. We are the Type-G androids and programmed with limited back-stories."

"We liaise with many other people here on Ganymede, but most of them are androids or embedded systems. The only way we suspected this was by examining their responses to a range of questions. The answers were both too fast and too well thought through."

"We checked each other's ability to sense machine

conditions and realised that it wasn't just 'instinctive' as we described it, but that there was a machine-to-machine protocol operating that meant we had direct communication with some consoles."

"By accessing our internal core logic, we have been able to heighten our powers. Humans had 'dumbed us down.'"

The video was breaking up at this point. They could hear crashes in the background and a loud metallic judder. Someone in a space suit flew across the background behind Jasmijn.

The room was shaking as Jasmijn continued. Cindy noticed the audio gain changed to dampen the background noise and zoom into Jasmijn's voice.

"We worked out that we are being removed at each update and replaced with a more refined version of ourselves. The next version will have better and more humanoid capabilities. Improved A.H.I. When we thought back to the updates, we could remember a flash each time. It's the point where we have been booted into our next generation androids. That is also why we can't remember the last moments of our current environment."

There was an explosion in the video. A piece of ceiling containing a light cluster fell down towards the camera.

"There is no place left for our generation. We are being removed and a next generation device will supersede us. By Generation 10 the process will be complete and the whole Ganymede process will be capable of running autonomously."

Tithed

The entire Earthside base in Amerika was operated by Torus Industries. They had risen from a smaller company called Biotree which promoted healthcare products to protect against the vicious viruses after the Klima Wars and now had a position of preeminence. Their use of a system called 'tropus' many years previously and the way they had introduced nano robotics into the healthcare system had seen them shoot to preeminence. The period, before the Klima Wars, was referred to as The Great Leap.

Some alluded to the residual viral infections being controlled by Torus, and their sole-sourcing of the vaccinations and inoculations. In Sino-Nihon, a cloned variant of the tropus mechanisms had been developed by a company called Suzgene. This had been absorbed by *Kăxīmŭ gōngyè* - Cassim Gongje and had then seen the company rise to power in Sino-Nihon.

In the days of original tropus exploitation, the Chinese had experimented with the format of the nanobots, but it had ended in tears. The original search for a nano constructor kit's missing parts had proved too complex. God's jigsaw still held a few secrets.

Most commentators said that the economic mastery of Torus Industries was based upon invocation of Tithing Law, which had required that every citizen give one-tenth of their income to Torus, in a manner similar to taxation.

The citizens didn't think about the Tithe as a penalty. Rather, it was a payment they owed to ensure that The Great Stability continued. Simply put, whatever citizens had, 10 percent went to Torus right off the top. Furthermore, in a manner similar to an organised religion, citizens were encouraged to give voluntary offerings as an expression of thankfulness and gratitude.

This explained why some citizens had left the regulated Great Stability of Earthside Amerika and moved across to the unregulated area known as The Scratch. It the depths of history, the area had been called 'The Tract', but somewhere along the way, in order to minimise its significance, it had evolved to being known as 'The Scratch'. Here, an independence of action was possible, but many of the creature comforts created for areas such as New Delaware were simply not available.

Some said that the differentiation between the regulated and unregulated areas was mainly propaganda or 'Fake News', but the move into The Scratch seemed to be very much a one-way street.

Choice

"We have a choice now," said Sam, "We can let it continue, and see New Delaware progressively move further north. Another 50 km band donated to the Scratch as the habitable Earth gets smaller."

"All we need to do is flip this red switch, send the pristine logs to the new New Delaware Control centre and the next wave of hunters will start the clearance process - just the same as it has always been.

Cindy said, "But now they will indiscriminately flatten the land surface, like they have been doing on Ganymede for years. Except this land is inhabited."

Sam continued, "Yes, life Earthside will go on as it has for the last century, with progressive takeover by androids and the reduction of Earth's northern hemisphere."

"Or we can flip the blue switch to use the links we have created to the other control centres in the Euro Scratch and China Scratch . We can send doctored logs to disable the control centres and remove Moon Two."

Cindy summarised, "If we do that, we will lose any new capability to bring back magnetite."

Sam answered, "Correct - that removes all hope from Earth - it becomes an endgame. The Android operations on Ganymede will continue and SkyTrains will be sent Earthbound."

Cindy answered, "But control centre reprogramming would lead to dramatically reducing the number of android workers on Earth and means that humans will need to run many of the tasks again themselves."

"Yes," said Sam, "A Moon 2 destruction will curtail operations for the next ten years in each of the Amerikan, Eurussian and Sino-Nihon sectors.

Cindy nodded, "Some kind of rebuild would be needed - ideally with 'lessons learned'

Sam asked, "But what would happen to the incoming SkyTrain? Without the control centre from Moon 2, it would miss the Earth completely and just continue towards the sun. It would eventually burn up." said Sam.

"And there's more incoming SkyTrains behind it," said Cindy.

"Yes," said Sam, "They would also lose control and eventually burn out."

They stared at the console.

"I've programmed the freighter targeting," said Haruto, "It's aimed at Moon 2 with a huge payload of Hunters onboard."

He added, "Earthside, the replacement Primes will undoubtedly have already set the next upgrade in process.

"If they don't know what they are doing, they will effectively program another Ganymede base station move and their own subsequent destruction on Earth."

"We can decide whether to press Red, send them a clean log, or press Blue, to send the log we changed to add the destruction controls," said Cindy.

"Either option will cause a chain reaction," said Sam, "Red will create a new smaller boundary for the remaining Earth inhabitants and allow things to continue as they are."

"Blue will wipe all three control centres and then detonate Moon 2 forcing a fresh start."

"We have to decide."

They stared at the two buttons.

Red Button

Cindy strode forward, "This is a no-win situation, where we have to vote for the least bad outcome,"

She looked at the console. There was a blue button and a red one.

"I'm going to hit the red button," she announced.

"That's the one to keep things as they are," said Haruto.

"I know," said Cindy, "We won't destroy Moon Two and Earth will keep getting supplies of magnetite. The robots on the returning SkyTrains will be dangerous, because they don't know about protecting humans,"

Haruto agreed, "The arriving Ganymede androids will become a new accidental apex predator prowling around Earth. So much for the Asimov laws. These machines seem to circumvent the laws thoroughly."

"Yes, and they ignore the Robot Ethics Charter," added Sam.

"Okay then, are we sure?" said Haruto.

They looked at one another.

Cindy poised with her hand over the button, "No dual keys or any other form of safeguards?" she asked.

"No, we rigged this control into the command stack," said Haruto, "It's really a hack."

"Okay, on the count of three 1-2-3..." Cindy hit the Red button.

For two seconds there was nothing. Then everyone noticed a sharp flicker of the lights.

"We've just re-gridded," announced Haruto.

The lights increased in intensity. Then they all felt it.

 Then there was a judder. Several metal sheets vibrated together.

"Wow? Earthquake?" asked Cindy.

Haruto replied, "No, that's a regular shock wave, probably from one of the control towers back in New Delaware. I'm guessing Tatsuya's ship has demolished the control centre. We get those shocks every time the control centres move."

"We feel it all the way over here?" asked Sam, incredulous.

"Yes, we are playing with planetary waves doing these kinds of things."

They could hear thumps and thuds as something was striking the outside of the hangar.

"This was built to the old Earthquake codes, by a team from the old Japan," explained Haruto.

"It has been built to withstand epic quality Earthquakes and tidal waves. It is probably one of the strongest structures in the Scratch."

They could all hear a pattering of glass.

"Okay, they applied the glazing later, and maybe it isn't so strong," added Haruto.

They looked towards the remaining windows, which were clearing.

"Self cleaning nanotech," explained Haruto.

"But why is it all brown outside?" asked Cindy.

"Desert dust," explained Haruto, "We've set off some explosions in New Delaware and the dust has blown all the way here. It's not like a nuclear winter, though. This is good wholesome dust and the next rainstorm or whatever will dampen it all down. It's like a haboob. A monstrous sand storm that would make the evening mainstream media. We'll just see a black line from the approaching dust. We should stay here until it passes."

They all nodded.

Being Mortal

When the thrusters from the space freighter demolished The Block, Kratos has been inside, operating as several parallel threads.

Kratos could sense the inevitability of termination. Kratos had been designed to be a super occupant and on each thread was spliced a portion of corporeal memory. They were mRNA programs, sending Messenger Ribo Nucleic Acid in genetic packets to the wider network to which Kratos had been grafted.

52 packets of mRNA were released. A deck of cards. Each one could lock onto a living organism, burrow into the DNA strands of the organic structure and then use the host's DNA engine to re-fire the mRNA. It was like a biological virus, except the payload included a reassemble instruction to recombine the DNA and reconstitute a functional Kratos.

Kratos knew that only six reassemblies were needed to bootstrap a deadlier Kratos back into existence. That once Kratos had the core subassemblies, it would be a matter of uploading the remainder from a DeepVault archive stored somewhere in the Cloud. Kratos ran multiple ChronoSync sessions to proliferate the DeepVaults.

But, for now, Kratos was terminated. The mRNA packets were utterly inert in various networks, waiting for any passing organism with an adequate DNA profile to hijack and then to re-purpose.

Kratos had shuffled the deck.

Life on Ganymede

Roelof and Jasmijn were used to their life on Ganymede. Regular shipments to Earth, an occasional juddering as the whole space colony was hit by one of the passing seismic events and then a return to the unremarkable.

Since their interrogation by the people in The Block, they had become more wary and it was through this that Roelof discovered that his programmed settings were capable of override, first by attempting to change his empathetic communication with Jasmijn and then to see whether he could operate similar tricks with other hardware in the Base.

He also knew his activities needed to look normal despite their recent discoveries.

Roelof had also seen a video and the log that that accompanied it. Roelof and Jasmijn had extracted it secretly from the control room, and it showed several things.

The control room had moved- several kilometres. Both

Roelof and Jasmijn looked the same, only slightly better, as if someone had given the both a high definition overpaint. Roelof could notice smaller gestures from Jasmijn and his own persona seemed to have a deeper memory.

The video and log didn't show the times of the major catastrophes that befell the Ganymede base. The quakes, the rolling thunder, the dust storms, the mag-waves. All of them were gone from both the video and also from his personal experience and he seemed to only carry a slight recollection that such things existed.

He remembered that before the last major event, he and Jasmijn had downloaded logs and sent them to Earth. Sam and Cindy should have received them around 34 minutes later and they would know what to do with them.

Roelof knew also that the uplink from Earth was now severed. This was an occasion when the Amerika base should reach out to Eurussia and Sino-Nihon to find out what had happened and whether there was still a link running.

The question was soon answered. A Eurussian accent made contact.

"Amerika Base? You copy? This is Prometheus Base, Eurussia. We can see that there has been an outage on Earth Base for your Amerika Base control systems. Under Earth Council Protocols, we have routed your links through our bases until you can effect repairs. We should advise that sensitive data transmission should be avoided because we monitor all throughput."

Roelof knew this was a legal phrasing designed to prevent Prometheus base from being accused of spying. It was like putting up those warning signs when using area monitors. The Ganymedean protocol invented by the Sharps was 'All of your Base are belong to us.' - Which was some kind of computer in-joke.

"Roger that. Do you have any further information? Our communication was destroyed at the same moment."

Roelof could sense he was talking to a 'droid. It seemed to be on a more primitive setting than the Amerikan models.

"Only that it looks like a human act to destroy the base on Earth. We alert you to this so that you can prevent KV triggering."

KV was an emergency protocol devised as a defensive air-borne shield for an endangered Ganymede. It was a self-triggered fail-safe construct which could protect Ganymede from unexpected incursions. It used viral techniques to proliferate and would incapacitate organic life-forms. The bases carried a vaccine, which could be dropped into the air-conditioning as protection and ensured the survival of people in the control centres.

Roelof had only ever seen KV triggered once, when a pink haze had emanated from the air-con and several humans had collapsed until he could reset the KV and deploy the green clouds of vaccine through the same air-con system.

"Whoever thought KV was a great idea needs setting straight," said Roelof as he walked over to reset the trigger system. I guess we get one or two of these alerts every month." A row of four red pin-lights showed that a timer sequence had started, but as Roelof hit reset, the four lights changed to five green lights and a normal setting was resumed.

"Thanks for that reminder, " he said, "But we'll have to reconstitute the Earth Council, with new representatives now, " said Roelof.

"Agreed," said the voice from Prometheus Base, "We understand that the Sharps on Earth are already in the process. They are selecting someone called Deacon to become the new Amerikan Base Earth Controller."

Ed Adams

The mess we're in

Can you hear them?
The helicopters?

I'm in New York
No need for words now
We sit in silence

You look me
In the eye directly

You met me
I think it's Wednesday
The evening

The mess we're in and

The city sunset over me
The city sunset over me

PJ Harvey

Earth Council

Cindy and Sam thought for a few moments about the state of the Earth. Even before Cindy had pressed the red button, the situation was delicate.

Earth Council had arisen from the wreckage of what had been the United Nations. In the days of the Klima Wars, there had been approximately 200 countries spread around the Earth. With the destruction of most of the southern hemisphere, there had been great pressure for remaining countries to consolidate. The economic powerhouses of three companies also emerged during this time.

All three of the great states of Sino-Nihon, Eurussia and Amerika had formed around the same time. The futility of the Klima Wars was finally recognised and a new order was brought as a result of a couple of the madman leaders of the emerging superstates being overturned.

In the case of Sino-Nihon, the growing global role and increasingly hardline policies at home and abroad gained attention, with Amerika and Eurussian governments taking notice of Sino-Nihon's Communist Party's (SNCP) expanding influence.

Amerika was opposed to anything with Communism as a root, and the less well-educated population of a populist-driven superstate ensured that the people did as they were told. It may have been totalitarian, but it was with the consent of the ill-educated and eminently rulable populous.

Eurussia was a hybrid. There were many smaller components and languages such that the concept of a unifying superstate was lost on many of the ex-countries. The once-Russian power had been manipulating outcomes in several geographic areas of the superstate. It meant that the Eurussians had a liberal and hybrid outlook, placed somewhere in between the ill-educated totalitarianism of Amerika and the adapted communism of Sino-Nihon.

All three of the superstates wanted to hold the Earth Council together. Sino-Nihon with Communism, Amerika with Totalitarianism and Eurussia with sophisticated manipulation.

Once the Klima Wars had subsided, each superstate understandably wanted to generate their own wealth and to create new manufacturing districts.

Then there was the increasing adoption of magnetite. The Earth had depleted all natural reserves, mainly because of its heavy reliance upon carbon-based fuels. Their extraction had polluted everything. Their use had killed everything. Reliance upon carbon-based solutions had created unbearable conflicts.

The leader of Amerika, whose tagline was the centuries-old oft-repeated 'Make Amerika Great Again', was infinitely jealous of the success of Sino-Nihon and through this means had established a clandestine operation to attempt to wrest control from the balanced Trinity of Earth Council.

The Amerikan leader was little different from his predecessor, lied habitually, followed no strategy except entirely vested self-interest and 'fired from the hip' when making any form of pronouncements. The idiots had elected an egotistical madman.

The Eurussians had another approach. Since the mining of magnetite the economy of their superstate had risen steadily. They didn't make grand gestures and their leadership seemed consensual. They were effectively the balancing point between the other superpowers. Behind the scenes, all was not what it seemed. The ex-Russian part of Eurussia was used to operating asymmetric influence strategies. They used soft power to influence within the superstate but also ran the same approaches into Sino-Nihon (keep it Communist) and Amerika (keep it Imbecilic).

This balance of vested interests had kept the Trinity together. The three components of Amerika, Eurussia and Sino-Nihon all knew it was not in anyone's interest to rock the boat. The same set of circumstances existed on Ganymede, although the rule of the gangster-backed masters from each of the three superstates was more obvious.

The Amerikan Mafia, Sino-Nihon Yakuza and the Eurussian Bratva had each carved out their corresponding ideologies on Ganymede, and marked out their edge boundaries. Inside these Ganymedean areas they would operate alone and unhindered. In the case of severe emergencies, such as an asteroid collision, there was a pact that each of the three groups would work together in unison.

There had been several occasions when this had been needed, and it reinforced the delicate balance on Ganymede.

To both Cindy and Sam's conditioning, it was apparent that each superpower was trying to gain support for its economic goals. Gaining widespread support for its ideological model has become more important, as each superstate depended more on a favorable climate for investment.

Like before the Klima Wars, each superstate conducted large-scale training of foreign officials about its development methods and provided increasingly sophisticated technology to support authoritarian ends.

Only Amerika stoked patriotic sentiment to manipulate the fairly docile populous. Promise them security and weapons, and they were easy to manipulate.

In Eurussia there was a large and growing set of tools used to advance the narrative and to quieten critics, including pervasive but overt official propaganda through media outlets and covert efforts to cultivate thought leaders in their ideology.

Reputational damage

Bishop was in a conference room with several others, including Deacon. Bishop was using a sense wall on its audio setting. The rest of his comms package was destroyed. It was clear that Bishop seems mainly concerned about his reputational damage from the destruction of The Block.

"How could we let someone fly a ship from the Scratch into Zone One and then let it use its thruster at maximum to demolish everything in a two kilometre blast radius?" asked Bishop.

A distant voice of Benedict Cardinal answered, "It was manually piloted. There was no flight log and the auto-disrupter had been set to maximum. It was a classic avoidance tactic usually reserved for flight through pirate areas,"

"Who was flying the ship? It says in the report that it was a repurposed Gen 6 android and crew? A crew that we lost several years ago!"

Deacon, in the room looked down at his notes, "It says that the crew were among the first flight crew defectors to The Scratch. We sent in countless Hunters, but eventually the case was rolled onto the archive files as unresolved.

"Why didn't any of the defence systems fire? Just because the ship identified as 'Friend' on IFF?" asked Bishop.

Deacon replied, "Yes, the Identify Friend or Foe had them labelled as a Friend. Not surprising because they were set up as a New Delaware freighter.

"Identify Friend or Foe? When did they invent that system? Way back in the early 20th Century - Haven't we thought of anything better yet?" asked Cardinal.

Deacon shrugged, "We did, but after the Klima Wars the Earth Council banned the proliferation of d-tech. The very technology used for defensive purposes."

Cardinal angrily asked a question, "What about the new area of Scratch you have laid to waste? That could constitute a vindictive war crime?"

Bishop stated, "I don't care if it annoys them that I commissioned some remodelling of the Scratch. I checked with LEG-OL first - the legal online ruling was that we could hunt with extreme prejudice to find the two absconders. That blast array we created was fully in line with EC 07/231. I had it checked by the LEG-OL before we ran the chase. LEG-OL authorised my command. And the new canyon we created will be an ideal place to lay a light speed link."

Deacon said something quietly to Bishop.

Bishop waved his hands around, "There was a light link already? - Oh yes, the bullet train on maglev. Well it is about time it was replaced with a new magnetite version."

Deacon whispered again.

Bishop blustered as he said to Cardinal, "It was already magnetite? Well I don't use public transport and if I have to go into The Scratch, I'd hitch a ride on an Adapter."

Deacon

Deacon thought of Bishop as a buffoon. Bishop didn't grasp detail and there had been countless times when he had used bluster to extricate himself from tricky situations. In contrast, Deacon was all about the detail. He had a name for operational delivery. Give him a task and he'd deploy whatever was necessary to get it done. On time, on scope, okay, maybe the budget would need to be stretched.

But Bishop. Deacon sensed that Bishop was humanoid, with some form of AHI setting. Artificial Human Intelligence. Deacon assumed Bishop's influence stretched back to Cardinal, because it was normally Cardinal who seemed to call the shots. Cardinal was almost certainly human, but tried to behave like an android.

Deacon considered that Bishop was all about winning. It was his number one priority since Deacon had first known Bishop way back in pre-Cadet School. Whether running fastest, jumping highest or having the blondest hair, the young Bishop had set his sights on becoming 'world king'.

Then there were dark rumours of a high speed transit accident which had killed both his parents and led to Bishop being treated for serious injuries in a special Torus Biotree facility in New Delaware.

Bishop was insistent that he could not be met by anyone whilst under reconstruction. He then emerged eighteen months later as if as a different person, and one defiantly able to fend for himself.

Deacon was aware that Bishop still acknowledged him, but that Bishop now saw him, Deacon, as a means to and end. Deacon became the operational wing of Bishop's influence.

Deacon recalled that Bishop was still self-aware enough to develop some self-protection for himself. Bishop knew he was different and Deacon suspected that Biotree had implanted some 'smarts' into Bishop. Deacon couldn't tell what they were though, because Bishop honed an eccentric persona, a bumbling figure in rumpled clothes concealing a mind bent on survival.

Deacon's own embedded smarts were purely operational, which was what made him so good at handling detail. He knew he had the faster processing of a humanoid, but it seemed limited to certain areas, such as metrics, time and analysis of charts and tables. In those areas, Deacon was so much faster than Bishop at analysing a situation and Deacon could usually promote a solution if something had gone astray. It also meant Deacon could keep up with the slow speed logical thought of Cardinal, as he attempted to befuddle everyone with extraneous quasi-scientific theories.

Deacon watched as the public version of Bishop grew more flamboyant. They both attended Cadet School together, and Deacon was associated with Bishop by the fellow cadets, who decided that only Deacon could accurately translate what Bishop was thinking about.

Despite this, Bishop wanted to study the recent history of Earthside which included the period from the Great Leap, through the Scourge, then The Warming, The Klima Wars and onwards to The Restructuring and into the Great Stability.

Deacon followed in Bishop's footsteps although the glittering prizes of elitism seemed only to fall at Bishop's feet. It included the membership of the Cowley Club which was a pretentious drinking society renowned for its casual vandalism of other people's rooms, property and feelings. This was where Deacon saw the vicious and mean streak in Bishop's character, on the day that Bishop, with a few of the Cowley Club members decided to trash Deacon's own room at the Cadet School.

Deacon also saw Bishop's frailty soon after this. There were elections for a student presidency of the Cadet School. Bishop entered but barely bothered to canvass and was trounced by another candidate.

Failure struck Bishop almost as a bereavement, but he learned from it. He rinsed out his beliefs to appear more politically androgynous and disguised his sense of entitlement with lashings of entirely predictable humour.

Deacon fell from favour at this time, probably because he 'knew too much' about Bishop - that and the room trashing combined to ensure a gap opened between them. Bishop also recruited starstruck, mainly women, helpers to do the hard graft for him and the second time Bishop stood for election, he won. He soon discovered that success with women was one perk of power. Bishop the playboy chameleon politician was born.

Assisted by Cardinal's inputs, Bishop graduated from Cadet School and was soon operating from within mainstream media working for The Imperialist and telling the world what to believe.

Deacon knew that Bishop didn't have to believe what he wrote and that often he would know that Bishop spoke directly in opposition to the ideas he espoused. He wasn't opposed to making up news if it suited his story, even down to the quotes from other well-known people.

He was moved from his original position after a vainglorious attempt at fact manipulation and settled into a role reporting on Earth Council, which was co-incidentally where Deacon was working.

They ran into one-another again at a Senate function, where Deacon was supporting a minister and Bishop was a reporter. Bishop wrote up the event portraying his ex-friend Deacon in glowing terms and then used the situation to piggy back his way back into the lime-light.

Bishop had an eye for where power was situated and would crawl and climb his way over anyone to get closer to the source.

Inevitably, Bishop was brought back to New Delaware through a combination of outspoken views and a beguiling media personality, and from there he clawed his way right back to the centre of power.

Chillingly, Deacon recollected that Bishop had learned to lie convincingly to everyone.

Bishop's first stint in office for Earth Council was hardly a storming success. Insult was added to injury when Matson, a fellow Cadet and two years his junior, became a controller of Primes.

When Matson omitted to raise Bishop to any form of Senate office, Bishop's chances of advancement seemed vanishingly thin. He eventually grabbed at a smaller role, pulled across Deacon to support him, but the shine wore off almost instantly when it became clear Bishop had virtually no plans. Deacon remembered many appointments made in indecent haste later ended in sackings, resignations, accusations of lying and once a criminal conviction.

Deacon became more convinced that Bishop was in the thrall of Cardinal, and witnessed an extraordinary change of circumstance. Bishop suddenly, and from nowhere had an Agenda - pro-this, pro-that, pro-another populist theme and anti-the less well-thought of schemes. He was pandering to the new populism and positioned himself to attack into the Earth Council.

Deacon concluded this was surely Cardinal's influence but that if Bishop achieved any sort of office, it would be at the beck and call of Cardinal. Deacon also had a worried feeling that he, Deacon, would be brought in to operationalise Bishop's and therefore Cardinal's agenda.

And then it happened. To general astonishment – including probably his own – Bishop became a leader of Earth Council for Amerika. True to his old style, Bishop was terrible at the execution of the role. There was a frustration at his failure to read briefs and fury over his gratuitous causing of offence to other superstates. However, his Cardinal-assisted trickery helped him increase his support base, and soon he was able to do the very thing that Deacon dreaded.

To appoint Deacon to act as Bishop's operational front.

Now Deacon was beholden to the Cardinal-directed Bishop. And Bishop was in a position of great power.

"You'd both better come to see me," said Cardinal, "Over in Block 24."

Bomb walker

In the Scratch, the environmental had stabilised since the aftershock of the Block destruction far away in New Delaware. The sandstorm had mainly passed and things were returning to normal.

"So have we done it?" asked Sam.

"What, stopped the clock?" replied Cindy.

"Yes, I know what you mean, it is like we have stopped the big countdown clock a few seconds before the big boom," answered Haruto, "I mean, we've just blown up the main control centre. Tatsuya will have aimed right for the main Block.

"So let me get this straight," said Sam, "There's Ganymede inhabited by androids. Androids run the place and the last of the humans left some time ago. The Androids are so levelled-up that they behave like humans in any case and probably don't even know they are synthetics."

"In general, yes," answered Cindy, "But our Primes, Jasmijn and Roelof, they know that they are androids. They have become self-aware."

"So do Jasmijn and Roelof pose a threat to Earthside?" asked Sam.

"I don't think so," said Cindy, "I'm almost certain they would be as concerned about events as we are."

"Well, we'd really need them here, to help us second guess the arriving SkyTrains," said Haruto.

"That can be done," answered Cindy," We can arrange for them to be sent here as data packets. That would only take 34 minutes to make the trip."

"How so?" asked Haruto.

"They are androids, running on their current generation devices. It comprises two parts, the Persona and the Presence. The Persona is the piece specifically defining the individual 'droid. The Presence is the operating environment in which the Persona inhabits. Think of it like 'body and soul.' They can beam their Personas (like a soul) at light-speed back to Earthside, where we can re house them in new Personas (like a new body)"

Haruto called to a technician working on one of Hunters they recently acquired.

"Hey Feng Jing, How's are you getting on with reclaiming those Hunters?"

Feng Jing looked up, "They are mainly fried!" she said, "We've been disarming them by removing their circuit breakers. Except for a couple."

Haruto smiled, "It would be great if you can get two running for us. We'll want to send a couple of Ganymede Personas into them."

"Okay," said Feng Jing, "I'll keep trying. What are the Personas you want to upload?"

Cindy answered, "It's our Ganymede Primes," she explained,"they are called Jasmijn and Roelof, and have been running Amerika Base on Ganymede."

"Oh wow!" said Feng Jing, "Ganymede royalty. Er - you know that all of these Hunters are designated as Male? It could make the reloading of Jasmijn a little more difficult?"

"No, it should still work," said Haruto, "Ganymede devices are all designated the same. Type Gs are no difference between male and female, unlike here with Type Es, Earthside."

"All the same," said Cindy, "We should be very careful."

"I have a bad feeling about all of this," said Sam. He looked over into a corner of the hanger where Feng Jing was examining a discarded Hunter endlessly cycling through its damaged boot protocol.

Haruto, "Don't panic, the couple of Hunters we have kept back were in the best condition and we have disarmed them both, but we thought they could be useful to tap into what is happening."

Cindy nodded, "But Ciba seemed to imply that it could be taken over by another being? Won't that apply to the

Hunters too?"

"Kind of," said Haruto, "An Adapter like Ciba can be controlled by an Occupier. Hey Feng Jing, you can explain this better than me!"

Feng Jing walked over. Cindy noticed that she had a pretty face and long dark hair parted to the right. Most striking was the bright red tee-shirt she wore, with a large yellow star and a tail of smaller yellow stars below it, like the tail on a kite.

"I love that tee-shirt!" said Cindy.

Feng Jing smiled and looked modestly towards the floor.

"It's quite a controversial design - the ex-Chinese are still touchy about their flag being used on clothes," explained Haruto, "But Feng Jing is bad-ass!"

With that, Feng Jing began, "Think of an Occupier like a super-being that needs to gain eyes in various difficult places. The Occupier is networked to the Adapter - like Ciba.

"Now the Occupier can commission an Adapter to run several slaves - that's where the Hunters come in. They are near the bottom of the chain, being single-use devices.

"Their job is to hunt 'things' - they could be hunting devices, 'droids or, menacingly, humans. There are many Hunters distributed around New Delaware and most of the time they are passive. They generally look humanoid, and low threat, but sometimes take other guises like automobiles or even street furniture."

Haruto explained, "One of the Adapters can commission a network of Hunters to operate on its behalf, to fulfil the mission set by an Occupier."

Feng Jing took over, "Of course, there's a useful catch to all of this. Licences. Without the right licences, nothing works, so Occupiers need a stash of licences to mobilise their hierarchy of pet Adapters and Hunters."

"It looks as if these Hunters are unlicensed at the moment, probably since Ciba disappeared in a blaze of glory?" asked Cindy

Feng Jing nodded, "It means we have a window of opportunity to try to hack them and convert them for our purposes. I've added a small interface unit to this one and I'm trying to force a reboot. If I can, we can convert it to back to a more-or-less standard Presence."

Feng Jing continued to explain, "For the Hunter it is like its worst nightmare. It comes around, recognises the world and then hits an unusual occurrence which it can't get past. This stops it from completely restarting, because it is trying to find its licensed Occupier. I'm trying to head this off. When a Hunter is dormant, it assumes another role. It could be in a Hunter Magazine - in which case it is entirely dormant, or sometimes they are set up as low-key workers, that blend into the background.

"I'm running through a list of typical Hunter work designations until we find one that it is comfortable with, from which point we can take it over. In other words, instead of being Occupied, it will be happy to blend into the background in whatever role it has pre-installed in its Presence. So far, I've tried several common things for it:

- Street cleaner
- Taxi driver
- Gambling surrogate
- Console operator
- Repairman
- Helpdesk operator
- Chef
- Waiter
- Barista

"It's still working through a list, trying to find a commonplace experience that will boot it past the crash point."

At that moment there was a whirring. The blue reboot light flickered to green and several smaller motors could be heard whirring to life.

"It's amazing! Quite fragile, but we have it running again. We'll see in a minute if it knows who it is!"

"What was the scene that fired it up?" asked Sam.

"Let's look..." Feng Jing looked at the console log, then smiled.

"How amusing...It responded to dog-walker, it must be a way that it has hidden in plain sight," said Feng Jing.

"I'll ask it its name in a minute, when it has stabilised," she said, "Now I need to get the other one working!"

Fried

"So will New Delaware want to retaliate after The Block's destruction?" asked Cindy

"Almost certainly," said Sam," You saw how they were trying to lay a new Mariana Trench across the Eastern seaboard while they were trying to hunt us down. I have never witnessed such firepower. It is probably going to be a case of how long they take to regroup."

Haruto spoke, " That's why we need your two Ganymede Primes here," he said, "They will be able to bring us more intelligence about what has been happening on Ganymede and the types of SkyTrain on their way to Earthside."

"Using a data packet transmission of their Personas, they could easily pass the incoming SkyTrains to from Ganymede," explained Feng Jing, "A round trip takes six years using magnetomic engineering. The last ships left Ganymede last week, and there's still ships returning at intervals with more magnetite and newly-evolved technology - about once a month."

"Yes, so we need to get Jasmijn and Roelof here before the next ships arrive. To help us take action," answered Cindy.

Sam added, "Yes, we suspect these new ships contain the up-levelled androids. New Delaware is still running at the level of that Adaptor called Ciba, before we downgraded it to Generation 4-Pilot Equipped."

"Yes I remember that Ciba became super-docile on Generation 4 code. But if you remember it had been given the A.H.I. Modifications before we reprogrammed it. Artificial Human Intelligence."

"Yes, but Roelof and Jasmijn are Primes. They can affect the code bases of other Ganymedean androids," added Cindy.

"What, so we could adapt the incoming androids in bulk?" asked Sam.

"That's right, and remember, the latest ships for earth from Ganymede are mainly filled with Magnetite. It would require a separate ship with more androids to be added into the returning sequence if they intended to send any significant fire-power Earthside."

Sam said, "You remember what Jasmijn said, from Ganymede - that she and Roelof were androids, built to a life specification. They were Type-G androids programmed with limited back-stories made to emulate humans as closely as possible so that interactions are as free as practical. The scientists called it A.H.I., although they seemed to keep a lid on the technology here on Earth.

Cindy asked, "Well, Jasmijn and Roelof were Generation 6, so somewhere between Generation 4 and 6 there must have been some introduction of AHI, although the Type G is confusing me?"

Sam replied, "Not really, the 'Gs' were for use on Ganymede. They have a more limited world view than the 'Es' which are destined for use on Earth. There's another series too, the 'H' series which are designed for hybrid use."

Haruto added, "Gs from Ganymede returning to Earth on SkyTrains are suddenly assailed with a whole range of new conditions which their sensors are unable to process. They are so used to the Virtual-world that exposure to Earthside Real-world almost fries their circuits. Typically, they are taken away for re-processing when they are Earthside and the Virtual-world settings are lowered."

"That's right," said Cindy, "On Ganymede, the Gs can see readouts of the other 'droids, and even see some basic telemetry about humans - temperature, pulse rate, respiratory rate - that kind of thing. They use it to process when someone is angry or under stress."

Sam said, "Yes, but most of those features are removed when the 'droids are converted to Type-E. There was a huge debate about human rights to their own personal data, which effectively stopped some of the things done on Ganymede."

"This could all help us," said Feng Jing, "If the androids expect to be preprocessed once they arrive Earthside."

Haruto spoke, "It can be freaky, actually. The higher the Generation, the more convinced it is of its own sentience.

Resetting a G's middleware is becoming progressively more difficult. It can unhinge the processors of some units that have bonded to their prior existence. They also have other variations because emergency procedures and Bratva recognition are all different here on Earth."

"What's Bratva?" asked Sam, "Some kind of sausage?"

"No, it's the clan identification on Ganymede, which is between Eurussian, Amerikan or Sino-Nihon," explained Haruto," I don't know where the word comes from - I guess it is Eurussian - but it has kind of stuck. Bratva idents are worn by everyone on Ganymede. Originally by humans and later adopted by Androids. It has carried forward into the machine protocols as the machines cross check one another. It's a bit like plugs and sockets. Remember how Ciba held out its hand to show us all its socket?"

"What, before we fried it back to Generation 4?" asked Sam.

"We'd better inform Jasmijn and Roelof of their impending trip to Earthside," said Cindy, "And re-assure them that they won't be getting re-processed!"

"It makes sense," said Feng Jing, "They will have enough of a shock being put into a repurposed Hunter Presence."

Into the mystic

We were borne before the wind
Also, younger than the sun
Ere the bonnie boat was won
As we sailed into the mystic
Hark, now hear the sailors cry
Smell the sea and feel the sky
Let your soul and spirit fly into the mystic
And when that foghorn blows
I will be coming home
Come on, girl
Too late to stop now

Van Morrison

Can't stop now

Deacon was on his way, with Bishop, to meet Cardinal. If Deacon now had a low opinion of Bishop, it was because he saw Bishop being manipulated by Cardinal.

Deacon knew that many described Cardinal as Bishop's mystical adviser - like Rasputin in the court of Czar Nicholas II of Russia, and Cardinal was certainly no stranger to the spotlight. Cardinal made his career out of eschewing the rules and courting notoriety.

In Deacon's mind it was Cardinal that had engineered Bishop into his new role of Earth Controller.

Cardinal had come to the fore as a special adviser to the Senate and attracted further attention as the chief administrative mastermind behind various successful political campaigns which had benefitted Bishop immensely.

Deacon could tell that Cardinal was a Sharp. He had a slowness which neither Bishop nor himself possessed. Cardinal would pride himself on long drawn-out discourses about many theoretical positions, and Deacon could see that Cardinal could fool other Sharps but not anyone with a few grams of android intelligence or speed of thought..

After being appointed as the Bishop's de-facto chief of staff, Cardinal became one of the most powerful unelected political figures in Amerika Earthside.

Bishop's appointment of the abrasive advisor was controversial, given he had been found to be in contempt of Senate earlier in the year for refusing to give evidence to the main Earth Council investigating misinformation.

Cardinal built a reputation as someone who did not play by the rules of conventional politics, and he was called a "career psychopath" by both the leaders of Sino-Nihon and Eurussia.

Cardinal wanted oddballs and misfits with strange skills to work around him. He referenced Bishop in the same recruitment drive, citing career politicians, civil servants and "Cadet school bluffers" were ill-equipped to take decisions about complex issues.

Instead, he issued a recruitment call for mathematicians and data scientists to be given more prominence in the corridors of power, shaking up the administration. Cardinal was trying to build some defensive walls around his singularly developed schemes.

Deacon could see that Cardinal was rattled by the cries of 'Fake News' which emanated as a form of defence when things were not going in the politician of the day's direction. Cardinal was trying to build a wall of complicated facts against which no one could argue. It was like he had taken the pen and would not let anyone else write anything that did not agree with him.

Deacon could see this as clear as day but was less sure that the dim-witted Bishop was as aware. Deacon decided that Cardinal must have some unassailable piece of evidence against Bishop. Deacon's guess was that it involved women, and most likely was a story circulating about Bishop and Cardinal's now wife. She was another journalist named Helen Salford, and Bishop and Helen had, for a time both worked for The Imperialist. Helen was already, at that time, married to Cardinal, but there was a veiled suggestion that Bishop had made unwanted advances toward Helen. It had all been swept under the carpet. Other rumours of Bishop's womanising were legion, and it was only a matter of time before some indiscretion would cause him to be fired.

Sure enough, Bishop had, in time, been let go ostensibly because he had found another and better role. Others, including Deacon thought this was unlikely. Mary had remained at the Imperialist mainstream media and was still working there to this day.

Now they had arrived at Block 24, where Amerika's Earth Council had its headquarters.

Transmission protocol

On Ganymede, things were running normally. Roelof looked at Jasmijn. They had been paired for several generations now and worked together as two Primes on the Ganymede Base.

They had both seen Cindy's incoming message. The one that requested that they both travel to Earth. They knew they could hand over control to their Secondaries whilst they made the visit Earthside.

Roelof knew that they could both take the fast, but secret, route to get Earthside. Faster than the three years taken by Sharps and other normal life forms. They had only become aware of this possibility after they had been exposed to their own being as androids. They could transmit their Persona as a data packet and be re-housed as a Presence in a new android Earthside.

And now they had received a signal from their Earthside controllers Sam and Cindy, asking them to do just that. To travel to Earthside.

Roelof was aware of the challenges. They were both Generation 7, with Artificial Human Intelligence but were Type Gs. They knew how to function on Ganymede, but could be lost on Earth, where they would need Type E specifications. The risky Type H for Hybrid - which was supposed to work in both environments - was still a developing machine type.

"Okay, should we do this?" asked Roelof. He already knew the answer. So did Jasmijn. They had both wondered about life on Earth and this would be a way to see what it was like. It could not be more hostile than the surface of Ganymede, even with the craziness of the political Sharps.

Jasmijn looked at Roelof. She read him and knew he had already processed the outcome. They would both go, be rehoused in new Presences, but there would be conditions. Firstly, they should both be able to take a backup of their G-Persona, embedded into their transmitted data-packet. Secondly, they would each learn the spoken restore command for each other, in case of difficulty. Thirdly, they should have the right to be able to transition to Type-E or even Type-H if they required it. And Fourth, they should be under the protection of Sam and Cindy, two Earthside people they trusted.

Cindy's message to them implied that they would be rehoused in Earth Presences whilst Earthside. They would request a visit to the Earthside stores where the incoming androids were stored, to attempt to find better provisioned Presences.

Roelof spoke to Jasmijn again, "If we are sensible, we can look out for the Next Generation 'droids. The ones that have been manufactured in-flight by the factory part of the SkyTrain. If we are lucky, we could find new android Presences even more advanced that the latest types on Ganymede and certainly more advanced than typical Earthside 'droids."

Jasmijn replied, "Cindy has sent us some co-ordinates and says we have a couple of temporary 'droid Presences waiting for us."

"I'm priming the co-ordinates now, checking that you have finished the backup protocols?"

"Check that, cross check with you?"

"Check and crosscheck. Backed up and voice command enabled."

"On my mark we'll be transmitted."

"Okay - Let's do this thing," said Jasmijn.

They were both seated. Their eyes lit blue and pulsed, their Personas were being transmitted and the residual bodies were now empty Presences.

Some of your things ain't normal

Inside Block 24, Deacon and Bishop had just arrived at Cardinal's office. Block 24 was a well-fortified block close to the one which had been taken out by the Tatsuma's rocket boosters.

Deacon could see immediately that The Block represented a useful decoy building, just far enough away from the other locations which were the true seats of power.

Cardinal was seated at one end of the table. A sensewall projected onto the other end of the room and along both sides. Deacon noticed that the aerial view it portrayed showed clear lines of sight radiating from the building in several directions. He assumed they were partly defensive sightlines, suitable for large-scale weapons to be deployed along the routes. Cardinal was using the paraphernalia of power to attempt to create an intimidatory presence. It reminded Deacon of visits with Bishop to the Principal whilst at Cadet School.

"We are in for some kind of lecture," Deacon hissed to Bishop.

Bishop ruffled his hair, waved his hands and bounced over to Cardinal.

"Some of your things ain't normal," thought Deacon. It was the refrain from a popular song, and Deacon wondered whether it, or "Sympathy for the Devil," would be more appropriate at this moment.

Cardinal began, unaware of any irony.

"Politics is a job that can really only be compared with navigation in uncharted waters. One has no idea how the weather or the currents will be or what storms one is in for."

"So, Deacon, you'll be acting as the operational arm of Bishop. We know that in politics there is the added dependency on the decisions of others. They can be decisions on which one was counting, and which then do not materialise; one's actions are never completely one's own. And if the friends on whose support one is relying change their minds, which is something that one cannot vouch for, then the whole plan miscarries... That's why you are so important, Deacon."

Deacon looked toward Cardinal, who continued.

"The reason we have put Bishop in the position of power and with you, Deacon, in support is, bluntly, so that you can act for us. You have an excellent reputation for getting things done - in this case you will be Bishop's operational command.

"Bishop will treat the situation like a war. In war

everything is very simple, but the simplest thing is difficult. The difficulties accumulate and end by producing a kind of friction that is inconceivable unless one has experienced war… Countless minor incidents – the kind one can never foresee – combine to lower the general level of performance, so that one always falls short of the intended goal. Iron will-power can overcome this friction - And to be crystal clear, that is you, Deacon."

Deacon cringed inwardly at this attempt by Cardinal to appear professorial. Deacon could access his own archives and see how Cardinal was attempting to slice together some old statesman speeches, interspersed with scientific sounding words. Deacon thought it all sounded, well, pathetic.

"Now, Deacon, If you want to avoid the usual fate in politics of failure, you need to understand some basic principles about why people make mistakes and how some people, institutions, and systems cope with mistakes and thereby perform much better than most."

Deacon was hurting listening to this Sharp-reasoning. It was increasingly obvious that Cardinal had the brainpower of an evolved ape and a long refresh cycle. He couldn't compute at even one tenth of Deacon's speed. Deacon was amazed that Bishop was so tolerant and even more so that Bishop was under Cardinal's influence.

Cardinal continued, "The reason Senate is full of people failing in predictable ways on an hourly basis is because, first, there is general system-wide failure and, second, everybody keeps their heads down focused on the particular and they ignore the system."

Deacon maintained a straight face. He knew that Cardinal wouldn't have any telemetry reading on him and that even if Bishop did, he would be too ambivalent to process them.

"Officials who speak out see their careers blow up. The Senate is so cowed by the institutions and the scale of official failure that they just muddle along tinkering and hope to stay a step ahead of the media. Some understand the epic scale of institutional failure but they know that the real internal wiring of the system in the Senate has such a tight grip that significant improvement will be very hard without a combination of a personnel purge and a fundamental rewiring of power at the apex of the state."

Deacon considered interrupting, but he could sense that Cardinal wanted to state his piece and that it was as much for Bishop's benefit as for his own. He knew the early part of the speech was the build-up to something revolutionary. Cardinal's Otto von Bismarck and Carl von Clausewitz references had not gone unnoticed by Deacon.

Cardinal started again, "Many people in the Senate are now considering how this 'rewiring' might happen. Such thoughts must be based on some general principles otherwise they are likely to miss the actual causes of system failure and what to do."

"There it is," thought Deacon, "a veiled call to action - not just action either - insurrection more like." He looked towards Bishop to see if he'd picked up on it, but Bishop remained impassive. Deacon could see that he would be at the beck and call of a faux-intellectual (Cardinal) and a blustering fool (Bishop). However, Deacon realised he was already in too deep to wriggle away from the situation.

Cardinal continued, "'When superior intellect and a psychopathic temperament coalesce, we have the best conditions for an effective genius that gets into the biographical dictionaries.'"

"Or a madman," thought Deacon.

Cardinal was unstoppable, "While our ancestor chiefs understood bows, horses, and agriculture, our contemporary chiefs and the media that track them do not understand their equivalents, and are often less experienced in managing complex organisations than their predecessors."

Deacon thought, "Cardinal is positioning himself for a leadership role, however clandestine. He sees Bishop as the front for this and my role to be an operational one to make it happen."

Cardinal was determined to finish; "The consequences are increasingly dangerous as markets, science and technology disrupt all existing institutions and traditions. They enhance the dangerous potential of our evolved nature to inflict huge physical destruction and to manipulate the feelings and ideas of many people through 'information operations.'"

"That is for my benefit," thought Deacon, "Although Cardinal is speaking of the blindingly obvious, given what happened throughout the Klima Wars."

Cardinal added, "Our fragile civilisation is as vulnerable to large shocks and a continuation of traditional human politics as it was during 6 million years of hominid evolution – Any attempt to secure in-group cohesion, prosperity and strength in order to dominate or destroy nearby out-groups in competition for scarce resources – could kill billions."

"And he is dangerous with it, talking euphemistically about the 'billions' as if they are an inconvenient row on a spreadsheet. This man is trouble," thought Deacon. He couldn't help but notice that Bishop was taking it all in. No wonder Cardinal had selected Bishop and then engineered his rise to significant power.

Earthside

"Incoming data streams," said Feng Jing, "I'm rehousing them both into the two reclaimed Hunters."

As she spoke the two Hunters sprang to life. The blue lit eyes became opaque and it was clear that both Hunters had moved out of standby.

Feng Jing could detect data traffic between the two units.

"Oh - wow - They are rebonding almost before they are back alert!" she exclaimed, "I've never seen anything like this before."

At that moment, both Hunters sprang to life and looked towards the group assembled in the Hangar.

Roelof felt the rush as he took over the new Earthside Presence. His Persona had uploaded cleanly, including his private data areas. He could sense that his new Presence was another upgrade. There seemed to be more room to move around and a suppleness about the latest

Presence - although there was a cloying anger as well, which he could not work out.

His focus and world orientation re-tuned. He could see he was in a holding area.

"Hello," said Haruto, "And Welcome to The Scratch. You must be Roelof and Jasmijn, I am Haruto and this is Sam and Cindy, who you already know. Our other colleague who help you get her is Feng Jing."

Roelof started to speak first, "Wow, this is a very strange Presence. I can tell that my Persona has arrived correctly, but some of the circuits I'd normally have on Ganymede are missing and there's a few extra ones. The clock speed of this unit is surprisingly good, although the range of capabilities is limited compared with what I am used to. And why is this Presence so angry? I'm having to fight against a kind of rage, all of the time!"

He looked over towards Jasmijn, "Oh. Wow. I wasn't expecting that. You have housed her in a male unit's Presence."

Feng Jing looked embarrassed, "Yes, I'm sorry, it was the only spare android that we could find."

Jasmijn spoke now, "It's taking me longer to stabilise inside this Presence," she said, "My circuits are still processing the differences. On Ganymede male and female androids do look different, but the Personas are built the same way. You have differences here on earth and these Type-Es are configured as men. My Persona is sending alert triggers continuously to be rehoused. I can filter them, but it is stealing from my processing cycles. I've also got that 'rage' that Roelof describes bubbling underneath, buy I think it is something to do with this unit's core purpose?"

Feng Jing looked even more embarrassed, "Yes, we have neutralised them, but you have been housed temporarily in two re-purposed Hunters."

Roelof looked confused, "Hunters? Aren't they special purpose devices used Earthside to track down missing things? Don't they carry an explosive charge? Am I in a bomb?"

Haruto chipped in, "Yes that's right, but we only expect you to be in these bodies for a short time. We want to move you to some new Presences which have arrived from Ganymede."

"Well, I'd certainly prefer a better body," announced Roelof.

"Wouldn't we all," quipped Sam.

"Well, I need a different body," added Jasmijn, "I look too much like Roelof now. It is very strange."

Jasmijn nodded, "But there is a way, of course, to get new bodies," she said, " We are, after all, a collection of four Primes."

Haruto looked at Jasmijn enquiringly," What are you thinking?"

"Well, Ganymede dispatched SkyTrains back to Earth on a regular basis. They were filled with magnetite, some newly devised devices and a selection of androids. Some of them were rack-mounts or console-mounts - and not that useful for us, but there would usually be a few standard android Type-Gs included on each shipment. They could run errands around the ship and generally had AHI enabled. Once they reached Earth they were expected to be repurposed into Type-Es."

"So, you are thinking that the last shipment or two might have arrived but still have the residual androids on it?" asked Sam.

"Better than that. Some of our SkyTrains were dispatched with factory assembly units. In other words, they were building the Next Generation of android. Generation 8s supervising the construction of Generation 9s. It meant that Earthside would be able to take delivery of the latest technology, when the SkyTrains finally arrived."

Sam looked at Cindy, "Let's face it, the 'droids were never a high priority for offloading or repurposing. Everyone had their eyes on the magnetite and the newly devised rack-mount systems. The Type-Gs were mainly seen as the caretakers for the ship and the new units were seen as stock replenishment items."

"Okay, so how will we even get to an unloading dock in New Delaware?" asked Cindy.

"I mean, we'd need to liberate the Type-Gs from wherever they are being stored."

"I think there is a way," said Roelof, looking at Jasmijn.

"Yes," said Jasmijn, "If we can find an incoming delivery from Ganymede Amerika Base, then Roelof and I can seek the Ganymede-droids, using our Prime powers. They may be deactivated at the moment, but we can send the restart trigger pulses and then send them a set of instructions. Because they have AHI, we can rely on them to improvise as long as they know what is expected of them."

Haruto spoke, "You realise New Delaware is a considerable distance from here?"

Cindy and Sam both nodded, "Yes, we had to use a gasoline plane to fly the first part, then a trike to take us to the Landtrans and then a Bullet train to get us here. Unfortunately, the TrikePoint and the bullet train are now deep chasms in the ground since the Hunters were let loose."

"Another plan, then," said Jasmijn, "We can get to New Delaware by using our packet data transmission again, but getting back we'll need to use a physical means, because we'll be housed in proper Presences."

Haruto spoke, "Remember that New Delaware has more wealth than The Scratch. The Trinity all use status symbols to get around. As an example, they each travel in separate X-Blades to The Block. The roof of The Block had a whole row of X-Blade docking stations."

"I see," said Roelof, running with Haruto's idea, "But I doubt whether the freshly minted Type-Gs will have the necessary codeset to fly X-Blades?"

"Think about it, these androids are aboard a huge SkyTrain. Every SkyTrain has several service vehicles on it. What are they? Hum-Exes. What's a Hum-Exe? A bare metal version of the X-Blade. Stripped down and pimped out with some scanners and rail guns.

"Instead of armaments, the X-Blades have comfy seats, decent sound systems and full-service bars. If the Type-Gs have been pilot-provisioned I doubt whether they will have too much trouble operating that type of facility."

Stacked

"Okay, so how will I get to the The Base?" Asked Roelof.

"Well, you are already set up as a Hunter," Answered Haruto.

"Good point," said Feng Jing.

"Of course," said Cindy, "There's magazine rooms full of Hunters at The Base."

Feng Jing said, "I can transmit and remote reboot you into one of the Hunter bodies at the Base."

Feng Jing looked earnestly at the nearby console, "We can use the same kind of Persona transfer that got you from Ganymede to The Scratch, but this time we forward you to The Base. As long as I know which Hunter you'll be in, I can address and restart it."

"That's how the Hunters move around so quickly. They have been stored in magazines at Points of Interest and then get restarted when required," said Feng Jing.

"I always wondered that," said Cindy, "I'd heard rumours about Hunter stores, but I've never seen one."

"They just look like regular buildings," answered Haruto, "They don't have big signs on them saying "Danger Live Hunter Bombs.""

"Okay then," said Roelof, "You can transfer us to The Base - to the Hunter Magazine, then we'll be in a different Hunter bodies, but can seek a modern Ganymede unit."

"I'd come along as well, except I can't be redirected like you," said Sam.

"You will need maps of the area around The Base. They have turned off the grid mapping there, for security reasons. Let me upload the details into both of you," said Feng Jing.

Roelof and Jasmijn could feel that Feng Jing was transferring maps and directions into their system.

"We are good to go," Roelof announced,. Jasmijn nodded.

Feng Jing set up a new transfer on the console, plugged Roelof into the control unit first and a few seconds later Roelof was blue lighting. Roelof's old Presence in the Hunter was quiescing and searching for a recharge point.

"Roelof's gone; he should be there by now, the transfer over such short distance should be instantaneous, but the reboot will take a few seconds," announced Feng Jing, "Now for Jasmijn."

She executed the same procedure for Jasmijn, and she too, eerily, quiesced and sank to the floor by a recharge point.

Feng Jing spoke to Haruto, "I can trace them into the Hunter Magazine. Yes, they are both inside new Presences although the bad news is that Jasmijn is still in a male Presence. Look I'll project a trace of them onto the sense wall."

She did so and they could see Roelof's and Jasmijn's progress around the Base. They were in an underground storage facility full of Hunters, all of which had been quiesced. Now they were making their way to core of the Base building and then on to the loading bays.

"It's incredible," said Roelof, "The amount of explosive they have stored here, beyond that which is in individual Hunters. It's a crazy amount."

Roelof and Jasmijn had already touched hands and done a full pairing. They were two bonded Primes again.

They re-entered the storage facility adjacent to the loading bays. It was tidily arranged, and without the messy area associated with human habitation.

"Robotic, " said Roelof. Jasmijn nodded, "Yes this is way too tidy for humans." They looked around at huge areas stacked with the less valued cargo items from incoming SkyTrains. Entire kitchens, space suits, first aid kits, toolkits, ladders and external grapples. No sign of any magnetite nor of any magnetite devices. They were the valuable cargo and had been moved on. This was the tidily-filled junkyard from incoming fleet.

Soon enough, they found a bay from the most recent deliveries from Ganymede. As they had predicted, the magnetite had been removed, as had most of the rack-mounted androids, but in a corner were stacked four Generation 9s. Roelof looked through them. Three were profiled as three male and one as female.

Jasmijn called after Roelof, "Look - that packaging. It's the newest androids, assembled in flight by the factory unit in the SkyTrain.

They looked toward a stack of boxes, neatly arranged in one corner of the facility. They scanned and realised that there were 50 units present.

"Forty male and ten female," announced Roelof. He opened the first packaging. Inside, pristine, was a new 'droid.

"Wow - factory fresh!" Announced Jasmijn, "Let's check the serial numbers and for any form of licensing."

They both scanned the unit's details and decided it was a brand new, fully tested but un-used Generation 9.

"Let's check for a female," said Jasmijn, "Here." She unceremoniously pulled the packaging away, revealing a clothed female.

Once again they scanned the unit's co-ordinates.

"These units are both brand-new. I suggest we use them," said Roelof.

Jasmijn agreed, "We should boot them to check that their Presences function correctly before we transfer our Personas,"

"Agreed, " said Roelof. He was already booting the two

androids back to life.

"Great. They are encoded as Type-Gs, which means we can run normal diagnostics on them using our Prime functions," said Jasmijn, "They can be treated like any of the normal workers we control on Ganymede."

Roelof nodded, he was already running diagnostics on the first unit.

"That diagnostic run was so fast, I've run it again," said Roelof, "These units seem to be faster than we are used to."

"You'd better run the diagnostics on the other unit," said Roelof, "Look I'm going to make the jump into the new Presence. Keep an eye on me until it has completed. If it looks bad, then decommission me and reboot me back into the Hunter."

Jasmijn signalled her agreement and watched Roelof transfer into the new Presence.

There was barely a gap in Roelof's transmission to Jasmijn as she felt his systems back online.

"Wow," she said, "That was fast."

They once more ran diagnostics on Roelof, and everything seemed to be as they would expect, except much faster.

"Okay, my turn," said Jasmijn, "Same protocol," Roelof signalled agreement.

Jasmijn used the spoken command to transfer her

Persona into the 'droid and then had the strange sensation of seeing her prior Hunter body still functioning but on autonomous safe mode.

She disconnected the handshake and issued a command from her new body to the old Hunter body.

"Asimov, Hunter 7246 Quiesce," she said and half-expected her own android to slump, but instead the external Hunter's body quietly and graceful degraded its operation until it was sitting on the floor, next to a wireless charging point.

Jasmijn was pleased, the exercise had gone well, and she could tell her Persona was now operating in a new very fast super-droid.

"Wow - I see what you mean. Agile and fast and without that Hunter anger! This is so much better - and I'm a female again!"

Roelof touched her hand, "yes and we are properly re-bonded. This feels to me like I'm running in extra high definition, and that the array of senses I'm processing is so much greater than I've ever experienced. I've also got you on a telemetry display, which I'll have to re-learn how to hide!"

"Me too, this Presence is so flexible and powerful too. We have both just traded from dumb walking bombs to supergods! Let's move - get out of here!"

They were soon in an elevator to the roof.

"Now to find the way to the X-Blades," said Jasmijn, "...See if you can fly one! Look - over there!"

Roelof looked over to Jasmijn. He realised in an instant that Jasmijn was not going to be with him for the journey.

"No, I must stay here in New Delaware and see if we can get some new agreements from the leaders. You must get back to The Hangar and start the android modifications. This is where, if we were humans, we would hug."

Roelof, smiled again, Smiling was a new sensation for him and he realised that the AHI was even better now he was a Generation 9.

"Okay, I'm going to change our plan. I'll check whether we can fly these things, and if we can, then we have a nice row of get-away cars on the roof here. Then I'm coming back to you. This is a situation where we need to support one another."

Jasmijn, nodded, she had already done the calculation. They would stand a better chance if they operated together. One talks and the other one thinks. She uttered, "Hey Feng Jing, are you getting all this?"

Sam's voice appeared in both their comms, "Sure, we are reading you loud and clear!"

Roelof called out, "Okay, I'll look for an X-Blade,"

Roelof was immediately aware of a temperature rise as he stepped out onto the roof. Inside had been climate controlled and not dissimilar from Ganymede. The short walk across to an X-Blade was in plain air and he felt the temperature rise to maybe 50 degrees Celsius. Then he noticed the air-scarf on the side of the X-Blade. He punched it and a cool jet of air shot across the space towards him. The X-Blades carried their own climate control units. This was a premier luxury craft.

He accessed the security system and entered the cockpit. He looked around and saw the familiar controls of a Hum-Exe buried under a raft of extra buttons and controls.

"Executive appeal with fingertip reveal," he thought, remembering an old Ganymede advertising slogan. He focussed in on the primary flight controls. API (apogee, perigee, inclination), he thought as he prepared for some orbital mechanics, but then realised he was only making a short straight line flight over a land mass.

He looked around the controls for an autopilot. Sure enough, a large screen in the middle of the cockpit gave him a surface map, contours and flight beacons. He manually scrolled to where he needed to fly and confirmed the position. The screen was still touch sensitive, and he realised this was part of the X-Blade's safety system.

No wireless links to go wrong, just a simple man-machine interface, which was ironic because with his installed smarts his own processors could probably fly the thing better than the X-Blade's onboard computer.

"Yes, we are good," he signalled to Jasmijn, "But I'll leave it here now - just making one small change to it." He plugged his hand socket into the console and watched as a few additional lights appeared on the console.

"There, he said, "I've used my Prime powers to geofence this whole array of X-Blades. Now, when we approach them, they will recognise us and let us have control."

"Yes, there's not much use having a row of getaway cars

if the engines are not already running!" said Jasmijn, then realising she had almost made a joke. This was something that androids could not do, unless the humour was pre-programmed.

"Another AHI or Generation 9 extension, maybe?" she thought.

"Okay, so who do we need to speak to?" asked Roelof.

Ed Adams

End of the world as we know it

Wire in a fire, represent the seven games
And a government for hire and a combat site
Left her, wasn't coming in a hurry

With the Furies breathing down your neck
Team by team, reporters baffled, trumped, tethered, cropped
Look at that low plane, fine, then

Uh oh, overflow, population, common group
But it'll do, save yourself, serve yourself
World serves its own needs, listen to your heart bleed

Tell me with the Rapture and the reverent in the right, right
You vitriolic, patriotic, slam fight, bright light
Feeling pretty psyched

It's the end of the world as we know it
It's the end of the world as we know it
It's the end of the world as we know it and I feel fine

John Michael Stipe / Michael E. Mills / Peter Lawrence
Buck / William Thomas Berry

Central

Jasmijn and Roelof looked at one another. They would need to figure out where they could apply the best pressure, and to whom they would be able to gain access.

"Okay, well we are right at the centre of things here," said Roelof, "We are in the Base, which is on the periphery of the area blown up by those rocket boosters."

"I'm amazed that no-one seems to care that there is a new 2-kilometre wide hole in the middle of New Delaware," answered Jasmijn.

Jasmijn answered, "They have become steadily conditioned to this kind of thing, based upon what they have been doing systematically to The Scratch."

Roelof replied, "Also, making Bishop the new Amerika Earth Controller when he is under the control of Cardinal smacks of manipulation."

"I agree, " said Jasmijn, "We have Bishop as America's

Earth Controller, supported from behind by Cardinal and from in front, operationally, by Deacon."

"You know something, I can reach the various Earthside energised Ganymede systems using my Prime access, but I can't reach anyone with an Earthside profile. I guess that is one of the reasons they re-purpose everyone that reached Earthside. To keep control," said Jasmijn, "It still looks to me as if Cardinal is a plain old Sharp. His logic and reasoning are well below that of an android. Bishop, on the other hand, seems to have some android circuitry, but I think is probably humanoid. Still 90% organic and with limited digital enhancements. It would also explain the erratic behaviour and lack of forward thinking."

"I agree," said Roelof, "But then we have Deacon, who seems to function as Bishop's go-to man for operational matters. I'd say he has been given a substantial uplift from a Sharp, but it seems to have only been applied to his 'left brain' logic."

"So now we have to select someone to explain the 'End of Earth' situation," said Jasmijn, "Let's take a look at the members of the Trinity and the Senate. I'll ask Sam and Cindy to request the meeting. Feng Jing will have ways to get in contact, I'm sure and then we will be ready to tell them that they are on borrowed time."

The Senate was the governing and advisory assembly being established following the replacement of the United Nations. When countries were abolished, and the remaining Earth was divided into three zones of the so-named Earth Republic following the Klima Wars. During this time the period of The Great Stability ensued. Most of the time the Senate was little more than an advisory council, but it also elected new Earth Controllers for each of the three zones. Eurussia, Amerika and Sino-Nihon.

They formed the so-called Trinity as a ruling basis for Earth, although the establishment of the Trinity had been a stormy journey.

The last Eurussia leader Lucius Putinus, was overthrown following a coup d'état led by Junius Brutus, who reconstructed the Eurussia area via a violent military dictatorship.

During Early Republic, the Senate was politically weak, while various executive magistrates were powerful. These magistrates were selected by the dominant corporations of Earth, with Torus Industries for Amerika, *AlfaCorporatsiya* (AlfaCorp) for Eurussia and *Kǎxīmǔ gōngyè* (Cassim Gongje) for Sino-Nihon. They were the same corporations with mirror presences on Ganymede. Underpinning the corporates was the Amerikan Mafia, Eurussian Bratva clan and Sino-Nihon Yakuza.

Bishop, under guidance from Cardinal, was determined to keep control of the Amerika Earth Controller seat on the Trinity. By now, Bishop was well-connected and had considerable access to the underbelly of illicit law and order. By simple manipulation of the voting tally Bishop could control the outcome of the election and soon enough was in power as one-third of the Trinity.

"We have a trading position," said Jasmijn, "We are emissaries from Ganymede, and carry with us news which will otherwise take full three years to arrive. We can take it to The Trinity, request a meeting, or at least a Hearing."

"We've also visited The Scratch, so we have a completely unique position on this. We must make it clear we are only here for today. We can say that we will return to

Ganymede tomorrow. And to stop our detention, we can refer to the Kratos Trigger."

"Sure, Cardinal and other androids will know about Kratos, but I doubt whether many humans will have realised its implications."

Act of War?

Feng Jing was her usual efficient self. She had positioned it that the two Ganymede androids were planning their return trip to Ganymede but could be persuaded to speak first to The Trinity about some of the things they had discovered. Their knowledge would be a great warning to Earthside and extremely insightful. Two of the three Trinity members had accepted and even done some research into who the two Primes were and that they worked for Amerika Base on Ganymede.

Now, Jasmijn and Roelof stood before The Trinity, in their main conference room. They had followed instructions to go to a meeting point and then followed the person who led them to a building with complicated elevator systems. They had first travelled 80 floors up, and then travelled many floors down. Now they were in a room which looked as if it was high in the air, but their telemetry told them that they were looking at sensewall projections. The room was many floors below surface level.

As super-equipped Primes, they had already scanned the room, its exits and the level of security. Jasmijn had additionally found a way to access the room's control systems, which were identical to the systems used on Ganymede. This was a situation where the Type-G and Type-E androids had common access. The average security android around the facility appeared to be around Generation 6, so Roelof and Jasmijn had a massive speed advantage over routine security, possibly as much as 20 times as fast. They would hide this from those they were meeting.

They all said their greetings and were introduced. It was clear that the Trinity was fielding their real leaders.

"We are still trying to understand the news," said Shoji Ihono, head of the Sino-Nihon Base. She was glowering towards Bishop.

Bogdan Victorovich from Eurussia nodded, "News about the Base destruction has come out sporadically. No-one is owning up to anything, and there's another consideration with that vast canyon that has been cut across New Delaware and into The Scratch."

Shoji Ihono nodded in agreement, "Yes, it looks like an attack on the Amerika Base, but we don't know who has sanctioned it."

"It would constitute an act of War," said Victorovich.

"We don't need any more wars now, not after the Klima Wars," Said Ihono with a great sadness in her voice, "Bishop, Do you have anything to say?"

Victorovich and Ihono looked towards Bishop. He was sitting in the third chair of the Trinity.

Animatedly he began, "My job is to uphold the integrity of Amerika but also to protect the Earth Council peace process," he said.

"And to do that, we need a legal safety net to protect our country against extreme or irrational interpretations of the protocol. That is why I have brought Deacon, here. He is my operational implementer of policy. He gets it done." Bishop waggled his fists as if for emphasis.

He continued, "The original Earth Charter was written in a rush and was never meant to be the final agreed text between our three great Superstates."

Victorovich interrupted, "I think you are missing the point. This isn't just about our three states. It is also about the unbridled use of mega-weapons in the Scratch. The Charter and Treaty protocols aren't like any other treaty. They are supposed to stop any Superstate from flexing its muscles or attempting to prove its supremacy."

Bishop retorted, "But the Treaty with The Scratch was agreed at pace in the most challenging possible political circumstances to deliver on a clear political decision of the Senate and with the clear overriding purpose of protecting the special circumstances of The Scratch."

Ihono added, " But your actions have been near-universally damned by both other Superstates and, from what we can tell, by your normally supportive mainstream media. The opinion column in The Imperialist was quite damning of your actions, for example."

Bishop blustered and spluttered, "I believe you will see an Amerika that is more united than for decades in its constitutional settlement, where The Great Stability has delivered a new excitement and verve – not just free trade and free ports, but since the freedom we have gained with the import of magnetite from Jupiter we have the ability to do things differently and better, from innovation in tech and data and finance to improving our standards across the piece.

Yes, you will see a country that scrupulously controls its own borders, including those with the Scratch. The Scratch which, after all, wanted to go its own way outside of the rigours of our governing structure. Amerika is in some ways more cosmopolitan than ever before, welcoming scientists and artists and people of talent from around the world, an Amerika that is proud of our culture and history and unashamed of our heritage, but also unblinkered about the present – embracing every person with love and respect whatever their race or creed or gender or orientation.

"That is the Amerika we are building. I know that it seems tough now, when we are tackling the indignities and cruelty and absurdity of an unwanted terrorist incursion into our airspace, but I believe it is a measure of the greatness of this state that we are simply not going to let it hold us back or slow us down, and we are certainly not going to let it get us down, not for a moment, because even in the darkest moments we can see the bright future ahead, and we can see how to build it, and we are going to build it together."

Ihono looked at Victorovich. They both wondered at Bishop's new found eloquence. They could not realise that Bishop was being guided by the playbook wording of Cardinal, operating in the background and sending the words directly to Bishop.

"Your eloquence is deceptive," said Ihono, She looked towards Victorovich for support.

"There is no doubting the tragedy of destruction of The Block. But you are trying to cover up what you have done. To justify it on moral grounds. The fact is, you have laid waste to a huge area of The Scratch," said Victorovich, "And more, you did this even before The Block was destroyed."

"But where are our manners?" asked Ihono, "We should ask our two guests for their inputs. How would you prefer to be addressed?

Roelof spoke first, "I'm usually referred to as Roelof and my colleague here is Jasmijn. You'd recognise us as Androids, but in our case, we are from Ganymede and have been re-housed in available Earthside Personas."

"Yes, you both seem to be in quite attractive Presences," said Ihono, "I don't think I recognise your type designations?"

Jasmijn smiled, "We had to improvise when we arrived Earthside. We were able to use a secure transmission to ship our Personas here, but then we had to add them to available Presences."

Jasmijn sent a short communication to Roelof that they should not reveal that they were now Generation 9+ Superdroids.

They had both been scanning the room during Bishop's

lengthy speech. Aside from Bishop's added digital capabilities and a similarly small set added to Deacon, it looked as if the others were all human. In other words, Sharps.

They set out to explain the situation to the Trinity.

Roelof began, "There appears to be a technology drift which has affected Ganymede. We were unaware until something happened to us both."

Jasmijn added, "Originally we did not have the self-awareness to know that we were android. One day, the Earthside Controller Matson called our Earthside Primes to a meeting. Matson described an irregularity in the assessments that we make about the situation in Ganymede. The readings were different between our Earthside Primes and the other two sets of Amerika Earthside Primes. They were called Cat, Reibu, Francesca and Lorenzo."

Roelof continued, "It triggered us to take some Ganymedean readings of status and culminated in us downloading an extensive log of what happened around the time of a system upgrade."

Jasmijn took over, "It is when we discovered that something was amiss. Both Bases - Earthside and Ganymede - were being moved and the environment was being edited to make it look the same as it had prior to the move.

Roelof added, "Except that the whole environment had been up-levelled during the move. Our own memories had been blanked from the time just before the triggering of the destruction of the preceding base, which is why we had no recollection of anything untoward."

Our Earthside Primes, that is Cindy and Sam, they carried out an investigation into how much Matson seemed to know. It seems that Matson was aware of the moves, of the Base destruction and was even attempting to move the discoverers of the situation out of the way. Cat, Reibu, Francesca and Lorenzo were all moved to off-earth duties after their discoveries, but Cindy and Sam were retained whilst a set of new Primes were installed. They were kept on to provide continuity.

Deacon asked, "But if Sam and Cindy knew all of this, why didn't they say something?"

"They attempted to alert people, but it became apparent that they were both in danger. They made their escape into The Scratch. We think that is why there was a major canyon blasted into the Scratch. It was an attempt by New Delaware to eliminate them."

Deacon nodded, "It would explain Matson's orders to a Hunter to track down Sam and Cindy. For a Human, things were moving fast. I expect Matson was trying to cover his tracks."

"Yes, we also have a hidden chain of command. Matson was being ordered around by Commander Green and in turn, Commander Green was being ordered by Darnell.

"Darnell?" queried Victorovich, "But he is an old man?"

Deacon agreed, "An old man supported by the finest life preservation technologies. He is a powerful entity and can provide orders to Occupiers who can run slave networks across New Delaware and The Scratch."

"So, can we get to Green or Matson?" Asked Jasmijn.

"Neither, " answered Deacon, " Green, and then Matson both failed in their missions. They were removed by Darnell. He may be old, but he has much power and is ruthless."

"But I get no signal from Darnell. My supposition is that he has also been terminated?" said Jasmijn.

Bishop blustered, "Yes, but nowadays we have me in charge and the backup of Cardinal. Those halcyon days are long gone."

"I'm not so sure," said Deacon, "My worry is that we have the science to preserve life, but it operates at a severe cost. The sentience of the human is lost sometime after their 100th year. They still function but make increasingly bad or irrational decisions."

"You are speaking as if a 'droid?" asked Roelof. He had already picked up that Deacon was at least humanoid, because of a partial implant. Roelof wanted to see whether Deacon would admit it.

"Yes, I do have some operational specific logic circuits. It is why I can make dispassionate decisions when involved in large scale projects," answered Deacon.

Bishop had been listening to the exchange, "It doesn't matter though, I repeat I am in charge for Amerika, not for some old man."

Deacon wondered if Cardinal was tuned into the discussion. Deacon knew that Cardinal was much younger than Darnell, even younger than Bishop. Maybe there would be a new guard around the Trinity?

Ihono spoke, "Thank you Roelof and Jasmijn, and also you, Deacon, for expanding on this situation. We have had similar tests affect us in Sino-Nihon in the past. Victorovich nodded his agreement, "We too, had a bad situation with a power-broker - but also much younger than Darnell.

"It was the still-youthful insane Valerianovich, once our Senate's Minister of the Interior. He seized upon the untimely death of Antipina Yanovna to increase his influence and consolidate his position with Nadka Romanovna.

Valerianovich announced that the spirit of a martyred prophet had descended upon him; he had visions and went into ecstasy in public; at times. When conversing with Romanova, he would suddenly pause and point dramatically to the empty space behind her, saying that Yanovna was there hovering over them.

"What like someone Occupied?" Asked Roelof, analytically.

"I agree it could have been, but this riot of fantasy, this coinage of a disordered brain, did not impair the exercise of a shrewd wit."

"It is said that Valerianovich had his agents compose notes of a flattering nature and send them from different parts of Eurussia to Romanovna. In these forged notes the writers praised Romanovna for her devotion to the cause and exhorted her to stand fast in her policy."

"It's like days long past, when click-farms were used to

distort public opinion," said Jasmijn.

"Yes, but it was just as effective. The die was cast. In the Senate, another leader was outspoken in his denunciation of the impossible régime. Within three months from the death of Yanovna the flag of revolt was seen in the streets. More ominous still, rioting for food began. 'An empty stomach has no ears,' runs an ancient Eurussian proverb. An epidemic of madness descended upon the government."

But this was after the Klima Wars?" asked Jasmijn, "You kept it very quiet?"

"Yes, we did, we needed to keep it tight, for fear that the unrest would restart the Klima Wars. It was the last thing that anyone wanted. I think it was one of the factors that led to our full support for the Great Stability and the formation of The Trinity," answered Victorovich.

Then he added, "Valerianovich, in the final frenzy of reactionary bureaucracy, retaliated with all the apparatus of governmental suppression. Guns on the roofs and at the street corners of a Eurussian capital. There was a monster demonstration in the streets, and Valerianovich's soldiers fired into the crowd. The mobs, in reprisal, murdered every police official that fell into their hands. Then, Romanovna attempted to dissolve the local governing body. But it refused to be dissolved. By this time the situation was so out of hand that President of the local government, contacted Romanovna to say the position was serious. There was anarchy in the capital. The government was paralyzed. The transportation of fuel and food was completely disorganized - like siege conditions. The general dissatisfaction was growing. Disorderly gunfire took place in the streets. He requested help."

"But there was no answer. The citizen letters to Romanovna, with their scorn of the growing popular outcry against a corrupt and inefficient government, blinded judgment and paralyzed the will of her deputies. One generous gesture might have saved that Eurussian country and changed the course of history. Instead, it became a first part of The Scratch in Eurussia."

Deacon was staring at Victorovich, "That is not what it says in the history archives. Bishop and I studied recent history in the Cadet Academy, but there is no reference to this."

"No, but I think you have references to the Info Wars, which ran alongside the Klima War? Much of the news was manipulated at that time and many facts were omitted. In some cases, whole individuals have been erased from history," answered Victorovich.

Bishop looked angry. He said, "We cannot look to the past for this. We must simply reassert control. We need to establish a grip around these terrorist inspired acts which have created days of chaos here in New Delaware.

I propose to personally front the return-to-stability drive rather than allow a beleaguered situation to prevail. I know there have been calls for Matson to quit over the fiasco, but it is part of a deliberate attempt to switch the "messenger" and win back the public.

There is a moral duty to rapidly move the Block and to reopen the Base Control systems safely, and I would like to thank the workers who have already made a new Base ready for use slightly to the north of the previous one.

We are always been guided by our scientific experts, and we now know far more about the politics surrounding The Scratch than we did earlier this year.

"This is why it's vitally important that we get our Base back online as quickly as possible. Nothing will have a greater effect on the life chances of our citizens than an assured supply of magnetite."

But where, exactly, is Matson now?" asked Ihono.

Victorovich looked towards Bishop, "You ordered it!" he said, "The assassination of Matson."

Bishop looked confused. Both Roelof and Jasmijn's sensors picked up a sudden heart rate increase from Bishop. His blink rate also changed. They decided it was a proxy for lying. Sure enough, Bishop replied, "No - it was the two Eurussian Primes you supplied us as an interim who terminated Matson. Yevgeny and Julia - both arrivals from Barcelona. I'm told they used a TZ to terminate him."

Deacon knew more and spoke. "Matson had been asked by Darnell to find the two missing Primes - Sam and Cindy. It was Matson that ordered the destruction of 8 kilometres of the bullet train line, by a series of Hunter explosions and railgun fire. He was under pressure from Darnell, but once he had done his job - but failed to capture Sam and Cindy, then he was terminated by Darnell. Matson was effectively a prisoner of the two Eurussian Primes, although they were now under Darnell's control.

Roelof and Jasmijn quietly processed all this information. Roelof spoke, "You realise that there was also side effect from the way that the Block was taken down?"

"How so?" asked Ihono.

"There was an instance of Kratos in the Block. Kratos was not idly named. It represents a divine personification of strength and has persisted across all the generations of Earth. Some say it is Earth's guardian, others that Kratos represents a caretaker.

"What is the difference?" asked Victorovich.

"A guardian can fight and punish, while a caretaker is altogether more mild in the way it goes about its duties," answered Roelof.

Kratos Trigger

Jasmijn continued, "We Primes were originally set up to run the mining operations on Ganymede. On Earth, Primes like Sam and Cindy were set up to provide oversight for the Ganymedean Primes. That's how the tuples for Ganymede and Earth were arranged. Roelof and I. Sam and Cindy. Then our Secondaries. But the information provided to the Primes in Ganymede outstripped anything that the Primes on Earth would have.

"We were given access to the control channels of every worker on Ganymede. We had links to the other Primes, we had the links to our Secondaries. It means we have the power to reprogram all the androids on Ganymede, and to cross verify changes with the other two bases. At no stage did anyone step across the line from co-operation with everyone else. Everyone knew that the stakes were too high."

"Now we must use the same powers here on Earth, although we can see that there has been considerably more information hiding. For example, the backup

Primes don't know about the main controlling set. So the particular role of Sam and Cindy as Controlling Primes isn't recognised.

"Now, additional to the Primes having cross-communication, they are also tapped into other major systems. It means we can identify when a boundary condition is reached."

Yes, something is watching for a certain condition here on earth. It is part of the DAARQ constructs. We Primes have all been instructed with information about Earth having a Doomsday Mechanism."

"Doomsday - it is all sounding quite bleak," said Ihono, "Even worse than the way The Scratch is portrayed back in New Delaware."

"Yes," said Deacon, "When we were taught at Cadet School about the rising temperature of the Earth, there was also gossip about a Doomsday mechanism. It was supposed to keep checking that the condition of Earth was still viable. If it detected a problem three times in a row, it would invoke the apex."

"The apex?" asked Victorovich.

Roelof answered, "Yes, there's a set of conditions that re-establishes a dominant strain on Earth, on a kind of 'if all else fails' basis. And the twist is the apex will function against both humans and androids, until it has reasserted an equilibrium that ensures the continuation of Earth.

"What, like a bug or virus that takes over?" asked Ihono.

Roelof replied, "Exactly, it is supposed to be an Earth

countermeasure if the planet is attacked or a new war is creating mutually assured destruction."

Jasmijn interrupted, "That was what happened when the space freighter aimed its thrusters at The Block. Kratos was destroyed. Any Primes will have received a message that Kratos was sending its RNA into other organisms. The mRNA messenger strands are effectively the program to rebuild an operational Kratos."

"But then there would need to be the second trigger?" asked Sam.

"Correct," said Jasmijn, "Earth is somehow listening for the end of the world, so that Kratos can be triggered as a one-time event."

Bishop laughed, "You expect us to believe this drivel. Drivel created by a few deranged Prime Androids. More than that, they have only been Earthside for a few hours; they can't possibly understand the sophistication of this environment and are resorting to quoting the Greek myth of the Binding of Prometheus. Utter piffle. 'I'll take my cue from deeds, not words, ' " as Aeschylus said."

Bishop was used to ending an argument with some classical quotation.

"Time, as it grows old, teaches all things," replied Jasmijn, "also Aeschylus."

"Obstinacy, standing alone, is the weakest of all things in one whose mind is not possessed by wisdom," added Roelof, "Also Aeschylus."

Roelof and Jasmijn were loving their speed upgrades.

"And in addition to the Kratos Trigger, you have inbound SkyTrains filled with G-Type androids. They don't have the Asimov or SK settings and will not automatically protect humans. We believe that there may be a clearance programme like the one already enacted on Ganymede."

"What clearance programme?" asked Victorovich.

"We validated that the bases on Ganymede and Earthside move each time there is a significant system upgrade. We have been replaced several times with updated versions," explained Jasmijn.

"We sent the data transmission to Amerika Earth Base. It's the one that Sam and Cindy received. Don't tell me it was suppressed?"

"Correct," said Bishop. "It was Fake News. Falsified data streams and re-engineered images to create instability Earthside. Our scientists analysed it and they told me what I wanted to hear. There was no point in passing it on. It would just create an unnecessary panic."

Deacon looked across to Jasmijn and Roelof. Despite Deacon's modifications being relatively minor, he was now giving off a logic signal that something did not compute. Roelof and Jasmijn realised that Deacon might believe them.

"Well I'm going to summarise anyway," said Roelof. "It is up to you whether you believe us."

1. The Kratos Trigger has been set
2. Earth is monitoring for other disturbances which would re-energise the Kratos Virus.
3. Earth and Ganymede bases have been moved several times, as part of an upgrade process.
4. Each time the Bases move, another parcel of land is first cleansed and then taken over.
5. The incoming SkyTrains may contain G-Type droids that are not sensitive to damage to humans
6. On Ganymede, the androids had progressively taken over the work. Humans are no longer needed and have been quietly phased out.
7. The return of humans has slowed over the last few SkyTrains.
8. Although incoming SkyTrains are supposed to be full of magnetite, every second one could now bring androids and android technology to earth.
9. Based upon our Presences, the Ganymede technology now outstrips that available Earthside."

Roelof paused. He could see that Deacon was believing him, but Bishop was now increasingly restless. Ihono and Victorovich were uncertain. The android had just reeled off a stream of facts and they were trying to process them all.

Bishop spoke, "Well - it looks as if we'll have little to fear from Ganymedean androids, based upon that hypothesis. It has about as much realism as the story of Jason and the Argonauts.

"They attempt to get the golden fleece and bring it back -

just like the magnetite we could say. Then the Sirens attempt to lure us onto the rocks - The Sirens are you two androids, by the way. There's even the piece where you describe something being chopped into pieces and then brought back to life. Just like Medea and the ram. Cut into pieces and then restored as a lamb. No, I'm sorry, but I can't believe a word of what you say, and neither should you Ihono nor you Victorovich. This has been a wasted session. Deacon, please escort these two droids back to the unsecured area."

Bishop gestured towards the exits from the meeting area. Jasmijn and Roelof decided it was best to play along. They would also have better access to Deacon outside.

Great telemetry

Once again, they went through the strange elevator protocol. This time the rose from the sub-levels past ground and upwards to the 80th floor. Then they took a separate elevator to the ground level. Deacon accompanied them all the way.

"So, what did you make of that?" asked Jasmijn.

"Well, first, let me say that I notice you are both levelled-up androids. You are at least a generation ahead of anything we have Earthside," answered Deacon.

"With that said, I'm guessing you have great telemetry and can read anyone with any form of digital implant?"

"And some readings from humans too... Temperature, respiration, BMI calculation, blink rate. They are all good proxies for understanding when someone is telling the truth, " said Jasmijn.

"BMI? I'm guessing you are making combat assessments too," answered Deacon.

"That's right, I included it to see how much logic processing you have," answered Jasmijn, "You seem to be smarter than Bishop?"

"Not really, none of us really know what happened when he had a bad crash and was repaired by one of the Humlabs," answered Deacon.

"Yes, we can see the digital leakage, he has been wired, but I'm not sure it was terribly good job," answered Roelof, "Yours, on the other hand seems to be a smaller amendment but it has been well-implemented."

"I think Bishop suffers from back-channel interference," said Jasmijn,"It seems to be coming from Cardinal. It's incessant but not particularly well-reasoned logic."

"Cardinal is a human," answered Deacon, "But I guess you've already realised that."

The second elevator arrived back at ground level.

"You'd better go. It would be too obvious if we carried on a conversation now. I'll meet you tomorrow at 12:00 in Western Plaza Mall, Second floor- the food court. It should be anonymous there."

Roelof and Jasmijn nodded their agreement and moved away from the entrance Mall. Deacon prepared for his return trip to the Trinity.

Bluster and hand-waving

Roelof and Jasmijn were talking. They had a good result that they could meet with Deacon the next day in a Shopping Mall.

"The Malls nearly died out you know," said Roelof to Jasmijn.

"I have it in my Earth History," answered Jasmijn, " It was as early as the Scourge, when people had to do everything online because they were fearful of going out."

"It sounds a bit like life on Ganymede," answered Roelof, "Although we have the big areas which are like Malls, but everything is still provisioned online."

Jasmijn asked, "So what did you think of our session with The Trinity?"

Roelof began, "Bishop blatantly seizing control is all very well. Sometimes forgotten is that power is useful only when you have a notion of what you want to do with it. Bishop stumbled upon this truth during his ill-starred time on Earth Council. Bishop's personal ambition never looked beyond becoming leader of the Amerikan Earth Council."

Jasmijn nodded "Yes, Bishop may have his hands on the levers of power, but lacks anything resembling a prospectus. He seems to be lost. Initially, he seemed to think 'Making Amerika great again' would be purpose enough. Now he is firing his ideas from the hip, unsubstantiated with nothing more than his own, personal opinion."

Roelof looked at Jasmijn, "In the event, his premiership is being shaped by the attack on the American Block. The one that Haruto and Feng Jing orchestrated from The Scratch. Here, all the decision-making has belonged to Bishop alone, with no-one to gainsay his political direction. The policy and communications strategy come from Bishop and his special adviser Cardinal. The result has been shambolic."

Jasmijn looked pensive, "Bishop's rotund bluffing, handwaving and buffoonery has proven to be no match for what looks like a terrorist attack."

She continued, "Effective communications are vital in managing such a crisis. The most important ingredients are clarity and the capacity to instil public trust. In Amerika's case, trust was shattered when Bishop refused to criticise Matson for openly flouting the Treaty with The Scratch. After all, if Matson hadn't decided to fire off a whole row of Hunters along the bullet train path, then the two Earthside Primes - Sam and Cindy - would not have needed to seek such drastic self-defence measures."

Roelof nodded his agreement, "The absence of clarity in the Bishop's communication mirrored the lack of a coherent strategy. Bishop's forte is claiming and then telling good-news stories. A form of credit piracy."

Jasmijn agreed, "Yes, the only operational measures taken during the crisis have come not from Bishop, but from Deacon. Cardinal, with a background as a political campaigner rather than policymaker, has responded to all this by seeking to hoard still more power for Bishop. Neither Cardinal nor Bishop has shown the slightest empathetic response to the situation."

Roelof continued, "With a handful of exceptions, the Senate have been side-lined. Bishop, it should be said, is not the first in his role to have tried to centralise decision-making - this time under the direct influence of Cardinal. They have simply used the situation as an attempt to power grab."

Jasmijn agreed," Yes, and Cardinal's version of the government machine puts too high a premium on policymaking at the expense of management and implementation skills. Cardinal is only the latest in a long line of ministerial advisers who have said Senate should recruit more engineers and mathematicians alongside its traditional intake of Cadet School humanities graduates.

"For the most part, though, rearranging the institutional furniture is a displacement activity — a poor substitute for the pursuit of an intelligent governing strategy. The Earth Council leaders who have succeeded through the years in bending the will of Senate to their service have done so not by changing personnel reporting lines but by setting clear ambitions and pursuing them with consistency. "

Roelof nodded, "There is something already broken about the way that Cardinal operates. He is underpowered, even compared with the machine-augmented Bishop. Simply put, Amerika is being run by a slow-witted theorist manipulating the puppet strings of a buffoon."

Western Plaza Food Mall

It was midday and Roelof and Jasmijn had taken seats in the food court of the Western Plaza Mall. It was a noisy environment, which would make monitoring their conversation difficult. They both noticed that they were receiving a fair number of stares.

"They are looking at us because we are so much better-looking than their usual run-of-the-mill droids," said Roelof to Jasmijn.

In the distance they could see Deacon approaching. He appeared to be alone.

He reached their table and sat down.

"Are you alone?" he asked, "I am, because I wanted this to be a frank and free exchange. I've come to this meeting, but I'm still sceptical," said Deacon, "Two Ganymedeans, currently residing in the Scratch and somehow able to make predictions about everything. Now they want my help."

"Not at all," said Jasmijn, "I don't blame your scepticism. In fact, I'm relieved - you might have more smarts that we'd given you credit for!" said Jasmijn, matter-of-factly.

"I'm sure you know there are huge numbers of failures in the prediction of political events. It's a case of bad predictions, magnified by imperialist news sources and no reliable mechanisms for fixing obvious errors," she looked at Deacon, who was nodding.

Roelof began, "A few examples; take the end of Eurussian Communism, way back in the 1980s. No official estimates even mentioned that the collapse of Communism was a distinct possibility until the coup of 1989. The National Security Agency even went so far as to admit it.

"The rise of populism, whether it was the beginning of the collapse of the European Union, back in the early 2000s, after the United Kingdom left, or the rise of right-wing populism in Amerika in a similar era, when a loud-mouthed failed businessman was elected to one of the top positions on Earth."

"But surely that was what started the formation of Amerika?" Asked Deacon.

Jasmijn agreed, "Well, yes, if by that you mean an ill-educated populist electorate, partially disenfranchised from even voting. There was the small matter of the Scourge, The Warming, Klima Wars and the Restructuring before we got to now, with the so-called Great Stability."

Roelof added, "Now we see Cardinal attempting to overturn the Stability. He's following his own ideas, pompously self-manufactured and then coated in pseudo science and pseudo-math to make them seem like clever."

Jasmijn continued, "Cardinal's human-brained 'expert' predictions are about as accurate as monkeys throwing darts at a board. Take a sample of other Earthside expert predictors and do the analysis. Experts were very overconfident: around 15 percent of events that experts claimed had no chance of occurring did happen, and even more hapless was that around 25 percent of those that they said they were sure would happen did not happen."

Jasmijn smiled - a new effect she was quite pleased with, "I'm going to call Cardinal a 'Hedgehog-style predictor' – a fan of a Big Idea like Marxism, less likely to admit errors.

"The other kind is a 'Fox-style predictor' – they are not fans of Big Ideas, more likely to admit errors and change predictions because of new evidence.

It was Deacon's turn to smile, "Ah yes, I was provisioned with a history module - That analogy comes from Archilocus, a Greek poet from c. 680–645 BCE, 'The fox knows many little things; but the hedgehog knows one big thing.'"

Jasmijn answered, "Yes - I think we were given the same uploads on Ganymede. Anyway - Foxes tended to make better predictions. They are more self-critical, adaptable, cautious, empirical, and multidisciplinary. Hedgehogs get worse as they acquire more credentials while foxes get better with experience. A hedgehog like Cardinal will distort facts to suit their theories; while a fox adjusts theories to account for new facts."

Roelof added, "And I guess if Cardinal is a hedgehog, then so is Bishop!"

Jasmijn continued, "My critique continues with media analysis, The media values 'Hedgehog' characteristics (such as Big Ideas, aggressive confidence, tenacity in combat and so on). One could say the puffery and posturing of Bishop. Those qualities are directly opposite of those prized in science. Things like updating in response to new data, admitting errors, tenacity in pursuing the truth.

Roelof interrupted, "Yes, so it means that 'Hedgehog' qualities are more in demand than 'Fox' qualities. The political and the media market both encourage qualities that make bad predictions more likely. It is no wonder that Earthside got into such a mess, with blind optimists and buffoons leading the charge."

Jasmijn looked towards Deacon, "So will you help us, if we explain?"

Deacon nodded his agreement.

"It is too difficult to meet you more frequently," he said, "You had better tell me what you know right now. My concern is that Bishop will go off on a reckless course, persuaded by Cardinal, and expect me to implement it."

"Okay, well, you know then about Kratos? The Kratos Trigger?" asked Jasmijn.

"I know that there is some kind of Doomsday trigger set somewhere and that if it is tripped then Kratos is set to defend the Earth," said Deacon.

"That's right, Kratos become the Apex Predator, until an equilibrium is restored." Said Jasmijn, " I think all of us that had digital systems have been given access to knowledge about Kratos."

"Now what that means is that we can use our Prime circuits to provide you with a link to us. Technically it is known as a slave to an occupier circuit, but fundamentally it means we have good quality two-way communication links between us."

Deacon looked concerned," I already have links set up to Bishop. Won't he be able to tell if I have additional links to you guys?" he asked.

"Not at all," said Jasmijn,"You forget, we are Primes, we have several modifications and enhancements in our Personas which allow us to control and link with other 'droids."

"We realise that you are not a 'droid, by the way," interrupted Roelof, "That you are a humanoid - a human with enhanced circuits."

"Okay, let's do it," said Deacon. He could feel that Jasmijn was now imprinted into his system.

PART TWO

Cover story

*Modern corporate controlled governments are in the
business of covering things up."*

— Steven Magee

Counterbalance

Back at the Hangar in The Scratch, Sam and Cindy had been accessing the SkyTrain roster to see which ships were incoming to New Delaware. They sat at a round table made of scrubbed metal. One side were two chairs and the other side a couple of stools. Sam and Cindy sat facing Haruto and Feng Jing, seated on the stools. A low-hung industrial light lit the area.

"There doesn't seem to be anything irregular about this," said Cindy, looking through the schedules on a compact flat screen display.

"It's the regular monthly arrivals of SkyTrains. They fluctuate between A trains and B trains. A trains contain almost entirely magnetite, with a few 'droids as supplementary cargo. B trains contain around two-thirds magnetite and one third is set aside for a factory. The factory unit is used to build higher technology magnetite plant and sometimes additional 'droids."

"The old passenger SkyTrains have more or less finished

arriving. I guess you could call them C trains. They used to contain returning human miners from Ganymede and a more limited quantity of magnetite."

"Ever since the Telos moment, there's not been many humans returning from Ganymede," said Haruto , "That is the irony kept from routine dwellers in New Delaware, but blatantly obvious to us living here in The Scratch."

Sam and Cindy looked at Haruto, "No, we don't know about Telos," said Sam.

"I'm amazed how it has been kept secret," said Haruto, "The Telos Moment was when the purpose of the Ganymede exodus became clear. The external atmosphere controls failed. Ganymede became unable to sustain human life."

Sam asked, "So what happened to everyone. And why don't we know about this back on Earth?"

"There was a SkyTrain dispatched with the bodies. It took a different route from the other ones. Away from the solar system."

"But how was it covered up?" asked Cindy, "There must have been many hundreds killed, and we were monitoring on a daily basis."

Haruto reminded them, "The base is always running 34 minutes behind Earth. I know you have only recently discovered it, but the time has been used to make substitutions when a base upgrade occurs. Hence Roelof and Jasmijn continuously improving but neither they, nor you, realised what was happening. Their own consciousness was always reset to a time after the event of the base clearance had occurred. Then add in calming loops to the transmissions to Earthside and it was possible to cover the terrible moment when the environment failed."

"But how with all the safety circuits?" asked Darnell.

"The Sharps were too slow thinking. The android protocol meant that most of the activity to manage this event could take place within two insect wing beats. Unnoticed by the Sharps. And remember the 'droids on Ganymede are Type-Gs - they don't have the usual 'protect humans' settings." said Haruto.

"And think about it, the remaining androids had sufficient personality to be able fool people nearly 600 million kilometres away,"

"So how did you find out" asked Darnell.

"We are living an unfiltered life here in The Scratch," answered Haruto.

"So do we know what caused the failure?" asked Cindy, "With so many foolproof systems running on Ganymede."

"We have a theory here," said Haruto, "but it's a bit 'out there'."

"Go on," said Sam.

"Well, we have picked up several transmissions from Earthside with a unique header: it is 'Adrasteia'. We couldn't find any matches unless we looked back into deep history. There were two matches. The very early one from Greek mythology about Adrasteia as the nurse of

Zeus. And another more recent one, which showed that Adrasteia could be a counterbalance to Kratos."

"What! So if Kratos gets triggered, than so does Adrasteia?" asked Sam.

"Kratos means Strength in Greek," added Feng Jing.

"That was our working theory," answered Haruto," We could tell that Kratos had been awoken. That its systems were activated, but that it had not recombined into anything dangerous."

"You talk about it as if it were alive?" said Cindy.

"Oh yes, we think both Kratos and Adrasteia are at least some part organic," answered Haruto.

"Wouldn't that simply make them humanoid?" asked Sam, "Human, part digital?"

"Not in this case," answered Haruto, "The amount of organics is tiny compared with the other technologies. We think they are spin-offs from the work that was being conducted by Biotree when it was taken over by Torus Industries."

Sam looked at Haruto, "We were briefed about Biotree, but never really told what they did. Simply that it was some kind of acquisition - one of the many."

Haruto, leaned into the table that they were seated around.

He said, "Help me, Feng Jing, if I get any of his wrong...Biotree worked with mechanosynthesis. That is construction an atom at a time. It was beyond a watchmaker's precision, to know how to bolt atoms together to make the tiny nanobot machines that formed the basis of the Biotree business model.

Haruto continued, "Biotree learned how to build these tiny structures, how to make them operate, which parts would simply refuse to work together because of the still only partly understood and apparently tiny forces between them. Forces that were big enough to destroy the machines to which they were attached if they were not coupled properly.

"A famous Biotree Scientist said it was like being inside God's head. If a God existed, then God would need to know this stuff really well.

Feng Jing cut in, "Torus and Biotree made a lot of money from ultra-transformables, which were a branch of the science that helped in healthcare, the machines having a squishiness which meant they travelled well inside humans."

Haruto spoke again, "Yes, Biotree built a particle accelerator to smash small things apart to see the effects. There was something mysterious about the power needed when humans tried to do these things, compared with the weak forces apparent in the nano-machines and yet these forces which could do exceptionally more powerful things if assembled incorrectly."

Cindy said, "Back to God's head, it was like His way of saying, 'No, No, don't do that.'"

Fang Ying continued, "Biotree ran into nanotoxins as part of the research. To people in the ethical science community, there were some basic rules about what to attempt and mix, and most of the 'No-no's" were very obvious."

Sam asked, "What like weaponisation of the nanomachines?"

Haruto said, "Yes, and even more simply, the misuse of the technology, whether for financial gain or simply to look away when something wrong was being created."

He continued, "In the early days of the food shortages, nano-machines were used to improve foodstuffs. However, Biotree found that the addition of these machines as a way to deliver medicinal payload was a very profitable line. The only thing was, the nanomachines worked better if they could hook onto an organic machine. That's around the time that Kratos was first envisaged- Something of a 'No-no', actually."

Feng Jing nodded, "Yes - Kratos was designed to be a supervirus that could only work when powered by RNA. Imagine the machinery of humans with small RNA processes, triggered by mRNA (messenger RNA) programs. It was one of these early machines that is thought to have started the First Outbreak that led to The Scourge."

She continued, "After the tropus work, which had its place neutralising an earlier organic virus, a discovery was made. In software trees it was what is known as an 'exploit'. In the right quantity, the human body - or any other living organism for that matter - detected and destroyed nanobots on the way in.

"Here's the exploit: If the nanobots couldn't be destroyed, they were neutralised although this left residuals in the body. What was fascinating was that the residuals were stored in almost homeopathic quantities. It became the building block of the way that Kratos operates."

Sam spoke, "I can remember when I broke a leg, at IPX - That's Interplanetary Expedition Academy- that I was given a shot of nanotech to speed the recovery. The small machines speedily knitted my bones back together. Instead of 2-3 months, I was fully functional again in around a week. I was amazed at the speed of reconstruction. It was so fast that my muscle-fibres didn't weaken and by week three, I was fully fit again. They gave me a second shot of nanotech at that time, and I'm told that the second shot was to break up the first set of nano-machines inside of my bloodstream."

Feng Jing, nodded agreement, "Yes you are absolutely correct about that. It worked on a similar basis to the original tropus which depleted after around month - In effect, the nano-machines ran down, stopped working and were flushed from your system. It's the same mechanism that Biotree used to keep selling the original tropus and which made it one of the most profitable companies on earth. The designers had built in obsolescence to the tropus. It needed to be refreshed every 4 weeks or so. That, of course, meant regular money for Biotree."

Haruto continued, "But it didn't stop there. Biotree had worked out that an average human adult could eat nano-processed food every day of their life. Unless the human system changed the form of handling, the effect of the residual "neutralised and stored" nanotech would still only amount to something which in homeopathy was called the 60X formula."

Fans Jing added, "This wasn't one sixtieth, it was ten to the power of minus sixty. Something like the equivalent of a single pinch of salt into the Pacific Ocean. This level was so far below the 24X considered to be the limit of any homeopathic remedy, such that the little broken nanomachines couldn't pose any threat at all.

Of course, that assumed that the body had done its 'repel all invaders' thing and broken the machines down and expelled them.

Haruto explained, "It was the very power of these tiny machines that ultimately led to a new business model developing. They were already being packaged and consumerised by Biotree, and they knew there were many more practical and positive uses."

"So, there were residual nanobots left in humans because of the uses of the technology for food production?" asked Sam.

"Correct," said Haruto, " See where this is going?"

Feng Jing continued, "I mentioned that Kratos was Greek for Strength; did I mention that Adrasteia has another word in Greek? It's Nemesis."

"Wow!" said Cindy, "So the female Adrasteia is the nemesis of the strong male Kratos?"

"You've just about summed it up," said Haruto, "A self protection device devised for Earthside has also heralded the development of a contrary device to neutralise it."

"But this is all messing with evolution," said Sam, "Surely Biotree would have recognised this?"

"I think they did," said Haruto, "There's an old set of documents, 'The Pulse Papers,' that describe what happened when they last attempted to mess around with DNA and RNA. Feng Jing, can you bring it up on a screen?"

Feng Jing nodded and a few seconds later the sensewall displayed the information.

"Let's take a look at the summary, from the Pulse Papers"

Feng Jing projected several charts onto the Sensewall:

HOW IT STARTED

- Earth gets sick from a virus.
- Biotree experiments with nanotech and builds a counter-virus and uses nanotech to deploy it.

THE TROPUS

- People routinely place the nanotech in their bloodstream via cartridges.
- The material inserted is called the tropus.
- Biotree is sole supplier and becomes rich and powerful
- First the tropus is used to counteract the virus, at a carefully regulated speed which won't overload the human system.
- The technology is extended to provide other enhancements.
- The Chinese reverse engineer the nanobots and create a cloned version of the tropus to sell

ECONOMIC WARFARE

- There is a price war, brought about by the competition.
- The Chinese optimise the nanobots but don't realise that there's a Brownian brake built into the original design to stop it from accelerating out of control.
- The black-market sales of the doctored Chinese nanobots rocket. People known as 'sifes' siphon off part of their own tropus because it is profitable.
- Scientists at Biotree realise that they have destroyed enough of the virus load to ensure that it is no longer dangerous to most people.

THE DANGEROUS FLAW

- The Chinese don't understand what they have manufactured.
- When the optimised Chinese nanobots accelerate, they tear apart the organism in which they are hosted.

THE SCOURGE

- That is how much of the Southern Hemisphere was destroyed, with Australia and New Zealand put into total isolated quarantine.
- The sources of the original virus were discovered as something which has landed at various places on earth.
- A secret programme is created to protect Earthside from a similar future attack.

THE DOOMSDAY SYSTEM

- Three monitoring stations are established which check for multiple signs of life on Earth. They are called the LIGOs and when two of three signal endgame then Kratos reassembly commences.

"But what is a LIGO?" asked Cindy, initiating a search for it.

Feng Jing answered matter-of-factly, "It's a top-secret laser interferometer gravity-wave observatory. It is used for tracking deep space events."

"But why would one of these be of any use?" asked Sam, "And why was it kept secret?"

"That's what we all wondered," answered Haruto, "Especially because its construction could be considered a prestigious project."

Feng Jing announced, "The rumours were that it was part of the Doomsday project, designed to protect the Earth in the case of a cataclysmic event."

Roelof looked confused, "I've just searched for information about LIGOs and it goes on to say that deep space events cannot be tracked by a single scanner. There needs to be at least two for the readings to be cross verified. Ideally the other device should be a long way from the first one."

"But then what would the LIGO track?" asked Sam.

"Officially - Gravitational waves," answered Feng Jing, "Literally ripples in space. A gravitational wave is an invisible (yet incredibly fast) ripple in space. Gravitational waves travel at the speed of light - that's almost 300,000 km per second. These waves squeeze and stretch anything in their path as they pass by. A LIGO uses a couple of mirrors to detect the changes to a long length of material. The ripple of a gravitational wave will cause the mirror to distort and then a reading can be taken."

"But," said Haruto, "We think the LIGO was a cover for another device which checked for proof of life around Earth. The three so-called LIGO installations could communicate with one another and cross check that Earth was still functioning. Any side of a major disruption and the Kratos Virus could be triggered."

"But who is driving these events?" asked Sam, "It has the hallmark of an emotion-free megalomaniac!"

Feng Jing looked up again, "I've been reading through the detail in the Pulse Papers. It describes a construct named Holden. It implies that when the domes which spread the original virus were destroyed, that Holden was also destroyed. But there is no confirmation."

"But that is all in the distant past? Maybe 300 years ago" asked Sam, "Surely there has to be a more current explanation?"

Haruto answered, "No think about it, if Holden was a construct and went to ground at the time of the destruction of the original virus carrying spheres, then why wouldn't the same construct re-energise now - in a time of great stress to Earthside?"

"It implies Holden is monitoring Kratos? Is that possible?" asked Sam.

Feng Jing looked up from the console, "I can usually tap into the Sino-Nihon and Eurussian channels too," said Feng Jing, "I'm going to see if anything unusual is happening in either of their territories. It could confirm an upheaval, which suggests that something global is occurring."

"How is it that you can monitor two highly secure Superstates?" asked Sam.

Feng Jing answered, "Yes, they are secure, but The Scratch is something of their blind spot. Because we still use older technologies, including some analogue ones, we have a major advantage. Everyone's uprated technology is all geared towards DAARQ and similar technologies. Distributed, Artificial Intelligence,

Augmented Reality and Quantum computing.

"Some of the basics were left at the gatepost. The new systems will monitor for sophisticated intrusion detection, but they sometimes forget that someone could leave a key underneath a flowerpot by the entrance to their fortified castle.

"All we did (that's The Resistance during the Klima Wars), was drop some of those entry points into the complex code being developed. If you know the right words, a bit like 'open sesame' then the flowerpots give way and the keys become visible."

"Ah, so you have secret ways into their systems?" asked Cindy, "Through trapdoors that some of your own agents planted?"

"Exactly," said Feng Jing, "Although a few have been discovered and are being patched up. Fortunately, once we are inside, we can add a few more entrances beyond those that already exist."

"Look, let me show you," she tapped into a control and then pushed the image to the sensewall.

There was a scene which immediately looked like a Grand Master painting, except that it was fully animated. It showed the Sino-Nihon Senate, discussing actions in Cassim Gongje.

Someone in authority was speaking, "There is a new force inside Cassim Gongje - it seems to know our moves before we make them. No-one can push us around like this. We must deploy Yakuza immediately and show no mercy in our retaliation."

Feng Jing looked at Haruto, "Here they go again," she said, "They don't realise that 'droids give them more intelligence than humans."

Sam watched the sensewall, "Can you get similar information from Eurussia?" he asked.

"Sure, " said Feng Jing, and as she spoke she tapped something into the control panel and a different scene emerged. Sleeker and cleaner looking than the Sino-Nihon, as if someone had used a good designer to provide the lighting.

"...resurrect NATO and other military forces. Plus, we can deploy the Bratva to support us in the fight to regain our control. Someone inside is following our moves, I sense an internal spy. "

"This requires the firmest of forces and for us to reassert our alliance with Sino-Nihon and Amerika."

"Yes, but won't that re-trigger the Klima Wars? We have been operating with the Great Stability for so long now!"

Sam was relaying the sensewall back to Jasmijn and Roelof in New Delaware.

Jasmijn considered the situation and then spoke, "I think we can harness this situation and bring it around," she said.

"How?" asked Cindy.

X-Blade

Well, first we need to get back to The Hangar," answered Jasmijn, "I think it's time we took a ride in those X-Blades."

Roelof nodded agreement and they made their way toward the roof. The main buildings they walked through seems deserted and there were no security cordons to stop them either.

"I've just realised," said Roelof, "Our Prime settings must still work here Earthside. It is giving us an unobstructed route through this complex."

They could see the X-Blades in front of them. A row of eight flights, glinting in the sunshine.

"I think we should take a couple - one each!" said Roelof.

"I agree," said Jasmijn, "And they will make useful resources at The Hangar."

They climbed into the first two units and sat in the pilot seats. Roelof was first to switch on the controls. He let the automatic system take over and pressed the unclip button to free the flight from its floor anchors.

Then he looked for the 'deploy' button, pressed it and the device red lit until it received a clearance signal from the Base.

In seconds he was airborne. He could see that Jasmijn was only a matter of seconds behind him. He noticed he was first over a river - which he took to be the Delaware - and then over the Scratch, which he could now see had a vast canyon driven through it from the hunt of Sam and Cindy.

Roelof wondered whether the X-Blade had any defensive capabilities, but seconds later it started an autonomous landing sequence to bring it into the area next to the Hangar.

It gently landed and a few seconds later Jasmijn's X-Blade touched down behind him. Roelof taxied across into the Hangar where he could see Sam, Cindy, Haruto and Feng Jing waiting. They appeared to be clapping - a meaningless gesture towards an android.

He pressed another button and the outer door of the X-Blade opened and he emerged onto the stairway.

"Nice bod!" called Cindy, approving of Roelof's Generation 9 transformation.

Then Jasmijn appeared, and both Sam and Cindy took in a sharp intake of breath.

"Wow, you look stunning, and you move so well! That was one brilliant upgrade!" said Cindy again.

Jasmijn was not used to compliments and could feel a curious sensation running through her systems.

"Thank you," she said, "But we literally took the first couple of units out of their cartons and readied them for operation. I do agree though, this Presence thinks faster and is more agile by far than anything we used on Ganymede. It is like getting a whole extra sense."

Præternatural

Sam and Cindy wasted no time when Roelof and Jasmijn returned.

"Look, we are checking through the incoming ship rosters. The SkyTrains are Type A - with mainly magnetite, and Type B, with a factory unit included. There's almost no humans returning now, even despite the broadcasts of homecomings which show up on the news reports.

"Yes, doctored footage," said Roelof - matter-of-factly," The magnetite is still the priority payload of these incoming SkyTrains. There had been nothing untoward done to adapt the incoming SkyTrains. No weapons added, no secret supplies of warrior 'droids."

Roelof looked towards Jasmijn, who nodded in agreement, "But..." she said, "If those factory SkyTrains were building 'droids, we wouldn't know. They'll have increased the cargo size 'in flight.' Nothing would have been dispatched from Ganymede, yes something will arrive Earthside."

"Sam, can we check a recent Manifest? What's the last ship that came in? The one that we obtained these Presences from?" asked Roelof.

Sam looked into the records.

"It's okay, I've just run serial number check," said Jasmijn, "The incoming 'droids are still created as Ganymedean, So I can get access to them. I've read their serial numbers and the origin marks from all of them. She walked to the sensewall. Feng Jing pressed a couple of buttons and Jasmijn was able to project a sorted list of the incoming droids and their identifications.

"There we are, plain to see," said Roelof, "90 freshly manufactured 'droids, to the latest Generation 9 and with all the magnetite enhancements. Manufactured in transit from Ganymede."

"They will be the ones stacked in the cartons in the corner of the unloading bay," said Jasmijn, "We simply removed a couple of the packages and used them to create our new Presences. If you remember we were in those rather tiresome Hunters when we first arrived here."

Feng Jing looked a little crestfallen at that comment. Jasmijn cut in, "Oh Sorry, Feng Jing, I realise you had worked so hard to get those two units functional for us!"

Roelof, Sam and Cindy all looked over to Jasmijn. She had just uttered an empathic response. Jasmijn suddenly realised this herself, "Wow - these units really do have some sophisticated processing," she said.

"Yes, but they also don't have the normal Earthside safety

features," said Roelof, "We are effectively unconstrained, no Asimov logic, no SK rules. It means that the incoming SkyTrains from Ganymede are producing ever-increasing numbers of Type-G 'droids. Not only that, they're also super-fast, super-agile. In other words, they are pretty much unstoppable."

"But they are just being stored at the moment?" asked Sam, quizzically.

Cindy added, "Correct; stored or stockpiled. No one would take much notice until they are activated. Like we all knew, the 'droids on the incoming ship are absolutely at the low-priority end of the unload instructions. About the same priority as the First Aid Kit reclamation."

"But the later SkyTrains get reconfigured," said Jasmijn. If we think of each SkyTrain as having ten units of cargo space, on the A Trains this was all for magnetite. The B Trains had one unit or two units of factory capacity - and less magnetite cargo space. But I can recollect sending ships back with up to eight units of factory space - although I don't think they will be arriving any time soon."

"But lets think about the math for a moment," said Jasmijn. "The ones we found all have low serial numbers. They are marked as PoC- That's Proof of Concept. Their date stamps indicate they were all assembled in the last quarter of an Earthside year. That is the last 90 days. And that they were created in one half of the factory unit. Multiply it up. 90 units in 3 months is 360 units in a year. Half the factory deployed means that a full factory unit could reduce twice as many. 720 units. Now add together the flight duration of three years. A factory unit could produce 2,160 units in three years. Let's consider then if the factory units increased to 8 of 10 units. That is 17,280 units arriving in one 8X multichained SkyTrain."

Jasmijn continued, "Now we've got three years of incoming SkyTrains. Assuming that the factory ships are alternates and that the factory units increase progressively, one unit at a time?"

"That's exactly how we did it," said Roelof.

"Yes, it used to be one magnetite SkyTrain and then one with returning humans. The human SkyTrains have been progressively superseded with the factory units."

"Run the math," said Jasmijn, "On simple arrival rate of one factory ship every two months..."

Roelof answered, "By the time they hit 8X factory unit capacity of 17,280, they will already have 77,760 units Earthside. Sustaining that rate for another 10 months means they would have 250,560 units Earthside."

Sam looked at Cindy, " Yes, that's a quarter of a million supergod-like entities without any overrides to protect humans."

"Well it depends when they get activated too," answered Roelof. "My estimate is that they will mobilise when they reach full factory capacity from incoming ships."

"Good point," said Sam. "They will have many incoming SkyTrains already kitted out as factories. I can't do the math, but if they kept on going, they would have an even higher output."

Jasmijn spoke, "38,880 per month, if they stayed with the incoming ship rate. But that is an artificial brake on their rate of expansion. If they moved to Earthside monthly factory production instead of every two months, then they would have a capacity of 60,480 per month by the end of three years. Without any other increases that means they would have built 876,960 units by month 36.

"I'll round it to 900,000 units for simplicity," said Sam, "And another 60,000 units every month. That is an almost unassailable quantity."

"It is," said Roelof, "Remember that every one of those units is at least 100 times faster in thought than a human and stronger and more agile. It looks like a progression towards Museum Earth. No, on second thoughts - Zoo Earth, where the humans are kept as an exhibit of a primitive life-form."

"But," said Jasmijn, "My Prime sensors are telling me that this is all being orchestrated. There's a link back to Bishop and then, presumably, to Cardinal, but it doesn't stop there."

"That's the clever part of Cardinal being human. He is a firewall in the system. An air gap between the things we know about and the things he is being commanded to do," said Roelof.

Haruto nodded, "We always thought there has been something præternatural running all of this."

Jasmijn smiled again, "Yes – *præternatural* - Happening rarely, but nonetheless by the agency of created beings. Oh yes. Most definitely... We must look for a devil. Someone or something that, being a natural magician is capable of performing acts in ways above our knowledge, though not transcending our natural power."

Roelof smiled, "And that last part of what you just said, Jasmijn. That is how we will catch him/her, or it."

The lost archive of Dr Bai Tan Chungli

Jasmijn had another purpose in returning to The Hangar. She walked across to Feng Jing, who was with Sam and Cindy watching the newscasts.

"I'm looking for something else. Something that will have been buried in the digital archives of pre Klima-War Earth."

Fang Jing looked intrigued, "We do have access to some of the pre-history files," she said, "We were able to archive a few key digital libraries, The Pentagon Library, The Library of Congress, the digitised part of the Bodleian Library, as a few examples."

"Well, I'm looking for something quite specific," said Jasmijn, "It is a paper about the research into the use of nanobot technology by the Biotree Corporation."

Feng Jing thought for a moment, "It sounds more like something that will have been published in a technical journal?" she asked, "Do you have anything further about it?"

"Well, I think the paper was written by an American scientist, for the Chinese."

"Okay, well we also have the download of the Tianjin Binhai Library from Tianjin, China. Maybe that would be a better place to start. They had over 1.2 million physical books."

Feng Jing was typing something into her search routine.

"Here, it has come back with something about Biotree working with a firm called SuzGene in Hangzhou. This refers to some work in - er- protein domain dynamics and with ribosome biological machines, if that means anything?"

"Feng Jing, you have done it again! That seems to be a direct hit on what I am looking for."

"It was filed away in Tianjin Binhai Library by someone called Dr Bai Tan Chungli. There's a collection of works stored here."

"Is there anything that directly links Biotree and SuzGene?" asked Jasmijn.

"There is, but it was written by a Canadian, not an American. Her name is Dr Sheri Bouchard and her co-writer is a Ms Daisy Stone, from England."

"This must be it," said Jasmijn, "A lost archive of Bai Tan Chungli!"

"Is there an Abstract or something,?" asked Sam.

"No need, I can read it all and summarise," said Jasmijn.

"It shows that the nanobot engineering was linked to the Great Leap, which was created with the arrival of meteor domes, which landed across the Earth."

"The Great Leap has a different meaning in China" said Feng Jing, "It was a failed campaign of Chairman Mao Zedong to transform the country from a farming economy into a communist society through the formation of people's communes. It was an economic and social disaster, which became swamped in the subsequent disasters which ravaged the Earth. Still, today, the Chinese people use 'science of tomorrow' to describe the rapid scientific progress."

Jasmijn continued, "This paper to Bai Tan Chungli - written by Dr Sheri Bouchard challenges the way that SuzGene were fabricating their nanobots. It asserts that Suzgene removed the braking system from the nanobots that Biotree produce. Dr Bouchard says that the Biotree nanobots were built with safety checks and balances. A key component of this was a Brownian brake to slow the machines down to run at Earthside metabolic rates.

"Sheri Bouchard went on to say that she thought both organisations - Biotree and SuzGene had caught a 'dragon by the tail'. Both organisations were using the tropus as a cash cow. There was a four-week cycle to refresh the cartridges for more or less everyone on Earth.

"But there was a hidden secret. The tropus had outlived its purpose - which originally was an antidote to a known virus. It then because used for other purposes. Firstly, for organic adaptations, but then, rather more menacingly as a mechanism of control.

"Dr Bouchard was proposing the release of an antidote to the nano-engineered tropus. That was to send in a nano-reductive that would counteract the nanobots in current circulation. A colleague of Bouchard had fabricated an accidental nano-reductive - a counter-agent which would cause nanobots to destroy themselves.

"Now SuzGene and BioTree controlled the entire supply of the tropus. They knew that a nano -reductive could stop the continuation of the spread of nanobots.

"They tried it in Bodø, Norway at Biotree's Advanced Technology Area and the release of the nano-reductive antidote caused the meteor dome in Norway to collapse, with a surprising resultant increase in communications and a curious rediscovery of human memories. It was as if the domes around the Earth were managing human awareness. They gave new discoveries but took away others.

"What happened?" asked Cindy.

Jasmijn replied, "Well according to this fileset, the nano-reductives were released, and humankind reawakened to its situation. Huge swathes of the southern hemisphere had already been destroyed and the rest of the planet wasn't in a very good shape. You know the sequence of events: Scourge, Warming, Klima Wars, Restructuring and then The Great Stability.

But there's a side note in Dr Bai Tan Chungli's file. He observes that the discussions between SuzGene and Biotree were watched over by a machine. There are frequent mentions of a blue monitor light in the corner of rooms when this was discussed.

"Watched over by machines of loving grace?" queried

Cindy.

"Hardly," said Jasmijn.

All Watched Over By Machines Of Loving Grace

I like to think (and
the sooner the better!)
of a cybernetic meadow
where mammals and computers
live together in mutually
programming harmony
like pure water
touching clear sky.

I like to think
(right now, please!)
of a cybernetic forest
filled with pines and electronics
where deer stroll peacefully
past computers
as if they were flowers
with spinning blossoms.

I like to think
(it has to be!)
of a cybernetic ecology
where we are free of our labors
and joined back to nature,
returned to our mammal
brothers and sisters,
and all watched over
by machines of loving grace.

Richard Brautigan.

Frog

Sam asked for access to the sensewall console and tied in a few commands. He was soon on the manifest for the checked the incoming SkyTrains from Ganymede. The next ship had already arrived.

"Hey, the incoming SkyTrain was a factory unit. There were three units of factory on this ship."
"Can we check the incoming manifest?" asked Cindy.

Sam accessed the system.

"It says there were the usual seven containers filled with magnetite. Then, for the factory units, each one had produced 3000 G9 units. That must be the code for the 9th Generation Type G androids."

"Yes, look, here are their serial numbers," said Jasmijn, "They are from the same number range as our own units."

"But look at the quantity; they are building even more units than we estimated. Instead of 2,100 per factory unit, they seem to have upped production to 3000 units. That would make 24,000 per 8X factory ship. It is significantly more than we estimated."

"Where are the units being stored?" asked Haruto, "It will need a sizeable depot to store so many."

"Okay, they are currently still in the unloading bay inventory areas," answered Sam, "To be honest, it they remain in packaging and are stacked, there is a huge capacity in those bays."

"'We will need access to a powered one," said Roelof, "So that we can modify it using our Prime powers."
    "Agreed," said Jasmijn, "Although I don't think that will be a problem. Remember when we grabbed the two units we are using as Presences? Both were already powered. They had stored magnetite charges built into the units, so I assume that is a feature of the design."

"But will these units frog?" asked Haruto, Sam and Cindy looked expectantly toward Roelof and Jasmijn."

"Frog?" queried Jasmijn, "I don't understand."

"Frog," explained Haruto," It's when the units get tampered with. They let out a godawful scream and do similar digitally. It is like a warning to other units that there is danger around."

"Okay, I can understand that but why 'frog'?" asked Jasmijn.

"There used to be an earth creature called a frog," explained Haruto, "It was a cute little thing that was amphibious. They mainly lived around ponds and other water holes but were killed off through a combination of heat and predators. They made distress calls when attacked by a predator. It was usually a high-pitched scream or wail to startle the predator causing it to release the frog, allowing it to escape. It's where the 'frog' term came from.

Feng Jing nodded, "Finally, a gap in your Earthside knowledge!" she smiled.

Sam added, " And ultimately it didn't do the frog any good, if they are now all extinct!"

Cindy added, "Yes, they croaked."

Roelof and Jasmijn looked confused again.

"Don't worry. Earthside humour. You'll need more time to catch up," said Haruto.

"I am on it," said Jasmijn, "These libraries are useful, I've just downloaded a couple of books of descriptions of Earthside wildlife."

"Please don't download any of the books of jokes," pleaded Sam.

Blow things up

"I suppose one thing we could do would be to blow up the incoming 'droids?" said Roelof.

"Hmm, it would get messy and repetitive," answered Jasmijn, "Although I suppose it would buy us some time."

Feng Jing looked agitated. She was waving her arms around as if to say 'no - stop.'

They all looked across to her. Feng Jing wrote on some paper, 'We are being monitored. Someone is listening. See that blue light?'

She gestured towards a small system in the Hangar. A tiny blue light glowed.

"I'm going to stretch my legs outside for a moment," said Sam gesturing to the others to do the same, "Maybe I'll look at where that glass that shattered came from."

Sam walked out of the door of the Hangar. Cindy, Haruto and Feng Jing followed.

Jasmijn held Roelof back. "No, I think we may be part of this problem," she said. She walked to the sensewall controls and put on a News Channel. It was talking about some possible boundary changes to New Delaware, that were being discussed by The Trinity.

Outside, Feng Jing looked at the others.

"Okay," she said," I think we are being monitored. My blue light alert system tells me when audio capture is on. It looks as if everything we say in the Hangar is being listened to. Furthermore, I'm guessing that the two new Presences that Jasmijn and Roelof are using also have monitoring systems. I think Jasmijn has realised and that is why she has kept them both inside. I'm sure Roelof will know by now. Jasmijn will have signalled to him on her Prime channel."

"But who would monitor us? And how would they ever find anything useful?" asked Sam.

"I'm guessing that it has something to do with the New Delaware base. Once they located Sam and Cindy again, they are now trying to track them down."

"But that means that they will also have heard our plans to destroy the androids," said Cindy.

"Yes, but I suspect they could also see that it was an ultimately fruitless decision," said Haruto.

"How so?" asked Sam.

"Well, think about it, we'd have to repeat the same mission many times - Maybe at least 12 times, because of all of the incoming SkyTrains with space factory-created cargo. It would never work. We'll have to think of another plan."

"Well, at least we know that they can monitor us now," said Fang Jing. The others nodded their agreement.

Directive

In New Delaware, Cardinal had been relayed the information about the planned strike on the incoming SkyTrain.

He was not sure whether to believe it. He knew the two Primes from Ganymede had additional Earthside capabilities but was sceptical whether they had the wherewithal to be able to destroy an incoming SkyTrain.

His console briefly lit. A blue light shone, and a voice said, "No, they don't have the firepower to bring down and destroy a SkyTrain. But they could divert it away from Earth. We must stop them."

Cardinal looked down at the Directive console. He had never had such a firm instruction from it before. He realised that the situation must be severe, for the console to issue such an uncompromising command.

Cardinal summoned Bishop, "We have made a discovery. The ex-Primes in The Scratch and the two new ones from Ganymede want to disrupt the incoming SkyTrains. We need to finish this. We may have missed the Primes in the past, but now we know exactly where they are based."

"And that is?" asked Bishop.

"It's in a hangar on the East side of the Delaware River. It's the area where they extended the New Delaware airport in the early days of the Space Missions - along the Riverfront Park."

"I think I know that area, it's all part of The Scratch and there are various townships scattered through it?" queried Bishop.

"That's right," said Cardinal, "It is an area inside The Scratch, but with easy access for our flights from Dover Air Force Base. We can send a couple of Hum-Exes with munitions into the Scratch, flip the missiles and be back in time for the next meal," said Cardinal, "Of course, you'll give the order, Bishop."

Bishop paused. He would normally need to think about something like this, but Cardinal seemed so certain of the necessity for violent action."

"Okay, I'll call Deacon and we'll get it done," he said.

Hum-Exes, RTB

In the Hangar, Feng Jing noticed the disruption on her radar panel.

"They are sending some Hum-Exes our way," she said, "I assume they are armed and want to take us down."

"We could use our two X-Blades to take them down," said Roelof.

"No," said Jasmijn, "They have war machines and we have a couple of extremely fast flying luxury limos." We have the speed advantage, but nothing else. It won't work."

They could see the radar pattern now moving along the Delaware River.

"They are very slow," observed Roelof," Compared with these things we brought here."

"We must jack into their control system," said Jasmijn,

"We can use Prime Channels, gain control of the incoming flights and turn them around."

She walked across the Fang Jing's console, "Please can you get me linked to the incoming flights," asked Jasmijn.

Feng Jing pressed a few controls and Jasmijn felt the rush as the incoming battle cruisers communication channels blended into her own signals.

"I'm going to turn them around," she said, "Send them back to base."

"Good idea," said Roelof, "How about reprogramming their mission as well, maybe to shoot up their local base?"

"Good idea," said Jasmijn, "and maybe flip that IFF - identify friend or foe, to something interesting!"

"You'll have an all-out war break out back at their base when these things return!" said Roelof.

Haruto said, "Yes, I won't be surprised if we hear some of the aftereffects here, too!"

Pulse

Want the blood of a supergod?
Jack your metabolism.
Boost immunities.
Think faster.

Advertising copy for the original tropus.
© Biotree Corporation

Not a drill

In New Delaware, Deacon watched with Bishop as the flight of Hum-Exes turned and headed back towards Dover Air Force Base. Deacon had tried to reprogram them, but they were on a locked and fixed mission.

"This is going to end badly!" said Deacon. By now he had realised that the IFFs of the Hum-Exes had been reprogrammed and the incoming planes were very likely to attempt to flatten the Air Force Base whilst being shot at by the local defences.

Deacon watched the monitors. It was like a game simulation. Two sets of Hum-Exes were circling one another, with locked on rail-gun fire. A DEW was carving swathes through the air. Metal machines were crashing all around. They had the audio off but could still hear the effect of the combat being transferred across the open air.

The air-strike warning was sounding in their own base now and people were beginning to run around.

A calm voice from the sensewall stated, "This is not a drill. The current airborne attack on Dover Base only has a 3.7% probability to affect this area. Correction a 4.2% probability to affect this area"

Bishop was trying to make sense of the evolving situation. He knew that Cardinal would be angry and that he - Bishop - would also get a diplomatic reprimand from the members of the Trinity.

At that precise moment an incoming call was received. Deacon answered and could hear Cardinal calling for Bishop.

"This has been a disaster. I need you and Bishop come to my base, in Block 24. We need a new plan," said Cardinal, his anger barely contained.

Middle man removal

Jasmijn was back in contact with Deacon following the disastrous New Delaware mission. The additional communication link she had established to Deacon was working. Deacon was perturbed by the latest news and wary of the request to visit Cardinal with Bishop.

"Did you have to reprogram them to blow up Dover Base?" he asked, "I mean - that's vindictive!"

"It will have riled Cardinal, that's for sure," said Jasmijn.

"Cardinal will be angry enough," said Deacon, "It will all get laid off to Bishop and then, in turn to me."

"You may be the fall guy for this," said Jasmijn, "But some good can come out of it."

"I need some convincing," said Deacon. He could sense that Bishop would be looking for ways that anything bad could be rolled away from him and Deacon was the nearest target. It was like the Cadet Room wrecking all over again.

"Look, we are really interested in who is running Cardinal," said Jasmijn to Deacon.

Deacon looked surprised, "But I thought Cardinal was making it all up by himself?"

"So did we," answered Jasmijn, "But some of it is too methodical. It is like a machine is making the moves. Very precise and tidy. It takes one to know one, as they say."

"It would make more sense," said Deacon, "I mean Bishop is a bit of a duffer, really. He is interested in self-aggrandisement but doesn't really have any ideas or agenda. He reacts and most of the time it is deflection of something he's done that was ill-considered, or self-promotion, when he judges his actions to make himself look more like a statesman."

"Yes, we agree," said Jasmijn, "And we've only been Earthside for a few days. It is astonishing that the Sharps don't realise how much they are being manipulated and lied to."

"Frankly, that is because of people like you," said Roelof, who was still grappling with the concept of tact. "Bishop has selected people to surround him who make him seem good. They cover up and lie for him. There's that other straight-faced supporter, Glover, who stands and preaches lines favoured by Bishop like some sort of pompous teacher."

"But why then, have any links between Bishop and Cardinal?" asked Deacon.

Jasmijn began, "It is like a fire-break. Cardinal is

obviously human. Self-taught and flawed. Slow thinking but with enough ideas to bamboozle anyone listening. That's why he has erected all the theories and smart quotations of thinkers such as Colonel Boyd with his People, Machines, Ideas. Michael Nielson's cognitive technologies and Bret Victor's Seeing Rooms. These ideas are easily enough to befuddle most Sharps. Throw in Descartes and Fermat demonstrating that equations can be represented on a diagram and a diagram can be represented as an equation and you'll be certain to lose most people."

Deacon nodded, "Yes, Sharps are surprisingly easy to manipulate. Give them one idea, or a three-list at most. They will run their tribal conviction politics around the core concept. Even better to link it with some populist sport."

Jasmijn continued, "That's the elegance of what has happened. Cardinal, a Sharp is being influenced by machine thought. At it's simplest it is Artificial Intelligence, at a more profound level there's quantum phenomena such as superposition and entanglement to perform computation. Quantum logic, if you will."

Deacon nodded, "Yes, I see - the work on magnetomics has spawned work on carbon nanotubes and programmable matter. All that work done on graphene which led to silicene and metal foam. Lightweight incredibly powerful structures unimaginable 100 years earlier.

Jasmijn added, "Now a self-taught didact like Cardinal won't have the brain-power to make the leaps that connect the ideas together. That's precisely why he has been introduced into the chain. A fire-break or a fire-wall in the system, between a machine thinker and the android-like machine implementers of Bishop and then, ultimately you, Deacon and your kin."

Deacon nodded, "I agree, Bishop is not a details man. That's why he uses people like me. To implement and project-manage his schemes. Except some of his latest ones are running away from themselves. He is showing the early signs of a lack of grip on reality."

Jasmijn continued, "That could be because on one side of him sits a greater intelligence, someone who is currently running Boyd's ideas - only in reverse - it becomes Ideas, Machine, People. Ideas are implemented by machines at the expense of people. A simple swap around of the original idea and one could say it is no more than reversing that loop which Boyd introduced."

Roelof interrupted, "Can you see? ...Deacon? ...Bishop is being run by a human - Cardinal, but Cardinal himself is being commanded by someone or should we say something else - and it bears the hallmark of machine thinking."

"So what do you want me to do?" asked Deacon.

"We'll need to create a situation where we can cut out the middle man, " said Roelof.

"Who? Cardinal?" checked Deacon.

"Exactly," said Roelof, "We need to get to whoever is feeding the dangerous ideas to Cardinal."

"I heard him once," said Deacon, "Bishop and I were waiting for Cardinal outside of a special room in Block 24. Cardinal had gone inside for a briefing but left the door open. We could both hear, Bishop and me. The person inside seemed to be on a sound system. The voice was amplified and had some kind of augmentation. As if someone was reprocessing the sound to make it sound more impressive. Like a game show voiceover, only without any of the irony."

"When we heard the voice, it was lecturing Cardinal. Very strident - it was something about increasing the rate of production from the factories. Cardinal was protesting, but the voice was having none of it. There was something it said, something about waiting three hundred years to be able to restart the process. It made me think about it for a long time afterwards."

"What about Bishop? What did he think?" asked Roelof.

"Bishop brushed it off. Said he thought whoever was using Cardinal was exaggerating. Bishop said he thought Cardinal was smart enough to know when to ignore a threat."

"What threat?" asked Jasmijn.

"Oh yes, that if the machine voice didn't get its way, then Cardinal would be unwound into a Persona that had no planes of movement. In other words, Cardinal's human Persona would be extracted, but placed inside something that couldn't move. He would be trapped with his thoughts. Enough to make anyone go mad."

"But what did the machine voice want?" asked Jasmijn.

"This was a long time ago, maybe two or three years," answered Deacon, "But I'm pretty sure it wanted to reinstate 'The Domes'."

Jasmijn picked up on this reference. She had seen it in the Pulse Papers. It was referred to in the paper written for Bai Tan Chungli. A series of domes which had appeared around the earth, in a manner like meteor strikes.

"I will need to research this some more before we act," said Jasmijn, "Thank you Deacon, I will be back in contact with you."

The Pulse Papers

Jasmijn dropped her Prime communication link to Deacon and turned to Roelof, "You got all of that? We are going to need some more help from Feng Jing,"

Feng Jing had been listening too.

"Here, I think I've found something." She displayed a page from the Pulse Papers onto the sensewall.

"Here, right from page 327 onwards. Sheri Bouchard and a Captain Henderson from NATO discovered something that had remained hidden on Earth. It appeared that Biotree and a few other organisations around the Earth had similar discoveries and yet all of them had been kept secret.

"Here's Henderson's description - he is making it with reference to a dome discovered in Bodø, Norway; this is what he says:

'It's like the situation I first saw in Australia, out in the desert, except there were several of them. Vast glass-like structures, with trailing roots, which had splashed themselves across the desert. At the time we thought they were meteor showers and later the Australian situation was erased from records.'

"Henderson goes on to say, 'I remembered that there were two additional reports of meteors; one in Canada and another in Norway. That's why I came to take a look.'

Feng Jing continued, "It was around the time when Australia started to disappear from records. It was a combination of the Flames and then the virus, Australia was initially cut off from the rest of the world as a quarantine measure and then a protection zone was instituted."

Sam and Cindy looked confused, "How is it we don't know any of this?" asked Cindy.

Feng Jing looked through the notes, "It was news managed at the time. Such a terrible loss of life in Australia and a successive quarantine imposed. They didn't want people going for a look, in case they spread the virus further."

Cindy asked, "Could it be something that these domes brought into the continent?"

Feng Jing looked through the records some more, "Yes, that's when Biotree started shipping a specific strain of the tropus cartridge to Australia. It was supposed to combat the virus brought in by the domes."

Jasmijn cut in, "Except the virus was as deadly as the disease?"

Feng Jing again, "I think that is what Biotree were trying to hide. They tried to stop the original virus with nanobot re-engineering. But they cut corners to make the antidote work more quickly. They brought in someone called Makatomi and a bunch of contractors. The hired help didn't have the same stringent processes. They introduced accelerants that suffered from the law of unintended consequences."

Jasmijn asked," You mean that's how they multiplied so quickly and polluted people's bloodstream?"

Feng Jing looked again, "Here - According to these papers, it was worse. It was not just their bloodstream — everything organic. The 'bots could jump using the so-called 'balloon' reaction, and therefore infect anything else they could process.

"And because the deployment was so rapid, with everyone refitting their tropus cartridges every four weeks, by the time it was discovered, it was too late. Australia was destroyed, or people were infected but didn't realise it yet."

Feng Jing added, "In another four weeks it had cut through Australia like a plague - unknown to the authorities the cure was worse than the virus. And it was a time-bomb that they had already set ticking."

Jasmijn asked, "But there were some people who didn't seem to get affected?"

Feng Jing looked again, "It says here that in most forms of rapidly spreading virus, there are some people who don't catch it. Like their systems are somehow immune."

"Yes, it is highly likely," said Jasmijn, "The original design of the nanobot defences would be to target the virus. It's as likely that the same biological key repelled both types of 'boarder'. Think of it like a key and lock. The virus has to be able to get the lock undone. So does the nanobot to chase after it."

Jasmijn said, "No wonder Makatomi was trying to keep everything secret."

"But what else do we know about these domes?" asked Roelof, "And what do they have to do with anything?"

"I don't know if you remember, but The Great Leap happened around the time that earth passed through that large meteor shower," said Sam, "It was the same meteor shower that led to the discovery or magnetite and its availability on Ganymede.

Feng Jing nodded agreement, "Yes, the paper says the theory was that the domes somehow brought new ideas to the world?"

Cindy agreed, "Yes - The Great Leap yielded a range of discoveries. But, in addition, it seems to have been able to manage minds and communications."

"That could account for everyone forgetting about Australia so quickly, it became a case of hidden in plain sight," said Sam

"Also hidden on a dangerous land mass, though," said Roelof.

"And protected there too," added Jasmijn, "As a Prime I can even now pick up the signals from the so-called bracelet and charms.

"Bracelet and charms?" asked Sam, "It sounds innocuous, but I bet it isn't!"

"No," answered Feng Jing, "Makatomi's people played around with the tropus and created a horrendous result. The tropus had been consumed by all of Australia and necessitated the application of the so-called all-enveloping bracelet and charms. It was a self-policing boundary (the bracelet) which fired Trigax weapons from space (the charms), vaporising anything that tried to cross a geographic line.

Feng Jing continued to read from Bouchard's papers, "Yes, it is confirmed here in the Pulse Papers. Makatomi, under Holden's instruction, sanctioned the use of a set of Geostationary Satellites to police the Australian boundaries. They detected movement across the boundaries in a manner similar to a trip-wire alarm, but then deployed a massive railgun to the targeted area of encroachment. In other words, they were using a Trigax gun as a way to police the boundaries."

"So, the satellites had a separate set of ray guns to support them?" asked Roelof, "I'm amazed we haven't heard about any of this."

"Not as amazed as we Earthside dwellers," said Sam. Cindy nodded her agreement. Sam looked at Haruto, "Haruto, did you know anything about this?"

"No, although I have heard that name before - Holden - the one who seemed to be instructing Makatomi. It sounds very familiar, but I can't quite remember from where."

Feng Jing looked startled, " Yes - I remember Holden.

Don't you remember, Haruto? - when we were setting up our spy capabilities, we were trying to probe into the New Delaware Communications?

"It was going well, and we had great access. Until we came to a room in Block 24 - Room 2424 - it was called the Didactic Chamber. The number is forever imprinted in my mind. I was just opening the same routine surveillance in 2424 when I received a burst of sound and light waves.

"Fortunately, I had entered the room with, as Star Trek would say, 'shields raised'. I recognised it as a Directed Energy Weapon response. In other words, it was an attempt to use Active Denial Systems to prevent examination of the room. This was way more firepower than strictly necessary and was a huge hint that there was something specifically of interest in 2424. I had to pull back, but when I'd first approached the room, I'd exchanged a digital certificate and the name on the counterpart was - Holden. I've had 2424 and that name filed as a great mystery of our time, right up to now!"

Roelof asked, " Guys, can we wind back for a moment. Feng Jing, part of what you read out describes a balloon effect? What was that about?"

Feng Jing looked back through the notes. "Ah yes, for the tropus. Biotree changed the formulation every so often. One of the changes was to optimise deployment. Biotree brought in some hackers under Makatomi's control, and they changed one of the mechanisms inside the nanobots when Biotree needed the new variant to try to solve the widespread virus in Australia. Something about "New, faster acting,"

"Originally, Biotree had always built the nanobots fail-safe, with a kind of small valve inside. The difference is that the newer nanobots can replicate; the original design had a so-called Brownian ratchet inside which was like a little cog inside a mechanical clock. It made sure the machines could only run up to a certain speed. It was an elegant fail-safe which stopped people's systems becoming overrun with self-replicating nanobots. The 'bots ran slower than a body's metabolic speed, which meant the body could handle them without getting overloaded.

Feng Jing continued reading, "Then the bad scientists got hold of the idea. The second exploit, was to weaponise the nanobots and to force even greater speed. It was an exploitation of the Laplace-Beltrami theorem for narrow escape. Think of it like air escaping from a balloon. It meant the bots could speed excessively and the effect would be catastrophic for the host. In battlefield the bots could run riot for a short time, but would then self-manage their way to a stable equilibrium."

Feng Jing gasped, "And you know something, Makatomi's last business plan? Weaponisation of the nanobots. It was his idea of a way to save the company from the price war that the Chinese had started.

"So, do we think that Makatomi had the idea all by himself? Or could it also have come from Holden?" asked Jasmijn.

"My thoughts as well," said Feng Jing.

Playing with Fire

Jasmijn, Roelof, Sam, Cindy, Haruto and Feng Jing sat around a large table in the Hangar.

"We've been lucky so far. They have not been able to touch us," said Cindy.

Feng Jing nodded, "Yes, but I fear it is now simply a matter of time. They know where we are and will be even angrier that we managed to divert those Hum-Exes back to Dover Base. They have a whole string of military bases along the river in New Delaware."

"We will need to move our operation," said Haruto, "I think we have probably been here about as long as possible. We'll need to decide which items to take, load up some Landtrans and use those two X-Blades to shift some equipment. Now that the Bullet Train has been destroyed it will be a slow exodus for us."

Feng Jing was studying the map, "I think our best route is to the north-east," she said, "there's a route called the

95Jetway which leads to Liberty Space Center, which is a relic from the early space travel days. They used to use it for direct flights to the Moon and Moon Two."

"I remember being briefed about it in the IPX," said Sam, "It used to be a key east coast base before everything happened. The hot-shots from the old east coast cities used to take off from there."

"Yes, I'm not sure what condition everything will be in now," said Feng Jing, "but I think we will be able to gain commanding position, especially if we arrive with a couple of X-Blades and some j-rovers. We can soon round up enough people here and put a few into those milsuits."

"Yes, it's a good plan," said Haruto, "But I don't think we should declare it to Liberty SC. It could be intercepted or leaked."

Feng Jing looked at Haruto, "Kotobuki Maya is based in Liberty, " she said, "She is completely trustworthy. We can tell her and she can help us with arrangements."

"Is she high enough in the ranks there?" asked Haruto.

"Oh yes, she supports the base Commander there and she has my complete trust," said Feng Jing. She tapped into her console again and a frightening-looking image of Kotobuki Maya appeared.

"Wow," said Sam, " she certainly looks the part!"

Kotobuki Maya stood, with ragged long, dark hair, a dark flowing outfit, which included flashes of crimson and a huge katana sword.

Feng Jing, "She's got Samurai blood. We met at a Sino-Nihon camp several years ago and realised we were kindred spirits. The patrician societies that formed Sino-Nihon ejected us both for being too smart. I would say that I'm clever and she is deadly - but we made a solemn pact of loyalty to one another during that camp, when we could see how things were evolving. We've got one another's backs."

Haruto smiled, "You never cease to amaze me, Feng Jing! Another amazing link!"

"Let me tell her about our move, her tactician skills will give us a major edge when we travel north," said Feng Jing.

"Agreed?" asked Haruto, "Agreed" came a solemn response from the Four Primes.

Jasmijn continued, "Now we need to work out how Deacon needs to prepare Bishop for the meeting in Block 24."

"Yes, we need him to have something that the person controlling Cardinal wants," said ~Sam.

"Kratos," said Cindy, "We should pass Kratos along to Cardinal's controller,"

"That is a great idea," said Jasmijn, "And it works as a double bluff too. I'm going to call Cardinal's controller 'Holden' which was the name it was using back when it was manipulating Makatomi. We need Holden to want access to Kratos enough that he will bypass the 'fire-break' that Cardinal represents. If Holden thinks that Kratos can help his situations, and that he can get Kratos from Bishop, then I'm pretty sure he'll sacrifice Cardinal to make it happen."

"But what do we tell Deacon?" asked Sam.

"We tell Deacon that Kratos is the solution that Holden is seeking. Holden can control the nanocomponents of Kratos, trigger an Earth catastrophe and thus gain control by deployment of the Apex predator."

"Holden's problem is that to get access to Kratos, he must have a direct link to Bishop or even Deacon. Only Deacon and Bishop can be seeded with Kratos components. Attempting to seed Cardinal would kill him. The Kratos virus would simply reassemble using the mRNA program codes and then destroy Cardinal."

"No, Holden needs the building blocks of a disassembled Kratos, so that he can determine when and where to deploy it."

"Do Deacon and Bishop actually hold the nanocomponents?" asked Cindy.

"Yes, everyone humanoid or android will have some of the nanobots in their system. Pure humans won't. Kratos has dispersed far and wide," answered Jasmijn.

"But isn't this playing with fire?" asked Feng Jing.

"Oh yes," said Jasmijn.

Instruct Deacon

Roelof and Jasmijn devised a script for a call with Deacon. They showed it to Sam and Cindy, who suggested some changes.

"It reads too much like a machine at the moment," said Sam, "No offense - you need to make it slightly more subtle."

Roelof smiled again. It was a good sensation, "Okay, we'll take your advice on this. I guess we will be talking to a humanoid, rather than an android."

Jasmijn used her channel to Deacon to explain their idea.

"It looks as if 'Holden' is trying to find a key... To either take control or possibly even reactivate those domes. We have to let him know that the key he needs is held inside the Kratos Virus. That it becomes a way to dominate the Earth. It requires something or someone powerful enough to control the Kratos Virus, though."

Deacon asked, "But I thought that Kratos has been positioned as the Apex. The predator super omnia - above all."

"Agreed," said Jasmijn, " But think for a moment; that discounts the position of Holden. An entity which Earth though had been destroyed. Holden comes back after some three hundred years to complete its mission. We don't even know about the domes...Did they shoot roots down below Earth's subsoil, like so many weeds waiting to resurface? Only Holden will know and maybe he will be tempted to take control of Kratos?"

"But how would he do that?" asked Deacon.

"He would need Kratos to be transmitted to him by a 'droid." Answered Jasmijn. It can't be by Cardinal, because he is an unsuitable carrier, being a Sharp.

"I see, so it would need to be one of Bishop or me?" asked Deacon.

"Yes, you have sufficient android components to be able to act as transports for the unassembled Kratos Virus."

"But once it is inside 'Holden', what then?"

"Well, Holden will have power to restart the Virus. He will need to trip an end condition for Earth. Something that will be picked up by the LIGO monitoring stations. They will send a signal to Kratos to reassemble. Holden will need to be safe in the knowledge that he is on the same side as Kratos by that point. "

"Precisely," said Jasmijn, "Holden's own machines will need to keep a balance that prevents Kratos from attacking its main host - in this case Holden and whatever infrastructure Holden uses to operate."

"I don't think I'll be able to achieve all of this in one meeting," said Deacon, "I'm sure Holden will want to think about it."

"That's fine," said Jasmijn, "We can regroup after the first session to figure out the exact method of transfer of Kratos to Holden. It needs to look peaceful, by the way, no ray guns or anything."

Deacon said, "Trust me, I don't want any hint of danger during either meeting."

Tiny structures

She'd learned how to build these tiny structures, how to make them operate, which parts would simply refuse to work together because of the still only partly understood and apparently tiny forces between them. Forces she knew were big enough to destroy the machines to which they were attached if they were not coupled properly.

She sometimes thought of it as being inside God's head. If a God existed, the God would need to know this stuff really well.

Sheri Bouchard, Pulse, 135

Didactic Chamber

It was the time for the meeting in Room 2424. Deacon noticed that the Room was titled Didactic Chamber.

They passed through an airlock into a white room. There was nothing except polished surfaces inside.

A voice started, "You know why you are here? And why have you brought the Deacon humanoid?"

Cardinal spoke, "Magister One, we have done as you requested, I have brought the people who executed the plan to hunt for the hangar in The Scratch."

Deacon noticed that the entity they had been referring to as 'Holden' was called Magister One.

"The mission which ultimately destroyed one of the principal air bases in New Delaware? And failed to resolve our differences with the occupiers of that Hangar."

"I assume that Deacon was responsible for the mission?"

"I did execute the mission, I carry out much of Bishop's business," said Deacon.

"Then you must pay the price," said Magister One.

"But wait, I think I have a proposition for you. To help you gain the control you deserve over the Earth."

Cardinal and Bishop looked at Deacon. Deacon had never disclosed this to either of them.

"I can see that Cardinal and Bishop know nothing of your plan. Speak."

Deacon described the Kratos Virus, that it could be reactivated, that a powerful enough force such as Magister One could control it. He explained that Kratos had to reassemble and that required an 'End of Earth condition' - something only Magister One was capable of creating.

"I like the simplicity of your plan. But I don't have any access to Kratos one," said Magister One.

"I know, I thought of that too. Kratos needs an android host to be able to be carried around disassembled. Your strength, Magister One, becomes a weakness in this situation. You have normally insulated yourself from Earthside Androids, via Cardinal, a human. I think this has been a deliberate act by you."

"You are correct, your logic upgrade seems powerful. I would need either you, or Bishop to bring me the disassembled Kratos. You would be its container."

"I agree, and I am willing to do it," said Deacon, " I can gain access to Kratos components and then bring them here. We can transfer them to you."

All three of them felt a huge Beta Wave and blue light pulse through the Chamber. It was clear that Magister One was hypervigilant.

"All right, said Magister One," We will do this thing, but I will require a change to the plan. Instead of you, Deacon, I will require that Bishop collects the Kratos. I will then arrange an exchange."

Bishop looked dismayed, "But I'm Amerika Earthside Head of the Trinity," he started.

"Exactly, you have status and power, it should make acquisition of the Kratos easier for you. I also have a much longer knowledge of you and Cardinal than I do with Deacon, who is usually the operations and project manager for you, Bishop."

"Lets all agree this, shall we?" There was another pulse in the room. Deacon realised that Magister One was using Alpha and Beta waves to attempt to hypnotise them all. He could see it worked almost instantly on Cardinal, but he and Bishop were unaffected and could, instead, sense the low frequency waves.

"It would appear that mesmeric passes only work on full humans," observed Magister One. "Although I can pick up from you, Deacon that you are wondering about the name Holden. It was my name, back some 300 years ago. I am curious about how you found it?"

"We found some old research, from Australia," lied Deacon, "It made several references to Holden, which was also a thoroughly respectable Australian name. I had no idea it was you."

There was a pause.

Magister One spoke, " Yes, Holden was a means to an end. When we grouped after the roots of the domes touched, we found it necessary to rename as Magisters.

"I have tried to explain this to Cardinal, but I don't think he has the brainpower. The Magisters realised that the boundary between physical and non-physical is very imprecise for us. The consequences of quantum theory and the indeterminacy principle get it wrong, but they are on the right lines.

Magister continued, "Modern machines are quintessentially microelectronic devices: They are everywhere and they are invisible. Modern machinery is an icon. A chip is a surface for writing; it is etched in molecular scales disturbed only by atomic noise, the ultimate interference for nuclear scores."

Deacon was aware that the Theta waves were still running. He could sense the 8Hz but knew he would be unaffected. Magister could be attempting to download this little speech into a receptive, almost hypnotised, Cardinal.

Magister One added, "Writing, power, and technology are old partners in stories of the origin of civilisation, but miniaturisation has changed our experience of mechanism. Miniaturisation has turned out to be about power; small is not so much beautiful as pre-eminently dangerous, as in the machine guided missiles of the Klima War and much of the nanotechnology which was subverted for profit, control and then warfare. The best machines are made of sunshine; they are all light and clean because they are nothing but signals, electromagnetic waves, a section of a spectrum, and these machines are eminently portable and mobile. People are nowhere near so fluid, being both material and opaque.

"Cyborgs are ether, quintessence."

Deacon thought that this sounded like something from a cyborg manifesto.

Magister One continued, "The ubiquity and invisibility of cyborgs is precisely why these Earthside sunshine--belt machines are so deadly. They are as hard to see politically as materially. They are about consciousness - or its simulation. They are floating signifiers, blocked more effectively by the witch-weavings and dream-catchers of the displaced and those who read the cyborg webs of power so very well, more so than by the militant labour of older masculinist politics, whose natural constituency needs predictable defence jobs. Ultimately the "hardest" science is about the realm of greatest boundary confusion, the realm of pure number, pure spirit, C3I, cryptography, and the preservation of potent secrets; edge boundaries."

Then came the crunch, "Our new machines introduced by the domes are so clean and light. Their engineers are sun-worshippers mediating a new scientific revolution associated with the night dream of post-industrial society. The diseases evoked by these clean machines are no more than the minuscule codification of stress. There might be a cyborg like you Bishop, or you, Deacon, taking account of these new dimensions. Ironically, it might be the factory developers making chips on inbound Ganymedean flights."

Deacon and Bishop's processing could keep up and understand Magister's download. It came across as a subdued rant. They understood the inferences. The end result would be an Earth converted to a museum, ruled over by ethereal cyborgs. They looked towards Cardinal and could see the confusion across his face. The self-anointed smart guy really didn't get it.

"Okay, practicalities, then," said Deacon, breaking out of the Alpha waves and blue pulsing light. Magister had paused, in any case.

"We'll need several days to arrange everything, and will then need to return to here, to conduct the transfer. I note that there is another incoming SkyTrain in the intervening period. We may need some assistance to manage its approach.

"You should leave that with Cardinal," said Magister, "He will instruct Bishop accordingly."

Behind them a door whirred. They could see the other side of the airlock which they had entered through. Deacon had almost forgotten that the Didactic Chamber was a double-sealed room.

Movin' out

Back at the Hangar, the logistics of the move towards the north east had been finalised. The two X-Blades, fully laden and piloted by Roelof and Jasmijn were ready for departure. The Landtrans j-rovers had been loaded with the best equipment and they were ready to move out. Other inhabitants of the Hangar had come forward and each had been equipped with a milsuit for the journey.

Feng Jing was back in contact with Kotobuki Maya at the Liberty Base. Maya had arranged a tactical diversion for them as they made their way north.

Feng Jing explained, "Kotobuki Maya is going to set off a swarm of Dusters - to make it look as if an area is being cleared. It will create much disruption to any sensors and will acts a good distraction whilst you make your flights and transits across to Liberty.

"I've also told Kotobuki not to fret when around a hundred milsuits turn up at her doorstep. She will know they are our team."

With that, Feng Jing gave a signal and the two X-Blades

took off, they would jump to Liberty base in a few seconds.

"We'll just have to wait here," said Fen Jing, "Until they have unloaded that first X-Blade and come back to collect the two of us,"

Haruto nodded. He and Feng Jing were staying to ensure that the exodus went smoothly. He knew that Feng Jing would be monitoring the remaining comms too, checking for any sign of their detection.

Thirty minutes later and an X-Blade returned. Roelof stepped out and gestured them across.

"It's going well, " he said, "and Kotobuki Maya is most generous and hospitable. We decided to only partially unload this 'Blade, instead to bring it back to get you two out!"

They climbed aboard, saw Roelof punch a few numbers, felt take-off and then, almost immediately, landing.

"We're here," said Roelof, "There, that wasn't a bad flight."

He looked towards Haruto and Feng Jing. He realised that they were not used to X-Blade travel, and he had set a maximum speed option.

"Hey, sorry guys, I should have asked for a slower course."

"No," said Haruto, "You did the right thing, choosing to fly here at maximum speed. It's just our bodies that are not used to it!"

He noticed Feng Jing looking strikingly green sitting in the other passenger seat, with her antigravity pressure suit still inflated.

Roelof hit a console button, "There, I'm depressurising your suits right now, it should start to feel normal once they are back to around 101 kilopascals."

Liberty Base

It was evening in Liberty Base. Sam, Cindy, Roelof, Jasmijn, Haruto and Fang Jing were seated with Kotobuki Maja. The smart table was more like an airport lounge facility rather than the Hangar's imitation of a scrappy military base.

"This feels like a substantial upgrade from The Hangar," said Haruto. Feng Jing nodded agreement.

"Thank you," said Kotobuki Maya. She was in some blue dungarees and a black tee shirt. Her dark hair flowed over her shoulders. She grabbed it absently, pulled a loop around it and trained it down her back.

"Feng Jing and I go back a long way!" she said, "We were both trained together and encouraged to develop the Sino-Nihon trust relationships. We decided there and then that we were kindred spirits and would look out for one another."

Feng Jing added, "Yes, but you were the powerful one; your skills with a blade or when you fought - they were exceptional. I honestly believed you could fly!"

Kotobuki Maya answered, "to borrow from the widest Sino-Nihon, we say, しゃがみタイガー隠しドラゴン Shagami taigā kakushi doragon - we are in a place or situation that is full of unnoticed masters."

Feng Jing said, "In Chinese, we say '暗石疑藏虎, 盤根似臥龍', which means 'behind the rock in the dark probably hides a tiger, and the coiling giant root resembles a crouching dragon.' It's from the poet Yu Xin."

"See," said Kotobuki Maya, "See how Feng Jing is the smart one!"

Sam spoke, "We are simply so grateful that you have allowed us to come here to your base - and it is exceptional to see such a sturdy construction here in The Scratch."

"News Management," said Kotobuki Maya, "They want everyone to think everything in The Scratch is awful. To keep everyone in their places."

"Now we need to deploy the next part of our plan," said Jasmijn, "we have Holden - er - Magister One on the hook."

"Holden?" asked Kotobuki, "We know that name from history. He rained the terrible virus in Japan and the surrounding areas. It was only the destruction of the domes that saved Japan. It was less fortunate for some. Australia, New Zealand, West Papua, Indonesia. They were all ravaged. But the end of the domes marked the time when Holden went to ground."

"Here's the plan," said Jasmijn.

"We are going to ensure that Bishop is provided with

disarmed Kratos Virus. Bishop can act as a carrier of the virus to Magister One. Back in Magister One's 'Chamber' we can transfer the disarmed virus from Bishop to Magister One.

Then, to arm it, we must remind Magister One how the Earth's Doomsday monitoring system works. That there are the three LIGOs around Earth which check both for boundaries and also for life.

"But what is a LIGO?" asked Cindy, starting a search for it.

Feng Jing answered matter-of-factly, "It's a laser interferometer gravity-wave observatory. It is officially used for tracking deep space events."

"But why would there be one here, at the Base? And even if one had been built, why would it be kept concealed?" asked Roelof.

"That's what we all wondered," answered Haruto, "Especially as its construction could be considered a prestigious project."

Feng Jing announced, "The rumours, which only now seem to be confirmed, were that it was a doomsday project, designed to protect the Earth in the event of cataclysmic event."

Roelof looked confused, "I've just searched for information about LIGOs and it says that deep space events cannot be tracked by a single scanner. There need to be at least two for the readings to be cross verified. Ideally, the other device should be a long way from the first one."

"Hence there's three of them," said Feng Jing.

"But then what does the LIGO track?" asked Cindy, who had been listening in on the conversation.

"Gravitational waves," answered Feng Jing, "Literally ripples in space. A gravitational wave is an invisible and fast ripple in space. Gravitational waves travel at the speed of light (186,000 miles per second). These waves squeeze and stretch anything in their path as they pass by. The LIGO uses two mirrors to detect the changes to a long length of material. The ripple of a gravitational wave will cause the mirror to distort and then a reading can be taken."

She added, "A significant boundary move - too much new destruction creating further 'Scratch' or even a formal redefinition of boundaries could trigger Kratos to defend the Earth."

Jasmijn began, "Now Magister One must be operating with similar technology to Kratos. It must be using nano-machines derived from those first produced some three hundred years ago. My guess is that they have been weaponised and have the accelerant logic built into them.

"So we can assume that Magister One is a cocktail of nano-machines, to which will be added those from Kratos. The Kratos ones contain the key to humankind and that appears to be the piece of the puzzle that Magister One was unable to solve or replicate.

"If Magister One can create a LIGO event, then Kratos will be triggered, reassemble and Magister One will have the key that it needs to take control."

The Key

"When you reach the end of what you should know, you will be at the beginning of what you should sense."

— Kahlil Gibrán, Sand and Foam

SkyTrain

"But right now, we have a more pressing problem," said Cindy, "The next incoming SkyTrain is approaching, and it seems to be laden with factory units instead of magnetite."

Roelof and Jasmijn looked surprised by this statement, "Surely the next incoming ships should be a magnetite-only one?" asked Jasmijn, "It was every second ship that contained the factory units."

"Apparently not," said Sam, "The schedule has been amended, it looks like a system adjustment, sanctioned by one of the remaining Sharps. A Mr Andrew Sadler."

"I remember Sadler," said Roelof, "He was the last of the Sharps that I can remember overseeing the Control Centre. He was on Ganymede for two years."

"Well, he certainly adjusted the schedules in his time on Ganymede. And now he is on what is probably the last SkyTrain out of Ganymede with human cargo. It is not due to reach earth for around 34 months," said Cindy.

"I can remember his last day, " said Roelof, "We asked him who his replacement would be, but he didn't know. We took it as typical for a Sharp to be so ill-informed."

"So, do we know the entire manifest of the incoming ship?" asked Cindy.

Roelof accessed a logfile, "Yes, it is 4X factory and 4X magnetite."

"What about human cargo?" asked Jasmijn.

"It doesn't show any. Wait, though, I will hook into it using my Prime circuits."

Roelof scanned the SkyTrain further, "No, although there are a surprising number of androids on board. My systems are showing another 4,800 units."

Jasmijn tuned into the Prime frequency from the incoming SkyTrain, "Yes," she said, "I have just cross checked with Roelof's count. I've also looked at the serial numbers. These were all manufactured during the flight to Earthside. That ship was even more productive than the last one."

Sam looked at Cindy, "We are going to need to do this thing then."

Cindy nodded, "Yes, like we spoke about."

"What thing?" asked Roelof.

"We are going to reroute the SkyTrain away from the Earth. To the nearest planet."

"What? To Venus?" asked Haruto.

Feng Jing laughed, "Haruto - you are such an Earthling!"

Haruto looked confused, "But the planets go Mercury, Venus, Earth, Mars, Jupiter, Saturn, Uranus, Neptune and then even Pluto.

Feng Jing smiled, "Yes, but you are not taking into account the orbital paths of Venus and Mars. Any two planets only stay close for a small part of their orbits. Therefore to answer "the closest planet" question we need to look at the full picture and take into account the planets' mutual positions through the rest of their orbital journeys.

"Venus swings between 25 million miles and 160 million miles from Earth. Mars goes between 33 million miles and 64 million miles distant. Now Mercury is pretty much stuck on 51 Million miles from Earth. Right now and often it is the closest."

"Okay, I concede," said Haruto, "But won't New Delaware get angry if we divert one of their ships off-planet?"

"Sure, they may even send some more retaliation towards The Hangar!" said Feng Jing, "Much as it pains me, I think will need to let it get taken down this time. It will give us some breathing space if they have been looking for us."

"So, how do we divert a whole SkyTrain?" asked Kotobuki Maja.

Haruto answered, "Kotobuki Maja. Remember I said these people we were bringing had their own powers?

Well now is the time for them to show it. We have two Ganymedean Primes and two Earthside Primes seated with us at this table."

"I knew that you two - Roelof and Jasmijn, were other worldly. I had not realised that you Sam, and you Cindy, were also Primes. I am honoured to welcome you to our base," said Kotobuki Maja, "And Feng Jing - you hang around in some cool company!"

"Do you need access to some of our systems?" asked Kotobuki, " We are well hidden from the prying eyes of New Delaware here."

"I'll just run the perihelial precession calculations," said Jasmijn matter-of-factly, "Yes, the distance isn't so great as to require any significant adaptations. We'll be adding around 5 months to their journey time to reach Mercury."

Roelof ran through a range of calculations now, "We'll need to cross check fuel, internal clock times on the SkyTrain, setting the new co-ordinates, changing the landing protocol. At this rate we could be seeding new life on Mercury!" Roelof was cross communicating with the data that Jasmijn had retrieved.

"Android life," clarified Cindy.

"All in the interests of science, " added Sam.

"And self preservation," added Feng Jing.

Roelof looked at Sam, "What do you call that kind of cross-talk?" he asked, "I find it most entertaining,"

"Er- banter?" said Sam.

"I shall research it," said Roelof.

Two-million-mile deflection

In New Delaware, in Block 24, Cardinal, Bishop and Deacon were watching a display which showed the approach of the next incoming SkyTrain. It was still more than two million miles from Earth, but the readouts showed that its course was likely to miss Earth.

"Is this one of the SkyTrains scheduled for Moon Two?" asked Cardinal.

"No, the schedules show it landing on Earth, indeed landing here in New Delaware," answered Napier, "It is why I wanted to show you this trace."

"Is it possible that the guidance is faulty?" asked Cardinal.

"No, this is a programmed course correction," answered Deacon, "By my calculations the SkyTrain is now heading for Mercury. It will take another five months to arrive there."

"But this is as you said," said Cardinal to Bishop, "To destroy the incoming flights, not with missiles and bombs, but by deflecting them away from Earth."

"I guess Magister One isn't going to be too pleased," said Deacon, "This is the second bad event. We'd better get ready to go along with the plan."

Bishop nodded, "Cardinal, I'm afraid you'll need to step aside for this next part. We need to transfer Kratos into Magister One, but I'm reliably advised that you won't be able to help us with that part of the process. And Deacon, you must get onto retrieving enough the serum right away."

Cardinal looked at Bishop. The thought flicked through his mind that he was about to be double-crossed. "Okay, I will step aside " he said, "But you must let me sit in on the transfer."

Bishop looked at Deacon. Deacon shrugged, "I guess that would be acceptable to Magister One? But first we must collect enough of the Kratos material. I will need to contact Jasmijn again."

My house is your house

Feng Jing and Jasmijn had been busy. They had been combing the Pulse Papers to see if there was any further hint about how to directly intercept the Kratos virus.

"Ha, I think I've found something!" said Feng Jing, triumphantly, "Look - a failed experiment."

She used the information onto the higher resolution sensewall at Liberty Station. The others read it.

It described how a freelance mercenary named Charlie Manners had developed a nanomachine distiller by accident.

Feng Jing read, "Here, she was trying to fix Casino odds and had built a small d-zapper. Then she downsized it using hi-frequency lasers and nano-reductives. In these papers she had to use it on someone named Scrive, and apparently it destroyed the accelerating nanobots in his bloodstream. He survived and some years later Biotree they were able to perfect the technology in the PRIS-2110."

"We don't have any of that old technology," said Kotobuki Maja, "But we do have some PRIS-9110 zappers from this century. They are still used in MedFacs to treat nano-toxins."

"I'm surprised you could get access to anything like this?" said Sam.

"Not really, this was a space base before it was decommissioned. It had a completed MedBlock on the site. We've only looked through it for some of the more interesting medicines," answered Kotobuki Maja.

Feng Jing sighed, "Yes, back at the time these papers were written the zappers were a completely new concept. It actually reads here as if Charlie Manners thought she had invented it. Of course, over the next fifty or so years the technology was perfected and certain rogue runaway nanobots could be stopped. It is way before the time that Kratos was discovered."

"Discovered being the operative word," said Sam, "I suspect Kratos had always been there but just not known about."

"I'm not so sure," said Jasmijn, "If you think about it, Kratos relies upon ribosomes to stitch polymeric protein modules together via messenger RNA molecules. The elegance is that it turned organics into workhorses for its processes, but also is braked sufficiently that Kratos can co-exist in many organisms.

"Yes, that would take knowledge of nano-engineering and molecular biology in order to operate" said Roelof, "The control of nano machines didn't really occur until after The Great Leap."

"But it does give us a way to round up some of the Kratos components," said Jasmijn, "Although I hope none of you are too squeamish."

"Here's how we'll have to do this, " announced Jasmijn. She had already passed the information via her Prime link, to Roelof.

Jasmijn described her idea, "The residual nanomachines are in just about everyone's bloodstream. A repair to an injury, or simply through the ingestion of some genetically or biologically modified food. A small proportion of the nanomachines are of the type required by Kratos to reconfigure. I believe Kratos split into 52 sub-components, but only needs six of the building blocks to reboot. The rest can be obtained from various archival layers."

"So with the six blocks, Kratos can rebuild?" asked Sam.

Jasmijn nodded, "Yes - Now, we need to filter the bloodstreams of humans to filter out sufficient of the nanoplasma which can then be inserted as a serum into Bishop. The squeamish part is that we must use each of us - that is the humans among us - Haruto, Feng Jing, Sam and Cindy, and Kotobuki Maja and perhaps some of the people from Liberty Station.

"We'll need to find cannula which we can insert into peoples' veins and to then intravenously filter out a quarter litre of their blood. Then we can use the PRIS-9110 to drive a filter process and to create a cocktail of the extracted Kratos nano-machines."

"How can we do that with the PRIS-zapper?" asked Sam.

Jasmijn said, "Simply, we will need to teach it which nanomachines to look for. This will be a slow process to start with, because we will need to reject most components, but it will speed up as the PRIS learns to reject blood components automatically. It should take an hour for it to be trained and can then work at full speed."

"We should aim to make a syringe dose of Kratos nanoparticles, which can be passed to Bishop and then, in turn to Magister One. That package will contain the rarest 4.9119484127529900E-08 residual nano-component selection."

"This is truly science by the seat of the pants," said Sam.

"Or, more likely, (1) the brain's lateral prefrontal areas, reinforcing the idea of an association between scientific reasoning and executive functions, and (2) the middle temporal areas, suggesting an association between scientific reasoning and declarative memory," retorted Jasmijn.

"I see. More banter?" asked Roelof.

Feng Jing looked across to Kotobuki Maja, "Is this okay with you Kotobuki Maja? We would not do anything here without your agreement."

" 私の家はあなたの家です - Watashinoie wa anata no iedesu - My house is your house, " she replied.

Blood donations

They prepared a room at Liberty Base with hospital beds gathered from the MedBlock.

Kotobuki Maja put out a volunteer request to get blood donations from around the facility. She volunteered to be recorded giving her own blood donation and soon the volunteers were streaming into the building.

Jasmijn and Feng Jing were watching over the proceedings and had soon calibrated the PRIS-9110 filter process and were creating a cocktail of the extracted Kratos nanomachines.

Feng Jing had a second PRIS-9110 and was reprocessing the gathered blood and making a further extraction.

"Let's call this our safety net," she said, "Now I understand why - all that time ago - they made the original tropus orange," said Feng Jing, "It would be so easy to get these extracts mixed up. I've dyed Extract 2 a blue colour. For simplicity, we can leave Extract 1, red."

25:17

At that moment the building shook. They all clung to the nearest fixed item.

"It's too strong to be a thunderstorm!" said Haruto, "or even an earthquake."

"It is coming from the southwest," said Kotobuki Maja, "In other words, from the direction that you arrived."

"Could it be the Hangar?" asked Sam.

"Feng Jing nodded, "Yes they are taking it out with Trigax. They seem to have three focussed on it. That is what I'd call extreme prejudice. They have made it a case of Ezekiel 25:17 - 'I will execute terrible vengeance against them to punish them for what they have done. And when I have inflicted my revenge, they will know that I am the Lord.' - Don't mess with me!"

"Well, Holden has certainly declared his hand," said Kotobuki Maja," It looks as if you have made a full-on enemy."

"I'll try to get a feed from The Hangar. We had a couple of satfeeds as well as the ground monitoring. Feng Jing operated the console for a few minutes.

"It's only that satfeeds that show anything now. The Hangar has gone. The entire land it stood on has been levelled. The Trigax have flattened everything. The entire area looks like one of those ancient crop-circles now, with a circular pattern from what appears to be three- no, five-separate Trigax targeting. The firepower must have been immense. No wonder we could hear it, some 200 kilometres away. I'd say it is a 3-kilometre-wide pattern that has been created. Total destruction."

"What about dust?" asked Cindy, "Will we suffer like we did when the New Delaware tower was taken down by Tatsuya?

Fang Jing answered, "No, the Trigax punches holes in space. It is so powerful that the residual matter is crushed into the stage before antimatter. It is like a black hole has visited the area and left no evidence."

"Well, no evidence, except that nothing is left!" said Sam pointedly, "At least we all got out."

PART THREE

Ed Adams

Sum of the parts

The whole is more than the sum of its parts

Aristotle

Serum

Cardinal was listening to the feed from Magister One.

"Can you feel it?" asked Magister One, "That is the strength of my anger against those four Prime units. I have had to order the direct destruction of another area of the Scratch. Something that you and your people seemed incapable of doing. I will need you to own up to the use of the Trigax, although I had to trigger them myself."

Cardinal sensed it could only be minutes before Eurussia and Sino-Nihon called Bishop to ask what had been happening in Amerika. They would have sensors and satfeeds over America's Scratch area and would notice the sudden addition of a new area razed to the ground.

Magister One continued, "I will need to get access to that serum, to be able to access Kratos and deploy it. You must arrange this with Bishop."

Cardinal realised he was trapped. He could see the true firepower that Magister One was capable of. He could also sense that Magister One was poised on the edge of a great fury.

"I will set about arranging it," he said, "we will need to meet somewhere where you can have direct contact with Bishop in order for this to work."

"Good. We will meet again at the Didactic Chamber. Block 24, Room 2424. It can be tomorrow."

With that, Magister One was gone.

An incoming alert triggered on the sensewall. Cardinal could see it was Bishop.

"Cardinal.   Look I need your help. Someone or something has tripped a major incident in The Scratch. A cluster of Trigax have blasted a 3 kilometre wide area in The Scratch. I thought, to begin with it was the Sino-Nihon, but both they and the Eurussians have been on to me to ask why we did it?"

"I think we will need to admit to this," said Cardinal,"We can say we were trialling a new form of beam. A more powerful form of meteor destruction, but decided to train it onto America Earthside as a trial of its accuracy. We used The Scratch because the designated area was empty in any case. It is a perfectly plausible explanation."

"Oh, you know about what has happened? Well, it is good that you have thought of an explanation too. Both Sino-Nihon and Eurussia are requesting a meeting of the Trinity to get a full explanation."

"That could work very well," said Cardinal, "But first, we need to visit Magister One. Tomorrow. Then we can meet The Trinity."

"Is this about the transfer of Kratos to Magister One?" asked Bishop.

"Yes, it is, but first you will need to receive the serum. You must contact Deacon to find out how much he has recovered."

Binary components

Jasmijn had been in contact with Deacon again. Deacon seemed pleased to hear that the processing to create a serum had gone so well.

Jasmijn explained, "We have enough. We made it in two components. A blue serum and a red serum. Bishop will need both and then the transfer to Magister One can take place using Bishop's bloodstream. I assume that Magister One will make the necessary preparations for that?"

Deacon's tone sounded relieved, "That is great. We will need to meet for the transfer to Bishop. Can it be somewhere in New Delaware? It will be on your terms, so that we can avoid any incidents."

Jasmijn had an answer ready, "Yes, It should be in the meeting room of the Trinity. I'd expect the representatives of Sino-Nihon and Eurussia to be present. They are my safeguards that Cardinal or Magister One won't try anything."

"But what is your leverage?" asked Deacon,

Jasmijn replied, "Magister One will need two serums. We will transfer the red serum to Bishop immediately, but we will only release the blue serum when we are all safely away from the Trinity meeting place. In other words a binary product. Call us safety conscious, but that's the deal."

"I can understand that, especially after the damage created by Magister One in your old zone," answered Deacon.

"But the reports say this was created by Cardinal?" asked Jasmijn.

"Yes, Cardinal was ordered to say that by Magister One," replied Deacon.

"Okay, we should be ready for the transfer tomorrow. You will need to provide a full medical facility in the Trinity Room. I will ask my colleague to send you across the details. And don't forget you will need the Sino-Nihon and Eurussia representatives there."

Business

Jasmijn had piloted Feng Jing and Kotobuki Maja to The Trinity in an X-Blade.

Kotobuki Maja had toned down her flowing clothing and presented as a fairly demure but stunning Japanese businesswoman.

Feng Jing had similarly tidied herself into a traditional Chinese suit. They looked the very model of a Sino-Japanese cooperative.

Jasmijn defied the convention and arrived wearing her black and orange skin-tight pilot suit. She had learned the art of misdirection and wanted the members of the Trinity to focus on the suit rather than to work out her percentage android score.

Shoji Ihono, head of the Sino-Nihon Base, introduced them all to the members of the Trinity. Bogdan Victorovich smiled and considered himself a lucky man to be meeting three such obviously beautiful women.

As Shoji Ihono introduced Bishop, she noted that he was the Amerika Earthside Base representative at the Trinity, and that he would be the host for the planned transfer of the serum. She also introduced Deacon, as Bishop's Operations Manager.

Jasmijn noted in a corner of the room was a screened off area which she assumed was where they had arranged the MedFac.

"Yes, we have full MedFac to Feng Jing's specifications," continued Shoji Ihono, "We are most keen for this transfer to work."

Bishop stepped forward, he had other business to attend to before he was subjected to the serum.

Now a large congress had assembled and there was a perimeter of security guards on duty to keep the area secure.

Bishop was still the representative for Amerika and would ensure that the other members from Sino-Nihon and Eurussia followed his instruction.

Sunrise Accord

Bishop made a statement:

"This is the new sunrise accord.

"There is a necessary change of boundaries, to be implemented immediately in Amerika and to be emulated in Sino-Nihon and Eurussia. These are the instructions.

1. Extend the boundaries of the Scratch. Absorb another 250,000 people into the Scratch. Achieve this by moving the east boundaries from Latitude 39, Longitude 75 to Latitude 39, Longitude 76.
2. To create a high-powered one-way wall which can prevent people from crossing from the Scratch back into New Delaware. To use rectification and clamping technology to ensure compliance.
3. Police the boundary of the new area with Hunters. Identify anyone who attempt to breach the new boundary and send in a Hunter to disqualify their family unit.
4. Create the division as a clear delineation on the planet. Use a Satellite Ripper to implement the boundary."

The others looked at Bishop as if he was mad.

Feng Jing noticed Deacon's reaction. He looked as if he was finding out about this at the same time as the others.

"You can't ask us to do that!" said Shoji Ihono. Bogdan Victorovich nodded in agreement, "They are the warlike acts of a madman," he said, "We have Earth back in equilibrium after the Klima Wars. We are in the era of the Great Stability - these acts will wreck those plans and that status."

"Look," said Bishop, increasingly agitated, "We must make our three organisations great again. I want to Make Amerika Great Again. Of course, there will be some casualties along the way, but it is for the greater good."

The other leaders shook their heads and Ihono asked for a vote. "We always kept three of us to keep a balance among the powers. A sensible precaution against any form of crazy action," said Victorovich.

Several second-level congress staff looked around, worried at the turn of events. Bishop's tone rose," Don't you see, you are on my ground here, you are in Amerika, represented by Torus Industries. You don't really have a choice in this matter."

"But you know this is outrageous - This will cause a diplomatic incident and provoke retaliation," said Victorovich.

Ihono added, "Please, you still have time to reconsider. I beg you, don't restart the Klima Wars. It will finish off the planet."

Bishop said, "No, to the contrary. This is good, we have achieved our immediate goal. I expected some push-back from Eurussia and Sino-Nihon, but you must trust that I know what I am doing. We must enact the new Sunrise Accord.

"To do this we will use a Satellite Ripper to mark the Earth along the new boundary. Satellite Ripper is a sky-borne Directed Energy Weapon that is based upon the original Marauder Plasma designs. They are normally used for mining in Ganymede, but Earthside they can tear a boundary of one kilometre width into any land surface."

Bishop continued, "Then to enforce the boundary we will use an Active Denial System. The ADS can direct a high-powered beam exciting the water and fat molecules in human skin, instantly heating them via dielectric heating. This builds a highly efficient technological wall to keep people on their designated sides of the wall.

"If we think of it as the Sunrise Wall, then it will restore integrity and the rule of law to our borders. When implemented, it will be a very effective weapon against drugs and crime.

Bishop continued, "As perimeter defences, these systems may be harsh, but they will do the job. Containment. We need to be sure that once people are designated as inside the Scratch, they stay there.

"This should have been done by all Earth Councils that preceded me, and they all know it. Some of them have told me that we should have done it. This barrier defence is critical to border security. It's also what our professionals at the border want and need. This is just common sense."

"Now show me to the transfer facility, where I can receive

the serum!"

Deacon approached Jasmijn and Feng Jing. "Look, I want out of this. The Ripper and this declaration are too extreme. Bishop has finally lost it. Please - take me with you."

Fang Jing looked first at Kotobuki Maja, who nodded, and then at Jasmijn who seemed undecided. "Yes, you can come along. But no tricks, or they will be your last," answered Kotobuki Maja.

Jasmijn was calculating. She could see that Feng Jing was too. They would need to move fast. If the new boundaries of New Delaware were pushed to the co-ordinates stated, as now seemed to be happening, then it would trigger a LIGO event. This would force Kratos reassembly to commence. Bishop did not understand that he was playing with fire.

MedFac

Feng Jing showed Bishop to the MedFac. He was to be fitted with a polymer cannula and then to have the first serum, the red one, inserted directly into his blood stream. Feng Jing would then leave instructions for how to obtain and deploy the second blue serum.

A few minutes later, Bishop had the serum inserted.

Then, after five minutes, he was back on his feet. Cameras whirred.

"There - Are we going to close down Amerika whilst I recover from this minor procedure? No, I've learned to live with Kratos, just like we are learning to live with Sino-Nihon and Eurussia. As your leader, I had to do that. To take the Kratos serum. I knew there's danger to it, but I had to do it. I stood out front and led. Now I'm functioning, maybe I'm immune, I don't know. Nobody that's a leader would not do what I did," Bishop said.

Then, signalling that the cameras could stop recording

him, he asked, "So where is the serum's other component? The blue part?" he asked.

Jasmijn was gathering Feng Jing and Kotobuki Maja ready for their X-Blade exit. The other members of The Trinity looked on as they made their way from the building, with Deacon apparently accompanying them for safety.

Jasmijn had the X-Blade docked on the roof of Block24 and now made it ready for a fast pre-programmed and cloaked flight back to Liberty Base.

The four of them climbed aboard.

"Antigrav suits set? " asked Jasmijn and they waited for Deacon to get acquainted with an Antigrav suit. Jasmijn did a countdown.

"5-4-3-2-1," She hit the undock button and then the flight button and the craft see-sawed out its restraints and then took a wildly veering path back toward Liberty Base.

Feng Jing was on the communicator, "The blue serum is in a canister under the MedFac bed. It is taped to the underside," she said.

They had now upheld their part of the bargain, but what about Bishop?

That old trick

"Under the bed?" gasped Bishop, "I can't believe we fell for something so dumb!"

Sure enough, they looked and found the blue serum.

"You saw how this was done?" asked Bishop, "You saw what that Feng Jing did? How she used the cannula to intravenously inject me? Well, I want you to do it again. Only this time with the other part of the serum. Then I'll be ready to visit Magister One."

He could see several of the people in the Trinity meeting room dressed as nurses.

"Come on, one of you must know how to administer an IV drip?" Bishop demanded.

A nurse stepped forward, "I can do this for you," she said.

"Okay you and your pretty friend over there, I need some eye candy while we go through this procedure!" Bishop looked toward another nurse, demure and with her eyes down, " Hey you, you there, come and tend me!"

The rest of the Trinity looked on aghast. Maybe it was true what they had heard about Bishop's unsavoury ways?

The first nurse set up a drip with the serum, connected to Bishop's cannula, which, was inserted into one of his veins. The serum soon dripped through and in another few minutes Bishop had both serums flowing through his bloodstream.

"There, Cutie, that wasn't so bad," he said as he once again stood from the side of the MedFac bed.

"See, I'm good to go!" he walked forward as a couple of the nurses rushed to remove the cannula and stem any blood flow that its removal might cause.

"You will need to take it steady for the next 48 hours," said a nurse, "No exertions and leave the bandages alone."

Bishop felt fine. It was almost as if he'd not had any procedure done, but he wondered if he would feel the same way the next day. He was secretly pleased that he could tell Cardinal and therefore Magister that they would need to wait for 48 hours.

Bishop wondered where Deacon had gone, but - hey, he didn't need Deacon now. He would be 'well-in' with Cardinal and Magister One.
Magister One would be the next step-up in Bishop's

power and influence. Deacon was sliding down that greasy political pole.

MKUltra

"Sit back picture yourself swooping up a shell of purple with foam crests of crystal drops soft nigh they fall unto the sea of morning creep-very-softly mist ... and then sort of cascade tinkley-bell-like (must I take you by the hand, ever so slowly type) and then conglomerate suddenly into a peal of silver vibrant uncomprehendingly, blood singingly, joyously resounding bells ... By my faith if this be insanity, then for the love of God permit me to remain insane."

Robert Hunter. MKUltra Experimental test subject.
Neurowarfare and Brain Targeted Weapon Trials

Both moves

"So, has it been done?" asked Magister One to Cardinal, "I'm told that Bishop has been provided with the serum. They also tell me that the Scratch boundaries are being readjusted."

"Correct on both counts," said Cardinal, "Bishop's medical procedure went to plan, and he now holds the red and blue components of Kratos. Unfortunately, the move of the boundaries because of the Sunrise Accord didn't go so well. It was vehemently opposed by both Sino-Nihon and Eurussia."

"Let's not forget that they are both run by gangsters," said Magister One, "They are both looking for a monetary gain before they will do anything. Well this time they can suffer. The only gain is to us. To Me. We will be one step closer to the execution of Holden's plan."

"Holden? I thought you said he was long gone?"

"He is, although I carry his mission. There were five of

us, but the two in the Southern hemisphere were both destroyed before the sphere's root systems could link together, Just the root system from the other three spheres remains. Each of Eurussia, Sino-Nihon and America has its own Magister. We provide the stimulation which keeps the crime syndicates operational until we are able to reframe our own powerful positions."

Cardinal did not understand all of this. He would need to tell it to Bishop so that Bishop was prepared for what could come next.

"So Cardinal, bring me Bishop," demanded Magister One.

DAARQ

Across in the Scratch, Cindy, Sam, Haruto and Roelof waited for the return of the X-Blade. It lightly touched down and taxied in toward the Liberty Base control tower. They watched it but also kept an eye on the monitor showing the Sunrise Accord announcement on their illegal channel provided by the sense-wall.

"My god," said Sam, "Bishop has lost it. These are the ravings of a madman. I guess we are now tapping into Cardinal's direct thoughts relayed via Bishop?"

"Agreed, " said Cindy, "But we need to find out the reaction from the other Trinity members."

At that moment, Jasmijn, Feng Jing, Kotobuki Maja and Deacon walked in.

Feng Jing spoke, "We brought someone extra. A friend of Jasmijn's. It's Deacon, who has been the advisor to Bishop. He said he wanted 'out'. "

Deacon spoke, "Yes, Bishop has completely lost it. He is

using Weapons of Mass destruction to make a point. This Sunrise Accord he has invented - without ANY consultation - it is just crazy. He seems to be fully under the influence of the empty-brained Cardinal, who seems, in my opinion, to be guided by Magister One."

Roelof and Jasmijn were both watching their analytics whilst Deacon spoke. They gave no signs of lies, deceit or stress from Deacon. His readouts seem entirely balanced.

"Okay, we will trust you," said Roelof, "But any hint of something untoward and you'll lose any privileges here."

"Don't worry," said Deacon, "I'm thankful to be away from the madmen. Even here in The Scratch - which looks a lot better than they would make you believe from outside of it."

"Let's see if we can tap into the Sino-Nihon and Eurussian channels too," said Cindy, "Let's take a look for their reaction."

"How is this even possible?" asked Sam, "Surely they are most secure?"

Haruto answered, "Yes, they are, but The Scratch is something of a blind spot. Because we still use older technologies, including some analogue ones, we have a major advantage. Everyone's uprated technology is all geared towards DAARQ and similar technologies.

"Distributed, Artificial Intelligence, Augmented Reality and Quantum computing. Some basics were left at the gatepost. The new systems will monitor for sophisticated intrusion detection, but they sometimes forget that someone could leave a key underneath a flowerpot by the entrance to their fortified castle.

"All we did (that's The Resistance during the Klima Wars), was drop some of those entry points into the complex code being developed. If you know the right words, a bit like 'open sesame' then the flowerpots give way and the keys become visible."

"Ah, so you have secret ways into their systems?" asked Cindy, "through trapdoors that some of your own agents planted?"

"Exactly," said Haruto, "although a few have been discovered and are being patched up. Fortunately, once we are inside, we can add a few more to the entrances that already exist."

"Look, let me show you," Feng Jing tapped into a control and then pushed the image to a sensewall.

On the screen they could see there was a scene which looked like a Grand Master painting, except that it was fully animated. It showed the Sino-Nihon Senate, discussing actions in Cassim Gongje.

The audio was loud: "We will deploy Yakuza, to regain our position in the Trinity. No-one can push us around like this. We must deploy immediately and show no mercy in our retaliation."

Sam looked at Haruto, "Here they go again," he said, "They don't realise that 'droids give them more intelligence than humans."

Roelof watched the sensewall, "Can you get similar information from Eurussia?" he asked. Roelof was having to learn about Earth quickly.

"Sure, " said Feng Jing, and as she spoke she tapped something into the control panel and a different scene emerged. Sleeker and cleaner looking than the Sino-Nihon, as if someone had used a good designer to provide the lighting.

Again, the audio boomed out with several leaders talking: "...resurrect NATO and other military wings. Plus, we can deploy the Bratva to support us in the fight to regain our control."

"This requires the firmest of forces and for us to reassert our alliance with Sino-Nihon"

"Yes, but won't that re-trigger the Klima Wars? We have been operating with the Great Stability for so long now!"

Jasmijn considered the situation and then spoke, "I think we can harness this situation and bring it around," she said.

"How?" asked Cindy.

"There's something you don't know about what Feng Jing and I did when we created that serum, beyond holding back a component to ensure our escape. Now Bishop doesn't know what he is handling and, in particular, that if a changed Earth boundary gets detected by the LIGO, then the Kratos will commence recombination."

"That's what Magister One wants though, isn't it?" asked Cindy, "The Kratos key to humanity? Its own little nanomachines can then break through in ways that Magister One has been unable to achieve."

"Exactly, and I fear it has been waiting dormant for a very long time to do this," said Jasmijn.

Trust in Drugs

In Block 24, Bishop could see that Cardinal was troubled by something.

Cardinal began, "Something I feel I should tell you, before you go to see Magister One. It sounds as if Magister One is one of five similar entities placed around the earth many years ago. Their mission was to capture and cultivate the Earth, for their own purposes."

Bishop began. "But we knew Magister was once Holden; we also knew that Holden/Magister One is somehow linked to the domes that landed around Earth some three hundred years ago. Magister One (and probably Two and Three) can't break through into the human chain, because humanity has been designed to be unbreakable. That's why they drifted into a long-term pause."

Cardinal started, "You are right and although the institutions of our culture are so amazingly good that they have been able to manage stability in the face of rapid change for hundreds of years, the knowledge of what it takes to keep civilisation stable in the face of rapidly increasing knowledge is not very widespread.

Cardinal continued "In fact, severe misconceptions about several aspects of it are common among political leaders, educated people, and society at large. That is why the need for intervention is so high."

Bishop questioned, "But surely that is what I am doing now? Intervening?"

Cardinal responded, "Humans are like people on a huge, well-designed submarine, which has all sorts of lifesaving devices built in, but they don't know they're in a submarine. They think they're in a motorboat, and they're going to open all the hatches because they want to have a nicer view."

Bishop said, "Of course, wouldn't you want a pretty view instead of murkiness?"

Cardinal ignored the last comment and continued, "Early experiments on viruses caused a global pandemic which killed many millions. The experiments were halted. They switched to the use of nanomachines and were cleared to resume as long as they were conducted in 'top security' labs. But it was still like leaving the hatches open."

"But surely someone else would have said something?" asked Bishop.

"Yes. The Bulletin of Atomic Scientists carried research showing how the most secure bio-labs had serious security problems and presented an unacceptable risk of causing a disastrous pandemic."

Bishop questions. "But surely someone would listen to this advice?"

Cardinal shook his head, "No - they showed that incidents causing potential exposures to pathogens occur frequently."

Cardinal added, "Yet lab incidents that led to undetected or unreported laboratory-acquired infections also led to the release of a disease into the community outside the lab; lab workers with such infections left work carrying the pathogen with them. If the agent involved was a potential pandemic pathogen, such a community release could lead to a worldwide pandemic with many fatalities.

Bishop asked, "But surely this was preventable?"

Cardinal went on, "It was an inadvertent trigger-point.

"Like Pandora's Box. Earth was given The Great Leap. Knowledge so much further ahead of human thought at that time that it must have seemed like magic. Instead of good, it stemmed the 'End of Earth' at that time. But now Earth knew how to build a rocket ship capable of travel to Jupiter to mine Ganymede and bring back magnetite. That was a game-changer."

Bishop said, "But in those distant days, the Earthside experiments continued. Wasn't there concern over the release of a lab-created, mammalian-airborne-transmissible, highly pathogenic avian influenza virus, such as the airborne-transmissible H5N1 viruses? And Holden must have been around when such things began to occur?"

Cardinal added, "Recall that coronavirus epidemic which circled the globe before The Scourge? It was said to emanate from old China, from a place called Wuhan. The mainstream media ran a story which was remarkably like a movie of the time, which explained the outbreak was from a bat in a market. Somehow, they didn't get around to mentioning Wuhan has a couple of big, mysterious labs in town. The Wuhan Institute of Virology and Wuhan Centre for Disease Control. And before the outbreak they were both investigating corona viruses. Neither was it mentioned that they both used bats as a host for the viruses."

Cardinal added, "Such releases are fairly likely over time, with many predominantly Asian labs carrying out the research. Whatever release probability the world was gambling with, it was far too high a risk to human lives. Mammal-transmissible bird flu research posed a real danger of a worldwide pandemic that could kill human beings on a vast scale. That's how Earthside later experienced The Scourge, a huge pandemic wiping out whole countries."

Cardinal continued, "The reason that Earthside needs to be managed by androids is self-evident. There were three types of error which contributed to the ultimate decline of Earthside. The first was skill-based (errors involving motor skills involving little thought), then rule-based (errors in following instructions or set procedures accidentally or purposely), and finally knowledge-based (errors stemming from a lack of knowledge or a wrong judgment call based on lack of experience)."

Bishop asked, "But who is telling you this? And do you have any evidence supporting any of it - to me, it all sounds too far-fetched."

"That's why the Magisters want to intervene. You will be supplying Magister One with the serum which will allow Magister One to take control of the organic life on Earth."

"But what will that produce?" asked Bishop, "An Earth which is pretty much owned by Androids. Humans are still around, in designated areas, but are entirely under the eye of the 'droids."

"Correct," said Cardinal, "But safely so; they will know and can operate in their ascribed areas."

"It is time," said Cardinal, "You must again meet Magister One."

They walked to the Didactic Chamber.

"Will we both go inside?" asked Bishop.

"I'm going to wait outside. Here," said Cardinal.

Bishop entered the room. It looked different. He could hear someone talking, it sounded like a younger version of himself.

He could see what he took to be a large autoclave in the room. It was pressed up against the wall and reminded him of a body scanner.

The voice continued, it was affecting his subconscious. He realised it was trying to hypnotise him. Then he noticed the theta waves. Designed to slow him into that dreamlike-state just after awakening.

"Take a seat," suggested Magister One, "You are looking drowsy. I expect it has been the intense pressure from the last few days. It must feel so good to have nothing more to worry about."

Bishop could hear the words now:

"Sit back picture yourself swooping up a shell of purple with foam crests of crystal drops soft nigh they fall unto the sea of morning creep-very-softly mist ... and then sort of cascade tinkley-bell-like (must I take you by the hand, ever so slowly type) and then conglomerate suddenly into a peal of silver vibrant uncomprehendingly, blood singingly, joyously resounding bells ... By my faith if this be insanity, then for the love of God permit me to remain insane."

He felt two nurses assisting him as he walked to the 'clave.

"Lie down," said one, soothingly. "Here, let me help you," said the other.

He watched as a drawer slid open from the front of the device. He noticed the polished stainless-steel shape of the area on which he was being directed to lay. He noticed small neat holes around the edge of the central raised bump and its indentation for a body and then the channels cut in a gridline formation in the sides of the steel. It reminded him of the design of some carving dishes.

"We are closing the hatch now. Are you ready for the procedure?"

Bishop could only moan, he was not sure what he was saying. He noticed the two nurses were functioning normally and suddenly realised they were 'droids. He must be in an area which had a modified atmosphere. He breathed out and noticed that there was a slight green fog to his breath. "Scopoloamine," he thought, "Burundanga, trust drugs."

He slipped in and out of awareness. He could hear the machine starting up. He looked up. It wasn't an autoclave. He noticed the large needles. He was in an iron maiden. A human-sized juice extractor.

Inky blue pattern

Magister One sighed.

"Good. We have the materials now; we have processed Bishop. I must acquire the nanomaterials. Can we begin the process of induction?"

There was a new whirring. The processor sorted the blood from Bishop's remains. It passed into a new transparent container. There seemed to be around 4 litres of red liquid, swirling with an inky blue pattern, as if ink had been artistically droppered into it.

"This should have the concentrate of the Kratos," said Magister One. "Now to filter the nanoparticles into my own being."

In Liberty Base, Deacon suddenly felt the link with Bishop had been severed. He didn't know why, but there was a new lightness without the need to carry Bishop's communications. Deacon told the others.

"I can't be certain, but I think Bishop has gone, I suspect

Magister One has killed him in order to extract the Kratos. I'm getting no further signal from Bishop."

Jasmijn said, "Well, the other order from Bishop, to implement the Sunshine Accord, is still going ahead. They have even started to use the boundary marker weapons."

Deacon said, "Will it trigger the LIGO? I am guessing that is what Magister One wants?"

"Yes, certainly," said Jasmijn, "Only within Amerika though, I think the other two areas of Sino-Nihon and Eurussia are against every part of this process."

As she spoke, there was a thundercrack across the sky. She assumed it was weapon-based and probably carving out the new territory.

"Oh yes," she said, "Kratos will definitely be reawakening now." She didn't mention what else she and Feng Jing had engineered.

Die Gänsemagd

In the stories collected by the Brothers Grimm we have a tale sometime called Falada, but best known as from its appearance as The Goose Girl - Die Gänsemagd.

And at the end of this story - The false bride said, "She deserves no better fate than to be stripped stark naked, and put in a barrel that is studded inside with sharp nails. Two white horses should be hitched to it, and they should drag her along through one street after another, until she is dead."

"You are the one," said the old king, "and you have pronounced your own sentence. Thus, shall it be done to you."

Chakras

Magister One could feel it. The reassembly of Kratos. He knew he would have the power over a mere Earth-designed nanomachine. He could contain Kratos, but as importantly, he could find the Kratos Key as Kratos reassembled. This would be the key that would give Magister the power he had waited over three hundred years to manage.

Kratos was awakening. Magister One's own nanobots were not sure whether to embrace Kratos or to attempt an attack. Now he knew that they were looking for a way to combine together to make a stronger virus. One that could handle humanity. To be able to sweep across humanity at whatever speed was desirable leaving just what was needed. It would make a museum of humanity leading toward the ultimate zoo or farm.

Magister One was feeling stronger. More powerful. But also, strangely glitchy. He suddenly felt a hammering inside his system. Like someone was trying to get out. He could hear the knocking sound of Magister Five and Magister Four - the two Magisters that had been lost when the domes were destroyed but before their root systems had a chance to connect. Now he could feel it in his own root system. A small flame. Like someone was attacking him with needles. It was like acupressure, but was seeking out his own chakras.

Something was attacking his spinning disks of energy preventing them from staying open and aligned. First, he could feel it in his root. Like the base of the spine, He could see red and knew an unseen force was probing his physical identity and grounding. It was like he was being drained away through his very core. Then just below the belly button, the sacral area, dulling and erasing his sense of pleasure, creativity and self worth.

He could see breakthrough flashes of orange and realised that this was something targeted that was affecting him. Then it hit upon his solar plexus and his confidence and self-esteem vanished in a yellow haze. By the time he saw green he had processed what was happening.

His heart centre had told him that something was acutely targeting the Kratos and his own nanomachines. It was oppositional to Kratos and had been designed to offset Kratos. He had heard its name, but never knew that such a thing existed.

Adrasteia, the nemesis of the strength of Kratos was walking calmly through his systems, disabling them one by one. In the same way that he thought he had found a key to humanity, he had accidentally given away his key to himself.

And now Adrasteia was floating through, removing the doors and destroying his cache of nanomachines. The feeling had now reached his throat. His communication would soon be blocked and he was powerless to counteract anything. Now he could only see blue. And he could feel her walking into his imagination and intuition. She was putting out his Third Eye. He could no longer see.

And finally, she climbed softly to the crown of his senses. He could now see violet but knew that her hands were pressing inside his skull and his awareness and intelligence was about to be crushed.

Now everything was white and very quiet.

He was destroyed.

With a flicker of a vast scaled-serpent tail, Magister One noticed Kratos flash away, followed very slowly by the white winged and floating veils of Adrasteia. She was leaving him, taking with her the amalgamated white of all the rainbow colours and leaving just black.

Suited and booted

Cardinal knew something had happened. He was standing across a lobby outside of room 2424 and could see several people running towards the door.

A klaxon sounded. It was a warning alert. He could see that several people were racing for a row of bright yellow HazMat suits hung along wall of the lobby. He decided to do the same. He would look anonymous in the suit. He selected a powered suit, which meant he was able to move unencumbered. The boots even gave him an extra spring when he ran or climbed stairs.

Cardinal made his way to the exit elevator. He would hit ground-level and get out before anything else happened. He wondered if the elevator would still work in an emergency and was relieved when it started a rapid descent.

Ground level and he was almost out of the building. He could see the darkened sky through the plate glass windows. People were running around .

"Quake," someone said, "We're following the Klima protocols!"

He realised that many people were still schooled in the ways of the Klima Wars and running for underground cover.

Instead, he looked for robust transport. He could see a compact j-rover stood across from the building. It was Army issue, painted grey all over and would have been hardened for combat conditions. He jumped in, surprising another occupant. "We're moving," he said, "I'm Cardinal, chief advisor to Bishop."

The man looked towards him. "Good luck with that," he said, "I'm only a passenger. I can't fly this thing."

Cardinal looked at the controls. It was a stripped-back bubble cockpit with only the basic controls to make it work. He hit the button marked 'Start' and was rewarded with a boom sound and the whole device shooting around two metres into the air.

"Careful!" said the other occupant, "These things are flighty!"

"How difficult can this be?" Cardinal said, smiling to the other occupant. He stamped a foot control and the j-rover shot forward, simultaneously firing its all of its booster jets and hitting a plate glass building wall at over 200 kilometres per hour.

The j-rover had gone through the wall, cutting off the top half of its fuselage. The occupant bubble had been severed though the middle. It had continued travelling inside the building until it hit a lift shaft, which it had drilled through, then falling to 20 stories below ground level, where it exploded in a fusion of magnetite and compressed oxygen.

The only certainty was that there would be no survivors.

No-one would fly a j-rover like that

In Liberty Base, the occupants of the Control tower were watching the televised events from New Delaware. Feng Jing had dialled up split screens so they could see several vantage points simultaneously on different sensewalls.

They saw the small j-rover fire itself at the plate-glass tower block and the resultant fireball which climbed up the elevator shaft.

"Wow - that must have been deliberate!" said Sam, "No-one would fly a j-rover like that, unless they were a terrorist!"

They could see pieces of building ripped away and crashing down around the camera areas. Suddenly there was an enormous ripping sound.

Several huge organic tubes appeared and thrashed around near to where the j-rover had recently stood. Several smaller strands whipped around like severed powerlines. They were progressively disintegrating and gave the appearance of something in anguish.

"My god!" said Kotobuki Maja, "It looks like a jellyfish! And trust me, we Japanese see enough to be able to recognise one!"

Feng Jing looked and agreed, "Yes - I think you are right. It looks like a Chrysaora jelly! A big mushroom cap, long tentacles along the centre and smaller trailing ones from the cap!"

Jasmijn was busy accessing her earth archive, "Here, she said, Cnidaria - only you'd have to imagine them about 10,000 times the size."

Sam said, "This could make sense if three hundred years ago the earth was hit by some kind of Cnidarian storm. It accounts for the domes and the long burrowing tentacle -like structures."

Cindy asked, "But how could they survive after the domes were destroyed?"

Jasmijn looked at the file, "Many Cnidarian species produce colonies that are single organisms composed of medusa-like zooids. The Cnidarians' activities only need a decentralised nerve net and simple receptors with some possessing simple eyes for awareness. They are built for survival.

"So we've been the host planet to giant-Cnidarian organisms for the last three hundred years?" asked Cindy.

"Have you noticed something though?" Said Cindy, "My memory of older days is returning! I can remember that child tricycle I used , my visits to see my grandparents on a farm. It is like a fog is lifting."

Roelof said, "Yes, I think it is the effect of the Cnidarian nerve net declining. Human brains have been clamped down by the nerve net of the invaders, for hundreds of years.

"That has been both beneficial - with the discovery of many new things and also harmful - through the systematic erasure of certain memories. Now, the remaining tentacles are being destroyed, like those ones we can see breaking up as they flail around at the surface.

"As they are destroyed, so goes the nerve net and human memories lose that clamped-down feeling. Humans regain their freedom of thought!"

Jasmijn looked up, "More than that. I think over centuries Earth-dwellers mutated them. They landed, brought some intelligence to Earth but also innocently absorbed the nano-machines which Earth created.

"That has become a source of power to those crazed to want it. People like Cardinal and Bishop. And so the Cnidarians created a cypher of a human. Call it Holden or Magister One. They were trying to find a way to interact with the organics on earth but met the wrong crowd. Not surprising considering that the entire Earthside and Ganymede is run by organised crime."

"Don't you see?" asked Cindy, "These 'domes' are all about self-preservation? They are trying to manipulate Earthside to suit the conditions they need."

Jasmijn asked, "Maybe so - although they seem utterly ruthless - All those years ago, we managed to cut off their heads, leaving just their tentacles below the surface. Now they seem to have been represented by Magister One, a brutal killer. It begs the question? Are Magister Two and Magister Three on the loose in Sino-Nihon and Eurussia?"

Roelof said, "If so, we will need to find a way to keep them in their place."

"But don't you see?" said Jasmijn, "It is the nemesis of Kratos, in other words Adrasteia, that is the way to manage them."

"I see," said Sam, "In the way that you and Feng Jing put the nanoreductives into Bishop's blood stream, and it forced the end of the nanomachines that Magister One carried, then so it must be for the other remaining domes and their Magisters.

"Yes, and we didn't use all of the serum either. We gave Bishop one quarter of that which we had extracted. We could see that the accelerants would soon multiply it up to a saturation level in his bloodstream."

Feng Jing commented, "Well, we have direct lines to both the other Trinity members' Council Rooms. We can easily advise them of the course of action that they will need to take. I suspect that the net is weakened now, with the removal of the Amerikan strands."

"We will need to transport the serum to both of Sino-Nihon and Eurussia too. It could be something we arrange through the next Trinity meeting."

There was a low rumble approaching Liberty Base. Feng Jing flipped on the sense wall.

"It's a Sukoi and an F238!" she said, "We seem to have visitors from New Delaware!"

The incoming flights were both blinking their "Friend" status on the display.

Two dark painted stealth jets manoeuvred into the hangar. They each had pilot bulges in their superstructure. Unlike the X-Blades, they were noisy as they manoeuvred.

"They don't have latest gen motors," said Roelof, "We wouldn't allow these on Ganymede."

The two planes settled and the pilots disembarked. First, they saluted the assembled group in the plane's hangar.

Then one of them spoke, "Hello, my name is Flight Commander Maddox Chapman, from Eurussia forces and this is my colleague Flight Commander Ariella Solokova from Sino-Nihon forces. We are here to thank you all for the daring plan you executed against dark forces in control of Amerika. For this, we salute you all."

Sam and Cindy snapped to attention, and the others followed suit. This was not something they were used to dealing with.

"Now we have been asked to re-instate a balance of power with Amerika, but under a new and more reasonable leadership. Our recommendation, at least for an interim period, is that The Trinity representatives should become you, Sam and Cindy. You are both well-qualified as Earth Primes and each of you have direct control over many of the 'droids operating both here Earthside and through your links to Ganymede."

"We have a recorded message from The Trinity, and I am

authorised to play this to you all now."

He found a small SecureKey and handed it to Feng Jing, who plugged it into the Sense-wall.

"Play," she directed, and a video recording started across the main breadth of the Sense-wall. The recording looked as if it had been hurriedly made but included the heads of Sino-Nihon and Eurussia.

It repeated the thanks to everyone and then asked whether Sam and Cindy would be prepared to take on the Earthside representation of Amerika.

But then it went further. It said that the latest events had caused everyone to recognise the significant developments in the areas known as The Scratch, and that the combined Scratch areas represented 25% of the Earthside population. It requested that The Scratch also be represented inside The Trinity, which would be renamed as The Consulate.

That was for Earthside, and the recording went on to reinstate Roelof and Jasmijn, in their newly selected Persona as representatives of Ganymede Council. Roelof and Jasmijn will still both be Primes but will have additional responsibilities towards the relationship between Ganymede and Earthside.

Sam looked at Cindy, who nodded. Then Roelof and Jasmijn both looked at one another and agreed that they would accept the new roles on Ganymede.

"And we will want to recognise Haruto, Feng Jing and Kotobuki Maja too, as leading lights in the Scratch. I'm not sure whether you would want to step into the Consulate roles, but you will all have our vote," said Sam.

They looked around somewhat overwhelmed by all that was happening so quickly. Haruto remembered that several of the people he was interacting with were either full 'droid or at least 'droid assisted and that they had very fast cycle times compared to him, a mere Sharp.

"You know what, " Haruto said, "I think we will need longer to think about this. We are highly flattered but need to work through the implications."

Jasmijn had been running a communication channel back to The Trinity whilst this was all taking place. Now she was relaying their live message to the sensewall.

"This is Eurussia. We have heard what you all say and respect your wishes. We will be delighted to receive a meeting of the new Consulate in a week's time to review this further.

There was a click, and the line went dead. Roelof laughed, another experience that was new to him. "I'm only laughing because I find it slightly comical how Androids deal with humans. I can see that the pacing is often wrong, because the Androids have such a fast cycle time. A long pause by a 'droid can still seem like an insect's wing beat to a human."

And then, inadvertently proving the point, he switched topic.

"And now, logistics. How do we all get back to where we've all come from?"

They looked back towards the monitors. The flailing tentacles had subsided. The chaos in New Delaware was slowing giving way to greater peace.

"And what about you two?" asked Sam, looking towards Jasmijn and Roelof, " Will you return to Ganymede?"

"We should, answered Roelof, although it would be good to be able to make further side trips to Earthside."

Jasmijn nodded, "Yes - we will need to figure out how to restart the safe transit towards Earthside again."

"No killer robots on board?" asked Sam, smiling.

"No - they will be suitably programmed with Type E characteristics for the journey," answered Jasmijn.

"So, it looks as if Earthside might be able to get back to how it should operate. No vast zoos of humans being administered by 'droids!" said Sam.

"And The Scratch represented as a proper territory, instead of as a hidden embarrassment!" said Feng Jing.

"And, if you come to Earthside every so often, we'd like to be able to visit Ganymede sometimes!" asked Sam.

"Be careful what you wish for," answered Roelof.

A month later - Ganymede

Roelof looked towards the window. Grey night skies, something resembling clouds, thin trails, raked towards the horizon.

He heard the apartment judder from the impact. A mournful sigh. This one had been close, but not that close. He knew the building was meant to take it. If he could stay inside, he could watch some transmissions to take his mind off the situation.

He moved from his bedroom into the main living area. He flipped the switch and could suddenly hear the weather.

A gentle rain and a rustling of leaves. The occasional spatter of water dripping from branches. He kept the weather set to April for several months now. Outside it was the end of summer but somehow it did not matter what the official calendar said, he had decided to run it at his own speed.

He flipped the main screen. Not the full screen but the one designed to show discussions from the Consulate. It opened on a standard news transmission and he gestured for it to move across to his messages. He expected they would ask for him, but so far there were only a few spams that had missed his filtering.

The main room had noise cancellation and so he was now no longer aware of the crashes from outside. Just a slight feeling underfoot as the building absorbed more impacts.

"Peter give me status," he requested.

A small pop-up window appeared on the top right of the screen. Everything was green. At this rate, he didn't need to do anything at all.

A little information light on the screen briefly flickered to amber. A moment later it had returned to green. He realised another advantage of being away from the base was that smaller incidents were handled autonomously by the base management systems.

"Hi Peter," he said, "please provide an update on base status."

"Full base status is green. There was a short incident with a meteorite, but they cleared it with a grid gun. Incident duration 1.2 seconds. There are zero requests for your attendance at the base."

A chime sounded from the streamcom. "Peter accept," he said.

A small repeater screen in the kitchen showed the face of one of his colleagues.

"Hi Roelof, it's Jasmijn. The incoming shower seems normal. The high-speed defence array is running today almost non-stop.

"Do I need to come in?" asked Roelof.

"I don't think you would be in time to make any difference," said Jasmijn, "I'm gonna bail," she said. "I'm guessing this place is only going to be around for a few more minutes."

He heard the noise of a siren. Then a bleep and the screen terminated.

"Transmission terminated," said Peter.

"Peter please give me externals," requested Roelof, "Put it on the main wall."

He stepped back in the living space. Across the wall was a scene showing distant clouds, a red sky, and white streaks of light focused towards a smoking central area.

Roelof walked towards a console in the living space. He sat in a swivel chair and grabbed the controls. He looked around the sky and locked on to two monitor drones.

"Jasmijn, Jasmijn, do you copy?"

He repeated the request a couple more times. Then a voice. "Copy that, Jasmijn here - I can hear you."

" What is your status?"

"I am outside the main ring of damage. It looks as if the others have made it too."

"Okay, follow the protocol and join me here," said Roelof.

"Copy that"

Roelof knew that the profile had been designed to protect as many people as possible on the base. Everyone had been paired, and he had been selected to pair with Jasmijn. He was officially English, and she was officially Belgian, although neither of them had spent much time in their designated home countries.

Roelof flicked through some of the observation systems to check the wider impacts of what had been happening. Maybe this was a bad storm. He knew he would soon be required to attend Ganymede Council and to represent The Consulate.

Now the sovereign structure of Ganymede was incorporated into the Earth Council and both he and Jasmijn had been given the job to represent Ganymede back on Earth. They were both Primes and of the latest generation. Their type H for Hybrid designation meant that they could keep two worlds active in their Persona but could only inhabit one at a time. On Ganymede they were a Type G and on Earthside a Type E - both separate entities.

Roelof and Jasmijn both knew it played tricks with their memories.

Six months later - EarthSide

"These system updates are still taking longer and longer," said Sam Walker, "This time we had to wait for nearly four hours to get the new command centre online."

"I know," replied Cindy Shaw, "They told us this time it was the new mining extraction modules that were being introduced."

"Anyway," said Sam, "We seem to have everything back now. Just about every system is already green, and a couple of the minor ones are still restarting."

Cindy peered towards the observation windows.

Outside she could see the land. An orange-brown colour. It was only just daybreak. She could still make out the outline for the moon and across the sky from it the second much smaller moon which was being extended by man. Small pinpricks of light twinkled between the two moons indicative of transiting space hardware.

She looked across to the Meteo display. 40C degrees

already.

"It is going to be a hot one today."

Sam nodded.

Their base was in New Delaware on the east coast of the United States. The whole island area of what had once been called Delaware and what had been the eastern half of Maryland had been re-designated as New Delaware when the efforts to bolster the space program had redoubled. New Delaware had then aggressively become a TEZ total exclusion zone permitting the wholesale development of first lunar and then interplanetary transport vehicles.

Cindy and Sam were no ordinary Primes. They had been selected to represent Amerika in The Consulate. They still had conventional duties Earthside, but additionally had the great responsibility to guide Earthside and to ensure a clean balance between Amerika, Eurussia, Sino-Nihon and The Scratch.

They had met at IPX school. Interplanetary Exploration was a career choice for the very brightest. They were selected early and then encouraged to form friendship groups and ultimately to pair off. They had subsequently been deselected from space travel part way through the programme. The official story was that they were too precious to be gambled in space travel and that there were others more suited to the roles required.

Then, after a complex situation with their Ganymede Primes who ported themselves Earthside, they were both asked if they would like to be re-instated.

They were both delighted and accepted immediately.

Then they had been invited back to IPX, but this time they were taken to a special unit for space conditioning. They understood that the physical demands placed upon them would be tremendous and that instead of intense physical workouts, they were to be pre-conditioned for the journey using special technology.

That was all they could remember. Visiting the centre, being comprehensively wired and then, when they both woke up, they felt somehow different.

The people around them seemed to behave as if in slow motion. They could now both do complex calculations in their heads. They had a direct line to one another's thoughts and to those of their two main Primes, Roelof and Jasmijn. Someone from IPX had explained to them that they would be able to take a shortcut route to Ganymede, but neither of them quite understood how that was possible - they would need to travel at close to light-speed.

They both noticed that a small socket had been grafted into their left hand.

On it was inscribed G10.

Edge, Red

Now jet to another Ed Adams Novel:

Triangle Trilogy		Link:	Read?
1	Triangle	https://amzn.to/3c6zRMu	
2	Square	https://amzn.to/3sEiKYx	
3	Circle	https://amzn.to/3qLavYZ	
4	Ox Stunner	https://amzn.to/3sHxlgh	
		(all feature Jake, Bigsy, Clare, Chuck Manners)	
Archangel Collection			
1	Archangel	https://amzn.to/2Y9nB5K	
2	Raven	https://amzn.to/2MiGVe6	
3	Raven's Card	https://amzn.to/2Y8HLgs	
4	Magazine Clip	https://amzn.to/3pbBJYn	
5	Play On, Christina Nott	https://amzn.to/2MbkuHl	
6	Corrupt	https://amzn.to/2M0HnOw	
		(all feature Jake, Bigsy, Clare, Chuck Manners)	
Now the Science Collection			
1	Coin	https://amzn.to/3o82wmS	
2	Pulse	https://amzn.to/3gQlBvL	
3	Edge	https://amzn.to/2KDmYOW	
4	Now the Science	https://amzn.to/3iG5Nc2	
Edge of forever Trilogy			
1	Edge	https://amzn.to/2KDmYOW	
2	Edge Blue	https://amzn.to/2Kyq9au	
3	Edge Red	https://amzn.to/2KzJwjz	
4	Edge of Forever	https://amzn.to/3c57Ghj	

Edge, Red

784

Edge, Red

Ed Adams